" This horse is decidedly a buttercup," drawled the stranger

THE THREE MUSKETEERS

The Windermere Readers

The Three
MUSKETEERS

By ALEXANDRE DUMAS

Translated and arranged by
PHILIP SCHUYLER ALLEN
The University of Chicago

Frontispiece by MILO WINTER

Windermere Readers
SCHOOL EDITION

RAND McNALLY & COMPANY

New York   Chicago   San Francisco

First printing, January 15, 1954
Second printing, September 1, 1955
Third Printing, September 15, 1956

THE CONTENTS

The Preface

CHAPTER

THE CONTENTS

THE PREFACE

The author of *The Three Musketeers* was born near Paris a hundred years ago. His father, who was one of the great Napoleon's generals, died when his child was only four years of age. The boy Alexandre grew up in extreme poverty and led a careless and neglected youth in his birthplace, the little village of Villers-Cotterets. But when he was twenty years old he ran away to Paris, and not long thereafter he had made himself famous by his stage-plays and romances.

Alexandre Dumas' life itself reads like one of his own incredible and galloping novels. He achieved his first brilliant success with the drama *Henry the Third,* written in his twenty-seventh year, and he followed this up with an unbelievably long procession of plays and romances. During his lifetime he published over three hundred sizable volumes. He was a human dynamo. He would acquire a large fortune, toss it recklessly away in absurd extravagances, become swamped with debts, only to receive new riches on his promises to write dozens of books. And then the scenes of his prodigality and poverty would be acted all over again. Sometimes he published under his own name novels which he had written only in part, but such was the magic of his touch, so did he change and make living everything that passed through his hands, that even in such cases the honor of the story belongs to him.

* * * * *

In the long ago when I was a boy, there were only three or four books that held me captive, and Dumas' *The Three Musketeers* was easily the first of these. I still recall the thrills of hot and cold, the shivers of fear, and the tremulous joy which possessed me when first I read the gallivanting and swashbuckling doings of young d'Artagnan.

Time after time, with intervals of years between, I have returned to this sprightly romance of those twilight days when knighthood was last in flower. And never have I yet laid down the story unrewarded by a new enjoyment as keen as was that with which I

THE PREFACE

first made its acquaintance. I have traveled through its immortal pages at least ten times, and I am sure I shall still find many an hour of breathless fun in its delightful company.

Well—in this book I have made a translation which I hope will carry home to a new generation of American boys and girls. Some of the French original I have omitted, notably one long episode that to my mind arrested the gay march of the narrative. Here and there I have cut out part of a chapter that was slightly soiling or unclean, and which seemed to dim the pure brightness of the rest of the book. And I have trimmed down the many historical allusions that are of slight interest to the young reader.

What have I left after my pruning?

I have left the story, as I imagine Dumas himself would have written it if he had lived in our later day. In the present volume the romance speeds straight to its goal with the swiftness of an arrow. There is no moment of hesitation in it now—not an instant of dullness. I have mined and minted the gold of it.

PHILIP SCHUYLER ALLEN

The University of Chicago

THE THREE MUSKETEERS

CHAPTER I

THE MAN OF MEUNG

On the first Monday of the month of April, 1626, a young man rode into the market town of Meung.

As the rider, imagine to yourself Don Quixote at eighteen, clothed in a woolen doublet that had faded to a nameless shade between dregs of wine and a heavenly azure. Face long and brown. High cheek bones, a mark of sagacity. Muscles of the jaws highly developed, an infallible sign by which a Gascon may always be detected. The eye open and intelligent. The nose hooked, but finely chiseled. Too big for a youth, too small for a grown man. And, like Don Quixote, wearing a long sword that dangled from a leathern baldric and struck against the calves of its owner as he walked, and against the rough side of his steed when he was on horseback.

The steed itself was the observed of all observers. It was a Béarn pony, yellow of hide and without a hair in its tail. Accustomed, though the pony was, to carry its head below the knees of its windgalled legs, it nevertheless never failed to do its eight leagues of travel every day. But, unfortunately, the good qualities of this horse were so well concealed that its appearance at Meung (where everyone was a connoisseur of horseflesh) produced an unfavorable impression which extended to its rider.

You may remember that Don Quixote mistook windmills for giants, and sheep for armies of men. And in such matters young d'Artagnan—for so was this second Don Quixote named—did not lag behind his great predecessor.

D'Artagnan took every smile for an insult, and every look as a provocation. Whence it naturally resulted that all the way from Tarbes to Meung his fist was constantly doubled or his hand rested on the hilt of his sword. Of course, the sight of the wretched pony did excite numerous smiles in the faces of passers-by. And yet these onlookers were quick to repress their hilarity, because against the side of the pony rattled a sword of respectable length. And above this sword there gleamed an eye that was ferocious rather than haughty. And, even when the merriment of those he met prevailed over prudence, they endeavored to laugh only on one side of their mouth— and that the side turned away from d'Artagnan. Thus our young hero remained majestic and intact in his irritability until he arrived at this unlucky city of Meung.

But here, as he was alighting from his horse at the gate of the Jolly Miller, he spied through an open window of the ground floor a gentleman, well built and of good carriage, who was talking with two persons who appeared to listen to him with respect. D'Artagnan was only partially mistaken in fancying himself the subject of their conversation—he was not in question, but his horse was.

Now, the gentleman was enumerating all the odd qualities of the wretched animal. And, as his auditors had great deference for the narrator, every moment or two they burst into guffaws of laughter. A half-smile was sufficient to arouse the irascibility of our young man. Therefore the effect produced upon him by this vociferous mirth may be easily imagined.

D'Artagnan fixed his haughty eye upon the stranger. He perceived a man of forty to forty-five years of age, with black, piercing eyes, pale complexion, a prominent nose, and a black mustache neatly trimmed. He was dressed in a doublet and breeches of a violet color, with aiguillettes of the same, without any other ornament than the customary slashes, through which the shirt appeared. The young man noted these facts with the rapidity of one who observes most minutely. And perhaps, too, he had an instinctive feeling that this unknown was destined to have a great influence over his future life.

At just this moment the gentleman of the violet doublet made one of his profoundest remarks about the Béarnese pony. And his two auditors laughed even louder, if possible, than before. Filled, then, with the conviction that he had really been insulted, d'Artagnan pulled his cap down over his eyes, placed one hand on the hilt of his sword and the other on his hip, and advanced. In this attitude he was endeavoring to copy some of the court airs he had picked up in Gascony from young traveling nobles.

But, unhappily, as the youth went to meet his mocker, his anger increased at every step he took. So, instead of the lofty speech he had prepared as a prelude to his challenge, he found nothing at the tip of his tongue but a gross personality, which he accompanied with a furious gesture.

"You, sir, who are hiding behind that shutter! Tell me what you are laughing at, will you, eh? Then we shall laugh together."

The gentleman raised his eyes slowly from the nag to the cavalier. And then, with eyebrows slightly bent, and with an accent of insolence impossible to describe, he replied to d'Artagnan, "I was not speaking to you, sir."

"But I am speaking to you!" shouted the exasperated young man.

The unknown looked at him again with a slight smile. He retired from his place at the window, came out of the hostelry with a slow step, and placed himself before the bedraggled yellow horse within two paces of d'Artagnan. His quiet manner and the ironical expression of his countenance redoubled the mirth of the persons who still remained at the window.

The young Gascon, seeing his tormentor approach, drew his blade a foot out of its scabbard. The unknown continued to address his remarks to his auditors at the window without paying the least attention to his victim's exasperation.

"This horse is decidedly a buttercup," he drawled. "Or rather, it was a buttercup when it was young. Yellow is a color well known in botany, but until the present time very rare among horses."

"There are people who laugh at the horse that dare not laugh at his master!" cried the young man.

"I do not often laugh, sir, as you may judge from the look of my face," replied the unknown. "Still I retain the privilege of making merry when I please."

"And I allow no man to make merry when it displeases me," asserted d'Artagnan. "Turn, Master Joker, lest I strike you from behind."

"Strike *me?*" asked the other, turning to survey the young hot-head with as much astonishment as contempt. "Why, my good fellow, you must be mad!" Then in a suppressed tone, as if speaking to himself, he continued, "What a godsend you would be for his Majesty, who is searching everywhere for brave fellows to recruit his Musketeers!"

He had scarcely finished, when d'Artagnan made a furious lunge at him. If he had not sprung nimbly backward, it is likely he would have jested for the last time.

Then, perceiving that the matter had gone far beyond raillery, the unknown drew his sword, saluted, and placed himself seriously on guard. But at the same moment his two auditors, seconded by the host, fell upon d'Artagnan with shovels, sticks, and tongs.

This caused so complete a diversion from the attack that d'Artagnan's adversary, while the youth turned about to face this shower of blows, sheathed his sword and became a spectator of the fight.

With his usual impassiveness he muttered, "A plague upon these Gascons! Put him back on his orange steed and bid him begone!"

"Not before I have killed you, poltroon!" cried d'Artagnan, not yielding a single step to his three assailants, who continued to shower blows upon him.

"Hark to another gasconade!" grumbled the gentleman. "Keep up the dance, then, since he will have it so. Let him but tell us when he grows tired."

But the Gascon was never the man to cry for quarter. The fight was therefore prolonged for some few seconds further. But at length d'Artagnan dropped his sword, which had been snapped in two by a blow from a stick. At the same moment another thwack full upon the forehead brought him to the ground. He was covered with blood and almost fainting.

From all sides people now came flocking to the scene of action. At the behest of the landlord of the Jolly Miller, servants carried the wounded man into the kitchen, where some trifling attentions were bestowed upon him.

"Your Excellency is safe and sound?" the host asked anxiously of the unknown a few moments later.

"Oh, perfectly sound, my good host. Has our young man fainted quite away?"

"Yes. But before he fainted he collected all his strength to challenge you and defy you."

"Why, this fellow must be the devil in person!"

"Hardly that, your Excellency," replied the host with a grin of contempt. "We have rummaged his valise and found no more than a clean shirt and eleven crowns. However, he swore you would have cause to repent of your action at a later period."

"Then," said the unknown coolly, "he must be some prince in disguise. Did he name no one in his passion?"

"Yes. He struck his pocket and said, 'We shall see what M. de Tréville has to say of this insult offered his protégé.'"

"De Tréville?" demanded the unknown, becoming at once attentive. "He put his hand upon his pocket while pronouncing the name of M. de Tréville. What was in his pocket, dear landlord?"

"A letter addressed to M. de Tréville, captain of Musketeers."

Now, the landlord was not endowed with great perspicacity, and so he did not observe the expression which his words had brought to the face of the unknown.

"The devil!" the latter murmured. "Can Tréville have set this Gascon upon me? A weak obstacle is sometimes sufficient to overthrow a great design."

"Host," he said aloud with a cold yet menacing air, "get rid of this frantic boy for me. He annoys me. He causes a disturbance in your hostelry which respectable people cannot put up with. Make out my bill and notify my servant. I gave the order to saddle my horse. Have they not obeyed me?"

"It is done. As your Excellency may observe, your horse is in the great gateway, saddled and ready for your departure." An imperious glance from the unknown stopped further speech on the part of the landlord. He bowed humbly and retired.

"It is not necessary for Milady to be seen by this fellow," the stranger continued. "She will soon be passing —she is already late. I'll mount and ride to meet her. I should like, however, to know what this letter to Tréville contains."

And the unknown, muttering to himself, directed his steps to the kitchen, where the doublet and bag and sword of d'Artagnan had been left when he had been carried upstairs.

Meanwhile the host, who did not doubt for one minute that it was the presence of the young man that was driving the unknown gentleman from his hostelry, went upstairs and found d'Artagnan again master of himself. So the host firmly insisted that, despite his weakness, the young Gascon should get up and depart at the earliest possible moment. D'Artagnan arose, half stupefied, without his doublet, his head bound up in a linen cloth. Urged on by the host, he began to descend the stairs. But when he got to the kitchen, the first thing he saw was his antagonist talking calmly at the step of a heavy carriage drawn by two large Norman horses.

His interlocutor, whose head appeared through the carriage window, was a woman of about twenty or two and twenty years. We have already observed how quickly d'Artagnan received an indelible impression of a face. He perceived then, at a glance, that this woman was young and beautiful, pale and fair, with long curls falling in profusion over her shoulders. She had large blue, languishing eyes, rosy lips, and hands of alabaster. She was talking with great animation to the unknown.

"His Eminence, then, orders me—"

"To return instantly to England, and to inform him the moment the duke leaves London."

"And as to my other instructions?" the fair traveler asked.

"They are contained in this box, which you are not to open until across the Channel. As for me, I am returning to Paris."

"What! Without chastising this insolent boy?"

The unknown was about to reply, but at this moment d'Artagnan, who had heard all, plunged across the threshold of the door.

"This insolent boy chastises others!" he cried. "Before a woman you will not dare to fly, I presume, poltroon!"

"Remember," said Milady quickly, as she saw the unknown lay his hand upon his sword, "the least delay may ruin everything."

"You are right," observed the gentleman. "Begone then! And I shall depart as swiftly."

He bowed to the lady and sprang into his saddle, while her coachman applied the whip vigorously to his horses. At full gallop, in opposite directions, the two friends departed.

"Here's your bill!" bawled the landlord, whose esteem for the traveler was changed to profound contempt as he saw him making off without settling his account.

"Pay him, booby!" cried the unknown to his servant, without checking the speed of his horse. And the man, after throwing two or three silver pieces at the feet of mine host, galloped in pursuit of his master.

D'Artagnan sprang forward in an attempt to seize the fleeing lackey. But, scarcely had he taken ten steps, when his ears began to tingle, a cloud of blood passed over his eyes, and he fell in the middle of the street, crying still, "Coward! coward!"

"He certainly is a coward," murmured the host, approaching d'Artagnan and trying by this flattery again to get into the good graces of the young fellow.

"Yes, a coward indeed," mumbled d'Artagnan, "but *she,* a beauty indeed."

And a second time he had fainted.

"That's all right," said the host to himself. "I've lost two of them, but I still have this one, whom I'm sure to keep at least several days. I'll still get eleven crowns out of it."

Now, it is to be remembered that eleven crowns was just the sum that remained in d'Artagnan's purse. Thus the landlord had counted on eleven days of confinement for his guest, at one crown a day. But he had reckoned wrongly.

For on the following morning at five o'clock the young Gascon descended to the kitchen without help. He asked for some oil, wine, and rosemary and a few secret ingredients. Of these, according to a recipe bestowed upon him by his mother, he composed a balsam. With this he anointed his numerous wounds, replacing his bandages with his own hands and refusing the services of a doctor. Thanks no doubt to the efficacy of this sovereign remedy, thanks also, perhaps, to the absence of a doctor, d'Artagnan walked abroad the same evening, and was almost cured by the morrow.

But when the time came to pay for the rosemary, oil, and wine—the only expense he had incurred, as he had strictly abstained from food—d'Artagnan found nothing in his pocket but his little old velvet purse with the eleven crowns in it. As to the treasured letter of recommendation he was bearing to M. de Tréville, it had disappeared.

The young man instituted a search for this writing with the greatest patience, turning out all his pockets over and over again. He rummaged and re-rummaged in his valise. He opened and reopened his purse. When he finally became convinced that the document was not to be found, he flew into a terrible rage.

"My letter of recommendation!" he cried. "Or, by the holy blood! I'll split you all like ortolans."

The host seized the bellows, his wife a broomstick, and the servants the same clubs they had used the day before. But they need not have bothered. For, unfortunately, there was one powerful obstacle to the accomplishment of d'Artagnan's threat, although he had forgotten the fact. His sword was broken in two. Hence he found himself armed only with the stump of a blade about eight or ten inches in length. As to the remainder of the blade, the landlord had slyly put that to one side to make himself a larding-pin.

"I warn you," shouted the Gascon, "that this letter is for M. de Tréville. And if you do not find it, he will know how to do so."

This threat completed the intimidation of the host. After the king and the cardinal, M. de Tréville was the man whose name was perhaps most frequently repeated in France.

"Does the letter contain anything valuable?" the disturbed host inquired after a few more minutes of useless investigation.

"Zounds!" cried the Gascon. "It contained my fortune."

"Bills upon Spain?" asked the landlord with a groan.

"Bills upon his Majesty's private treasury," answered d'Artagnan, who believed this was not exactly a falsehood.

"But the money is no matter.   I should have given a
thousand pistoles not to have lost the letter."

He might as well have said twenty thousand—it would
have cost no more.   But a certain juvenile modesty restrained him.

All at once a ray of light penetrated the tormented
mind of the host.   "It is not lost," he said, "but stolen
by the gentleman who was here yesterday.   He came down
to the kitchen where your doublet lay.   He stayed there for
some time.   I would lay a wager that he took it."

"Then he's my thief," asserted d'Artagnan.   "I shall
complain to M. de Tréville, and he to the king."

He then drew two crowns majestically from his purse
and gave them to the landlord, who, cap in hand, accompanied his guest to the gate.   Without delay the Gascon
mounted his yellow horse, which bore him without any
further accident to the gate of St. Antoine in Paris, where
his owner sold him for three crowns—which was a very
good price, considering that d'Artagnan had ridden him
hard during the last stage of the journey.   The dealer
did not conceal the fact that he gave this enormous sum
only because of the originality of the beast's color.

Thus our young man entered Paris on foot, carrying
the little packet of clothes under his arm, and walked about
until he found an apartment to rent on terms that suited
the scantiness of his means.   This chamber was a sort of
garret in the Rue des Fossoyeurs, near the Luxembourg
palace.

As soon as the earnest money was paid, d'Artagnan
took possession of his lodging, and passed the remainder

of the day in sewing on his doublet and breeches the lace his mother had secretly ripped from a garment of his father.

Next, he went to the Quai de Ferraille to have a new blade put to his sword, and then on his way back to the Louvre he inquired of the first musketeer he met the location of M. de Tréville's residence. This proved to be in the Rue du Vieux-Colombier, that is to say, in the immediate vicinity of the lodging hired by d'Artagnan—a fact that seemed a happy omen for the success of his journey.

Thereafter, satisfied with the way he had conducted himself at Meung, without remorse for the past, confident in the present, and full of hope for the future, our hero retired to bed and slept the sleep of the brave.

CHAPTER II

THE ANTECHAMBER OF M. DE TRÉVILLE

M. de Tréville had really begun life in Paris as
d'Artagnan now did, that is to say, without a sou in his
pocket, but with a fund of audacity and intelligence which
makes the poorest Gascon gentleman ofttimes the peer
of the richest noble from another province.

Louis XIII had a real liking for Tréville—a royal,
self-interested sort of affection, it is true, but still a liking.
At this unhappy period of French history it was important
that a sovereign surround himself with such men as
Tréville. Now, many might take for their device the
epithet of *strong,* which formed the second part of the
motto on this nobleman's coat of arms, *fidelis et fortis,*
but very few gentlemen could lay claim to the *faithful*
which formed the first part. Tréville was one of these
latter.

At last the king made him the captain of his Musketeers, who were to Louis XIII in devotedness what his
Ordinaries had been to Henry III, and his Scotch Guard
to Louis XI.

Nor was the cardinal behind the king in this respect.
When he saw the formidable picked body with which Louis
surrounded himself, Richelieu, this second (or rather,
this first) king of France, became desirous that he, too,
should have his guard. He maintained his musketeers,
therefore, as the king did his. And these two powerful

rivals vied with each other in procuring the most celebrated swordsmen, not only in all the provinces of France, but also in all the countries abroad. Each boasted the bearing and the courage of his own mercenaries. And it was not uncommon for Richelieu and Louis XIII, during their evening game of chess, to dispute regarding the relative merits of their military servants.

Loose-lived, half-drunk, swaggering bullies, the king's Musketeers (or rather, M. de Tréville's) spread themselves about in the cabarets, in the parks, and in the places of public sport. They shouted boisterously, twisted their mustaches, clanked their swords, and took the greatest pleasure in annoying the Guards of the cardinal whenever they could fall afoul of them. They drew their blades in the open streets, as if this were the best of all possible pastimes. Sometimes they were killed, but they were always sure in that case to be both bewept and avenged. Frequently they killed others, but then they were certain not to lie forgotten and rot in prison, for M. de Tréville was invariably there to claim them for his own.

The day on which d'Artagnan presented himself at the court of the captain's mansion in the Rue du Vieux-Colombier the assemblage was an imposing one. It was especially so to a provincial just arriving in Paris.

True, this provincial was a Gascon. And, especially at this period, the compatriots of d'Artagnan bore the reputation of not being easily intimidated.

When he had once passed the massive entrance door of the building, he found himself in the midst of a troop of swordsmen who were crossing swords as they passed, calling one another to mock duels, quarreling, and playing pranks of a somewhat violent order. To force one's way through these turbulent human waves, it was necessary to be an officer, a great noble, or a pretty woman.

Our young man advanced with a beating heart, ranging his long rapier closely to his lanky leg. He kept his hand at the edge of his cap, with that half smirk of the embarrassed provincial who wishes to put a good face on a doubtful situation.

When he had passed the first group, he began to breathe more freely. He could, however, not help but observe that they turned around to stare at him. And d'Artagnan, who had until that day entertained a very good opinion of himself, for the first time in his life felt ridiculous.

At the staircase things were still worse. There were four musketeers on the bottom steps amusing themselves with a definite exercise in swordplay, while ten or twelve of their comrades waited upon the landing to take their turn in the sport.

The exercise was this: One of them, stationed upon the top step, naked sword in hand, prevented (at least, he endeavored to prevent) the other three from ascending.

These three others, of course, fenced against him with their agile swords. D'Artagnan at first believed these weapons to be foils with buttons at their ends. But he soon perceived, because of certain scratches that were in evidence, that every weapon was pointed and specially sharpened. And as, one after the other, these scratches were incurred, not only the spectators but the recipients themselves laughed and capered about like madmen.

The man who at the moment was occupying the upper step kept his opponents marvelously in check. A circle was formed around him. The rules of the sport were that, at every hit, the man touched should quit the game, yielding his place to the adversary who had pinked him.

In five minutes three had been slightly wounded—one on the hand, another on the chin, and the third on the ear— by the defender of the staircase, who himself remained untouched.

However difficult it might be to disconcert our young Gascon, this pastime really amazed him. He had seen at home in his province—that land in which brains become so easily heated—a few of the preliminaries to duels. But the daring of this quartet of fencers seemed to him the greatest he had ever heard of, even in Gascony.

He could almost fancy himself transported to that famous country of giants of which Gulliver tells and which frightened him so much. And yet, the youngster suddenly realized that he had not gained the goal of his search, but still had to storm the landing and the antechamber.

On the landing they were no longer fighting, but amusing themselves with stories about women. And in the antechamber they were whispering loose tales about the court. When he reached the landing, d'Artagnan blushed. When he entered the antechamber, he trembled.

"Certes, these fellows will all be either imprisoned or hanged," thought the terrified Gascon, "and I, no doubt, with them. What would my good father, who so strongly pointed out to me the respect due the cardinal, say if he but knew I was in the company of such pagans?"

Nevertheless, as he was a perfect stranger in the crowd of M. de Tréville's courtiers, he was at length noticed, and somebody came to ask him what he wanted.   D'Artagnan gave his name very modestly, emphasized the fact that he was the captain's compatriot, and requested a moment's audience of him.

The Gascon, a little recovered from his first surprise, had now leisure to study the costumes and faces about him.

The center of the most animated group of all was a musketeer of great height and haughty countenance.   He was dressed in a way so peculiar as to attract general attention.   He did not wear the uniform cloak of the regiment, but a cerulean blue doublet, slightly faded and shabby.   Over this was a magnificent baldric, worked in gold, which shone like water-ripples in the sun.   A cloak of crimson velvet fell in graceful folds from his shoulders, disclosing in front the splendid baldric, from which was suspended a gigantic rapier.

This musketeer apparently had just come off guard. He complained of having a cold, and coughed from time to time affectedly.   It was for this reason, he said to those around him, that he had put on the cloak.   And while he was speaking with a lofty air and twisting his mustache disdainfully, all admired his embroidered baldric, and d'Artagnan more than any one else.

"What would you have me do about it?" said the musketeer.   "The fashion is coming in.   It is a folly, I admit, but still it is the fashion.   Besides, one has to spend his inheritance somehow."

"Ah, Porthos!" cried one of his companions. "Don't try to make us believe you obtained that baldric through paternal generosity. It was given you by that veiled lady I met you with the other Sunday near the gate St. Honoré."

"No, 'pon honor and the faith of a gentleman! I bought it with the contents of my own purse," answered the soldier designated by the name of Porthos. "And the proof is that I paid ten pistoles for it, didn't I, Aramis?"

The other musketeer, to whom Porthos had turned for confirmation of his statement, formed a perfect contrast to his interrogator. This Aramis was a young man, of about two or three and twenty, with an open, ingenuous countenance, a black mild eye, and cheeks rosy and downy as an autumn peach. His delicate mustache marked a perfectly straight line upon his upper lip. He appeared to dread lowering his hands lest their veins should swell, and he pinched the tips of his ears from time to time to preserve their delicate transparency. Habitually, he spoke little and slowly. He bowed frequently, laughed without noise, showing his teeth, which were fine and of which, as of the rest of his person, he seemed to take great care.

He answered Porthos' appeal by an affirmative nod of his head. This appeared to dispel all doubts with regard to the baldric. The soldiers continued to admire it, but said no more as to its origin.

"What do you think of the story told by Chalais's esquire?" suddenly asked a musketeer, addressing nobody in particular.

"And what does he say?" demanded Porthos in a self-sufficient tone.

"He says that at Brussels he met Rochefort, the servile tool of the cardinal, disguised as a Capuchin monk. He also relates that this cursed Rochefort, thanks to his disguise, had tricked M. de Laigues, like the ninny that he is."

"Ninny is the right word!" said Porthos. "But are you sure of your news?"

"I had it from Aramis," replied the musketeer.

"Ah, indeed?"

"Why, you knew it, Porthos," declared Aramis. "I told it to you yesterday. Let's say no more about it."

"Say no more about it! *Peste!* You come to your conclusions quickly, my friend. What! The cardinal sets a spy upon a gentleman. He has the man's letters stolen by a traitor, a brigand, a rascal. With the help of this spy and the stolen correspondence, the cardinal has Chalais's throat cut, pretending that he wished to kill the king and marry Monsieur to the queen! Nobody in Paris knew how to solve the riddle of Chalais's murder, until yesterday you unravel it to the satisfaction of all. And, while we are still agape with wonder at the news, you come and observe, 'Let us say no more about it.' "

"Well, then, let's say a lot about it," replied Aramis patiently.

"If I were the esquire of poor Chalais," cried Porthos, "this Rochefort would pass a very uncomfortable minute with me!"

"And you would then pass rather a sad quarter of an hour with the Red Duke," added Aramis.

"He calls the cardinal the Red Duke!" exclaimed Porthos, clapping his hands and nodding his head. "Bravo,

bravo! The Red Duke is capital! I'll spread that saying, dear fellow; be assured of that. Who dares to say our Aramis is not a wit? It's a misfortune he did not follow his first vocation. What a delightful abbé he would have made!"

"I shall be one some day," drawled Aramis. "You know very well, Porthos, that I'm continuing to study theology for that very reason."

"Yes, he's only waiting for one thing to determine him to resume his cassock," said a musketeer.

"Well, what is he waiting for?" asked another.

"Only till the queen has given an heir to the crown of France."

"No jesting upon that subject, gentlemen," objected Porthos. "Thank God, the queen is still of an age to give one!"

"And they say M. de Buckingham is in France," replied Aramis with a significant smile.

"Aramis, my good friend," interrupted Porthos, "this time you are naughty. Your wit is always leading you beyond proper bounds. You would have cause to repent of your saying if M. de Tréville heard you."

"Are you trying to teach me a lesson, Porthos?" cried Aramis, whose usually mild eye now flashed lightning.

"My dear fellow, be a musketeer or an abbé," replied Porthos. "Be one or the other, but not both. You know what Athos told you the other day: you eat at everybody's mess—Madame d'Aiguillon's, Madame de Bois-Tracy's, Madame de Chevreuse's. Ah, don't be angry. That would be useless! You know what is agreed upon between you,

Athos, and me. All the world knows your discretion.
Now, since you possess that virtue, why the devil don't
you make use of it with respect to her Majesty? The queen
is sacred. And if any one speaks of her, let it be respectfully."

"You know I hate moralizing, Porthos, except when it
is done by Athos," announced Aramis. "I shall be an
abbé if it suits me, good sir. Meanwhile, I am a musketeer.
And in that capacity I say what I please. And at this
moment it pleases me to say that you weary me."

"Aramis!"

"Porthos!"

"Gentlemen! Gentlemen!" cried the surrounding
group.

"M. de Tréville awaits M. d'Artagnan," called a
servant, throwing open the door of the inner room.

CHAPTER III

THE AUDIENCE

M. de Tréville was at the moment in quite a bad humor. Nevertheless, he politely greeted the young man, who bowed to the very ground. And he smiled on receiving d'Artagnan's greeting, the Béarnese accent of which recalled to him both his youth and his country—a double remembrance which makes a man smile at all ages.

The captain made a sign to the Gascon as if to ask his permission to finish other business before taking up his case. And then he stepped toward the antechamber and called three times in a tone of thunder, "Athos! Porthos! Aramis!"

The two musketeers with whom we have already made acquaintance entered, and the door was closed behind them.

M. de Tréville then paced, in silence and with a frowning brow, the whole length of his room, to and fro. Each time he passed before Porthos and Aramis, who were as upright and silent as if on parade. All at once he stopped full in front of them and covered them with an angry look from head to foot.

"Gentlemen," he cried, "do you know what the king said to me yesterday evening?"

"No, sir. But I hope you will do us the honor to tell us," said Aramis in his most polite tone and with a graceful bow.

"His Majesty informed me, sirs," continued M. de Tréville, growing warmer as he spoke, "that his daredevils, his braggart Musketeers, had started a riot in a cabaret of the Rue Férou and that the cardinal's Guards (I thought the king was going to laugh in my face!) had been forced to arrest the rioters. *Morbleu!* Arrest Musketeers! You were among the rioters—the king named you. But it's all my fault, yes, it's all my fault, because it is I myself who select my men."

The two musketeers reddened to the whites of their eyes. Poor d'Artagnan did not know which way to look. He wished himself a hundred feet under ground.

"You, Aramis, why the devil did you ask me for a uniform when you would have been so much better suited with a cassock? And you, Porthos, do you wear such a splendid golden baldric only to suspend a sword of straw from it? And Athos—I don't see Athos. Where is he?"

"Sir," answered Aramis in a sorrowful tone, "he is ill, very ill."

"And of what malady?"

"It is feared that it may be smallpox, sir," said Porthos, desiring to take his turn in the conversation. "And the worst of it is that it will certainly spoil his face."

"That is a great story to tell me, Porthos! Sick of the smallpox at his age! No, no, but wounded, without doubt—killed, perhaps. Ah, if I but knew! S'blood! Messieurs Musketeers, I will not have occasion given the cardinal's Guards, who never allow themselves to be arrested, to laugh at you. They would prefer dying on the spot to being arrested or taking a backward step. To

save yourselves, to scamper away, to scurry off in flight—
that is good for the king's Musketeers, I must say!"

Porthos and Aramis trembled with rage. They stamped
upon the carpet with their feet, they bit their lips till the
blood came, they grasped the hilts of their swords with
knotted fists.

And their comrades outside the room had guessed
from the tone of his voice that M. de Tréville was very
angry about something or other. Ten curious heads were
glued to the tapestry of the antechamber, and these became
pale with fury. For their ears did not lose a syllable of
what their captain was saying. And they repeated all
this officer's insulting expressions to the people about them.
In an instant, from the door of the inner room to the
street gate, the whole place was boiling.

"Six of his Eminence's Guards arrest six of his
Majesty's Musketeers!" continued M. de Tréville, raging.
"Morbleu! My mind is made up. I go straight to the
Louvre. I give in my resignation as captain of the king's
Musketeers. I apply for a lieutenancy in the cardinal's
Guards. And if he refuses me, *morbleu,* I shall turn abbé!"

At these words the murmur without became an ex-
plosion. Nothing was to be heard but oaths and blas-
phemies. The *morbleus,* the *sang Dieus,* the *morts de touts
les diables,* filled the air. D'Artagnan hunted for a rug to
hide behind. He felt an overpowering inclination to crawl
under the table.

"Well, my Captain," said Porthos, quite beside himself
with fury, "the truth is we were not captured by fair
means. Before we had time to draw our swords, two of

us were dead and Athos grievously wounded. He endeavored to get up and fell again twice. We did not surrender, not we! They dragged us away by force, and on the way we escaped. They left Athos on the field of battle because they did not think it worth the trouble to carry him away."

"And I have the honor of assuring you that I killed one of them with his own sword," said Aramis, "since mine was broken at the first parry. Killed him or poniarded him, sir, as is most agreeable to you."

"I did not know that," replied M. de Tréville in a somewhat softened tone. "The cardinal exaggerated the story for the king, I perceive."

Seeing the captain becoming appeased, Aramis ventured to risk a petition. "Pray, sir, do not acknowledge that Athos is wounded. He would be in despair if the fact should come to the ears of the king. His condition seems very serious because the wound after crossing the shoulder penetrates the chest—"

At this instant the tapestry was raised. A noble and handsome head, albeit a frightfully pale one, appeared under the fringe.

"Athos!" cried M. de Tréville.

"You sent for me, sir," remarked Athos in a feeble but perfectly calm voice. "I am here, sir, to receive your commands."

With these words the musketeer, belted as usual and in irreproachable costume, with a tolerably firm step entered the room. M. de Tréville, moved to the bottom of his heart by this proof of courage, sprang toward him.

"I was about to say to these gentlemen," he observed, "that I forbid my Musketeers to expose their lives needlessly. For brave men are very precious to the king, and his Majesty knows that his Musketeers are the bravest fellows on earth. Your hand, Athos!"

The door had remained open, so strong was the excitement produced by the arrival of Athos. A burst of satisfaction greeted the last words of the captain. M. de Tréville was about to censure this breach of military etiquette, when he felt the hand of Athos stiffen in his grasp and realized that he was on the point of fainting. Athos, who had rallied all his energies to struggle against the terrible pain that held him, was at length overcome by it and fell upon the floor as if he were indeed dead.

The whole assemblage of the antechamber now rushed in and crowded around the sorely wounded man. But all this eager attention would have profited little had not a surgeon chanced to be in the house. He required, as the first and most urgent thing, that the musketeer be carried into the adjoining chamber. Thither Porthos and Aramis bore their comrade in their arms. M. de Tréville and the surgeon followed them, and the door was closed.

The chamber of M. de Tréville, generally held in such holy awe, at once became the annex of the public rooms outside it. Everyone shouted, vociferated, and harangued —consigning the cardinal and his Guards to eternal torments in the life to come.

An instant afterward Porthos and Aramis reëntered. Quite a little later M. de Tréville and the surgeon returned. The injured soldier had recovered his senses, and the physician declared that his situation need not render his friends uneasy, his swoon having been caused simply by loss of blood.

Then the captain waved all the intruders away, and the crowd vanished in its entirety except d'Artagnan, who had not forgotten he was promised an audience. And with the tenacity of a Gascon he remained where he was.

The event which had occurred had in some measure broken the thread of M. de Tréville's ideas. When he discovered himself alone with the persevering young man, he inquired what might be the will of his visitor. D'Artagnan then repeated his name, and with this the captain immediately grasped the business in hand.

"Pardon me," he apologized, smiling, "but I had quite forgotten your presence. Soldiers are big children, are they not? But, as I maintain, the commands of the king, and more particularly the orders of the cardinal, should be observed."

D'Artagnan could not restrain a smile. Because of this fact M. de Tréville judged that he was not dealing with a simpleton. So he went straight to the point.

"I respected your father extremely," he said. "Tell me what I can do for his son."

"Monsieur," said d'Artagnan, "it was my intention to request of you, because of the friendship which you have not forgotten, the uniform of a musketeer. I comprehend that such a favor is enormous and tremble lest I should not merit it."

"It is indeed a favor, young man," replied M. de Tréville, "but it may not be so far beyond your hopes as you appear to believe. His Majesty's consent is always necessary, of course. And I inform you with regret that no one becomes a musketeer without the preliminary ordeal of several campaigns, certain brilliant performances, or a service of two years in some other regiment less favored than ours."

D'Artagnan bowed without replying, feeling his desire to don the musketeer's uniform vastly increased by the considerable difficulties which preceded the attainment of it.

"But," continued M. de Tréville, fixing upon his compatriot a look so piercing that it might be said to penetrate to the depths of his heart—"but, on account of my old companionship with your father, I shall do something for you, young man. Our recruits from Béarn are not very rich. I dare say that you have not brought too large a stock of money to Paris with you?"

D'Artagnan drew himself up with a proud air which plainly said, "I ask no alms of any man."

"Oh, that's all very well," continued M. de Tréville. "I know these youthful airs. I myself came to the capital with four crowns in my purse. And I should have fought with any one who had ever hinted I was not in condition to purchase the Louvre."

D'Artagnan's bearing had become still more impressive. Thanks to the sale of his yellow nag, he was commencing his career with four crowns more than M. de Tréville possessed at the beginning of his.

"I shall write a letter today to the director of the Royal Academy, and tomorrow he will admit you without any expense to yourself. Do not refuse this slight service.

Our richest and best-born gentlemen often solicit entrance there without being able to attain it. You will learn there to ride, to fence, and to dance. You will also make some desirable acquaintances. And from time to time you can call on me to inform me of your progress and to say whether I can be of further service to you."

Stranger though he was to all the manners of a court, d'Artagnan could not but perceive a little coldness in this reception.

"Alas, sir," he said, "I realize only too well how sadly I need the letter of introduction which my father gave me to present to you."

"I am surprised that you should undertake so long a journey without that necessary passport."

"I had one, sir," cried d'Artagnan, "but it was perfidiously stolen from me."

He then related the adventure of Meung, describing the unknown gentleman with the greatest minuteness and with a warmth that delighted M. de Tréville.

"That is all very strange," said the latter after the tale was ended. "You mentioned my name, then, aloud?"

"Yes, sir. And I hope I did not thereby commit an imprudence. But what should I have done otherwise? A name like yours was a buckler to me on my way. Judge if I should not place myself under its protection."

At this period flattery was very current, and M. de Tréville was as fond of its incense as any king or cardinal. He could not refrain from a smile of visible satisfaction.

"Tell me," he continued, "had not this unknown of Meung a slight scar on his cheek?"

"Yes. Such a one as would be made by the grazing of a bullet."

"Was he fine looking and of lofty stature?"

"Yes, yes."

"Of pale complexion and brown hair?"

"Yes, that is he to the dot. How comes it, sir, that you are acquainted with this man? I swear I shall find him again if searching will do it and if it be in hell itself!"

"He was waiting for a woman?" continued M. de Tréville.

"He departed at once, after having conversed for but a minute with her whom he awaited."

"Did you overhear the subject of their conversation?"

"He gave her a box containing her instructions and asked her not to open it until she reached London."

"Was this woman English?"

"He called her Milady."

"It is he, it must be he!" murmured Tréville. "I believed him still at Brussels."

"Oh, sir," cried d'Artagnan, "if you know who this man is, tell me his name and where to find him. I shall then release you from all your promises, including that of my admission to the Musketeers. For, above all else, 1 must be revenged."

"Beware, young man!" counseled Tréville. "If you see him approaching on one side of the street, pass by on the other. Do not hurl yourself against this rock. He will break you like glass."

"That is all one to me," replied d'Artagnan with a shrug, "if I but succeed in finding him."

All at once the captain was struck by a sudden suspicion. This unusual hatred which the young traveler manifested so loudly for this man who—a fairly improbable yarn!—had stolen his father's letter—was there not some perfidy concealed under this pretended hatred? Was this d'Artagnan not an emissary of the cardinal, sent to Tréville's house to win his confidence, and afterward to ruin him? He fixed his eyes upon d'Artagnan even more earnestly than before. "I know he is a Gascon," he reflected, "but he may be one for the cardinal as well as for me. Let us try him out."

"My friend," he said slowly, "the king and the cardinal are the best of friends. Their apparent bickerings are only feints to deceive fools. I am unwilling that a brave youth like yourself should become the dupe of such artifices. Be assured that I am devoted to both these all-powerful masters, and that I have no other aim than to serve the king and also the cardinal—one of the most illustrious men of genius that France has ever produced."

With shining face the young Gascon cried, "I venerate your sentiments, sir, and I echo them."

"Now, young man," Tréville continued, watching his companion narrowly, "be pleased to regulate your conduct accordingly. If you entertain, for whatever reason, such an enmity as we constantly see breaking out against the cardinal, bid me adieu and let us separate."

Tréville was rather proud of himself as he finished this harangue. "There," he said to himself, "if the cardinal has set this young fox upon my trail, he will certainly not have failed to inform his spy that the best means of getting into my good graces is to rail at the cardinal. Therefore, in spite of all my protestations of loyalty, if d'Artagnan is a spy, he will assure me that he holds his Eminence in holy horror."

But d'Artagnan answered, with the greatest simplicity, "I came to Paris with just such intentions, M. de Tréville. My father advised me to stoop to nobody but the king, the cardinal, and yourself—whom he considered to be the first three personages in France."

D'Artagnan's father, as a matter of fact, had said nothing to him about M. de Tréville in any such connection. But the son thought this addition would do no harm.

"I have the greatest veneration for the cardinal," he continued, "and the most profound respect for his actions. And, sir, if you are speaking, as you say, with frankness, so much the better for me, for then you will do me the honor to appreciate the similarity of our tastes. But if you entertain any doubts, which is, of course, quite natural, I am ruining my chances by speaking the truth, and so much the worse for me, for you will then have no respect for me, and respect is what I want above all else in this world."

M. de Tréville was surprised to the greatest degree. So much penetration on the part of the youth compelled his admiration, but did not remove his suspicions. For, the more this Gascon was superior to others, the more he was to be dreaded if he intended to deceive. Nevertheless, he pressed d'Artagnan's hand and said to him, "You are an honest youth. But just at present I can do no more for you than I have already suggested. My house will always be open to you."

"That is to say," observed d'Artagnan, "you are forced to wait until I have proved myself worthy of obtaining what I desire. Be assured, sir, that you shall not wait long."

And he bowed as if about to retire and as if he considered the future was already well within his grasp.

"But wait a moment," said M. de Tréville. "I promised you a letter for the director of the Royal Academy. Are you too proud to accept it, my dear sir?"

"No, indeed," replied d'Artagnan, "and I shall agree that this one does not fare like the other. I shall guard it so carefully that it spells death to him who tries to take it from me."

M. de Tréville smiled at this flourish. He wrote the letter and rose from his desk to hand it to his young compatriot. But at the very moment when d'Artagnan stretched out his hand to receive it the captain was highly astonished to see him make a sudden spring, become crimson with passion, and rush from the room crying, "S'blood, he shall not escape me this time!"

"And who?" asked M. de Tréville.

"He, my thief!" cried d'Artagnan. "Ah, the traitor!"

And he disappeared like a flash of light.

"The devil and all his minions seize this madman!" muttered M. de Tréville. "Unless," he added, "this be but a cunning mode of escaping, seeing that he has failed in his purpose of trapping me!"

CHAPTER IV

THE BALDRIC AND THE HANDKERCHIEF

D'Artagnan crossed the antechamber in three bounds. He was darting down the stairs when, in his heedless course, he ran head foremost against a musketeer who was coming out of one of M. de Tréville's private rooms. He struck the man's shoulder violently, making him utter a cry, or rather a howl.

"Pardon me," said d'Artagnan, endeavoring to resume his course, "but I'm in an awful hurry."

A hand of iron seized him by the belt and stopped him.

"So you are in a hurry?" asked the musketeer, as pale as a sheet. "You say, 'Pardon me,' and believe that is sufficient? Let me disabuse your mind of that error, young man. Do not fancy, because you have heard M. de Tréville speak to us a little cavalierly today, that other people treat us carelessly."

"My faith!" said d'Artagnan. For he had recognized Athos, who was returning to his apartment after having his wounds dressed by the doctor. "My faith, sir! It seems to me that my apology is sufficient. I am in great haste. Unhand me, I beg, and let me go where my business calls me!"

"Monsieur," said Athos, releasing his captive, "you are not polite. It is easy to see that you come from a distance and are not at home with us."

D'Artagnan had already jumped down three or four stairs, but at this last remark of Athos he stopped short.

"*Morbleu,* Monsieur!" he cried.   "However far I may have come, it is not for you to give me a lesson in good manners."

"Perhaps!" said Athos drily.

"Ah, if I were not in such haste and if I were only not running after some one!" gasped d'Artagnan.

"Monsieur Man-in-a-hurry, you can find me without running—*me,* you understand?"

"And where, if you please?"

"Near the Carmes-Deschaux."

"At what hour?"

"About noon."

"About noon? That will do nicely. I shall be prompt."

"Endeavor not to make me wait! For at a quarter past twelve I shall cut off your ears as you flee from me."

"Suits me!" cried d'Artagnan. "I'll be there at ten minutes to twelve."

And he started running as if the devil possessed him, hoping that he might yet find the unknown, whose slow pace could not have carried him far.

But at the street gate Porthos was talking with the sentry. There seemed to be just room for a man to pass between the two. But our Gascon had reckoned without the wind. As he was about to pass, a sudden breeze blew out Porthos' long cloak, and the unhappy youth rushed straight into the middle of it. Apparently the musketeer had good reasons for not abandoning this part of his garments, for, instead of quitting his hold of the flap in his hand, he pulled it toward him. Thus it came that d'Artagnan entangled himself in the velvet by a movement of rotation caused by the odd persistency of its owner.

The young fellow heard the musketeer swear an awful oath. He wished to escape from the cloak which was blinding him and he sought to find his way from under the folds of it. He was particularly anxious to avoid marring the freshness of the famous baldric. But, upon timidly opening his eyes, he discovered that his nose was fixed between the two shoulders of Porthos, that is to say, exactly on the baldric.

Alas! Like most things in the world that have nothing in their favor except outward appearance, this baldric (which glittered with gold on the front side) was nothing but simple buff behind. Vainglorious as he was, the musketeer, who could not afford to have a thing entirely of gold, possessed at least the half of it.

One could now understand the pretense of the cold and the urgency of the cloak.

Porthos was making herculean efforts to disengage himself from d'Artagnan, who was wriggling about his back.

"Bless me!" he cried. "You must be fair mad to run against people in this manner."

"Pardon me," said d'Artagnan, that moment reappearing under the shoulder of the giant, "but I am in such haste—I was running after some one, and—"

"And do you always forget your eyes when you run?"

"No," retorted the Gascon, piqued. "And thanks to my eyes, I can see what other people cannot."

Perhaps Porthos understood the allusion, perhaps he did not. At any rate, he yielded to sudden anger.

"Monsieur," he said, "you stand a chance of getting chastised if you rub musketeers in this fashion."

"The expression is a strong one," said d'Artagnan.

"It is used by a man accustomed to look his enemies in the face."

"Ah, *pardieu!* I know full well that you don't turn that back of yours on either enemies or friends."

Porthos foamed with rage and made a movement to pursue the saucy Gascon, who, delighted with his joke, went away laughing loudly.

"Presently, presently," the latter called, "when you haven't your cloak on."

"At one o'clock, then, behind the Luxembourg."

"Suits me all right," replied d'Artagnan as he turned the corner of the street.

As there was no longer any question of finding his tormentor of Meung, he began to reflect upon the events that had passed. Here it was scarcely eleven o'clock in the morning, and yet the day had already brought him into disgrace with M. de Tréville, who could not fail to think the manner in which d'Artagnan had left him very peculiar, to say the least. Besides this, he had drawn upon himself duels with two men, each of whom was capable of killing three d'Artagnans. The outlook was sad.

While walking and soliloquizing thus, he had arrived within a few steps of the d'Aiguillon residence and in front of this building he perceived Aramis, chatting gaily with three gentlemen of the king's Guards.

On his part, Aramis perceived d'Artagnan. But, as he had not forgotten that it was in the presence of this

young man M. de Tréville had been so angry, he pretended
not to see him. The young Gascon, quite full of his plans
for conciliation and courtesy, approached the soldiers with
a profound bow, accompanied by a most gracious smile.
Aramis returned the bow slightly, but he did not smile.
Besides, all four of the friends immediately broke off their
conversation.

D'Artagnan was not so dull as not to realize that he
was one too many. He was seeking in his mind for the
least awkward means of retreat, when he remarked that
Aramis had let his handkerchief fall and by mistake, no
doubt, had placed his foot upon it. This seemed to the
youth a favorable opportunity to repair his intrusion.
Therefore, with the most gracious air he could assume, he
stooped and drew the handkerchief from under the foot
of the musketeer, despite the latter's efforts to prevent him.

He held the dainty thing out to Aramis and said, "I
believe, Monsieur, you would be sorry to lose this?"

The handkerchief was indeed richly embroidered. At
one of its corners it had a coronet and arms. Aramis
blushed—excessively—and snatched (rather than took)
it from the hands of the Gascon.

"Aha! And also aha!" cried one of the guards. "Will
you still persist, most discreet musketeer, that you are not
on good terms with Madame de Bois-Tracy, when that
gracious lady has the kindness to lend you one of her most
valuable bits of lace?"

Aramis darted at poor d'Artagnan one of those looks
that inform a man he has acquired a mortal enemy. Immediately, however, he resumed his mild air.

"You are deceived, gentlemen," he said. "This bit of lace is not mine, and I cannot fancy why Monsieur has taken it into his head to offer it to me rather than to one of you. As proof of what I say, here is my handkerchief in my pocket."

So saying, he pulled out his own bit of cambric—a very dear article at that period—but a handkerchief without embroidery and without arms, ornamented only with its owner's monogram.

"If the case were as you pretend it to be," said one of the companions of Aramis, "I should be forced to reclaim the thing myself. For, as you know, Bois-Tracy is an intimate friend of mine. And I really cannot allow the property of his wife to be exhibited abroad as a trophy."

"You say your piece badly," complained Aramis. "So, while I acknowledge the justice of your reclamation, I refuse it on account of the form in which you couch it."

"The fact is," d'Artagnan hazarded timidly, "I did not actually see the handkerchief fall from the pocket of M. Aramis. But I thought from his having his foot on it that the thing must be his."

"And you were deceived, my dear sir," announced Aramis coldly.

Then he turned to that one of the guards who had declared himself the friend of Bois-Tracy.

"Besides," he continued, "I have reflected, my dear intimate of Bois-Tracy, that I am no less tenderly his friend than you can possibly be. So this handkerchief is as likely to have fallen from your pocket as mine."

"No, 'pon honor, no!" cried his Majesty's guardsman.

"Now, here you're swearing on your honor and I on my word! It is pretty evident that there's a lie somewhere about. We shall do better than dispute the case if we each take half of the bauble."

"A Solomon has come to judgment!" exclaimed the other two soldiers. "Aramis, you are as full of wisdom as a nut is of meat."

The four young men burst out laughing and the affair had no other sequel. A moment later the group had separated with much cordial hand-shaking, the guardsmen going one way and Aramis another.

"Now is my time for making peace with this gallant fellow," said d'Artagnan to himself. And, although the musketeer was departing without paying any attention to him, he said, "Monsieur, you will excuse me, I hope."

"Permit me to observe," answered Aramis, "that you have not acted in this business as a gentleman should."

"Sir!" cried d'Artagnan. "And do you suppose—"

"I suppose, Monsieur, that you are not quite a fool, and that you know, even though you hail from Gascony, that people do not tread upon handkerchiefs without a reason. The devil, sir! Paris is not paved with cambric!"

"Monsieur," said d'Artagnan, "you speak of my birthplace. Very well, then, it is not necessary to tell you that Gascons are not patient animals. When they have begged to be excused once, they feel they have already done twice as much as they should."

"Monsieur," retorted Aramis, "I am seeking no quarrel. I am not a bravo, thank God! Being a musketeer only for a time, I fight simply when forced to do so, and always with great repugnance. But this time, let me tell you, the matter is serious. The name of a lady has been compromised by you."

"By *us,* you mean."

"You stupidly restored to me the handkerchief, I believe?"

"You stupidly let it fall."

"I have said, Monsieur, and I repeat that it did not fall from my pocket."

"Thereby lying twice, Monsieur. I saw it fall."

"Aha! So you adopt that tone with me, Master Gascon! Well, I shall teach you how to behave yourself better."

"And I shall send you back to your mass book, Master Abbé. Draw, if you please, and instantly—"

"Not so, sir! Can you not see we are opposite the d'Aiguillon mansion, which is full of the cardinal's creatures? And it may be that his Eminence has honored you with the commission to procure for him my head. Now, I entertain a ridiculous fondness for my head, Monsieur; it sets so correctly on my shoulders. I wish to kill you— please do not worry on that score—but to kill you quietly in some snug, remote place where you cannot boast of your death to any one. At two o'clock I shall have the honor of expecting you at the residence of M. de Tréville. There I shall indicate to you the best place and time."

The two young men bowed and separated, Aramis ascending the street that led to the Luxembourg. D'Artagnan, noticing that the appointed hour of noon was nigh, took the road to the Carmes-Deschaux, saying to himself, "Decidedly, I cannot draw back. But, at least, if I am killed. I shall have been killed by a musketeer."

CHAPTER V

KING'S MUSKETEERS AND CARDINAL'S GUARDS

D'Artagnan possessed that invincible stock of resolution which the counsels of his father had implanted in his heart: "Endure no slight from any one alive, except the king, the cardinal, and M. de Tréville."

He flew, then, rather than walked to the convent of the Carmes-Deschaux. This turned out to be a sort of building without a window, surrounded by barren fields. And it was generally employed as the meeting place for the rencounters of men who had no time to lose.

By the time the young Gascon arrived in sight of the bare spot of ground that stretched along the foot of the monastery, Athos had been waiting about five minutes and twelve o'clock was striking.

He was still suffering grievously from his wound, although it had been bandaged anew by M. de Tréville's surgeon. He was seated on a post and awaiting his adversary with that placid countenance and noble air that never forsook him. At sight of the young arrival he arose and came a few steps to meet him.

D'Artagnan, on his side, saluted his antagonist with hat in hand, his feather even sweeping the ground.

"Monsieur," said Athos, "I have engaged two of my friends as seconds, but they are late in coming. I am amazed at this, as delay is by no means their habit."

"And I, Monsieur, have no seconds whatever," replied

the Gascon. "Because of my fresh arrival in Paris, I know as yet no man but M. de Tréville, to whom I was recommended by my father, who has the honor to be one of his friends."

"Why, then, if I kill you," remarked Athos, reflectively, "I shall have the air of being a boy-slayer."

"Not at all, sir," observed d'Artagnan, with a bow that was not deficient in dignity, "since you are good enough to draw a sword with me while suffering from an inconvenient wound."

"Inconvenient is the proper term, sir. And you hurt me most devilishly, I can tell you. Do not fancy, however, that I am doing you a favor by using my left hand in our encounter. I use either right or left easily. It will even be a disadvantage to you. A left-handed man is quite troublesome to people who are unprepared for it. I regret I did not inform you sooner of this circumstance."

"I assure you I am very grateful for your courtesy, Monsieur."

"You confuse me," said Athos with his gentlemanly air, "so let us talk of other things, if you please."

"But first, Monsieur," suggested d'Artagnan timidly, "may I not speak of a miraculous balsam for wounds that my mother gave me? I have made trial of it upon myself, and am therefore sure that in less than three days it would entirely heal your painful shoulder. And then, sir, when you were quite cured it would still do me great honor to be your opponent." The young Gascon spoke these words with a simplicity that did honor to his gentle heart without throwing the least doubt upon his courage.

"*Pardieu,* Monsieur!" exclaimed Athos, "thus spoke the gallant knights of the time of Charlemagne, in whom we all should seek our model of chivalry. Unfortunately, three days hence, however well the secret might be guarded, it would be known that we were to fight and the meeting would be prevented. Oh, will those lazy fellows of mine never come?"

"If you are in haste to dispatch me, Monsieur, do not inconvenience yourself by waiting, I beg," said d'Artagnan.

"My young friend," cried Athos with a gracious nod to the Gascon, "I love men of your kidney. I plainly foresee that if we do not kill each other, I shall hereafter find much pleasure in your conversation. But here comes one of our gentlemen now, I believe."

At the end of the Rue Vaugirard the gigantic Porthos appeared.

"What!" gasped d'Artagnan. "Is your first witness M. Porthos?"

"Yes. And that disturbs you?"

"Not the least in the world, Monsieur."

"And here approaches our second witness, as if worked by the same string."

"What!" cried the young Gascon a second time, as he turned in the direction indicated by Athos. "Your second witness is M. Aramis?"

"But certainly. Are you not aware that no one of us is ever seen without the others? We are called by Musketeers and Guards, at court and in the city, the Three Inseparables."

In the meantime Porthos had come up, waved his hand

to Athos, and then on turning toward d'Artagnan stood stock-still in much astonishment. (Let us say, in passing, that he had changed his baldric and relinquished his cloak.)

"This is the gentleman I am going to fight," said Athos, saluting his comrade and indicating the young Gascon with the same gesture.

"Why, I have a small affair on with him, too," declared Porthos.

"But not before one o'clock," d'Artagnan reminded him.

"I also am anticipating some lively conversation with this young stranger to Paris," said Aramis as he reached the spot.

"But not until two o'clock," replied the Gascon with the same calmness as before.

"What is the cause of your duello, Athos?" asked Aramis.

"I' faith! I have forgotten, except that he wrenched my shoulder," responded the eldest musketeer. "And what is your pretext, Porthos, my son?"

"*Morbleu!* I am going to fight—because I am going to fight. And who knows a better reason?" answered Porthos, reddening.

Athos, whose keen eye lost nothing, noted the faintly sly smile that appeared on the lips of the Gascon as the latter returned, "We had a slight argument about clothes."

"And how about yourself, Aramis?" inquired Athos.

"Oh, ours was a theological quarrel," retorted Aramis, making a sign to d'Artagnan to keep secret the cause of their duel. Again the elder musketeer marked a smile on the lips of the young firebrand.

"We could not agree upon the meaning of a certain passage from St. Augustine," explained the Gascon.

"Decidedly, this is a clever bantam," murmured Athos.

"And now that you are all assembled, gentlemen," said d'Artagnan, "permit me to offer you my apologies."

At this terrible word *apologies,* a cloud passed over the brow of Athos, a haughty smile curled the under lip of Porthos, and a negative sign was the only reply of Aramis.

"Ah, you do not understand me, sirs," said the Gascon, throwing up his head, the sharp and bold lines of which were at that moment gilded by a bright ray of the sun. "I asked simply to be excused in case I should prove unable to discharge my debt to all three of you. For M. Athos has the right to kill me first, which must lessen your valor in your own estimation, M. Porthos, and renders yours almost nil, M. Aramis. And now, gentlemen, I repeat, excuse me—but on that account only. On guard, sir!"

It was now a quarter past midday. The sun stood at its zenith, and the spot chosen for the scene of the duel was exposed to its full ardor.

"It is very hot," said Athos, drawing his sword, "and yet I cannot remove my doublet. For I feel my wound is starting to bleed afresh, and I should not willingly annoy Monsieur with the sight of blood which he has not drawn from me himself."

"Whether drawn by myself or another, Monsieur, I assure you I shall always view with regret the blood of so brave a gentleman. I shall therefore fight in my doublet, myself."

"Here, here! Enough of such compliments," cried Porthos. "Remember that we are awaiting our turns."

"Speak for yourself when you are inclined to utter such incongruities," counseled Aramis. "For my part, I consider what they say to be very well spoken."

But scarcely had the two rapiers clashed, when a company of the Guards of his Eminence, commanded by M. de Jussac, turned the corner of the convent.

"The cardinal's henchmen!" called Aramis and Porthos in a single breath. "Sheathe your swords, gentlemen!"

But it was too late. The two combatants had already been seen in a position which left no doubts as to their intentions.

"Halloo!" shouted Jussac, advancing toward them and commanding his men to do likewise. "Halloo, musketeers! Fighting again, are you? And the edicts, what is to become of them?"

"You are very generous, gentlemen of the Guards," said Athos, full of rancor, for Jussac was one of the aggressors of the preceding day. "If we were to catch you fighting, I swear we should make no effort to prevent it. Let us alone, therefore, and you will enjoy a little amusement with no cost to yourselves."

"It is with much regret that I pronounce such action impossible, my friends," returned Jussac. "Duty before everything, is my motto. Sheathe then, if you please, and follow us."

"Monsieur," declared Aramis, parodying Jussac's tones to perfection, "it would afford us great pleasure to obey your invitation if we consulted our own wishes in the matter. But, unfortunately, M. de Tréville has forbidden it. Pass on your way, please. It is the best thing to do."

This mockery exasperated Jussac. "We shall charge upon you, sirs, if you disobey me."

"There are five of them," reflected Athos, half aloud, "and we are but three. We must die on the spot, for I swear I shall never again appear before the captain as a conquered man."

D'Artagnan turned in a flash toward Athos. "Monsieur," he said, "permit me to correct your words, if you please. You said you were but three, and it appears to me that we are four."

"Withdraw, young man," cried Jussac, who by the expression of the Gascon's countenance had guessed his design. "You may retire. Save your skin—begone quickly!"

D'Artagnan did not budge.

"*Peste,* but you are a brave fellow!" said Athos, pressing the youngster's hand. "But at best we should be only three, one of whom is wounded, with the addition of a boy. And yet, none the less, it would be said that we were four men."

"In heaven's name try me, gentlemen!" cried the Gascon. "And I vow to you by my honor that I shall not go hence if we are conquered."

"What is your name, my dear fellow?" asked Athos.

"D'Artagnan, Monsieur."

"Well then, Athos, Porthos, Aramis, and d'Artagnan, forward!" called the eldest musketeer.

"Ah, you resist, do you?" cried Jussac.

"S'blood! Does that astonish you?" asked Aramis.

Athos fixed upon a certain Cahusac, a favorite of the cardinal's. Porthos had Bicaret, and Aramis found himself opposed by two adversaries. As to d'Artagnan, in the assault he had drawn Jussac himself.

He fought like a furious tiger, turning ten times around his adversary and changing his ground and his guard twenty times. Jussac was a fine blade and had had much practice. Nevertheless, it required all his skill to defend himself against this young whirlwind. The Gascon, active and energetic, each instant departed from the accepted rules of fence. He attacked his quarry from all sides at once, and yet parried like a man who had the greatest possible respect for the safety of his own epidermis.

This style of contest at length exhausted Jussac's patience. Furious at being held in check by one whom he had considered a boy, he grew hot under the collar and began to make mistakes.

At this point d'Artagnan, who though wanting in practice was sound in theory, redoubled his agility. Jussac, anxious to put an end to this dancing about like a dervish, sprang forward and aimed a terrible blow at his adversary, who parried it. And while Jussac was recovering his balance, the Gascon glided like a serpent beneath the guardsman's blade and ran his sword through his body. Jussac fell like a dead mass.

D'Artagnan then cast an anxious glance over the field of battle. Aramis had killed one of his enemies, but the other was pressing him warmly. Nevertheless, the musketeer was in good situation and able to defend himself. Bicarat and Porthos had just made counter hits. The latter had received a thrust through his arm, and Bicarat one through the thigh. But neither of these two wounds was serious, and the two opponents only fought the more earnestly because of them. Athos, wounded anew by Cahusac, was growing visibly paler, but did not yield a foot of soil. He had changed his sword hand and was fighting with his left.

Athos would have died rather than appeal for help, but his look asked assistance of the young Gascon. In fact, the soldier's glance was one of supreme eloquence. D'Artagnan interpreted it rightly. With a terrible bound he sprang to the side of Cahusac, crying, "At me, Monsieur Guardsman! I shall slay you."

Cahusac turned. It was time. For Athos, thus happily relieved, sank upon his knees. His great courage alone had supported him.

"S'blood!" he cried to d'Artagnan. "Do not kill him, I beg. I have an old affair to settle with him when I am on my feet again. Disarm him—make sure of his sword. That's it! Very well done!"

This exclamation was drawn from Athos by seeing the sword of Cahusac fly twenty paces from him. D'Artagnan and Cahusac sprang forward at the same instant, the one to recover, the other to obtain the weapon. The youngster, being the more active, reached it first and placed his foot upon it.

Cahusac immediately ran to the guardsman whom Aramis had killed, seized his rapier, and returned to face d'Artagnan. But on his way back to the fray he met Athos, who had somewhat recovered his breath, and who, for fear that the Gascon might slay his enemy, wished to resume the fight.

The young man, perceiving that it would disoblige Athos not to leave him to his own devices, held his hand. And in a few minutes Cahusac fell with a sword-thrust through his throat. At the same moment Aramis placed his sword point against the breast of his fallen foe and forced him to beg for mercy.

There remained, then, but Porthos and Bicarat. The great musketeer was making a thousand flourishes with his blade. He asked Bicarat what time it was getting to be. He offered him congratulations on his brother's having just obtained a company in the regiment of Navarre. But, jest as he might, he gained nothing thereby. For Bicarat was one of those iron men who just don't know how to fall down dead.

Jussac, who had now managed to rise upon his elbow, cried out to the guardsman to yield. But Bicarat was a Gascon, as d'Artagnan was, and turned a deaf ear to his captain. He contented himself with laughing and, between parries, found time to point with his rapier to a spot of earth at his feet. Parodying a verse from the Bible, he cried, "Here shall Bicarat die. For I alone am left, and they seek my life."

"But there are four against you, idiot!" gasped Jussac. "Leave off, I command you."

"Ah, if you command it, that's another thing," answered Bicarat.

And, springing backward, he broke his sword across his knee to avoid having to surrender it. He threw the pieces of it over the convent wall and crossed his arms, whistling a cardinalist air.

Bravery is always respected, even in an enemy. The musketeers saluted Bicarat with their swords and returned these to their sheaths. D'Artagnan did likewise.

Then, assisted by his fellow Gascon, the young man carried Jussac, Cahusac, and one of Aramis' adversaries, who was only wounded, beneath the porch of the convent. The fourth enemy was dead.

Thereafter the four victors rang the bell of the monastery to summon help and medical care for the vanquished. Carrying away four swords out of five, intoxicated with joy, they took the road toward the residence of M. de Tréville.

Arm in arm they marched, occupying the whole width of the street and taking in every musketeer they met. So, in the end, their progress became a triumphant procession. The heart of d'Artagnan swam in a delirium of joy. He walked between Athos and Porthos, pressing them tenderly at every third step.

"For," he said to his new friends as he passed through the gateway of the mansion, "if I am not yet a musketeer, at least I have entered upon my apprenticeship, have I not?"

CHAPTER VI

HIS MAJESTY THE KING

This affair caused a great deal of talk.

M. de Tréville scolded his musketeers in public and congratulated them in private. Then he hastened to report himself at the Louvre in order to bring the first news of the encounter. But it was already too late for that.

"Come here, Monsieur Captain," said the king. "I wish to scold you. Do you know that his Eminence has been complaining of your Musketeers with so much emotion that tonight he is indisposed? Your soldiers are the devil, Captain. They should be hanged."

"On the contrary, sire," replied Tréville, "they are as meek as little lambs. And they have but one desire, I'll warrant you, which is never to draw sword but in your Majesty's service. But what are they to do? The Guards of Monsieur the Cardinal are forever seeking quarrels with them. And for the honor of the corps the poor young men are simply obliged to defend themselves."

"Hark to him!" laughed the king. "One would think he was speaking, not of dogs of war, but of a religious community. I've a good mind, Captain, to give your commission to Mademoiselle de Chemerault, to whom I promised an abbey."

Then Louis XIII turned away from the gaming table. He had been winning money and was thus in an excellent humor. He walked with M. de Tréville toward the embrasure of a window.

"Well, Monsieur, I am called Louis the Just because I always wish to hear both sides of a matter. You say his Eminence's Guards sought the quarrel with your Musketeers?"

"Yes, sire, as they always do."

"How did the thing happen, Tréville?"

"Good Lord! In the simplest manner possible. Three of my best soldiers, Athos, Porthos, and Aramis—you know them, sire—had made a pleasure party with a young fellow from Gascony. The excursion was to St. Germain, I think, and they had agreed to meet at the Carmes-Deschaux. There they were disturbed by de Jussac, Cahusac, Bicarat, and two other guardsmen, who certainly did not go there in such a numerous company without some intention of breaking the edicts."

"You incline me to believe they went thither to fight among themselves," the king said.

"I leave your Majesty to judge what five armed men could be going to do in such a deserted place as the Convent des Carmes."

"You are right, Tréville!"

"Upon seeing my musketeers, they changed their private anger for partisan hatred. For the poor Musketeers, who belong to the king and to nobody else, are the natural enemies of the Guardsmen, who belong to the cardinal."

"True, Tréville," declared the king. "And it is very sad, believe me, to see thus two parties in France, two heads

3

to royalty. You say, then, that the guardsmen sought the quarrel?"

"I cannot exactly swear to it, sire. You know how difficult it is to discover the truth of such a business. And, unless a man be endowed with that admirable instinct which causes Louis XIII to be named the Just—"

"Again, you are right, Tréville. But they were not alone, your musketeers. They had a youth with them?"

"A boy, and one wounded man. So that three of the king's Musketeers—one of them wounded—and a young stripling not only maintained their ground against five of the most terrible of the cardinal's Guardsmen, but absolutely brought four of them to earth."

"Why, this is a victory!" cried the king, all radiant. "A complete triumph."

"Yes, sire, as complete as that of the Bridge of Cé."

"And what does the stripling call himself?"

"D'Artagnan, sire. He is the son of one of my oldest friends, a man who served under the king your father, of glorious memory, in the civil war."

"And tell me how this young man behaved himself, Tréville. You know my delight in accounts of war and fighting."

Louis XIII twisted his mustache proudly and placed one hand upon his hip.

"M. d'Artagnan, sire, is little more than a boy. And, as he has not the honor to be a musketeer, he was dressed as a citizen. The guards of the cardinal, noting his youth and that he did not belong to the corps, invited him to retire before they attacked."

"So you may plainly see, Tréville," interrupted the king, "that it was they who attacked."

"They called upon him, then, to retire. But he answered that he was entirely devoted to your Majesty and would therefore remain with the musketeers."

"Brave young fellow!" murmured the king.

"And your Majesty has in him so firm a champion that it was he who delivered to Jussac the terrible sword thrust, which has made the cardinal so angry."

"He, a boy! Tréville, that's impossible."

"It is as I have the honor to relate to your Majesty."

"I shall see this young man, Tréville. We shall make it our business to see if something cannot be done for him."

"When will your Majesty deign to receive him?"

"Tomorrow, at midday, Tréville. Bring me all four together. Devoted men are rare and must be recompensed. And by the back staircase—it is useless to let the cardinal know our affairs. Besides, an edict is still an edict, and it is forbidden to fight, after all."

"But this encounter, sire, is quite out of the ordinary conditions of a duel. It is a brawl. And the proof is that there were five of the cardinal's Guardsmen against my three musketeers and M. the young Gascon."

"That is true, Tréville," said the king. "But never mind, come by the back staircase just the same."

That evening the three musketeers were informed of the honor accorded them. As they had long been acquainted with the sovereign, they were not vastly excited at the prospect. But d'Artagnan, with his Gascon imagination, saw in it his future fortune, and passed the night

in golden dreams.   By eight o'clock in the morning he was
in the apartment of M. Athos.

He found the soldier dressed and ready to go out.   His
host had an engagement to play tennis in a court near the
stables of the Luxembourg and invited the young Gascon
to accompany him, which the latter was only to glad
to do.

They found Porthos and Aramis already there playing
together.   Athos, who was very expert in all bodily exer-
cises, passed with d'Artagnan to the opposite side of the
court and challenged the other Inseparables.   But at the
first effort he made, although he was using his left hand,
he discovered his wound was still too recent to permit of
such exertion.

D'Artagnan, therefore, was left alone to play against
two.   Since he declared himself too ignorant of the game
to engage in a regular contest, they served balls to one
another without counting points.   But one of these shots,
launched by the herculean paw of Porthos, passed so
close to the Gascon's face that it barely missed flooring
him.   D'Artagnan did not wish to tempt fate by trusting
that Porthos would miss a second time.   So he saluted his
two opponents politely, saying that he would not resume
the game until he was prepared to play with them on more
equal terms.   He then went and took his place near the
cord and in the gallery.

Unfortunately for him, among the spectators was one
of his Eminence's Guardsmen, who believed the opportunity was now come of avenging the defeat of his companions the day before.   He addressed his new neighbor,

therefore, in rough tones, "It is not astonishing this young man is afraid of a ball, for he is doubtless a musketeer apprentice."

D'Artagnan turned as if a serpent had stung him and fixed his eyes intently upon the guardsman who had just made this speech.

"*Pardieu,* little gamecock," resumed the latter, twisting his mustache, "look at me as long as you like, I said what I said."

"Your words are too clear to require explaining," replied the young Gascon. "I beg you to follow me."

"And when?" asked the gentleman with the same jeering air.

"At once, if you please."

"You know who I am, perhaps?"

"I am beautifully ignorant of your identity, nor does the fact disquiet me much."

"That's where you are wrong. For if you knew my name, I doubt if you would be so pressing. I am Bernajoux, at your service."

"Well, then, M. Bernajoux," said d'Artagnan tranquilly, "I shall await you at the door. But do not hurry after me too soon. You must be aware that, for our undertaking, company would be in the way, and therefore we must escape observation."

"That's true," said the guardsman, astonished that his name had produced no effect upon the young bantam.

Indeed, the name of Bernajoux was known to all the world, d'Artagnan alone excepted, perhaps. For he was one of those who figured most frequently in the daily brawls which all the edicts of the cardinal could not suppress.

The Inseparables did not see their companion go out. An instant later the guardsman descended in his turn. The young Gascon cast his eyes around him and, seeing that the street was empty, said to his antagonist, "My faith! It is fortunate for you, although your name is Bernajoux, that you have to deal with only an apprentice musketeer and not with a real one. Never mind, be content! I shall do my best to amuse you. On guard!"

"But," replied the soldier whom d'Artagnan thus provoked, "it strikes me this place is badly chosen. We should be better off behind the Abbey St. Germain or in the Pré-aux-Clercs."

"You are right enough," retorted the Gascon, "but unhappily I have very little time at my disposal because of an important appointment at twelve precisely. On guard, Monsieur!"

Bernajoux was not a man to wait for a second bidding. In a second his sword glittered in his hand. He sprang straight at his adversary, whom, because of his evident youthfulness, he hoped to intimidate.

But d'Artagnan had served his apprenticeship on the preceding day. Fresh-sharpened by that victory, full of hopes of future favor, he was determined not to recoil a single step.

So the two blades were crossed close to their hilts and, as the lad did not budge an inch, it was his opponent who took the retreating step. Now, the young Gascon seized the moment at which, during this movement, the sword of

Bernajoux deviated from the line. He freed his weapon, made a lunge, and touched his enemy on the shoulder.

D'Artagnan immediately took a backward step and raised his sword—but Bernajoux cried out that it was nothing and, rushing blindly upon him, positively spitted himself on the Gascon's blade.

As he did not fall, however, and did not declare himself conquered, the young man was ignorant of the seriousness of the last wound his adversary had received. Bernajoux broke away toward the residence of M. de la Trémouille, in whose service he had a relative. D'Artagnan pressed him warmly, and doubtless would soon have completed his work with a third blow but for an unexpected interruption.

The noise in the street had been heard inside the tennis court, and two friends of the guardsman suddenly remembered that they had seen him go out after exchanging some words with the stripling. So they rushed from the court, sword in hand, and fell upon the conqueror.

But Athos, Porthos, and Aramis were not far in the rear. And the moment the two guardsmen attacked their companion, they whipped out their blades and drove the intruders back. Bernajoux now fell to the pavement, and as the guardsmen were only two against four they began to howl at the top of their lungs, "To the rescue! The Hôtel de la Trêmouille!"

On hearing these shouts, all who were in the place rushed forth and fell upon the four companions, who on their side cried aloud, "Help now, Musketeers!"

This cry, too, was generally heeded. For the Musketeers were known to be enemies of the cardinal and were beloved on this very account. Thus the soldiers of other companies than those of the Red Duke (as Aramis called him) often took part with the king's Musketeers in these quarrels. Of three guardsmen of the company of M. d'Essart who were passing, two came to the assistance of the four Inseparables, while the other ran toward the residence of M. de Tréville, crying, "To the rescue, Musketeers! To the rescue!"

As usual, this mansion was full of soldiers of this company, who hastened to the succor of their comrades. The *mêlée* became general, but numerical strength was on the side of the Musketeers.

The cardinal's Guards and M. de la Trémouille's people retreated into the building, the doors of which were closed just in time to prevent their assailants from entering with them. As to the wounded man, he had been taken in at once in a very bad condition of health.

The Musketeers and their allies now began to deliberate whether they should not set fire to the edifice to punish the insolence of M. de la Trémouille's domestics in daring to make a sortie upon them. But nothing came of this suggestion, for d'Artagnan and his companions suddenly recalled their audience, and it was then eleven o'clock. So the Inseparables made their way toward the abode of M. de Tréville, whom they found waiting for them.

"Quick!" he said. "To the Louvre without losing an instant! Let us try to see the king before he is prejudiced by the cardinal. We shall describe this thing to him as a sequel to yesterday's affair, and the two will pass off together."

To the great astonishment of the captain of Musketeers, when with his four young fellows he had reached
the Louvre, he was informed that the king had gone stag
hunting in the forest of St. Germain.

"Had his Majesty," he inquired darkly, "any intention
yesterday of holding this hunting party?"

"No, your Excellency," replied the valet de chambre.
"The master of the hounds came this morning to inform
him he had marked down a buck. At first the king said
he would not go. But he could not resist his love of sport."

"And the king has seen the cardinal?" asked M. de
Tréville.

"In all probability he has," replied the valet. "For I
saw the horses harnessed to his Eminence's carriage this
morning, and when I asked where he was going, they told
me to St. Germain."

"He is beforehand with us. Gentlemen, I shall see
the king this evening. But as to you, I do not advise you
to risk doing so."

This advice was too reasonable to allow the four young
men to dispute it. M. de Tréville recommended them
every one to return home and wait for further news.

And then, the moment that he had got rid of his companions, the great captain arrived at one of those brilliant
decisions which played so great a rôle in his success. He
repaired immediately to the residence of M. de la Trémouille and had himself announced.

"Monsieur," he said, "we imagine that we have cause
to complain of each other. And I am come to endeavor
to clear up this affair."

The address of the great Protestant duke was polite, but cooler than usual. No friendship existed between him and M. de Tréville, but there was at least esteem. Both were men of courage and probity.

"I have no objection to receiving new light," M. de la Trémouille replied to the captain's suggestion. "But I warn you that I am well informed. All the fault is with your Musketeers."

"How is M. Bernajoux, your esquire's relative?"

"Why, Monsieur, very ill indeed!"

"But has the wounded man retained his senses?"

"Perfectly."

"Does he talk?"

"With difficulty, but he can speak."

"Well, Monsieur, my proposal is that we go to him. Let us adjure him, in the name of that God before whom he must perhaps soon appear, to speak the truth. I shall take him for judge in his own cause, Monsieur, and shall believe whatever he says."

M. de la Trémouille reflected for an instant. Then, as it was difficult to suggest a more reasonable proposal, he agreed to it.

Both descended to the chamber in which the wounded man lay. The latter, on seeing these two noble lords come to visit him, endeavored to raise himself up in bed. But he was too weak and, exhausted by the effort, he fell back again almost senseless.

The Protestant duke approached him and made him inhale some salts, which recalled him for the moment to vigor. Then M. de Tréville, unwilling to have it thought

that he had influenced the wounded man unduly, requested
M. de la Trémouille to interrogate him himself.

That happened which the captain of Musketeers had
foreseen. Hovering between life and death as Bernajoux
was, he had no idea of concealing the truth for a moment.
And he described to the two nobles the affair exactly as
it occurred.

Ah, this was all that M. de Tréville wanted. He told
Bernajoux that he wished him a speedy convalescence,
took leave of M. de la Trémouille, returned home, and
immediately sent word to the four friends that he awaited
their company at dinner.

M. de Tréville entertained excellent company. That
the group was always anti-cardinalist goes perhaps without
saying. The talk during the entire dinner turned upon
the two checks that his Eminence's Guardsmen had
received.

Now, as d'Artagnan had been the hero of these two
fights, he was the target for all the felicitations. Athos,
Porthos, and Aramis gladly abandoned the praise to him,
not only as good comrades, but also as men who had had
their turn so often that they could well afford to dispense
with it for once.

About six o'clock M. de Tréville excused himself to go
to the Louvre. At that moment the young Gascon felt
himself tremble to the very marrow of his bones. In all
probability the captain's interview with the king would
decide the remainder of his life. His eyes therefore remained fixed in a sort of agony upon the door through
which M. de Tréville had vanished. But Athos was less

concerned about temporal matters apparently. He contented himself with smiling whimsically and remarking, "Things aren't going very well, I fancy. I doubt if we'll be made Chevaliers of the Order at just this session."

M. de Tréville entered the king's cabinet boldly and found his Majesty in a very bad humor. He was seated on the arm of a chair, beating his hunting boot with the handle of his whip.

"Monsieur, I am vexed with you," the king finally said sulkily.

"In what have I been so unfortunate as to displease your Majesty?" asked the captain, feigning the most profound astonishment.

"Perhaps," continued the sovereign, "in my haste I accuse you wrongfully. Without doubt the rioters are in prison, and you come to tell me that the ends of justice have already been met."

"Sire," replied M. de Tréville calmly, "on the contrary, I have come to demand justice of you."

"Ha-ha! This is something new!" cried Louis XIII. "Do you mean to tell me your three damned musketeers and the Gascon lad did not fall upon poor Bernajoux and maltreat him in such fashion that he is probably dead? Who has told me this fine story, you ask me? Who should have done so but that individual who watches while I sleep, who labors while I amuse myself, who conducts all business at home and abroad—in France as well as in Europe?"

"Your Majesty must be referring to God," said M. de Tréville. "For I know no one else who can be so far above your sovereign self."

"Oh, no, Monsieur. I speak of the real prop of the State, of my only trusted servant, of my one friend—of the cardinal."

"How can he be your one friend, sire, and still unjustly accuse your Majesty's Musketeers?"

"The accusation comes from M. de la Trémouille, from the duke himself. And what do you say to that, my captain?"

"I say to you, sire, let the duke come here. Interrogate him as seems best to you, without witnesses. Then, please you, let me see you immediately afterward."

"Granted!" cried the king. "And you will accept his judgment?"

"Willingly."

"La Chesnaye," said Louis XIII, "let some one go instantly and find M. de la Trémouille. I wish to speak to him this evening."

"Your Majesty gives me your word that you will not see any one in this matter between M. de la Trémouille and myself?"

"Nobody, by the faith of a gentleman."

"Tomorrow then, sire?"

"Tomorrow, as early as you like. But beware if you and your Musketeers are guilty."

"If the fault lies with them, sire, the offending ones shall be placed in your Majesty's hands to dispose of at your good pleasure. Does your Majesty require anything further? Speak, I am ready to obey."

"No, Monsieur, no. I am not called Louis the Just without reason. Tomorrow, then."

"Till then God preserve your Majesty!"

However ill the king might sleep, M. de Tréville slept still worse. He had ordered the three musketeers and their companion to be with him at half-past six in the morning. He took them with him to the Louvre without encouraging them or promising them anything. For their luck, and even his own, depended upon this one cast of the dice.

On arriving at the king's private antechamber, the captain found La Chesnaye, who told him that they had not been able to reach M. de la Trémouille on the previous evening and that he was at that very moment with the king.

This fact pleased M. de Tréville greatly, as he could thus be certain that no foreign suggestion could insinuate itself between the duke's testimony and his own.

Ten minutes had scarcely passed away when the door of the king's private room opened and M. de la Trémouille came out. The duke went straight to the captain and said, "Monsieur, his Majesty has just sent for me to inquire respecting the brawl which took place yesterday at my residence. I told him that the fault lay with my people and that I was prepared to offer you my excuses. I beg you to receive them now, and in the future to hold me always as one of your friends."

"Monsieur," said M. de Tréville, "I knew that I required no other defender before his Majesty than yourself. I thank God there is one man in France who is utterly loyal and true."

"Well said!" cried the king, who had heard these compliments through the open door. "Only tell him, Tréville, that I also wish to be one of his friends, but he neglects me. It is nearly three years since I have seen him."

"Thanks, sire," said the duke, "but your Majesty may rest assured it is not those you see at all hours of the day who are the most devoted to you."

Louis XIII advanced to the door of his room and stood upon the threshold. "Ah, Tréville," he said, "where are your musketeers? Why have you not brought them with you as I wished?"

"They are waiting below, sire. With your permission, La Chesnaye will bid them come up."

The duke saluted and retired. At the moment he opened the door the three musketeers and d'Artagnan appeared at the top of the staircase, conducted by La Chesnaye.

"Come in, my braves," called the king. "I am going to scold you."

The musketeers advanced, bowing. D'Artagnan followed close behind them.

"What the devil!" continued the king. "Seven of his Eminence's Guards placed *hors de combat* by you four in two days! If you do not stop, his Eminence will be forced to get a new company together three weeks hence—and I shall have to put the edicts in force in all their rigor. One fellow now and then, I don't say much about. But seven in two days, it is too many, gentlemen! I repeat, it is far too many!"

"Therefore, sire, they are come quite contrite and repentant to offer you their excuses."

"Ahem!" said the king. "Do you know. Tréville, I

place no confidence in their hypocritical faces? There is one yonder of a Gascon look. Come hither, Monsieur."

D'Artagnan approached, assuming what he considered to be a most deprecating mien.

"Why, you told me he was a young man, Tréville! This is a mere boy. Do you mean to say it was he who bestowed that naughty thrust upon Jussac?"

"And two equally fine ones at Bernajoux, sire."

"Without reckoning," said Athos, "that if he had not rescued me from the hands of Cahusac, I should not now be having the honor to make my very humble reverence to your Majesty."

"Why, he is a devil, this Béarnais! *Ventre-saint-gris!* At this sort of work many doublets must be slashed and many swords broken. And Gascons are always poor, are they not, M. de Tréville?"

"They have discovered no gold mines in their mountains, sire. Yet it would seem that God owed them this miracle in return for the manner in which they supported the king your father."

"Well, happily I agree that the Gascons made a king of me, seeing that I am my father's son. La Chesnaye, go and see if by rummaging in all my pockets you can find forty pistoles. And now, young man, place your hand on your heart and tell me how all this trouble came to pass."

D'Artagnan related the adventure of the preceding day in its every detail.

"That is all very well," murmured the king. "Yes, it is just the account the duke gave me of the affair. Poor cardinal! Seven men in two days, and those of his very best. Please to understand, gentlemen, that is quite enough. You have taken your revenge and you ought to be satisfied."

"We are, sire," said Tréville.

"And so am I," added the king, taking a handful of gold from La Chesnaye and putting it into the hand of d'Artagnan. "Here is a proof of my contentment."

At this time a gentleman might receive money from the hand of his sovereign and not feel in the least humiliated. So the young Gascon put his forty pistoles in his pocket without scruple, thanking his Majesty devoutly.

"I am grateful for your devotion, gentlemen. I may continue to rely upon it, may I not?"

"Oh, sire!" cried the four companions with one voice. "We will allow ourselves to be cut to pieces in your Majesty's service."

"Tréville," whispered the king, as the others were retiring, "since a novitiate is necessary before entering your corps, place the Gascon boy in the company of the Guards of M. d'Essart, your brother-in-law. *Pardieu!* I enjoy beforehand the face the cardinal will make. He will be furious, but I don't care. I am only doing what is right."

The king waved his hand to Tréville, who left him and rejoined the musketeers, whom he found sharing the forty pistoles with d'Artagnan.

As his Majesty had said, the cardinal was so furious that for eight days he absented himself from the royal gaming table. But this did not prevent the king's being as complacent toward him as possible. And whenever they met, Louis would ask in his kindest tone, "Well, Monsieur Cardinal, how fares it with that poor Jussac and that nice Bernajoux of yours?"

CHAPTER VII

HOW THE MUSKETEERS KEPT HOUSE

When d'Artagnan was out of the Louvre, he consulted his friends as to the best use to make of his share of the forty pistoles. Athos advised him to order a good dinner at the Fir Cone, Porthos to engage a lackey. The repast was carried into effect that very day, and the lackey waited on the table. The spread had been ordered by Athos, the servant had been engaged by Porthos. The fellow was from Picardy, and the glorious musketeer had picked him up on the Tournelle bridge, where he was making circles in the water by splashing his feet in it.

Porthos thought that this occupation was a sign of a reflective disposition, and he had carried the lackey off without further recommendation. Planchet (such was the Picard's name) had been won by the noble exterior and demeanor of this gentleman, by whom he considered himself to be engaged. He had been slightly disappointed when he discovered he must enter the service of the young Gascon.

When he waited at the dinner given by his new master, however, and saw him take out a handful of gold to pay for it, he thanked heaven for having brought him into the service of such a Croesus. But when, in the evening, he made his master's bed, Planchet's dreams faded away. This one couch was the only one in the apartment, which consisted of an antechamber and a bedroom. Planchet slept in the antechamber upon a coverlet from the bed of d'Artagnan, and the young Gascon from that time made shift to do without it.

Although Athos was scarcely thirty years old and was of great personal beauty and intelligence, no one knew about his intimate affairs. He never spoke of women. His reserve, his lack of sociability, and his silence almost made an old man of him. In order not to disturb his habits he had accustomed Grimaud, his valet, to obey him at a simple gesture or at a single movement of his lips. He never spoke to him except under most extraordinary circumstances.

Sometimes Grimaud, who feared his master as he did fire or pestilence, thought he understood perfectly what Athos wanted done and flew to execute the command as he thought right, only to discover that exactly the opposite thing had been desired. The master would then shrug his shoulders and, without putting himself into a passion, would thrash Grimaud soundly. Either despite this fact or because of it, the servant entertained a strong attachment for his master's person and had a great respect for his talents.

Porthos had not so noble an air as Athos. And at the beginning of their intimacy the consciousness of his inferiority in this respect had often rendered him unjust toward that gentleman, whom he endeavored to eclipse by his splendid dress. But, by the very manner in which he threw back his head and advanced his foot, Athos instantly took the place which was his due. Even when dressed in his simple musketeer's uniform he consigned the ostentatious Porthos to the second rank.

Porthos consoled himself by boasting in the ante-chamber of M. de Tréville and the guardroom of the Louvre of his love affairs, of which Athos never spoke. And just at the present moment, after having passed from women of the street to military wives, from lawyer's spouse to baroness, Porthos now would look at nothing less than the foreign princess who (according to Porthos) was enormously fond of him.

Mousqueton was a Norman, whose pacific name of Boniface his master had changed to the more sonorous title of Mousqueton. He had entered the service of Porthos upon condition that he should only be clothed and lodged, though in a handsome manner. He claimed two hours a day for himself, and devoted them to an employ-ment which provided for his other wants.

Porthos, of course, agreed to this bargain, and the arrangement suited him wonderfully well. He had doublets cut out of his old clothes and cast-off cloaks for Mousqueton and, thanks to a highly intelligent tailor who made his clothes look as good as new by turning them, the valet cut a very fashionable figure.

The lackey of Aramis was called Bazin. Because of the hopes which his master entertained of some day enter-ing into orders, Bazin was always clothed in black, as became the servant of a churchman. He was a Berrichon man, thirty-five or forty years of age, mild, peaceable, and sleek. He employed his leisure in the perusal of pious works and he knew how to provide an excellent if simple dinner. He was of unimpeachable fidelity and as secretive as if he were in reality blind, deaf, and dumb.

Athos dwelt in the Rue Férou, within two steps of the Luxembourg. Some fragments of past splendor appeared here and there on the walls of his modest lodging. There was, for example, a sword richly embossed and, to judge by its make, belonging to the times of Francis I, the hilt of which alone might be worth two hundred pistoles. It was incrusted with precious stones, and yet in his moments of greatest financial distress Athos had never pawned it or offered it for sale. It long had been an object of ambition for Porthos.

One day, when he had an appointment with a duchess, he tried to borrow it from Athos. Without saying a word, Athos emptied his pockets, collected all his jewels, purses, and gold chains, and offered them to Porthos. But as to the sword, he said it was sealed to its place and should never quit it until its master himself should seek other lodgings.

In addition to the sword, there was a portrait representing a nobleman of the time of Henry III, dressed with the greatest elegance and wearing the Order of St. Esprit. And between this portrait and Athos there were certain resemblances, certain family likenesses, which indicated that this great noble, a henchman of the orders of the king, was his ancestor.

Porthos lived in an apartment, large in size and of a very sumptuous appearance, in the Rue du Vieux-Colombier. Every time he passed with a friend before its windows, at one of which Mousqueton in full livery was sure to be standing, Porthos raised his head and his hand and said, "That is my abode." But he never was to be found at home. He never invited anybody to go up with him. And no one could form an idea of what this magnificent dwelling contained in the shape of real riches of appointment and furniture.

As to Aramis, he dwelt in a little lodging composed of a boudoir, dining room, and parlor. The rooms were on the ground floor and looked out upon a fresh green garden which was shady and impenetrable to the eyes of his neighbors.

D'Artagnan, who was by nature very curious, did all he could to discover who his friends might really be, for under their pseudonyms each of these young men concealed his family name. The young Gascon found the oldest of the three Inseparables particularly intriguing, Athos, who savored of nobility a league away. D'Artagnan addressed himself to Porthos to gain information about Athos and Aramis, and to Aramis to learn something of Porthos.

Unfortunately, Porthos knew nothing about the life of his silent companion except what revealed itself. It was rumored he had met with great misfortunes in love and that a frightful treachery had forever poisoned the life of this gallant man. What could this treachery be? Every one was ignorant of it.

As to Porthos, except his real name, with which no one but M. de Tréville was acquainted (as was also the case with those of his two comrades), his life was easily known. Vain and indiscreet as he was, it was as simple to see through him as through a crystal. The only way the investigator could be misled would be for him to believe all the amazing facts the man related about himself.

With respect to Aramis, although he conveyed the impression of possessing no secrets, he was a young man made up of mysteries. He answered little to questions asked about others, and eluded all those which concerned himself. For instance, "It seems to me," said d'Artagnan one day, "that you are tolerably familiar with coats of arms. I refer to a certain embroidered handkerchief to which I owe the honor of your acquaintance."

This time Aramis was not angry, but assumed the most modest air in replying.

"My dear friend, pray do not forget that I wish to enter the church and therefore I avoid all mundane opportunities. The handkerchief you saw had been forgotten and left at my house by one of my friends. I was obliged to pick it up in order not to compromise him and the lady he loves. As for myself, I neither have, nor desire to possess, any women friends, following in this respect the very judicious example of Athos."

"But what the devil! You are not a priest, you are a musketeer!"

"A musketeer against my will, but a churchman at heart, believe me. Athos and Porthos dragged me into the uniform to occupy my mind. I had at the moment of being ordained a little difficulty with—But that would not interest you, and I am taking up your valuable time."

"Not at all! It interests me greatly," cried d'Artagnan. "And at this moment I have absolutely nothing to do."

"Yes, but I have. First, repeat my breviary. Then some verses to compose, which Madame d'Aiguillon begged of me. Then I must go to the Rue St. Honoré to buy some rouge for Madame de Chevreuse. So you see, my dear friend, that if you are not in a hurry, I am."

The life of the four young fellows was joyous enough. Athos was devoted to gaming, but seldom won. Nevertheless, he never borrowed a sou of his companions, although his purse was ever at their service. And when he had played upon honor, he never failed to awaken his creditor by six o'clock the following morning to absolve the debt incurred the evening previous.

Porthos was subject to varying moods. On the days when he won, he was insolent and ostentatious. If he lost, he disappeared completely for several days, after which he returned with his face pale and drawn but with money in his purse.

Aramis never staked a wager. He was the worst musketeer and the least convivial companion imaginable. He always had something or other to do. Sometimes in the midst of a dinner when everyone, under the influence of wine, believed he had two or three hours longer to spend at table, Aramis would consult his watch, arise with a bland smile, and take leave of the company. His pretexts on such occasions would sound fairly thin, as when he said he must go to consult a scientist with whom he had an appointment; or he must return home to write a treatise and requested his friends not to disturb him.

At this Athos would smile with the charming, melancholy expression that so became his noble countenance. But Porthos would bury his nose disgustedly in his flagon, swearing that Aramis would never be anything but a village *curé*.

Planchet, d'Artagnan's valet, supported his good fortune nobly. He received wages of thirty sous a day, and for a month he returned to his lodgings gay as a chaffinch and affable to his master. But when the wind of adversity began to blow upon the household of the Rue des Fossoyeurs, he commenced complaints which Athos thought nauseous, Porthos indecent, and Aramis ridiculous. Athos counseled the young Gascon to dismiss the fellow, Porthos believed in giving him a good thrashing first, and Aramis contended that a master must hear only the pleasant things that were said about him.

"The situation is serious," the three friends united in feeling. "It is a family affair. It is with valets as with wives—they must be placed at once upon the footing on which you wish them to remain."

D'Artagnan reflected well, and finally resolved to thrash Planchet provisionally. He did this with the conscientiousness that he carried into everything. After having thoroughly dusted him, the Gascon forbade Planchet to leave his service.

"For," he added, "the future cannot fail to mend. I look for better times which seem inevitable. Your fortune is therefore made if you remain with me, and I am too good a master to allow you to miss such a chance by granting you the dismissal you desire."

This manner of acting aroused much respect for d'Artagnan's policy among the Musketeers. Planchet, equally seized with admiration, said no more about going away.

The life of the four young men had become fraternal. It was quite easy for the Gascon to fall into the habits of

his friends, as he had come from his province into the
midst of a life all new to him and thus had no settled
notions of his own.

They arose about eight o'clock in winter, about six
in summer, and went to receive the countersign of the day
and see how things were going on at M. de Tréville's.
D'Artagnan, although he was not a musketeer, performed
the duty of one with remarkable punctuality. He mounted
guard, because he always kept company with whichever of
his friends was on duty. He was well known at the head-
quarters of the Musketeers, where everyone considered
him a good comrade. M. de Tréville, who had appreciated
him at the first glance and who bore him a real affection,
never ceased recommending him to the king.

On their side the three musketeers were much attached
to their young comrade. The friendship that united these
four men caused them to be continually running after one
another like shadows. They felt the need of seeing one
another three or four times a day, whether for dueling,
business, or pleasure. And the Inseparables were constantly
to be met with, seeking one another from the Luxembourg
to the Place St. Sulpice, or from the Rue du Vieux-Colombier to the Luxembourg.

In the meantime M. de Tréville was making progress
with his promises finely. One morning the king commanded M. le Chevalier d'Essart to enroll d'Artagnan as
a cadet in his company of Guards. The young Gascon,
with a sigh, donned this uniform, which he would have
exchanged for that of a musketeer at the expense of ten
years of his life.

But M. de Tréville promised this favor after a novitiate of two years. This period of apprenticeship might, he thought, be abridged if an opportunity should present itself for the young man to render the king a signal service or for him to distinguish himself by some brilliant action. Upon this promise d'Artagnan withdrew and the next day entered on his new service.

Then it became the turn of Athos, Porthos, and Aramis to mount guard with d'Artagnan when he was on duty. The company of M. le Chevalier d'Essart thus received four men instead of one when it admitted the young Gascon.

CHAPTER VIII

A COURT INTRIGUE

The forty pistoles of King Louis XIII, like all other things in the world, not only had a beginning but also had an end. And after this end our four companions began to be somewhat embarrassed.

At first Athos supported the association of friends for a time out of his own means.

Porthos succeeded him. And, thanks to one of those disappearances to which he was accustomed, he was able to provide for the wants of all during a fortnight. At last it became Aramis' turn. He performed his office with good grace and succeeded—as he said, by selling some theological books—in procuring a few pistoles.

At length, when they discovered they were likely to be really in want, they collected, as a last effort, eight or ten pistoles, with which Porthos was sent to the gaming table. Unfortunately he was in bad vein. He lost all, together with twenty-five pistoles for which he had pledged his word.

Then inconvenience became distress. Athos was invited to dinner four times, and each time he took his friends and their lackeys with him. Porthos had six opportunities, and in the same manner contrived that his friends should partake of them. Aramis had eight invitations— he was a man who made but little noise and yet was much sought after.

As to d'Artagnan, who as yet knew nobody in the capital, he found only one chocolate breakfast at the house of a priest from his own province and one dinner at the house of a cornet of the Guards. He took his army to the priest's, where they devoured as much provision as would have lasted him for two months, but, as Planchet said, "People do not eat at once for all time even when they manage to surround a great deal."

The young Gascon thus felt humiliated in having procured only one meal and a half for his companions. He fancied himself a burden to the society, forgetting that he had (with the forty pistoles) already supported them for a month.

One day he was sitting in his room seriously racking his brain for a solution of the common poverty, when some one tapped gently at his door. D'Artagnan awakened Planchet and ordered him to open it.

Because of this phrase—d'Artagnan awakened Planchet—one must not suppose it was night or that day had hardly come. No, it had just struck four in the afternoon. But Planchet, two hours before, had asked his master for some dinner and the Gascon had retorted with the proverb, "He who sleeps, dines." And Planchet dined by sleeping.

A man of simple mien was introduced. He had the appearance of a tradesman or a peddler. Planchet, by way of dessert, would have liked to hear the conversation, but the citizen declared that what he had to say was important and confidential.

"I have heard M. d'Artagnan spoken of as a very brave young man," said the citizen after Planchet had been dismissed. "And this fact has decided me to confide a secret to him."

"Speak freely and with trust, Monsieur," replied the Gascon, who instinctively scented something advantageous.

The visitor made another pause and then continued, "I have a wife who is seamstress to the queen, Monsieur, and who is deficient neither in virtue nor in beauty."

"Well, sir!"

"Well, Monsieur," resumed the citizen, "my wife was abducted yesterday morning as she was coming out of her workroom. I do not know that I ought to tell you what I suspect to be the cause of this kidnaping."

"Monsieur, I beg you to observe that I ask you absolutely nothing. It is you who have come to me. Act then as you think proper — there is still time for you to withdraw."

"No, no, Monsieur, I have confidence in you. I believe, then, that it is not on account of any intrigues of her own that my wife has been arrested, but because of those of a lady far greater than herself."

Now, the young Gascon wished to appear, in the eyes of his visitor, to be posted on court affairs, so he said, "Aha! Can it be because of the amours of Mme. de Bois-Tracy?"

"Higher, sir, higher."

"Of Mme. d'Aiguillon?"

"Still higher."

"Of Mme. de Chevreuse?"

"Higher, much higher."

"Of the —" d'Artagnan checked himself.

"Yes, Monsieur," replied the terrified citizen in a tone so low as to be scarcely audible.

"And with whom?"

"With whom can it be, if not with the Duke of—"

"But how do you know all this? No half-confidence, or—you understand!"

"I know it from my wife, Monsieur."

"Who learns it from whom?"

"From M. La Porte, her godfather. He is the confidential man of the queen. Well, M. La Porte placed my wife near her Majesty in order that the poor queen might have at least some one in whom she could place confidence. She is, as you know, abandoned by the king, spied upon by the cardinal, and betrayed by everybody."

"Ah, the plot begins to thicken," murmured d'Artagnan.

"Now, my wife came home four days ago, Monsieur, and confided to me that the cardinal is pursuing and persecuting her more than ever. He cannot pardon her the story of the Saraband. You know that story?"

"*Pardieu,* know it!" replied d'Artagnan, who knew nothing about it, but who wished to appear to understand everything that was on the tapis.

"And the queen believes that some one has written to the Duke of Buckingham in her name."

"In the queen's name?"

"Yes. To make him come to Paris. And when he has once come to the capital, to draw him into some snare."

"The devil! But your wife, Monsieur, how is she affected by this?"

"Her devotion to the queen is known. And they wish

either to remove her from her mistress, or to intimidate her in order to obtain her Majesty's secrets, or to seduce her and make use of her as a spy."

"That sounds likely," said d'Artagnan. "But do you know the man who has abducted her?"

"I do not know his name. But what I do know is that he is a creature of the cardinal's, his evil genius. My wife pointed him out to me one day."

"Is there anything remarkable about him by which one can recognize him?"

"Oh, certainly. He is a noble of very lofty carriage, has black hair, swarthy complexion, piercing eye, white teeth, and a scar on his temple."

"A scar on his temple?" cried d'Artagnan. "And with that, white teeth, a piercing eye, dark complexion, black hair, and haughty carriage! Why, that's my man of Meung."

"Your man, you say?"

"Yes, yes. But that only simplifies matters. With one blow I shall obtain two revenges. Do you know where he lives?"

"No. One day I was conveying my wife back to the Louvre. He was coming out as she went in, and she showed him to me."

"But you have learned nothing from M. La Porte or any other quarter regarding the abduction of your wife?"

"Yes, I have received—but I fear I am committing an imprudence."

"You always come back to that. But I must make you see this time that is is too late to retreat."

"I do not retreat, *mordieu!*" cried the citizen, swearing in order to arouse his courage. "Besides, by the faith of Bonacieux—"

"You call yourself Bonacieux?" interrupted the Gascon.

"Yes, Monsieur, that is my name."

"Pardon me, but have I not heard that title before?"

"Possibly, Monsieur. I am your landlord. And up to now I have not tormented you, although for three months you have forgotten to pay me my rent. I thought you would appreciate my delicacy."

"My dear Bonacieux, I am truly grateful for such unparalleled conduct," replied d'Artagnan.

"I believe you, Monsieur. And, as I was about to say, by the faith of Bonacieux, I have confidence in you."

The citizen took a letter from his pocket and handed it to his lodger. D'Artagnan opened it and, as the day was beginning to decline, he approached the window to read it.

"Do not seek your wife," read the young Gascon. "She will be restored to you when there is no longer occasion to use her. If you make a single attempt to find her, you are lost."

"That's pretty positive," continued d'Artagnan. "But after all it's nothing but a threat, and possibly an empty one."

"Yes, but the menace terrifies me, Monsieur. I am in no sense a fighting man. And I am afraid of the Bastille."

"Hum!" said d'Artagnan. "I have no greater affection for the Bastille than you. If it were nothing but a sword thrust, why then—"

"I have seen you constantly surrounded by musketeers of a very superb appearance, sir. And I knew these soldiers belonged to M. de Tréville and were consequently enemies of the cardinal. So I thought you and your friends might enjoy rendering justice to our poor queen and at the same time playing his Eminence an ill turn."

"Without doubt."

"And then I thought that considering three months' lodging about which I have said nothing—"

"Yes, yes. You have already given me that reason and I find it a most excellent one."

"Reckoning still further, that as long as you do me the honor to remain in my house, I shall never speak to you about rent—"

"Better and better!"

"And adding to this, if there be need of it, meaning to offer you fifty pistoles. You might just chance to be short of funds at the present moment—"

"Admirable! You are rich, then, my dear Monsieur Bonacieux?"

"I am comfortably well off, Monsieur—But!" cried the citizen, "whom do I see yonder?"

"Where!"

"In the street, facing your window, in the embrasure of that door—a man wrapped in a cloak."

"It is he!" cried d'Artagnan, springing to get his sword. "This time he shall not escape me."

Drawing his sword from its scabbard, he rushed out of the apartment. On the staircase he met Athos and Porthos, who were coming to see him. They separated quickly, and the young man rushed between them like a dart.

"Hey! Where are you going?" cried the two musketeers in a breath.

"The man of Meung!" panted d'Artagnan, and vanished.

Now, the young Gascon had more than once related to his friends his adventure with the unknown at the Jolly Miller, and so they understood from the single phrase that had escaped d'Artagnan's lips what affair was in hand. They thought that after overtaking his man, or after losing sight of him, either, their friend would return to his lodging. So they kept on their way up the stairs.

When they entered his chamber, it was empty. The landlord, dreading the consequences of the encounter which was doubtless about to take place, had judged it prudent to decamp. This action was consistent with the character he had given himself.

CHAPTER IX

D'ARTAGNAN SHOWS HIS METTLE

At the expiration of half an hour d'Artagnan returned.

He had again missed his man, who had disappeared from the earth as if by enchantment. The would-be avenger had run, naked blade in hand, through all the neighboring streets, but had found nobody remotely resembling the man he sought.

Then he did what he should have done at first; he knocked at the door against which the unknown had been leaning. But no one answered, and some of the neighbors who put their noses out of their windows assured him that the house, all the openings of which were tightly closed, had not been inhabited for six months.

While d'Artagnan had been making the tour of the neighborhood, Aramis had joined his companions. So, on returning home, the young host found the gathering complete.

"*Peste!*" he cried, throwing his sword upon the bed. "This man must be the devil in person. He has disappeared like a phantom, a shade, a specter. And his flight has caused us to miss a glorious affair, gentlemen—a business by which there were a hundred pistoles to be gained, and perhaps more."

"How is that?" cried Porthos and Aramis in a breath.

Athos, faithful to his inclination to reticence, contented himself with interrogating d'Artagnan by a look.

"Planchet," said the young Gascon to his domestic, who had just insinuated his head through the half-opened door to catch some fragments of the conversation, "go down to my landlord, M. Bonacieux, and ask him to send me half a dozen bottles of Beaugency wine."

"Aha!" exclaimed Porthos, smacking his lips. "You have credit with your landlord, then? But, come, what is this about?"

"Yes," said Aramis, "impart it to us, my dear friend. That is, unless the honor of a lady be compromised by this confidence. In that case you would do better to keep it to yourself."

"Be satisfied," replied d'Artagnan. ."The honor of no one will be hazarded by what I have to tell."

He then related to his friends word for word all that had passed between him and his host, and how the man who had abducted poor Madame Bonacieux was the same with whom he had had the difference at the hostelry of the Jolly Miller.

"Your affair is not bad," said Athos, after having tasted like a connoisseur and indicated by a nod of his head that he thought the wine good. "One might drag fifty or sixty pistoles from this good mercer. It only remains to ascertain whether these pistoles are worth the risk of four heads."

"But," cried d'Artagnan, "there is a woman in the case, a woman tortured, perhaps, because she is faithful to her mistress."

"Beware, hot-head!" warned Aramis. "You wax a little too warm, in my opinion, about the fate of Madame

Bonacieux. Woman was created for our destruction, and it is from her that we inherit our miseries."

At this speech of his friend the brow of Athos became clouded, and he bit his lips.

"It is not Madame Bonacieux about whom I am anxious," replied the young Gason, "but her Majesty the queen."

"Why does she love what we hate most in the world, the Spaniards and the English?"

"Spain is her native land," retorted d'Artagnan. "And I have heard it said she does not love the English, but an Englishman."

"And by my faith!" remarked Athos, "it must be acknowledged that he is worthy of being loved. I never saw a man with a nobler air."

"Without reckoning that he dresses as nobody else can," said Porthos. "I was at the Louvre on the day he scattered his pearls. And *pardieu!* I picked up two that I sold for ten pistoles each. Do you know him, Aramis?"

"Yes, I was among those who arrested him in the garden at Amiens. The adventure appeared to me to be cruel for the king."

"Which would not prevent me," said d'Artagnan, "from taking the Duke of Buckingham by the hand and conducting him to the queen, were it only to enrage the cardinal. For our true, our only, our eternal enemy, gentlemen, is his Eminence. And if we could find means of playing him a sharp trick, I vow I should voluntarily risk my head in the doing of it."

"My friends," said Aramis suddenly, "listen to this.

Yesterday I was at the house of a doctor of theology whom I sometimes consult about my studies."

Athos smiled.

"He resides in a quiet quarter," continued Aramis. "His tastes and his profession require it. Now, at the moment I left his house—"

Here the would-be abbé paused. He appeared to be thinking hard, like a man who, in the full relation of a falsehood, finds himself stopped by some unforeseen obstacle. But the eyes of his three companions were fixed upon him, their ears were wide open, and there was no way to retreat.

"The doctor of theology has a niece," stammered Aramis, "a very respectable lady."

The three friends burst into laughter.

"Ah, if you laugh like that," said Aramis, offended, "you shall know nothing further."

"We shall believe you as Mohammedans believe their prophet; we shall be mute as tombstones," promised Athos.

"This niece by chance was at her uncle's," resumed the musketeer, "at the same time I was. It was my duty to conduct her to her carriage. All at once a tall, dark gentleman—just like your unknown, d'Artagnan—came toward me. He was accompanied by five or six men who followed ten paces behind him. In the most polite sort of tone he said to us, 'Monsieur Duke, and you, Madame, enter this carriage without offering the least resistance or making the least noise.'"

"He mistook you for Buckingham," cried d'Artagnan, "and the doctor's niece for the queen!"

"The fact is," said Porthos, "that Aramis is of the same height and has something of the shape of Monsieur the duke. Still, it would seem to me that the uniform of a musketeer—"

"I wore an enormous cloak," explained Aramis.

"In the month of July? The devil you did!" croaked Porthos. "The doctor must be afraid you will be recognized. Well, anyway, I can see that the spy might be deceived in your person, but the face—"

"I wore a large hat low upon my brow," said Aramis weakly.

"Oh, good Lord! What precautions for the study of theology!" shouted Porthos.

"Gentlemen," counseled d'Artagnan, with a slight frown, "let us not lose time in jesting. We must find the mercer's wife—she is the key to the situation."

"A woman of such inferior position! I can't believe it," answered Porthos, protruding his lip in contempt.

"She is the goddaughter to La Porte, the confidential valet of the queen. Besides, it may have been deliberate calculation on her Majesty's part to seek for so lowly support on this occasion. High heads expose themselves from afar, and the cardinal is farsighted."

"Well then," advised Porthos, "we must first make a bargain with the mercer, and a good one, too."

"Absolutely not necessary, in my opinion," replied the young Gascon. "For if he does not pay us, we shall be well enough paid by another party, I'll wager."

At this moment a sudden noise of footsteps was heard upon the stairs. The door was thrown violently open, and the frantic mercer rushed into the chamber as if pursued by the Evil One.

"Save me, gentlemen!" he cried. "Four men have come to arrest me. For the love of heaven, save me!"

"Leave d'Artagnan to act as he thinks best," said Athos sharply, as Porthos and Aramis sprang to their feet with swords half drawn. "It is prudence, not courage, that is needed here. The young scamp has the longest head of the four of us, and I declare that I shall obey his suggestions."

The Gascon turned at once to the cringing mercer. "We can only save you by being free ourselves," he said quickly in a low tone. "If we seemed inclined to defend you, we should ourselves be arrested. Trust me utterly and you will not be betrayed."

At this instant the four guards appeared at the door of the antechamber, but, seeing four musketeers standing and their swords at their sides, the newcomers hesitated to proceed further.

"Come in, gentlemen," called d'Artagnan, "you are in my rooms. We are all faithful servants of the king and the cardinal."

"You will not oppose our executing the orders we have received to arrest this fellow Bonacieux?" asked the leader of the party.

"On the contrary, gentlemen, we should assist you, were it necessary. I have no motive for defending Monsieur. I saw him for the first time today, when he came to demand the rent for my lodging. Is that true, M. Bonacieux? Answer!"

"That is the very truth," cried the mercer. "But Monsieur does not tell you—"

"Silence, sir! Come, come, gentlemen, remove the fellow."

And d'Artagnan pushed the half-stupefied landlord among the guards, saying chidingly, "You are a shabby old fellow, my dear. Coming to demand money of me—of a guard of M. d'Essart! To prison with him, and keep him under key as long as possible. That will give me time to pay him my trifling debt."

The officers were full of thanks and took away their quarry. As they were going down the stairs, d'Artagnan laid his hand upon the shoulder of their leader.

"May I not drink to your health?" asked the canny Gascon, filling two glasses with Beaugency wine.

"That does me great honor," said the leader, "and I accept gratefully. My name, Monsieur, is Boisrenard. Your name, if you please?"

"D'Artagnan. To your health, M. Boisrenard!"

"To yours, M. d'Artagnan!"

"And, above all others," cried the young Gascon, as if carried away by his enthusiasm, "to the health of the king and the cardinal!"

The leader of the posse might perhaps have doubted the sincerity of this toast if the wine had been bad. But the wine was very good, and he was convinced.

"D'Artagnan," said Aramis when the officer had rejoined his companions outside, "you are a great man. And when you occupy M. de Tréville's place, I shall come and ask your influence to secure me an abbey."

"Well, I am in a maze," remarked Porthos, "to see a gentleman hobnob with a bailiff. Athos, do you approve of what our young friend has done?"

"More than that," replied Athos, "I congratulate him."

"And yet—" grumbled Porthos.

"Hold out your hand and swear!" cried Athos and Aramis at once.

Overcome by force of example, muttering to himself nevertheless, Porthos stretched forth his great paw. And the four friends repeated with one voice the formula dictated by d'Artagnan, "All for one, one for all!"

"That's good! And now let each one retire to his own home," said the Gascon, as if he had done nothing but give orders all his life. "And attention! From this moment we are at feud with the cardinal."

CHAPTER X

A MOUSETRAP

What is a mousetrap?

Four or five men are placed in ambuscade in the front room of a house. The door is opened to all who knock. It is closed after them and they are arrested. At the end of two or three days the police have in their power almost all the habitués of the establishment.

Such a mousetrap had the apartment of M. Bonacieux become. Whoever appeared there was taken and interrogated by the cardinal's people. Now, as a separate passage led to the first floor, in which d'Artagnan lodged, those who called to see him were exempted from this detention.

As to the young Gascon, he did not budge from his rooms. He converted his chamber into an observatory. From his windows he saw all the visitors who were caught. Then, having removed a plank from his floor, he heard all that passed between the inquisitors and the accused. This was possible, since nothing but a simple ceiling was between him and the room on the ground floor beneath in which the interrogatories were made.

First, a minute search of the persons arrested was undertaken. Then invariably they were asked:

1. "Has Madame Bonacieux sent anything to you for her husband or for any other person?"

2. "Did Monsieur Bonacieux send anything to you for his wife or for any other person?"

3. "Has either of them confided anything to you by word of mouth?"

"If the cardinal's secretaries knew anything definite, they would not question people in this manner," d'Artagnan said to himself. "Now, what they want to know is whether the Duke of Buckingham is in Paris, and whether he has had an interview with the queen or not."

It was the evening of the day after the arrest of poor Bonacieux. Athos had just left d'Artagnan's apartment to report at M. de Tréville's, nine o'clock had just struck, and Planchet was beginning his task of making the bed. A knocking was heard at the street door. Immediately the door below was opened and shut. Some one was taken in the trap.

D'Artagnan flew to his hole, laid himself down at full length upon the floor, and listened. Cries were soon heard, then moans, which some one was endeavoring to stifle.

"The devil!" said the Gascon to himself. "It seems to me it is a woman. They search her, she resists, they use force—the scoundrels!"

"But I tell you that I am the mistress of the house, gentlemen," he heard the unfortunate woman cry. "I tell you I am Madame Bonacieux and that I belong to the queen."

"Madame Bonacieux!" murmured the eavesdropper.

"Can I be so lucky as to find what everybody is seeking?"

The voice became more and more indistinct, a violent struggle made the partition shake. The woman was resisting as much as a woman can resist four stout ungentle men.

"Pardon, gentlemen, par—" murmured the voice, which could thereafter be heard only in inarticulate sounds.

"They are binding and gagging her! They are going to drag her away!" cried d'Artagnan to himself as he sprang up from the floor. "Good! My sword is at my side. Planchet!"

"Monsieur?"

"Run like the wind and find Athos, Porthos, Aramis. One of the three will certainly be at home, perhaps all three. Tell them to arm themselves, to come and come flying. Ah, I remember, Athos is at M. de Tréville's."

"Oh, Monsieur, do not go below! You will be killed!"

"Hold your tongue, stupid fellow! Put back the boards, sweep the floor, go out at the door, and leg it! I'm going down by the window to get there the sooner."

D'Artagnan laid hold of the casement and let himself gently down from the second story. This fortunately was not very elevated, and he reached the ground without injury. He then went straight to the entrance door and knocked, murmuring, "I'm going to get caught in a mouse-trap, but woe to the cats that pounce on such a mouse as I!"

The knocker had scarcely sounded under the hand of the young man before the tumult within ceased. Steps approached, the door was opened, and, sword in hand, d'Artagnan rushed into the rooms of M. Bonacieux. The door, doubtless moved by a spring, closed behind him.

Then those who dwelt in this unfortunate house, together with the nearest neighbors, heard loud cries, stamping of feet, clashing of swords, and smashing of furniture.

A moment later those who had gone to their windows to learn the cause of this amazing tumult saw the entrance door swing open and four men clothed in black fly out like so many frightened crows. And they left behind them on the ground feathers from their wings; that is to say, patches of their clothes and fragments of their cloaks. The Gascon had done a thorough job.

D'Artagnan was conqueror without much effort, it must be confessed. For only one of the officers was armed, and even he defended himself for form's sake. It is true that the others had tried to knock the young man down with chairs, stools, and crockery. But two or three scratches administered by the Gascon's sword were enough to terrify them. Ten minutes sufficed for their defeat, and d'Artagnan remained the master on the field of battle.

The neighbors who had opened their windows, with the coolness peculiar to Parisians in these times of perpetual riot, closed them again the moment they saw the four men in black flee. Besides, it began to grow late and people went to bed early in this quarter of the Luxembourg.

On being left alone with Madame Bonacieux, d'Artagnan turned toward her. The poor woman was reclining upon an armchair, where she had been left half fainting. With a rapid glance the youth examined her.

She was a charming woman of twenty-five or twenty-six years, with dark hair, blue eyes, and a nose slightly turned up. She had admirable teeth and a complexion marbled with rose and opal. There, however, ended the signs which might have confounded her with a lady of rank. The hands were white, but without delicacy. The feet did not bespeak the woman of quality.   Happily d'Artagnan was not yet acquainted with such niceties.

While d'Artagnan was studying Madame at close range, he saw on the floor a fine cambric handkerchief. He picked it up, and at the corner of it he recognized the same cipher he had seen on the handkerchief which had so nearly caused Aramis and him to cut each other's throat.

From that time on he had been cautious with respect to dainty handkerchiefs with arms on them, and he therefore tucked into the pocket of the swooning lady the one he had just discovered.

At that moment Madame Bonacieux recovered her senses. She opened her eyes, looked around her in terror, saw that the apartment was empty and that she was alone with her liberator. She extended her hands to him with a smile. She had the sweetest smile in the world.

"You have saved me, Monsieur," she said. "Permit me to thank you from the bottom of my heart."

"Madame," answered d'Artagnan, "I have done only what every gentleman would have done in my place. You owe me no thanks."

"Oh, yes, I do, Monsieur. And I hope to prove to you that I am no ingrate. But what could these men want of me and where is Monsieur Bonacieux?"

"Madame, these men are the agents of the cardinal. Your husband is not here because yesterday evening he was lodged in the Bastille."

"Oh, my God! What has he done? Poor dear man, he is innocence itself!"

"I believe, Madame, that his only crime is to have at

the same time the good luck and the misfortune to be your husband."

"But, Monsieur, then you know—"

"That you have been abducted, yes."

"And do you know by whom? Oh, tell me, if you do!"

"By a man of forty to forty-five years of age, with black hair, a dark complexion, and a scar on his left temple. His name I do not know."

"And did my husband discover I had been carried off?"

"He was informed of it by a letter written by the abductor."

"And does he suspect the cause of it?" Madame Bonacieux inquired with some embarrassment.

"He attributed it, I believe, to a political cause."

"At first I doubted that fact, but now I think as he does. Then my husband has not suspected me a single instant?"

"So far from it, Madame, that he boasted of your virtue, and above all of your love."

A second smile, almost imperceptible, stole over the rosy lips of the pretty young woman.

"Tell me," continued the Gascon, "how did you escape?"

"I took advantage of a moment when they left me alone. And, as I had known since morning the reason for my abduction, with the help of some knotted sheets I let myself down from a window. Then I hastened hither, where I thought to find my husband."

"Pardon me, Madame, if I say that this is not a safe place for confidences. The men I put to flight will return shortly, reinforced. If they find us here, we are lost. Let us withdraw."

Without taking the trouble to close the door behind
them the two young people passed down the Rue des Fossoyeurs rapidly, turned into the Rue des Fossés-Monsieur-
le-Prince, and did not stop until they had reached the Place
St. Sulpice.

"Now where do you wish me to conduct you?" asked
d'Artagnan.

"My intention was to get into communication with M.
La Porte through my husband in order that I might learn
precisely what has taken place at the Louvre during the
last three days and whether there is any danger in my
presenting myself there."

"But I can inform M. La Porte in your husband's
stead."

"The gate would be closed against you, Monsieur,
unless I gave you the password. And if I should do this,
would you forget it the moment you were admitted?"

"By my honor and the faith of a gentleman!" said
d'Artagnan with an accent so truthful that no one could
mistake it. "I shall do conscientiously all I can to serve
the king and to be agreeable to the queen. Dispose of
me, then, as a friend."

"But I—where shall I go meanwhile? I can trust
nobody."

"Stop," said d'Artagnan, "we are near the door of
Athos, my friend, who lives two steps from here in the
Rue Férou. He is not at home, and I shall carry away
the key after having placed you in his apartment."

"Suppose he should return?"

"I feel sure that he will not. But if he should, he will

be told that I have brought a lady with me and that she is in his rooms."

"You know that will compromise my good name sadly."

"Of what consequence is it? Nobody knows you. Besides, we are in a situation that demands that we overlook ceremony."

"Come then, let us go."

Both resumed their way. As d'Artagnan had foreseen, Athos was not within. He took from the concierge the key, which was customarily given him as one of the family, ascended the stairs, and ushered Madame Bonacieux into the small lodging which we have already sufficiently described.

"Make yourself at home," he said. "Remain here, fasten the door when I have gone, and open it to nobody unless you hear three taps—two taps close together and fairly hard, the other after an interval, and lighter."

"All right," answered Madame Bonacieux, "and now let me give you my instructions. Present yourself at the gate of the Louvre on the side of the Rue de l'Échelle and ask for Germain. Say to him the two words 'Tours' and 'Bruxelles,' and he will at once put himself at your orders. Command him to go and fetch M. La Porte, the queen's valet de chambre. And send him to me here."

"That shall be done promptly and to the letter, Madame. But where and how shall I see you again?"

"Are you so sure you wish to see me again, Monsieur?"

"Certain of it."

"Well, then, let that care be mine and be at ease."

"I depend upon your word."

"You may."

D'Artagnan bowed to Madame Bonacieux, darting at
her a glance which was perhaps unconsciously very ardent.
While he was descending the staircase he heard the door
closed and double-locked.   In two bounds he was at the
Louvre—as he entered the gate of l'Échelle, ten o'clock
struck.   All the events we have described had taken place
within a half hour.

Everything fell out as Madame Bonacieux prophesied.
On hearing the password, Germain bowed.   In a few minutes La Porte was at the lodge.   In two words the young
Gascon had informed him where Madame was.   La Porte
assured himself of the accurate address and set off on a
run.   Hardly, however, had he taken ten steps when he
returned.

"Young man," he said, "a suggestion.   You may get
into trouble by what has taken place.   Have you any friend
whose clock is slow?"

"Well, sir, and if I have?"

"Go and call upon him in order that he may give evidence of your having been with him at half-past nine.   In
a court of justice that is called an alibi."

D'Artagnan found the advice to his liking.   So he
took to his heels and was soon at M. de Tréville's.   But,
instead of going into the drawing-room with the rest of
the crowd, he asked to be conducted to the captain's office.
As the young Gascon so constantly frequented the house,
no difficulty was made in complying with the request.   And
a servant went to notify M. de Tréville that his young
compatriot had something important to communicate and

solicited a private hearing. Five minutes later the captain was asking d'Artagnan what he could do to serve him and what caused his visit at so late an hour.

"Pardon me, Monsieur," said the guardsman of M d'Essart, who had profited by his moment alone to put back the hands of M. de Tréville's clock some three quarters of an hour, "but I thought, as it was only twenty-five minutes past nine, it would not be too late for me to wait upon you."

"Twenty-five minutes past nine!" cried Tréville, looking at the clock. "Why, that's impossible!"

"Glance at the clock again and see!" said d'Artagnan.

"True enough!" admitted M. de Tréville. "I had thought it much later. But what can I do for you?"

Then d'Artagnan proceeded to tell the captain a long story about the queen. He related what he had heard of the projects of the cardinal with regard to Buckingham, and all with a tranquillity and candor of which M. de Tréville was more the dupe for having observed some fresh friction between the cardinal, the king, and the queen.

As ten o'clock was striking, d'Artagnan left M. de Tréville, who thanked him for his information, recommended him to have the service of the king and queen at heart, and returned to the drawing-room.

But at the foot of the stairs d'Artagnan suddenly remembered he had forgotten his cane. He consequently ran back upstairs again, reëntered the office, and with a turn of his finger set the clock right that it might not the next day be perceived to be out of order. Certain from that moment that he had a witness to prove his alibi, he ran down to the street and started home.

CHAPTER XI

THE INTRIGUE GROWS TANGLED

His visit with M. de Tréville over, the pensive d'Artagnan proceeded to take the longest way to the Rue des Fossoyeurs.

Of what was the young Gascon thinking that he strayed thus from his path, gazing at the stars of heaven, and sometimes sighing, sometimes smiling?

He was thinking of Madame Bonacieux. For this apprentice musketeer the young woman was almost an ideal person to fall in love with. Pretty, mysterious, initiated into almost all the secrets of the court, it might be surmised that she was not altogether without emotional capacity and experience. And this is an irresistible charm to novices in love.

Moreover, d'Artagnan had delivered her from the hands of the demons who wished to search and illtreat her. And this important service had established between them one of those sentiments of gratitude which so easily assume a more tender character.

Paris for two hours past had been dark and was becoming deserted. Eleven sounded from all the clocks of the Faubourg St. Germain. It was delightful weather. D'Artagnan was passing along a lane on the spot where the Rue d'Assas is now situated. He was breathing into his lungs the balmy emanations that were borne upon the wind from the Rue de Vaugirard and that arose from the gardens refreshed by the evening dews and the night breeze. From far away could be heard the drinking songs of the tipplers who were making merry in the cabarets scattered along the plain.

When he arrived at the end of this lonely lane, d'Artagnan suddenly recalled that he was near the house of Aramis. And he turned to the left, for the dwelling of his friend was situated between the Rue Cassette and the Rue Servandoni.

The young Gascon had just passed the first of these two streets and had already glimpsed the door of his friend's habitation, shaded by a mass of sycamores and clematis which formed an enormous arch opposite the front of it. Of a sudden he caught sight of something like a shadow issuing from the Rue Servandoni.

This something was wrapped in a cloak, and d'Artagnan at first believed it to be a man. But by the smallness of the form, the hesitation of the walk, and the indecision of the step, he soon discovered it was a woman. D'Artagnan was perplexed.

"Shall I offer my services?" he wondered. "No, by my faith, no! For a woman who wanders in the dark streets at this hour ventures out only to meet the man she loves. If I should disturb a meeting, that would not be the best way of commencing an acquaintance."

Suddenly—why, he did not know—d'Artagnan's mind reverted to the niece of the theologian of whom the would-be abbé had spoken.

"*Pardieu!*" he said to himself. "It would be droll indeed if this young maid should be in search of our friend's house. But, on my soul, that's the way it looks! Ah, my dear Aramis, this time I shall find you out."

He made himself as small as he could, and hid himself on the darkest side of the street near a stone bench that was placed back in a niche. The young woman continued to advance. And, in addition to the lightness of her step, which had betrayed her sex, she emitted a little cough which denoted a sweet voice. D'Artagnan believed this catching of the breath to be a signal.

All at once the woman drew near Aramis' shutter and tapped on it at three equal intervals with her bent finger.

"This is all very fine, dear abbé," muttered the young man. "Ah, Monsieur Hypocrite, I understand now how you study theology."

The three light blows had scarcely been struck when the inside blind was opened and a light appeared through the panes of the outside shutter.

"Aha!" said the eavesdropper. "This visit was expected. We shall now see the windows open and the lady enter by escalade."

But to the great astonishment of the secret witness the shutter remained closed. What is more, the light that had shone for an instant disappeared, and all was again in Stygian darkness.

D'Artagnan felt sure this condition could not last long. So he continued to look with all his eyes and listen with all his ears. He was right. At the end of some seconds two sharp taps were heard inside. The young woman in the street replied by a single knock and the shutter was opened a little way.

D'Artagnan (Gascons have eyes like cats) then saw
that the young woman took from her pocket a white object
which she unfolded quickly and which assumed the shape
of a handkerchief. She showed the person behind the
shutter the corner of this unfolded object.

Of course this immediately recalled to the mind of
the young man the bit of napery he had found at the feet
of Madame Bonacieux, which in turn reminded him of
that which he had dragged from under the feet of Aramis.

"Now what the deuce could that handkerchief signify?"

Placed where he was, d'Artagnan could not perceive the
face of Aramis. We say Aramis because the young Gascon
entertained no doubt but that it was his friend who held
the dialogue from the interior with the lady of the exterior.

Curiosity prevailed over prudence. Profiting by the
preoccupation into which the sight of the handkerchief
seemed to have plunged the two actors on the scene, the
young man stole from his hiding place. As quick as lightning, but stepping with the utmost caution, he ran and
placed himself close to the angle of the wall, from which his
wary eye could pierce the interior of Aramis' room.

When he gained this advantage, d'Artagnan almost
uttered a cry of surprise. For it was not Aramis who was
conversing with the nocturnal visitor—it was a woman!
The secret witness, however, could see only enough to
recognize the form of her garments, not enough to distinguish her features.

At the same instant the woman inside drew a second
handkerchief from her pocket and exchanged it for that
which had just been shown to her. Then some words

were spoken by the two women, and at length the shutter closed. The woman who was outside the window turned around and passed within four paces of d'Artagnan, pulling down the hood of her mantle. But the precaution was too late. The Gascon had already recognized Madame Bonacieux.

But was it on her own account or on that of another that she exposed herself to such hazards? This was the lightning question he asked himself, this young man whom the demon of jealousy was now devouring.

D'Artagnan ran after her. It was not difficult for him to overtake a woman hindered by her cloak. He came up to her before she had traversed a third of the length of the street. The unfortunate creature was exhausted, not by fatigue, but by terror. And when the unrecognized man placed his hand upon her shoulder, she sank upon one knee and cried in a choking voice, "Kill me, if it please you. But I swear you shall learn nothing."

D'Artagnan raised her sinking form immediately by passing his arm around her waist. He spoke to her gently. And at the sound of his voice she reopened her eyes, cast a quick glance at the man who had terrified her so, and uttered a cry of joy.

"Oh, it is you, it is you! Thank God!"

"Yes, it is I," answered d'Artagnan, "whom the angels have sent to watch over you."

"Was it with that intention that you followed me?" asked the young woman with a tremulous smile.

"No," replied the Gascon. "It was chance that threw me in your way. I saw you knocking at Aramis' window."

"This is the first time I ever heard that name."

"It is the first time, then, that you ever went to that house? And you did not know that it was inhabited by a musketeer? It was not he, then, whom you came to seek?"

"Not the least in the world. Besides, you must have seen that the person to whom I spoke was a woman."

"That is true. But this woman must be a friend of Aramis, since she lodges with him."

"That is not my concern."

"But who is she?"

"Oh, that is not my secret!"

"My dear Madame Bonacieux, you are charming. But at the same time you are one of the most mysterious of women."

"Do I lose by that in your estimation?"

"No, on the contrary, you are adorable."

"Give me your arm, then."

"Most willingly. And now?"

"Now escort me to where I am going."

D'Artagnan offered his arm to Madame Bonacieux, who took it willingly. Half laughing, half trembling, they gained the top of the Rue de la Harpe. When they had arrived there, the young woman seemed to hesitate, much as she had previously done in the Rue Vaugirard. By certain signs, however, she appeared to recognize a door. She approached it hesitantly.

"And now, Monsieur," she said, "it is here that I have business. A thousand thanks for your honorable company, which has saved me from all the dangers to which, alone,

I was exposed. The moment has come for us to part. I have reached my destination."

"And you will have nothing to fear on your return?"

"I shall have nothing to fear but robbers."

"But that seems to me a great deal."

"Why, what could they take from me? I have not a penny about me."

"You forget the beautiful handkerchief with the coat of arms."

"What?"

"That which I found at your feet and replaced in your pocket."

"Hold your tongue, imprudent man! Do you wish to destroy me?"

"You see very plainly that there is still danger for you, since a single word makes you tremble. And you confess that if that word were heard you would be ruined. Come, come, Madame!" cried d'Artagnan, seizing her hands and surveying her with an ardent glance. "Be more generous. Confide in me. Have you not read in my eyes that there is nothing but devotion and sympathy in my heart?"

"Yes," replied Madame Bonacieux. "Therefore, ask my own secrets and I shall reveal them to you. But those of others—ah, that is quite another thing."

"Very well," said the young Gascon, "I shall discover them. As these secrets may have an influence over your life, they must become mine."

"Beware of what you do!" cried the woman in a manner so serious as to make d'Artagnan start in spite of himself.

'Oh, meddle in nothing that concerns me! Do not seek to help me in what I am accomplishing. Place faith in what I tell you. Have no more thought of me. I exist for you no more than if you had never seen me."

"Must Aramis do as much, Madame?" demanded d'Artagnan, who was deeply piqued.

"That is the second or third time, Monsieur, that you have repeated that name, and yet I have told you that I do not know him."

"You do not know the man at whose shutter you knocked? Indeed, Madame, you believe me too credulous!"

"Monsieur!" said the young woman, supplicating him and clasping her hands together. "In the name of heaven, by the honor of a soldier, by the courtesy of a gentleman, depart! There, midnight sounds! It is the hour when I am expected."

"Madame," said her companion, bowing, "I can refuse nothing when asked of me in such terms. Be content. I shall go."

"And you will not follow me? You will not watch me?"

"I shall return home at once."

"Ah, I was sure you were a good and brave man," declared Madame Bonacieux, holding out her hand to him and placing the other upon the knocker of a little door almost hidden in the wall.

"Oh, I wish I had never seen you!" cried d'Artagnan with that ingenuous roughness which women often prefer to the affectations of politeness, because it betrays the depths of the thought and proves that feeling has conquered reason.

And, as if he felt strength to detach himself only by a violent effort from the hand he was holding, the young man sprang away and started to run, while Madame Bonacieux knocked, as previously, upon the shutter with three light and regular taps. When d'Artagnan had gained the corner of the street, he turned. The door had been opened and closed again. The mercer's pretty wife had disappeared.

Five minutes later the Gascon was in the Rue des Fossoyeurs.

"Poor Athos!" he said to himself. "He will never guess what all this means. He will have fallen asleep waiting for me, or else he will have returned home to learn that a woman has been there during his absence. A woman with Athos! After all," continued d'Artagnan, "there certainly was one with Aramis. All this is very strange and I am curious to know how it will end."

"Badly, Monsieur, badly!" replied a voice which the young man recognized as that of Planchet. For, soliloquizing aloud, as very preoccupied people do, he had entered the alley at the end of which were the stairs that led to his chamber.

"How do you mean, badly? What has happened, you idiot?" asked d'Artagnan.

"All sorts of misfortunes. In the first place, M. Athos has been arrested."

"What for, and by whom? Quick—are you dumb?"

"He was found in your lodging, so they mistook him for you, Monsieur. He was taken by guards who were brought by the black men you put to flight."

"Why did he not say right out who he was, and that he knew nothing about the affair?"

"He took care not to do so, Monsieur. On the contrary, he came up to me and said, 'It is your master who needs his liberty at this moment and not I, because he knows everything about this matter and I know nothing. They will believe he is arrested and safe in jail, and that will give him time. In three days I shall tell them who I am, and they cannot fail to let me go.' "

"Bravo, Athos, thou noble heart!" murmured d'Artagnan. "I could have sworn he would act in such a way. And what did the officers do?"

"Four conveyed him away to the Bastille or Fort L'Éveque. Two stayed behind with the men in black, who rummaged every place and took all the papers they found. The last two mounted guard at the door during the examination. Then, when all was over, they went off, leaving the house empty and open."

"And Porthos and Aramis?"

"I could not find them, Monsieur d'Artagnan. They did not come."

"Still they may come at any moment now, for you left word that I awaited them. So don't you budge from here. If they show up, say they can wait for me at the Fir Cone cabaret. Here it would perhaps be dangerous for them to remain, as the house may be watched. I'm off now to see M. de Treville and shall meet them later at the cabaret."

And with all the swiftness left in his legs, somewhat fatigued by the perambulations of that day, d'Artagnan directed his course toward the Rue du Vieux-Colombier.

M. de Tréville was not at home. His company was on
guard at the Louvre—he was at the Louvre with his company. The young Gascon immediately decided to find
him there. His costume of guardsman in the company
of M. d'Essart should be his passport for entering the
palace.

He therefore walked down the Rue des Petits Augustins
and came up to the quay in order to cross the New Bridge.
His first idea had been to ferry across the Seine, but, on
gaining the riverside and putting his hand mechanically
into his pocket, he had discovered he did not have the
wherewithal to pay his passage.

As he reached the top of the Rue Guénégaud he saw
two people coming out of the Rue Dauphine, and their
appearance struck him at once. One was the figure of a
man, the other of a woman. The latter had the outlines
of Madame Bonacieux; the man resembled Aramis so
much that anyone would consider him to be that person.
Furthermore, the man wore the uniform of a musketeer.
The woman's hood was pulled down over her face, and
the man held a handkerchief before his eyes. Both, as this
double precaution sufficiently indicated, had an interest in
not being recognized. They mounted the bridge. This was
now d'Artagnan's shortest route to the Louvre. So he
followed them.

D'Artagnan did not reflect that he had known the
mercer's pretty wife for only three hours. He did not
remember that she owed him nothing but a little gratitude
for having delivered her from the men in black who wished
to carry her off. She had promised him nothing. And

yet he considered himself somehow a betrayed and a ridi-
culed lover.   Blood mounted to his face as he resolved to
unravel this mystery.

The man and woman saw they were being watched and
redoubled their speed.   The Gascon decided at once what
course to pursue.   He passed them, and then returned so
as to meet them exactly before the Samaritaine, which was
illuminated by a lamp that threw its light over all that
section of the bridge.   The three came to a halt.

"What do you wish, Monsieur?" demanded the man,
recoiling a step.   He spoke with a foreign accent which
proved to d'Artagnan that one of his conjectures was false.

"It is not Aramis!" he cried.

"By your exclamation I see that you have mistaken me
for another," said the unknown.   "Allow me, then, to
pass on, since it is not with me that you are concerned."

"You are right, Monsieur, it is not with you that I
have anything to do.   It is with Madame."

"You do not know her, either," declared the stranger.

"Pardon me, Monsieur.   I know her very well."

"Ah," cried Madame Bonacieux in a tone of reproach.
"I had your promise as a soldier and a gentleman not to
follow me."

"And I, Madame!" said d'Artagnan, much embarrassed.   "You promised me—"

"Take my arm, Madame," interrupted the stranger,
"and let us continue on our way."

But d'Artagnan, stupefied and astounded by all that
had happened, stood with crossed arms, barring the path
to the musketeer and Madame Bonacieux.   The man

dressed in musketeer's uniform advanced two steps and pushed the Gascon aside with his hand. D'Artagnan made a lightning spring backward and drew his sword. At the same time and with the rapidity of light itself the unknown drew his.

"In the name of heaven, my Lord!" exclaimed Madame Bonacieux, throwing herself between the two combatants and seizing the swords with her hands.

"Did you say 'My Lord'?" asked d'Artagnan, enlightened by a sudden idea. "Pardon me, Monsieur, but are you not—"

"The Duke of Buckingham," said the mercer's wife in a swift undertone. "And now you may ruin us all."

"My Lord and Madame, I ask a hundred pardons for my folly. But I love her, Monsieur, and was consumed by jealousy. Tell me how I may risk my life to serve your Grace."

"You are a brave young man," said Buckingham, holding out his hand to the young man, who pressed it respectfully. "You offer me your service, sir. With the same frankness I accept it. Follow us at a distance of twenty paces as far as the Louvre. And if any one spies upon us, slay him!"

D'Artagnan placed his naked sword under his arm. He allowed the duke and Madame Bonacieux to take twenty steps ahead, and then followed. He was ready to execute the instructions of the noble and elegant minister of Charles I of England.

Fortunately he had no opportunity to offer the duke this proof of his devotion, and the young woman and the handsome musketeer entered the Louvre by the wicket of the Échelle without interference of any kind.

As for d'Artagnan, he immediately repaired to the cabaret of the Fir Cone, where he found Porthos and Aramis awaiting him. He could give them no explanation of the alarm and inconvenience he had caused them. He told them only that he alone had terminated the affair in which for a moment he believed he should need their assistance.

CHAPTER XII

GEORGE VILLIERS, DUKE OF BUCKINGHAM

Once within the interior of the courtway of the Louvre, Madame Bonacieux pushed a little servants' door which was ordinarily closed at night. The door yielded.

She took the duke by the hand, for they were now in darkness, and after a few groping steps grasped a balustrade, placed her foot upon the bottom step, and began to ascend the staircase. The duke counted two flights.

His guide then turned to the right, followed the course of a long corridor, descended a flight, walked a few paces farther, and inserted a key in a lock. She then pushed the duke gently into an apartment that was lighted only by a night lamp, saying, "Remain here, my Lord Duke. Some one will come."

She then went out by the door they had entered, locking it behind her. The Englishman found himself literally a prisoner.

But not for an instant did he experience the slightest fear. One of the salient points of the duke's character was the search for adventures and a love of romance. Brave, reckless, and venturesome, this was by no means the first time that he had risked his life in such attempts as the present undertaking.

He had learned, of course, that the pretended message from Anne of Austria which had brought him to Paris was a snare. But instead of hurrying back to England he had taken advantage of the position in which he found himself placed, and had declared to the queen that he would not depart without seeing her.

At first the queen had positively refused this demand. But at last she became afraid that the duke, if exasperated, would commit some folly. She had already decided to see him in order to urge his immediate departure from Paris, when on the very evening of coming to this decision Madame Bonacieux was abducted. She was the one charged with going to fetch the duke and bringing him to the Louvre. For two days no one knew what had become of this confidential messenger, and all plans were in suspense, but once she was free and placed in communication with La Porte matters resumed their course. Thus Madame Bonacieux had just accomplished the perilous enterprise which, but for her arrest, she would have executed three days earlier.

Buckingham, left alone, walked toward a mirror. His musketeer's uniform became him marvelously.

At thirty-five, which was then his age, he passed with just title for the handsomest gentleman and the most elegant cavalier of France or England.

The favorite of two kings, immensely rich, all-powerful in a kingdom that he disordered at his fancy and calmed at his caprice, George Villiers, Duke of Buckingham, had lived one of those fabulous existences which astonish posterity. He went straight to the object at which he aimed, even if it were so elevated and dazzling that another man would be considered mad even to contemplate it. It was thus that he had succeeded in approaching the beautiful and proud Anne of Austria and in making himself loved by dazzling her.

At this moment a door concealed in the tapestry opened and a woman appeared. Buckingham saw this apparition in the glass and uttered a cry. For it was the queen.

Anne of Austria was then twenty-six years of age and in the full splendor of her beauty. Her carriage was that of a goddess. Her eyes, which shone with the brilliance of emeralds, were at the same time full of sweetness and majesty. Her mouth was small and rosy. And although her underlip, like that of all princes of the House of Austria, protruded slightly beyond the other, it was eminently lovely in its smile and as profoundly disdainful in its contempt.

Her skin was admired for its velvety softness. Her hands and arms were of such surpassing beauty that every poet of the time sang of them as incomparable. Lastly, her hair, whose color had been light in her younger years, had now become chestnut in hue. She wore it curled very plainly and with much powder. It admirably set off her face, in which a rigid critic might have desired a touch less of color, and a fastidious sculptor a little more fineness in the modeling of the nose.

Buckingham stood for a moment blinded.

Anne of Austria took two steps forward. The duke threw himself at her feet and before the queen could prevent him had kissed the hem of her satin robe.

"Duke, you already know that it is not I who caused you to be written to."

"Yes, Madame!" cried the duke. "I must indeed have been mad to believe that snow would become animated or marble warm. But those who love believe easily in love. Besides, I have lost nothing by this journey, because I see you."

"Ah, but you know why I see you," replied Anne. "It is because, insensible to my sufferings, you persist in remaining in a city where you risk your life and endanger my honor. I see you to tell you that everything separates us: the depths of the sea, the enmity of kingdoms, the sanctity of vows. It is a sacrilege to struggle against so many things, my Lord. In short, I see you to tell you that we must never see each other again."

"Speak on, Madame," said Buckingham. "The sweetness of your voice covers the harshness of your words. You talk of sacrilege! Why, the only sacrilege is to separate two hearts which have been formed by God for each other."

"My Lord," said the queen, "you forget that I never said I loved you."

"But you have never told me that you did not love me. And, truly, to speak such words would be on the part of your Majesty too great an ingratitude. For, tell me, where can you find a love like mine—a glow that neither time, nor absence, nor despair can extinguish—a tender passion that contents itself with a lost ribbon, a stray look, or a chance word?"

"Such protestations are easily made," breathed the queen.

"Wait, Madame! It is now three years since I saw

you for the first time. Shall I tell you how you were dressed when I then saw you? You were seated upon cushions in the Spanish fashion. You wore a robe of green satin embroidered with gold and silver, hanging sleeves knotted upon your beautiful arms with large diamonds. You wore a close ruff, a small cap upon your head of the same color as your gown, and in that cap a heron's feather."

"What folly to feed a useless passion with remembrances!" murmured Anne of Austria. But she did not have courage to find fault with the duke for having preserved so well her portrait in his heart.

"And upon what, then, can I live? I have nothing but memory. It is my happiness and my hope. Each time I see you is a fresh diamond which I inclose in the treasure casket of my heart. This is the fourth that you have let fall and I have picked up. The first I have just described to you; the second, at the mansion of Madame de Chevreuse; the third, in the garden at Amiens."

"Duke," said the queen, blushing, "never speak of that evening."

"On the contrary, Madame, let us speak of it—the most happy evening of my life. How soft and perfumed was the air, how lovely the star-enameled sky! Take my wealth, my fortune, my glory, all the days I have to live, but give me back that moment. For that night, Madame, you loved me, I can swear it."

"And yet, my Lord, you saw the queen come to the aid of the woman who was faltering. At the first word you dared to utter, at the first freedom that I had to check, I called for help."

"Yes, that is true. Any other love but mine would have sunk beneath this ordeal, but mine became only the more ardent and eternal. Eight days afterward I was back again. That time you had nothing to say to me. I had risked my life and my favor to be with you but a second. I did not even touch your hand."

"No, but calumny seized upon all those follies of yours, in which I played no part, as you well know, my Lord. The king, spurred on by the cardinal, made a terrible clamor. Madame de Vernel was driven from me, Putange was exiled, Madame de Chevreuse fell into disgrace. And when you wished to come back as ambassador to France, the king himself opposed it."

"And France is about to pay for her sovereign's refusal with a war. What object, think you, have this expedition to Ré and this league with the Protestants of Rochelle? The pleasure of seeing you. This war will bring about a peace, this peace will require a negotiator, and that negotiator will be I. Thousands of men, it is true, will have to pay for my happiness with their lives, but what is that to me, provided I see you once again and am happy for an instant? This is folly, perhaps—even insanity. But tell me what woman has a lover more truly in love—what queen a servant more ardent?"

"My Lord, you invoke in your defense proofs of love that are almost crimes."

"Because you do not love me, Madame! If you loved me, you would see all that with other eyes. Madame de Chevreuse, of whom you just spoke, was less cruel than you. Holland loved her, and she responded to his love."

"Ah, but she was not queen," murmured Anne of Austria, overcome in spite of herself by the expression of so profound a passion.

"Thanks for those sweet words, Madame! You would love me, then, were you not queen. Oh, my beautiful sovereign, a hundred times, thanks!"

'You have wrongly interpreted, my Lord. I did not mean to say—"

"Silence!" cried the duke. "If I am happy in an error, do not undeceive me. You have yourself told me, Madame, that I have been drawn into a snare. Perhaps I may leave my life in the noose of it, for, strange though it be, I have for some time had a presentiment that I should shortly die."

And the duke smiled with an expression at once sad and charming. Anne of Austria cried out suddenly with an accent of terror that innocently proved how much greater an interest she took in her friend than she ventured to acknowledge.

"Oh, but I," she said, "I also, Duke, have had presentiments. I even dreamed I saw you lying bleeding, wounded."

"In the left side, was it not, and with a knife?" interrupted Buckingham.

"Yes—just so it was."

"Would heaven send the same visions to you if you did not love me? Ah, you will weep for me, my beautiful queen?"

"This is more than I can bear!" cried Anne. "If you are struck down in France, if your love for me is the cause of your death, I shall go mad. Take pity on me, then, and go! Come back, if you will, as ambassador, surrounded by guards who will defend you, with servants who will watch over you. And then I shall no longer fear for your days, and I shall be happy in seeing you."

"Is this true that you say?"

"Yes."

"Then give me some pledge of your indulgence, some object that comes from you and may remind me that I have not been dreaming. Something you have worn, that I may wear in turn—a ring, a necklace, a chain."

"If I yield to your demand, will you depart on the instant and return to England?"

"I swear it to you."

Anne of Austria reëntered her apartment and came out again almost immediately, holding in her hand a rosewood casket on which her monogram was incrusted with gold.

"Here, my Lord," she said, "keep this in memory of me."

Buckingham took the casket and a second time fell to his knees.

"You have promised to go," said the queen.

"And I keep my word. Your hand, Madame, and I depart!"

Anne of Austria stretched forth her hand, closing her eyes, for she felt that her strength was about to fail her. Buckingham pressed his lips passionately to her beautiful hand, and then, rising, said, "Within six months, Madame, if I am not dead, I shall have seen you again—even if I have to overthrow the world!"

And, faithful to the promise he had given, he rushed out of the apartment.

In the corridor he met Madame Bonacieux, who was waiting for him. And with the same precautions and the same good luck as before, she conducted him out of the Louvre.

CHAPTER XIII

MONSIEUR BONACIEUX

It may be observed that we have appeared to take but small notice of one person concerned in our story, despite his precarious position. This personage was M. Bonacieux, the respectable martyr of the political and amorous intrigues which are entangling themselves so nicely.

But we have by no means forgotten him.

The officers who arrested him conducted him straight to the Bastille, where he passed tremblingly before a party of soldiers who were loading their muskets. Thence, introduced into a subterranean gallery, he became the target for the grossest insults and the harshest treatment on the part of those who brought him. The officers saw that they were not dealing with a gentleman, and so they treated him like the lowest type of peasant.

At the end of half an hour or so a clerk came to put an end to his tortures, but not to his anxiety, by giving the order to conduct M. Bonacieux to the Chamber of Examination. Ordinarily prisoners were interrogated in their cells; not so our poor mercer.

Two guards attended the prisoner across a courtway. They entered together a corridor in which three sentinels were standing, opened a door, and pushed him unceremoniously into a low-ceilinged room where the only furniture was a table, a chair, and a commissary. The commissary, seated in the chair, was writing at the table.

This clerk was a man of repulsive mien, with a pointed nose, with yellow and prominent cheek bones, and small eyes that were keen and penetrating. The expression of his face resembled that of both the polecat and the fox. His head, supported by a long and flexible neck, issued from a loose black robe and balanced itself with a motion much akin to that of a tortoise thrusting his head out of his shell.

He began by asking M. Bonacieux his name, age, occupation, and place of dwelling.

The accused replied that he was Jacques Michel Bonacieux, that he was fifty-one years old, a retired mercer, and lived at Rue des Fossoyeurs, No. 14.

Instead of continuing to interrogate him the commissary then made him a long speech upon how dangerous it is for an obscure citizen to meddle with public matters. The clerk completed this exordium by an exposition in which he painted the power and the deeds of the cardinal whom none might thwart with impunity.

After this second part of his discourse, fixing his hawk's eye upon M. Bonacieux, he bade him reflect upon the gravity of the situation in which he now found himself.

At bottom the character of the mercer was one of profound selfishness mixed with sordid avarice, the whole seasoned with extreme timidity. The love with which his young wife inspired him was a secondary sentiment, and not strong enough to contend with the primitive feelings we have just enumerated.

"But, Monsieur," Bonacieux said calmly to the commissary, "believe that I know the merit of his incomparable Eminence by whom we have the honor to be governed."

"How came you then in the Bastille?"

"I do not know. But to a certainty it is not for having disobliged Monsieur the Cardinal."

"You must, nevertheless, have committed a crime, since you are here and accused of high treason."

"But how is it possible for a poor mercer who detests Huguenots and abhors Spaniards to be arrested for high treason? Consider, Monsieur, the thing is absolutely impossible."

"M. Bonacieux, you have a wife?"

"I had one, Monsieur, but they abducted her."

"Ah! They have nabbed her? And do you know the man who has committed this deed?"

"I suspect," said Bonacieux, who thought that by confessing all he might prove his good will, "I suspect a tall, dark man, of haughty carriage, who has the air of a great lord. He has followed us several times when I have waited for my wife at the wicket of the Louvre to escort her home."

The commissary now seemed to experience a slight uneasiness.

"And his name?" he asked.

"Is unknown to me, Monsieur. But I should recognize him in an instant if he were among a thousand persons."

The face of the commissary grew still darker.

"That is enough for today," he said. "Before we proceed further some one must be informed that you know the ravisher of your wife."

"But I didn't tell you I knew him!" cried Bonacieux in despair. "I told you, on the contrary—"

"Take away the prisoner," said the commissary to the guards.

"Where shall we put him?" demanded the chief.

"In a dungeon."

"Which one?"

"Good Lord! In the first one that's handy, provided it's safe," answered the clerk, with an indifference which filled the cowardly mercer with horror.

"Alas!" he said to himself. "Misfortune hangs over my head. My wife must have committed some dreadful crime. A night is soon passed, and tomorrow to the wheel, to the gallows! Oh, my God, have pity!"

Bonacieux could not close his eyes—not because his dungeon was so disagreeable, but because his uneasiness was so great. He sat, the whole night through, on his stool, starting at the least noise. And when the first rays of the sun penetrated his chamber, the dawn itself appeared to his disordered mind to have assumed funereal tints.

All at once he heard the bolts in his prison door drawn. He made a terrified bound. He thought they had come to lead him to the scaffold, at least. So when he saw instead of the executioner he awaited only his commissary of the preceding evening, attended by his assistant, he was ready to embrace them both.

"Your affair has grown worse since yesterday, my good man. I advise you tell the whole truth."

"I'll tell you anything," cried Bonacieux.

"Where is your wife?"

"But I said she was stolen from me!"

"All right. But yesterday afternoon at five o'clock she escaped, thanks to you."

"But, Monsieur, if she is free, that's not my fault."

"What business had you, then, to go to the room of M. d'Artagnan, your neighbor?"

"Why, to beg him to assist me in finding my wife. I thought I had a right to try to find her. He promised to help. But I soon discovered he was betraying me."

"You impose upon justice. In virtue of your compact together, M. d'Artagnan put to flight the police who arrested your wife and has placed her beyond reach."

"Well, I'll be hanged!"

"Probably. But, fortunately, M. d'Artagnan is in our hands. And I am going to confront you with him."

"By my faith, I ask nothing better," cried the poor mercer.

"Bring in the last one," said the commissary to the guards. The two soldiers led in Athos.

"But," exclaimed Bonacieux, "this is not M. d'Artagnan whom you are showing me—not the least in the world!"

"What is the gentleman's name, then?"

"How do I know? I have seen him repeatedly, but I don't know his name."

"Your name?" asked the commissary of the new captive.

"Athos," replied the musketeer.

"But didn't you say your name was d'Artagnan?"

"No. Somebody said to me, 'You are M. d'Artagnan.' And I replied, 'You think so?' My guards said they were convinced of it. I did not wish to contradict them. Besides, I might be deceived as to my identity."

"And I tell you, Monsieur Commissary," cried Bonacieux in his turn, "there is no doubt about the matter. M. d'Artagnan is my tenant, although he does not pay the rent—and I ought to know him even better on that account. He is a young man scarcely nineteen or twenty, and this gentleman is thirty at least. M. d'Artagnan is in M. d'Essart's Guards, and this gentleman is in the company of M. de Tréville's Musketeers. Look at his uniform!"

"*Pardieu!* That is true," murmured the commissary.

At this moment the door was opened quickly and a gate-keeper's messenger handed a note to the clerk.

"Oh, unhappy woman!" cried the commissary. "Yours is a pretty business now!"

"But," said the agitated mercer, "in case the note concerns my wife, how can it affect me when I am already in prison?"

"Because her actions are part of a plan concerted between you—an infernal plan!"

"I swear to you, Monsieur Commissary, that if she has committed any follies, I renounce her, I abjure her, I curse her."

"Bah!" said Athos to the clerk. "If you have no more need of me, send me elsewhere. Your M. Bonacieux is very tiresome."

The commissary designated by the same gesture both Athos and the mercer. "Let them be guarded more closely than ever," he ordered.

Athos shrugged his shoulders and followed his guards

silently, while M. Bonacieux uttered lamentations enough to break the heart of a tiger.

They locked the latter in the same dungeon where he had passed the previous night, and left him to himself during the day. Like a true mercer, Bonacieux wept intermittently for hours. But about nine o'clock in the evening, just as he had made up his mind to go to bed, he heard steps in the corridor outside. The door of his dungeon was thrown open and the guards appeared.

"Follow me," said the officer who came behind the guards.

"Ah, merciful heavens," muttered the mercer, "I am lost!" but he followed the guards mechanically and without resistance.

At the gate of the entrance court he found a carriage surrounded by four warders on horseback. The officer placed himself beside Bonacieux in the carriage and they were left in a rolling prison. Through the closely fastened windows the captive could perceive the houses and the pavement, that was all. But, true Parisian as he was, the mercer could recognize every street by the milestones, the signs and the lamps. When they came to St. Paul—the spot where they executed those condemned in the Bastille—he was near fainting away and crossed himself twice. He thought the carriage was going to stop there, but it passed slowly on.

Farther on, a still greater terror assailed him when they got to the edge of the cemetery of St. Jean, where state criminals were buried. The only thing that reassured him was his recollection that before people were buried here their heads were generally cut off and put in a basket, while he could feel that his cranium was still above his shoulders.

But when he saw the carriage take the way to La Grève, when he caught sight of the pointed roof of the Hôtel de Ville, and the carriage rolled beneath the arcade, he believed that then all was over with him. He tried to confess to the officer on the seat beside him and, upon the latter's refusal to listen, uttered such pitiable cries that the officer informed him if he continued to deafen the world thus a gag should be put in his mouth.

This somewhat quieted Bonacieux. If they were intending to execute him at La Grève, it would be scarcely worth their while to gag him as they had nearly reached the place of execution. Indeed, the carriage crossed the fatal spot without stopping. There remained, then, no place to fear but the Traitor's Cross. The carriage was taking the direct route to it.

This time there was no longer any doubt. It was at the Traitor's Cross that lesser criminals were hanged. Bonacieux apparently had flattered himself by believing himself worthy of St. Paul or the Place de Grève. It was here that his journey and his destiny were about to end! When they were within twenty paces of the dreadful cross, he heard a noise of people and the carriage stopped. This was more than the poor mercer could endure, depressed as he was by the successive emotions which he had experienced. He uttered a feeble groan which might have been the last sigh of a dying man and fainted.

CHAPTER XIV

THE MAN OF MEUNG

The crowd was caused, however, not by the expectation of seeing a man hanged, but by the contemplation of a man whose neck was already wrung and broken. The equipage, which had been stopped a moment by the curious throng, resumed its way through the press of people, threaded the Rue St. Honoré, turned into the Rue des Bons Enfants, and stopped before a low door.

This door was opened. Two guards received the limp form of Bonacieux from the officer who was supporting him. They dragged him through an alley, up a flight of stairs, and deposited him in an antechamber.

All these movements had been effected mechanically so far as he was concerned. He had walked as one drifts along in a dream. He glimpsed objects as if through a fog. His ears received sounds without interpreting them. He might have been executed at that moment without offering a single gesture in his own defense or uttering a cry for mercy.

He remained draped upon the bench where he had been deposited, his back against the wall and his hand hanging down.

A little later, however, on looking around him, he could perceive no threatening object. He saw nothing which indicated that he was running any real danger. The bench where the guards had placed him was covered with a well-stuffed cushion. The wall was ornamented with beautiful Cordoban leather. Large red damask curtains, fastened back by gold clasps, hung in front of the window. He perceived that his fears were exaggerated, and he began to turn his head right and left to make sure it was still properly hung on its hinges.

When he found that nobody objected to this movement, he gained an added bit of courage and ventured to draw up one leg and then the other. At length, with the help of his two hands he lifted himself painfully off the bench and tottered to his feet.

Just then an officer with a pleasant face opened a door, continued for a while to exchange some words with a person in the next chamber, and then approached the prisoner.

"Is your name Bonacieux?" he asked.

"Yes, Monsieur Officer," stammered the mercer, more dead than alive. "Bonacieux, at your service."

"Come in," said the officer.

He entered a large room, close and stifling. Its walls were furnished with a perfect arsenal of arms, offensive and defensive. There was a brisk fire in the hearth, although it was scarcely the end of September. A square table covered with books and papers occupied the center of the room. Unrolled upon the table was an immense plan of the city of La Rochelle.

Standing before the chimney breast was a man of medium height, of a proud and haughty mien — a man with piercing eyes, a large brow, and a thin face which was made still longer by an imperial beard surmounted by a pair of mustaches. Although this individual was scarcely thirty-six years old, hair, mustaches, and imperial all were turning gray. Except that he lacked a sword he had entirely the look of a soldier. And his buff boots, still slightly covered with dust, indicated that he had been on horseback in the course of the day.

This man was Armand Jean Duplessis, Cardinal Richelieu. Here he was not such as he is so often represented— broken down, suffering like a martyr, buried in a large armchair as in an anticipated tomb. Here he was an active and gallant cavalier, already weak of body but sustained by that moral power which made of him one of the most extraordinary men that ever lived. And at this moment, after having supported the Duc de Nevers in his Duchy of Mantua, after having taken Nîmes, Castres, and Uzès, Richelieu was preparing to drive .the English from the island of Ré and to lay siege to La Rochelle.

At first sight nothing denoted the cardinal. And thus it was impossible for those who did not know his face to guess in whose presence they were.

The poor mercer remained standing at the door while the eyes of the personage we have just described were fixed upon him as if they wished to plumb even the depths of his past. The officer took papers from the table and gave them to Richelieu, bowed to the ground, and retired.

Bonacieux recognized in these papers his interrogatories of the Bastille. From time to time the man by the chimney breast raised his eyes from the writings and plunged them like poniards into the heart of his shrinking victim. At the end of ten minutes of reading and ten seconds of examination, the cardinal had decided on his course. "You are accused of high treason," said he slowly.

"So I have been told, Monseigneur!" cried Bonacieux, giving his interrogator the title he had heard the officer accord him. "But I swear to you that I know nothing about it."

The cardinal repressed a smile. "That head has never conspired," he said to himself, "but no matter. We shall see." Aloud he continued, "You have conspired with your wife, with Madame de Chevreuse, and with my Lord Duke of Buckingham."

"Indeed, I have heard her pronounce those names, Monseigneur."

"On what occasion?"

"She said that the Cardinal de Richelieu had drawn the duke to Paris to ruin him and the queen."

"She said that?" cried the cardinal with violence.

"Yes, Monseigneur. But I told her she was wrong to talk about such things. And that his Eminence was incapable—"

"Hold your tongue! You are stupid."

"That's exactly what my wife said, Monseigneur."

"You have suspicions as to who carried off your wife?"

"Yes, Monseigneur. But these suspicions were disagreeable to Monsieur Commissary. And I no longer have them."

"Your wife has escaped. Did you know about that?"

"No, Monseigneur. I learned it while in prison and from the conversation of Monsieur Commissary—an amiable man."

Richelieu repressed another smile.

"Then you are ignorant as to where your wife is now?"

"Absolutely, Monseigneur. She has perhaps returned to the Louvre."

"At one o'clock this morning she had not come back."

"God knows what can have become of her then!"

"We shall know, too, before long. Nothing is concealed from the cardinal. The cardinal knows everything."

"In that case, Monseigneur, do you suppose the cardinal will be so kind as to tell me what has become of her?"

"Perhaps he may. But first you must reveal to the cardinal all you know of your wife's relations with Madame de Chevreuse."

"But, Monseigneur, I know nothing about them. I have never seen the lady whom you mention."

"When you went to fetch your wife from the Louvre, did you always return directly home?"

"Scarcely ever. She had business to transact with linen drapers."

"And how many were there of these people?"

"Two, Monseigneur."

"And where did they live?"

"One in Rue de Vaugirard, the other in Rue de la Harpe."

"Did you enter these houses with her?"

"Never, Monseigneur. I waited at the door."

"What excuse did your wife give for going in alone?"

"She gave me none. She said to wait and I waited."

"You are a very complacent husband, my dear M. Bonacieux. What are the numbers of these places?"

"No. 25 in Rue de Vaugirard, 75 in Rue de la Harpe."

At these words the cardinal took up a silver bell and rang it. The officer appeared at once.

"Find Rochefort," Richelieu said in a subdued voice. "Tell him to come to me immediately."

"The count is here," the officer replied, "and requests to speak to your Eminence instantly."

"Let him come in, then."

"To your Eminence!" murmured Bonacieux, half choked by terror and amazement. And he kept rolling his eyes around as he thought of how he had been conversing with the cardinal.

Five seconds had scarcely elapsed when the door of the cabinet opened and a new personage appeared.

"It is he!" cried Bonacieux.

"What 'he' are you talking about?" asked the cardinal.

"The man who abducted my wife."

The cardinal rang a second time. The officer reappeared.

"Take away that fool!" said Richelieu.

The newly introduced personage followed Bonacieux impatiently with his eyes until the door had closed behind him. Then he approached the cardinal eagerly and said, "The queen and the duke have seen each other at the Louvre. I am sure of it, for Madame de Lannoy, who is devoted to your Eminence, has just informed me."

"Why did she not let me know sooner?" cried Richelieu.

"Whether by chance or from mistrust, the queen made Madame de Surgis sleep in her chamber and detained her all day."

Well, we are beaten! How did it come about?"

"At half-past twelve the queen was with her women in her bedchamber when some one came and brought her a handkerchief from her laundress."

"And then?"

"The queen exhibited strong emotion and, despite the rouge with which her face was covered, turned pale—"

"And then, and then?"

"She arose and said with altered voice, 'Ladies, wait for me ten minutes, I shall soon return.' She went out the door of her alcove."

"Madame de Lannoy should have informed me instantly."

"Nothing was sure. Besides, her Majesty had ordered her to wait, and she dared not disobey."

"How long did the queen remain away from her chamber?"

"Three quarters of an hour, and then returned only to take a small rosewood casket with her cipher on it and went out again."

"And did she bring that casket back?"

"No. And Madame de Lannoy knows that it contained the diamond studs which his Majesty gave the queen. She is sure her Majesty gave them to Buckingham."

"How can she be certain?"

"In the course of the day in her capacity as tirewoman of the queen she looked for this casket, appeared uneasy at not finding it, and at length sought information from the queen."

"What then?"

"The queen became exceedingly red, and replied that she had broken one of these studs and sent it to her goldsmith for repair."

"He must be called upon to ascertain if this be true."

"I have just visited the goldsmith. He had heard nothing of it."

"Well, well! Rochefort, all is not lost. And perhaps —perhaps everything is for the best."

"The fact is, I do not doubt but that your Eminence's genius will repair the blunders of your agent, Monseigneur."

"Meanwhile, do you know where the Duchesse de Chevreuse and the Duke of Buckingham are now concealed?"

"No, Monseigneur. My people could tell me nothing on that head."

"Let me inform you, then. They were, one in the Rue de Vaugirard, No. 25, the other in the Rue de la Harpe, No. 75."

"Does your Eminence command they be arrested?"

"It is too late. They will both be gone."

"Still, we can make sure of that fact."

"Take ten guardsmen and search the two houses thoroughly."

The moment the cardinal was left alone by the departure of his agent, he rang the bell a third time.

"Bring back the prisoner," he said to the officer.

M. Bonacieux was introduced afresh, and upon a sign from the cardinal the officer retired.

"You have deceived me!" the cardinal said sternly.

"Your wife in going to Rue de Vaugirard and Rue de la Harpe was not seeking for linen drapers."

"Just God! Then why did she go there?"

"To meet Madame de Chevreuse and the English duke."

"That must be it!" cried Bonacieux. "I told my wife it was odd linen drapers should live in such houses, which had no signs. But she only laughed at me. Ah, Monseigneur! How truly you are the great cardinal, the man of genius whom all the world reveres!"

However contemptible might be the triumph gained over so vulgar a being as Bonacieux, the cardinal enjoyed it for an instant. Then, as if a fresh thought had occurred to him, a smile played upon his lips, and he said, offering his hand to the mercer, "Rise, my friend. You are a worthy man and must not kneel to me."

"The cardinal has touched me with his hand!" cried Bonacieux. "The great man has called me friend."

"Yes, my friend, yes," said the cardinal, with that paternal tone that he could on occasion assume, but which deceived none who knew him. "And as you have been unjustly suspected, well, you must be indemnified. Here, take this purse of a hundred pistoles and grant me your pardon."

"I pardon you, Monseigneur! But you are able to have me arrested—tortured—hanged! You are the master. You cannot mean you really wish to have me pardon you!"

"Ah, my dear M. Bonacieux, you are generous in this matter. I thank you for it. You will, then, take this bag of money and go away, not too malcontent?"

"I go away delighted!"

"Au revoir, then. We shall meet again frequently, I assure you. I find something quite agreeable in your conversation."

"Oh, Monseigneur! I am always at his Eminence's orders."

The cardinal made a sign with his hand, to which Bonacieux replied by bowing to the ground. He then went out backward, and when he was in the antechamber the cardinal could hear him, in his enthusiasm, crying aloud, "Long life to Monseigneur! Long life to his Eminence!"

Richelieu listened with a smile to this vociferous manifestation of the feelings of the mercer. And then, when Bonacieux's shouts were no longer audible to him, he said, "Good! That man would henceforth lay down his life for me."

And the cardinal began to examine with the greatest attention the map of La Rochelle which lay opened on his desk. He traced with a pencil the line to be followed by the famous dyke, which eighteen months later shut off the port of the beleaguered city. He was deeply immersed in his strategic meditations when the door opened and Rochefort appeared.

"Well?" called the cardinal eagerly.

He rose with a promptitude that proved the degree of importance he attached to the commission with which he had charged the count.

"They had lodged at the two houses pointed out by your Eminence. But the woman left last night and the man this morning."

"And now it is too late for pursuit!" chafed the cardinal, looking at the clock. "By now the duchess is at Tours and the duke at Boulogne. It is in London we must seek for them."

"What are your Eminence's orders?"

"That not a word of what has passed be spoken. Let the queen remain in perfect security, ignorant that we possess her secret. At most, she shall believe we are in search of some conspiracy or other."

"What has your Eminence done with the prisoner?"

"I have made him a spy upon his wife. Send me Séguier, the keeper of the seals."

The Comte de Rochefort bowed like a man who acknowledges the superiority of his master as great, and retired. Left alone, the cardinal seated himself again and wrote a letter, which he secured with his special seal. He rang. The officer entered.

"Tell Vitray to come to me," he said. "And order him to get ready for a journey."

An instant later the man he asked for was in the room before him, booted and spurred.

"Vitray," the cardinal said, "you will proceed with all haste to London. You must not stop a minute on the way. Deliver this letter to Milady. Here is an order for two hundred pistoles—call upon my treasurer and get the money. You shall have as much again if you are back within six days and have executed the commission well."

Without replying a single word, the messenger bowed, took the letter, with the order for two hundred pistoles, and retired.

Here are the contents of the letter:

MILADY:

Be at the first ball at which the Duke of Buckingham shall be present. He will wear on his doublet twelve diamond studs. Get as near to him as you can and cut off two. As soon as they are in your possession, inform me.

CHAPTER XV

SÉGUIER CONDUCTS A SEARCH

On the day after these events had taken place the cardinal sought the king. Without prelude he said to him, "Sire, Buckingham has been in Paris five days and left only this morning."

It is impossible to form an idea of the impression these few words made upon Louis XIII. He grew pale and red alternately, and the cardinal saw at once that he had regained by a single stroke all the ground he had lately lost with his Majesty.

"Buckingham in Paris!" the king cried. "And what does he come for?"

"No doubt to conspire with your enemies, the Huguenots and the Spaniards."

"*Pardieu,* no! Rather, to conspire against my honor, together with Mesdames de Chevreuse and Longueville, and with the Condés."

"Sire, what an idea! The queen is virtuous and besides, she loves your Majesty too well."

"Woman is weak, Monsieur Cardinal," said the king. "Moreover, I have my own opinion as to her love for me."

"I maintain," said Richelieu, "that the Duke of Buckingham came to Paris in the interest of a purely political project."

"And I assert, Monsieur Cardinal, that he came for another purpose. If the queen be guilty, let her tremble."

"Ah, indeed!" mused Richelieu. "Whatever repugnance I have in directing your mind to such a treason, your Majesty compels me to consider it. For Madame de Lannoy, whom, according to your Majesty's command, I have frequently interrogated, told me this morning that her Majesty sat up very late night before last. This morning she wept much and has been writing all day."

"To him, no doubt, Cardinal. I must have the queen's papers."

"But how to secure them, sire? I believe neither your Majesty nor I can engage in such a mission."

"What was done in the case of Maréchale d'Ancre?" cried the king in the highest state of anger. "First, her closets were searched, and then for good measure they searched her."

"She was no more than the Maréchale d'Ancre, sire, a Florentine adventuress. But the august spouse of your Majesty is Anne of Austria, queen of France."

"She is none the less guilty, Monsieur Duke! The more she forgets the high position in which she is placed, the more degrading is her fall. Besides, I long ago determined to put an end to these petty intrigues of the queen's. She has near her person a certain La Porte."

"And I confess I believe him the mainspring of all this."

"You think, then, that she is deceiving me?"

"I believe that the queen is conspiring against the power of the king, but not against his honor."

"And I—I tell you it is against both. The queen does not love me, she is infatuated with Buckingham. Why did you not arrest the infamous fellow here in Paris while yet there was a chance?"

"Arrest the prime minister of King Charles I! Think of the scandal, sire! And suppose that the suspicions of your Majesty, which I still am inclined to doubt, should prove without foundation—what a terrible disclosure!"

"But the duke exposed himself like any vagabond or thief. And so he should have been—"

"Just what should have been done, sire?"

"Oh, nothing, I suppose! Nothing. But, of course, all the time that he was in Paris you did not lose sight of him?"

"No, sire."

"Where did he lodge?"

"Rue de la Harpe, by the side of the Luxembourg."

"You are certain he did not see the queen?"

"I think she has too high a sense of her duty, sire."

"But they are in correspondence. It is to him that she has been writing all day. I must have those letters, Monsieur. At whatever price, I must have them."

"I should, however, beg your Majesty to observe—"

"Do you then also join in betraying me, Monsieur Cardinal, by thus opposing my will? Are you in accord with Spain and England, with Madame de Chevreuse and the queen?"

"Sire," replied the cardinal with a sigh, "I believed myself secure from such a suspicion."

"Yet you have heard me, Monsieur. I shall have those letters."

"There is but one way of getting them."

"What way is that?"

"To charge M. de Séguier, the keeper of the seals, with this mission. The matter enters completely into the duties of his post."

"Let him be sent for instantly."

"He is most likely at my residence. I requested him to call upon another business, and when I came to the Louvre I left orders to have him wait."

"Have him brought here at once."

"Your Majesty's command shall be executed, but—"

"But what?"

"The queen will quite probably refuse to obey."

"My orders?"

"Yes, if she is ignorant that these orders issue from the king."

"Well, that she may have no doubt on that head, I shall go and inform her myself."

"Your Majesty will please not forget that I have done everything in my power to prevent a rupture."

"Yes, Duke, yes. I know you are very indulgent toward the queen. Too indulgent, I fear. We shall have occasion to discuss that at some future period, I warn you."

"Whenever it shall please your Majesty. But I shall always be proud and happy, sire, to sacrifice myself to the harmony which I desire to see prevail between you and the queen of France."

"Very good, Cardinal! But, meanwhile, send for Monsieur the Keeper of the seals. I am on my way to the queen."

And Louis XIII, opening the door of communication,

passed into the corridor which led from his apartments to those of Anne of Austria.

The queen was in the midst of her women, Mesdames de Guitaut, de Sablé, de Montbazon, de Guéménée. In a corner was the Spanish companion, Donna Estefania, who had followed her from Madrid—the only one of her Majesty's Spanish women who had not been driven from her side by the jealousy of the king or by the persecutions of Richelieu.

Madame de Guéménée was reading aloud, and every-body was listening to her with attention except the queen. The latter had desired the reading only in order that she might be able, while feigning to listen, to pursue the thread of her own thoughts.

These meditations of hers, gilded as they were by a last reflection of love, were none the less sad.

Anne of Austria was deprived of the confidence of her husband and pursued by the hatred of the cardinal, who could not pardon her for having repulsed a more tender feeling on his part. She had had before her eyes the example of the queen mother, whom that hatred of Riche-lieu's had tormented all her life—although Marie de Médicis, if the memoirs of her time are to be believed, had begun by according the cardinal that sentiment which Anne of Austria always refused him.

The queen had seen her most devoted servants fall around her. Like those unfortunate persons endowed with a fatal gift, she brought misfortune upon everything she touched. Her friendship was a fatal sign that called down persecution. Madame de Chevreuse and Madame de

Vernel were exiled, and La Porte did not conceal from his mistress the fact that he expected to be arrested at any instant.

It was at the moment when she was plunged into the darkest of these reflections that the door of the chamber opened and the king entered.

Mme. de Guéménée immediately ceased reading. All the ladies rose, and there was a profound silence. As to the king, he made no demonstration of politeness, but stopped abruptly before the queen.

"Madame," he said, "you are about to receive a visit from the chancellor. He will communicate to you certain matters with which I have charged him.

The unfortunate queen, who was constantly threatened with divorce, exile, and even legal trial, turned pale under her rouge, and could not refrain from saying, "What can the chancellor have to say to me that your Majesty could not better say himself?"

The king turned upon his heel without reply, and almost at the same instant the captain of the Guards, M. de Guitaut, announced the visit of the Chancellor Séguier.

The latter entered, half smiling, half blushing. Her Majesty was still standing when he entered. But scarcely had she noticed him, when she reseated herself in her arm-chair and made a sign to her women to resume their cushions and stools. With an air of supreme hauteur she asked, "What do you desire, Monsieur, and with what object in view do you present yourself here?"

"To make, Madame, in the name of the king, and without prejudice to the respect which I have the honor to entertain for your Majesty, a close examination into all your papers."

"How, Monsieur? An investigation of my papers—mine? Truly, this is an indignity!"

"Be kind enough to pardon me, Madame. In this instance I am but the instrument which the king employs. Did not his Majesty just leave you? And has he not himself asked you to prepare for this visit?"

"Search, then, Monsieur! I am a criminal, it appears. Estefania, surrender the keys to my drawers and my desks."

For form's sake the chancellor paid a visit to the pieces of furniture indicated. But he well knew that the queen would not place in any piece of furniture the important letter she had written that day.

When the Chancellor Séguier had opened and shut twenty times the drawers of the secretaries, it became necessary to come to the conclusion of the affair, that is, to search the queen herself. The chancellor, therefore, advanced toward Anne of Austria and said with a very perplexed and embarrassed air, "And now it remains for me to make the principal examination."

"What is that, Monsieur?" asked the queen.

"His Majesty is certain that a letter has been written by you during the day. He knows it has not yet been sent to its address. The writing is not in any table or secretary, and yet it must be somewhere."

"Would you dare lift your hand to your queen?" demanded Anne, drawing herself up to her full height and fixing her eyes upon Séguier with a threatening expression.

"I am a faithful subject of the king, Madame, and all that his Majesty commands I shall do."

"The spies of the cardinal have served him faithfully," said Anne of Austria. "It is true I have written a letter today and that it has not yet gone. The letter is here."

And the queen laid her beautiful hand upon her bosom.

"Then give me that letter, Madame," said Séguier.

"I shall give it to none but the king, Monsieur."

"If the king had required the writing of you direct, Madame, he would have demanded it. I repeat to you, I am charged with reclaiming it. And if you do not surrender it—"

"Well?"

"He has, then, charged me to take it from you. I am authorized to seek for the suspected paper, Madame, even on the person of your Majesty."

"This is an unnamable horror!"

"Be kind enough, Madame, to be more compliant. The king commands it."

"I shall not suffer it. I would rather die!" cried the queen, in whom the imperious blood of Spain and Austria began to rise.

Séguier made a profound reverence. Then, with the patent intention of not drawing back a foot from the accomplishment of his object, he approached Anne of Austria as the attendant of an executioner might have done in a chamber of torture.

The commission of the chancellor might be called delicate. But the king had reached, in his jealousy of Buckingham, the point of not being jealous of any one else.

Anne took one step backward, grew so pale that it might be said she was dying, and leaned with her left hand upon a table behind her to prevent herself from falling. With her right hand she drew the letter from her bosom and held it out to the keeper of the seals.

"There is the letter, Monsieur," she cried with a broken and tremulous voice. "Take it and rid me of your odious presence."

The chancellor carried the letter to the king without having read a single word of it. Louis XIII received it with shaking hand, looked for the address—which was absent—became very pale, and opened the paper slowly. By the first words he saw that it was addressed to the king of Spain. He ran through it rapidly.

Quite delighted, the king inquired if the cardinal was still at the Louvre. He was told that his Eminence awaited the orders of his Majesty in the business cabinet.

The king went straight to him.

"There, Duke," he called. "You were right and I was wrong. The whole intrigue is political, and there is not the slightest question of love in this letter. But, on the other hand, there is abundant talk of you."

The cardinal took the letter and read it with the closest attention. He even read it a second time.

"Well, your Majesty," he commented, "you see how far my enemies go. They menace you with two wars if you do not dismiss me. If I were in your place, sire, I believe I should yield to such powerful entreaties. And, for my part, it would be a great happiness to withdraw from public affairs."

"What words are these, Duke?"

"I say, sire, that my health is sinking under these excessive struggles, these never-ending labors. In all probability, I shall not be able to undergo the fatigues of the siege of La Rochelle. It would be far better that you should appoint there M. de Conde, M. de Bassompierre, or some valiant gentleman whose business is war. Do not rely upon me, sire, who am a churchman, and who am constantly turned aside from my real vocation to look after matters for which I have no real aptitude. You would be the happier for it at home, sire, and I do not doubt you would shine the more greatly because of it abroad."

"Monsieur Duke, I understand you. Be satisfied. All who are named in that letter shall be punished as they deserve, even the queen herself."

"What are you saying, sire? God forbid that the queen should suffer the least inconvenience on my account! She has always believed me to be her enemy, although your Majesty can bear witness that I have always taken her part warmly, even against you."

"That is true, Monsieur Cardinal."

"Oh, if she betrayed the honor of your Majesty, that would be quite another thing; then I should be the first to say, 'No grace for the guilty one.' But, happily, there is nothing of the kind and your Majesty has just acquired a new proof of it."

"You are right, Duke, as you always are. But the queen, none the less, shall feel the weight of my anger."

"I fear it is you, sire, who have now incurred hers. Your Majesty has treated her with a severity—"

"It is thus I shall always treat my enemies and yours, Duke, however high their station."

"The queen is my enemy, sire, but she is not yours. She is a devoted and irreproachable wife. Allow me to intercede for her."

"Let her humble herself, then."

"On the contrary, sire, set the example. You have committed the first wrong, since it was you who suspected the queen."

"What! I make the first advances?" said Louis. "Never."

"Sire, I intreat you to do a thing which you know will be agreeable to her. You know how much the queen loves dancing. Give a ball. I'll answer for it—her resentment will not hold out against such an attention on your part."

"Monsieur Cardinal, you remember I do not go in for worldly pleasures."

"She will only be the more grateful to you, sire, since she knows your antipathy to that amusement. Besides, it will be an opportunity for her to wear those beautiful diamonds which you gave her recently upon her birthday. She has since had no occasion to adorn herself."

"We shall see, Monsieur Cardinal, we shall see," said the king. In his joy at finding the queen guilty of a fault he cared little about, and innocent of a fault which he greatly dreaded, he was ready to forget all differences with her. "But, upon my honor, you are too indulgent to her."

"Sire," replied the cardinal, "leave severity to your ministers. Clemency is a royal virtue. Employ it, and you will find you derive advantage therefrom."

Hearing the clock strike eleven, the cardinal bowed low and asked permission to retire.

Anne of Austria, who expected reproaches because of the seizure of her letter, was much astonished the next day when the king made overtures toward a reconciliation. Her first emotion was one of repulsion. Her womanly pride and her queenly dignity had been too cruelly offended for her to yield to the king's first advances. At last, however, persuaded by her women, she showed signs of beginning to forget. The king took advantage of this favorable occasion to tell her he intended shortly to give here a fête.

A fête was so rare an occurrence in the life of poor Anne that at this announcement, as the cardinal had predicted, the last trace of her resentment disappeared, if not from her heart, at least from her face. She asked upon what day this fête would take place, but Louis XIII replied that he must consult the cardinal upon that matter.

Now every day the king asked Richelieu when the fête might be expected, and each day on one pretext or another the cardinal deferred fixing the date. Ten days passed away thus.

On the eighth day after the scene we have described Richelieu received a letter with the London stamp. It contained only these lines:

I have them, but am unable to leave England because of lack of money. Send me five hundred pistoles, and four or five days after I have received them I shall be in Paris.

On the same day that the cardinal received this writing the king put the customary question to him. Richelieu counted on his fingers and said to himself, "It will take four or five days for the transmission of the money, and the same amount of time for her to reach here—that's ten days. Allowing for contrary winds, accidents, and a woman's whims, there are twelve days."

"Well, Monsieur Duke," said the king, "have you made your calculations?"

"Yes, sire. Today is the 20th of September. The aldermen of the city are giving a fête on the 3rd of October. That will fall in wonderfully well. You will not appear to have gone out of your way to please the queen."

Then, evidently as an afterthought, the cardinal added, "By the way, sire, do not forget to tell her Majesty the evening before the fête that you would like to see how her diamond studs become her."

CHAPTER XVI

BONACIEUX AT HOME

It was the second time the cardinal had mentioned the diamond studs to the king. Louis XIII was struck by the insistence and began to fancy that this recommendation concealed some mystery.

More than once Louis had been humiliated by the cardinal, whose police were better informed than their king even upon what was going on in his own household. He hoped, then, through a conversation with Anne of Austria to obtain some information regarding current intrigues. Afterward he could come upon his Eminence with some secret which the cardinal either knew or did not know, but in either case he would be raised infinitely in the eyes of his minister.

So he went to visit the queen, and according to his custom accosted her with fresh menaces against those by whom she was surrounded. Anne of Austria lowered her head and allowed the threatening torrent to flow on without replying. She hoped it would thus soon cease of itself, but this was not what Louis XIII wanted. He wished a discussion from which sparks of light would flash. For he was convinced by now that the cardinal was preparing some sort of mine to spring. And he knew by experience how skilful his Eminence was in arranging terrible surprises.

At last Louis XIII arrived at the desired end by his sheer persistence in accusation.

"But," cried Anne of Austria, weary of these vague attacks, "you are not telling me everything you have in mind, sire. What is it that I have done? It is impossible your Majesty can be making all this to-do about a letter written to my brother."

Attacked in a manner so direct, the king scarcely knew what to answer. And he thought this was perhaps the moment for expressing the desire which he was not to have made until the evening before the fête.

"Madame," he said with dignity, "there will shortly be a ball at the Hôtel de Ville in honor of our worthy aldermen. I wish you to appear in ceremonial costume and above all ornamented with the diamond studs I gave you on your birthday. That is my answer."

The answer was frightful.

Anne of Austria was now convinced that Louis XIII knew all, and that the cardinal had persuaded him to employ this long dissimulation of seven or eight days, which was likewise a characteristic act. She grew excessively pale, and placed her beautiful wax-like hand upon a console to steady herself. She looked at the king with terror in her eyes, unable to reply with a single syllable.

"You hear, Madame?" asked Louis XIII, who was enjoying her embarrassment to the fullest extent, although he was far from guessing the cause of it.

"Yes, sire, I hear," stammered the queen.

"And you will appear at this ball?"

"Yes, sire."

"With the diamond studs?"

"Yes, sire."

The queen's paleness, if possible, increased. Louis perceived it and enjoyed it with that cold cruelty which was one of the worst sides of his character.

"Then that is settled," he said. "That is all I had to say."

"But on what day will this ball take place?" asked Anne.

Louis XIII felt instinctively that he ought not to pleasure her by answering this question, for she had asked it in an almost dead voice.

"Oh, very shortly, Madame," he said. "But I do not precisely recollect the date of the affair. I shall ask the cardinal for you."

"It was his Eminence, then, who informed you of this fête?"

"Yes, Madame, it was," replied the astonished king. "But why do you ask me that?"

"It was he, was it not, who told you to invite me to appear there with these studs?"

"That is to say, Madame—"

"It was he, sire, it was he!"

"Well, and what the devil does it signify, Madame, which of us it was? Is there any crime in the request?"

"No, sire."

"That is well," said Louis XIII, retiring. "I shall count upon your ceremonial appearance."

The queen made a curtsy, less from etiquette than because her knees were sinking under her. The king went away in high spirits.

"I am lost," moaned the queen. "For the cardinal knows all, and it is he who urges on the king, who is ignorant as yet, but will himself soon understand. Heaven has forsaken me!"

She knelt upon a cushion and prayed with her head buried between her throbbing arms.

In fact, the position was terrible. Buckingham had returned to London, Madame de Chevreuse was at Tours. More closely watched than ever, the queen felt certain that one of her women had betrayed her, but she could not tell which one. La Porte could not leave the Louvre. She had not a soul in the world in whom she dared confide. She broke out into sobs and tears.

"Can I be of service to your Majesty?" said a voice full of sweetness and pity.

The queen turned sharply around, for there could be no deception in the expression of that voice. It was a friend who spoke thus. At one of the doors which opened into the queen's apartment appeared the pretty Madame Bonacieux. When the king entered she had been engaged in arranging the dresses and linen in a closet. She could not escape unseen, and so she had overheard all.

Anne of Austria uttered a piercing cry at finding herself surprised, for in her deep trouble she did not readily recognize the young woman who had been given her by La Porte.

"Oh, fear nothing, Madame!" said the young woman, clasping her hands and weeping in sympathy for the queen's sorrows. "I am your Majesty's, body and soul. And, despite the vast inferiority of my position, I believe I have found a means of extricating your Majesty from your trouble."

"I am betrayed on all sides!" cried Anne of Austria. "How may I be sure I can confide in you?"

"There are traitors about you, Madame. But by the holy name of the Virgin, I swear there is none so devoted to your Majesty as I. Those studs which you gave the Duke of Buckingham in the little rosewood box—well, we must have them back again."

"Oh, my God!" murmured the queen, whose teeth fairly chattered with fright. "How can that be effected?"

"Put your trust in me, Madame. I shall find the messenger to send to the duke."

"But who, who? And I shall have to write."

"Oh, yes, that is indispensable. Two words from your Majesty's hand will be enough, and your seal."

"But those two words might bring about divorce and exile!"

"If they fell into infamous hands. I'll answer for their honest delivery to their address. You must place your reputation, your life, your honor in my hands. And I shall save them all."

"But how? Tell me at least the means."

"My husband, Madame, is an honest man who entertains neither hatred nor love for any one. He will do anything I wish. He will carry your Majesty's letter, without even knowing from whom it is, to the address you give."

The queen gazed at Madame Bonacieux as if to read her very soul. She saw nothing but sincerity in her beautiful eyes and embraced her tenderly.

"Do that," she breathed, "and you will have saved my life indeed!"

"Do not exaggerate the service I have the happiness to render your Majesty. You are but the victim of perfidious plots. Give me, then, the letter, Madame; time passes."

Anne of Austria ran to the table and wrote hurriedly two lines. She sealed the letter with her private seal and gave it to Madame Bonacieux.

"And now," said the queen, "we are forgetting all about money. And I have none." (Those who have read the memoirs of Madame de Motteville will not be surprised at this statement.) "But wait a minute."

"Here," she continued, running to her jewel case, "is a ring of great value. It is mine, and I am at liberty to dispose of it. Raise money with it at the Piete, and let your husband set out."

"In an hour you shall be obeyed."

Madame Bonacieux kissed the hands of the queen, hid the letter in the bosom of her dress, and disappeared with the lightness of a bird.

Ten minutes afterward she was at home. She found her husband alone. With much trouble the poor man was restoring order in his house, the furniture of which was mostly broken and the closets nearly empty. Justice was not one of the three things which King Solomon names as leaving behind no traces of its passage.

Even the servant had run away at the moment of her master's arrest. Terror had lent such wings to the flight of the frightened girl that she never stopped going until she reached Burgundy, her native land.

This was the first time for the five days that followed Bonacieux's liberation that his wife could steal away from her duties to pay him a visit. Under other circumstances the delay would have appeared long to the mercer. But he had in the visit he had made to the cardinal, and in the calls which Rochefort had since paid him, ample subjects for reflection, and so the time had passed quickly.

His meditations were all rose-colored. Rochefort called him friend, and never ceased to inform him of the great respect Richelieu entertained for him. He fancied himself on the high road to honors and fortune.

Now, on her side, Madame Bonacieux had also reflected. In spite of herself, her thoughts dwelt constantly on that handsome young man who was so brave and fancied himself so much in love. She had married at eighteen and always remained insensible to vulgar attractions. But the title of gentleman had great influence with the citizen class, and d'Artagnan was a gentleman. He was, we repeat, handsome, young, and bold. And he spoke of love like a man who felt the tender passion.

At sight of his wife, Bonacieux manifested real joy and advanced to meet her with open arms. She presented her cheek for a kiss.

"I have something of the highest importance to tell you," were her opening words.

"True," said Bonacieux. "Tell me about your abduction.

"Oh, that's of no consequence now," she replied.

"And what does concern you, then—my captivity?"

"I knew you were not guilty of any crime, my dear, and so I attached no more importance to that event than it merited."

"Did you know I spent a day and a night in a dungeon of the Bastille?" inquired the husband, hurt at the slight interest his wife seemed to take in him.

"Oh, a day and a night soon pass away. Let us return to the object that brings me here."

"I fancied it was the wish to see again a husband from whom you had been separated for a week," said the mercer, touched to the quick.

"Yes, that first, of course. But there is something else of the highest interest on which our future fortune may depend."

"The complexion of our fortune has changed greatly for the better, since I last saw you, Madame. In a few months it will excite the envy of many folks, let me tell you."

"It certainly will, my dear, if you follow my instructions. There is a good and holy action to be performed, Monsieur, and much money to be gained at the same time."

Madame Bonacieux knew that in mentioning money to her husband she was taking him on his weak side. But even a mercer, after he has talked for ten minutes with Cardinal Richelieu, is no longer the same man.

"You would receive a thousand pistoles, perhaps," continued the temptress. "You must go away immediately. I shall give you a paper which you must not part with on any account, and which you will deliver into the proper hands in London."

"You are jesting. I have no possible business in London."

"But others wish you to go there. An illustrious person

sends you, an illustrious person awaits you. The recompense will exceed your highest expectations, so much I promise you."

"More intrigues! Nothing but intrigues! I am aware of them now, thank you, Madame, since Cardinal Richelieu has enlightened me on that head."

"The cardinal sent for you!" cried Madame Bonacieux. "And you responded to his bidding, you imprudent man?"

"I rather had to respond, my dear, for I was dragged to him by two guards. At that time I should have been delighted to dispense with the visit."

"He illtreated you—threatened you?"

"He gave me his hand and called me friend, his friend. I am the friend of the great cardinal. Perhaps you would contest my right to that title, Madame?"

"I should contest nothing. Am I to understand, then, that you serve his Eminence?"

"Yes, Madame. And in my capacity of servant I shall not allow you to be concerned in plots against the safety of the State, or to join in the intrigues of a woman who is not French and has a Spanish heart."

Poor Constance Bonacieux! She had reckoned blindly upon her husband and had answered for him to the queen. And yet, knowing the weakness of the man and more particularly his cupidity, she still did not despair of bringing him around to her purpose.

"And what do you know about the State you talk of so glibly?" she demanded, shrugging her shoulders. "Be satisfied to be a plain, straightforward citizen and turn to that side which offers you the most advantages."

"Eh, eh!" replied Bonacieux, slapping a plump bag which replied with the chink of money. "What think you of this, Madame Preacher?"

"Where does that come from?"

"From his Eminence and my friend, the Comte de Rochefort."

"Rochefort! And you take money from the villain who abducted me?"

"Did you not say the ravishment was entirely political?"

"Yes. But its object was to draw from me by torture confessions that might compromise the honor and perhaps the life of my august mistress."

"Madame," replied Bonacieux, "your august mistress is a perfidious Spaniard, and what the cardinal does is well done."

"Monsieur," cried the young woman, "you are an infamous creature. You sell yourself, body and soul, to the devil for money!"

"Hold your tongue! You may be overheard!"

"Yes, you are right, Bonacieux! For I should be ashamed if any one heard of your baseness."

"What is this thing that you require of me? Let us see."

"I have told you. If you accomplish the commission loyally, I pardon everything. I forget everything—and what is more, I restore to you my love." And she held out her hands to him.

Bonacieux was cowardly and avaricious in the extreme, but he loved his wife. He was softened by her appeal. A man of fifty cannot long bear malice against a wife of twenty-three.   Madame Bonacieux saw that he was hesitating.

"Come! Have you decided?" she asked softly

"Hold on, my dear," said the mercer. "I positively refuse—intrigues frighten me to death. I have seen the Bastille. Whew! It makes my flesh crawl just to think of it. They threatened me with torture—wooden points that they stick in between your legs until the bones protrude. No, I positively shall not go. *Morbleu,* why do you not go yourself? I really believe, after all, that you are a man and a violent one, too."

"You are a woman, fast enough, Bonacieux—and a stupid and brutal one. You are afraid, are you? Well, if you do not start this instant, I shall have you arrested by the queen's orders and thrust back into that Bastille you dread so much."

"If you have me arrested on the part of the queen, my little one," said Bonacieux, "I shall appeal to his Eminence."

The young woman saw at once that she had gone too far, and she was terrified at having communicated so much of her secret. For a moment she contemplated with fright that countenance impressed with the invincible resolution of a fool who is overcome by fear.

"Well, be it so!" she said. "Perhaps, considering all things, you are right. In the long run a man knows much more about politics than a woman does, particularly men who, like you, have conversed with the cardinal. And yet it is very hard," she added mournfully, "that a man on whose affection I thought I might depend treats me thus unkindly and will not comply with any of my fancies."

"That is because your fancies wander too far," replied the triumphant Bonacieux, "and I mistrust them."

"All right, I'll give them up, then," promised the young woman with a sigh. "Say no more about it."

"At least you had better tell me what I should have had to do in London," teased Bonacieux, who was remembering a little too late that Rochefort had desired him to try to surprise his wife's plans.

"There's no use for you to know anything about it now," answered the young woman, whom an instinctive mistrust now impelled to hang back. "It was about one of those purchases that interest only women—a purchase by which much might have been gained."

But the more she excused herself, the more important her husband thought the secret which she declined to confide to him. He resolved to hasten at once to the residence of the Comte de Rochefort and tell him that the queen was seeking a messenger to send to London.

"Pardon me for quitting you, my dear," he said to his wife. "But, not knowing you would come to see me today, I have made an engagement with a friend. I shall be gone only a few minutes, and if you will await my return I shall conduct you back to the Louvre."

"Thank you, Monsieur, but you are not brave enough to be of any use to me whatsoever," replied Madame Bonacieux. "Although it is somewhat late, I shall return to the Louvre very safely all alone."

"As you please, my dear. Shall I see you again soon?"

"Next week I hope my duties will afford me a little liberty. I'll take advantage of my freedom to come and put things in order here, as they seem to be terribly disarranged."

"Very well, I shall expect you.   You are not angry with me?"

"Not the least in the world."

Bonacieux kissed his wife's hand and set off at a quick pace.

"Well," said his wife, when he had shut the street door and she found herself alone, "that imbecile lacks only the wit to become a thorough cardinalist.   And I, who have answered for him to the queen—I, who have promised my poor mistress—ah, my God!   She will take me for one of those poor wretches with whom the palace swarms, who are placed about her as spies.   Ah, M. Bonacieux, I never did love you much, but now it is worse than ever.   I hate you, and I promise you shall pay me for this!"

At the moment she spoke these words a tap on the ceiling made her raise her head, and a voice that reached her through the ceiling cried, "Dear Madame Bonacieux, open for me the little door on the alley and I shall come down to you."

CHAPTER XVII

LOVER AND HUSBAND

"Ah, Madame," said d'Artagnan, entering by the door which the tearful young woman opened for him, "allow me to tell you that you have a poor sort of a husband, indeed."

"You have overheard our conversation?" Madame Bonacieux demanded eagerly and looking at the young Gascon with disquiet.

"I did not miss a single word of it."

"But how on earth is that possible?"

"By a mode of procedure known only to myself and by which I likewise overheard the more animated conversation you had with the cardinal's police."

"And how did you construe what we talked about?"

"First of all, that your husband is a simpleton and a fool. Next, that you are in trouble. This makes me very happy, for it gives me an opportunity of placing myself at your disposal, and God knows that I am ready to throw myself into the fire for you. Finally, that a queen needs a brave, intelligent, and devoted man to make a journey to London for her. I have at least two of the three qualities you stand in need of. Behold me!"

Madame Bonacieux made no reply. But her heart was beating with joy, and secret hope shone in her eyes.

"And if I consent to confide this message to you," she asked, "what guarantee will you give me?"

"My love for you, Constance Bonacieux! Speak—out with it! What have you for me to do?"

"Oh, God!" murmured the young woman. "Ought I to confide such a secret to you, Monsieur? You are almost a boy."

"I see that you require some one to answer for me."

"I admit that this would reassure me greatly."

"Do you know Athos?"

"No."

"Or Porthos?"

"No."

"Or Aramis?"

"No. Who are these gentlemen?"

"Three of the king's Musketeers. Let us see—do you know their captain, M. de Tréville?"

"Oh, yes, I know him! Not personally, it is true, but from having heard the queen speak of him more than once as a brave and loyal gentleman."

"You would not fear lest he betray you to the cardinal?"

"Oh, no, certainly not."

"Very good, then! Reveal your secret to him, and ask him whether you may confide it to me, no matter how valuable or important or terrible it may be."

"But this secret is not mine, and I cannot reveal it in the manner you suggest."

"You were going to confide it to M. Bonacieux," said d'Artagnan with much chagrin.

"Only as one confides a letter to the hollow of a tree, to the wing of a carrier pigeon, to the collar of a dog."

"And yet, I—you see so plainly that I love you."

"You say so."

"I am an honorable man."

"I have your word for it."

"I am a gallant fellow."

"I believe that from my heart."

"I am brave."

"Oh, I am sure of that."

"Then put me to the test!"

Madame Bonacieux looked sharply at the young Gascon, restrained for a moment by a last hesitation because so much was at stake. But there was such an ardor in his eyes, such persuasion in his voice, that she felt herself constrained to confide in him. Besides, she was in a situation where everything must be risked for the sake of everything. The queen might be as much injured by too great reticence as by too much confidence. And, we must admit, the involuntary sentiment she felt for her young protector decided her to speak.

"Listen," she said. "I surrender to your protestations. I yield to your assurances. But I swear to you before God who hears us that, if you betray me, I shall kill myself while accusing you of my death."

"And I swear to you, Madame, before the same Witness that if I am captured while accomplishing the orders you give me, I shall die sooner than do anything or say anything that may compromise any one."

Then the young woman confided to him the terrible secret of which chance had already communicated to him a part in front of the Samaritaine. This was their mutual declaration of love.

D'Artagnan was radiant with joy and pride. This secret which he possessed! This woman whom he loved! Confidence and love made him a giant.

"I go," he cried, "I go at once."

"How can you start without notice?" asked Madame Bonacieux. "What about your regiment, your captain?"

"By my soul, you had made me forget all that, dear Constance! You are right—a furlough is necessary."

"Still another obstacle," moaned Madame Bonacieux.

"As to that," cried d'Artagnan after a moment of reflection, "I shall surmount it, rest assured."

"How can you be so certain?"

"I shall go this very evening to Tréville, whom I shall request to ask this favor for me of his brother-in-law, M. d'Essart."

"Another thing we must not forget, Monsieur. You have, perhaps, no money."

"*Perhaps* is just one word too many, Madame."

"Then," said the young woman, opening a cupboard and taking from it the very bag which a half hour before her husband had caressed so affectionately, "take this!"

"The cardinal's!" cried d'Artagnan. He broke into a loud laugh, for thanks to the broken boards he had heard every syllable of the conversation between the mercer and his wife.

"Yes, the cardinal's," replied Madame Bonacieux. "You see, it makes a very respectable appearance."

"*Pardieu!*" exclaimed d'Artagnan. "It will be a doubly amusing game to save the queen with the cardinal's money."

"You are an amiable and charming young man," said Madame Bonacieux. "You will not find her Majesty ungrateful."

"Oh, I am already richly recompensed!" declared the Gascon. "I love you; you permit me to tell you of the fact — that is far greater happiness than I have dared to hope for."

"Silence!" said Madame Bonacieux, starting.

"What is it!"

"Some one is talking in the street outside."

"It is the voice of —"

"My husband! Yes, I recognize it!"

D'Artagnan flew to the door and pushed the bolt.

"He shall not come in before I am gone," he said. "The moment I'm out the alley door, you can open to him."

"But I must be gone, too. How can I justify the disappearance of his beloved money if I remain?"

"You are right, we must both go out."

"But how? That's the question. He is sure to see me."

"Then you must come up to my room."

"Ah," said Madame Bonacieux, "you say that in a tone that frightens me."

She pronounced these words with tears in her eyes. D'Artagnan saw this evidence of her disturbed condition and, softened by it, he threw himself at her feet.

"With me you will be as safe as in a temple. I give you my word as a gentleman."

"I have every confidence in you, my dear friend," the young woman said. "Let us make haste."

With much precaution d'Artagnan drew back the bolt. And both of them, light as shadows, glided through the interior door into the passage, ascended the stairs as quietly as possible, and entered the young man's chambers.

Once there, for greater security the Gascon barricaded the door. They both approached the window, and through a slit in the shutter they saw Bonacieux talking with a man in a cloak.

At sight of this man d'Artagnan started forward and, half drawing his sword, sprang to the door.

"What are you going to do?" cried Madame Bonacieux. "You will ruin everything."

"But I have sworn to kill that man," said the young Gascon.

"From this moment your life is devoted to another and does not belong to you. In the name of your queen I forbid you to throw yourself into any peril which is foreign to your journey."

D'Artagnan drew near the window and listened to what was being said below him.

The husband had opened the door of his house and, seeing the rooms empty, had returned to the man in the cloak, whom he had left alone for the moment.

"She has gone," he said. "She must have returned to the Louvre."

"Are you sure that she did not suspect your intentions when you left the house?" asked the stranger.

"She is too superficial a woman to do that," replied Bonacieux with a self-sufficient air.

"Is the young guardsman at home, do you think?"

"I don't think so. His shutter is closed, although the night is warm. And you can see no light shining through the chinks of it."

"Just the same, suppose we make certain by knocking at the door and asking his servant. Go ahead."

Bonacieux reëntered the house, passed through the same door that had already been used by the two fugitives, went upstairs to the young guardsman's room, and knocked.

No one answered. Porthos, in order to make a greater display at a dinner that evening, had borrowed Planchet.

The moment the hand of the mercer sounded on the panel, the two young people felt their hearts turn over within them.

"There is nobody inside," Bonacieux called down to his companion.

"All right, then. Let's go into your chambers. We'll be safer there than in the doorway to the street."

"Oh, now we shall hear no more," whispered Madame Bonacieux.

"On the contrary," said the Gascon, "we shall hear all the better."

D'Artagnan raised the three or four boards which made his chamber another ear of Dionysius, spread a rug on the floor, went down upon his knees, and made a sign to his comrade to stoop toward the opening as he did.

"You are sure there's nobody upstairs there?" asked the unknown.

"I'll answer for it," replied Bonacieux.

"And you think your wife's gone back to the Louvre without speaking to any one but yourself?"

"Positively."

"That is an important point, you understand? Are you sure that your wife mentioned no names in her talk with you?"

"No, she only told me that she wished to send me to London to serve the interests of an illustrious personage."

"The traitor!" muttered Madame Bonacieux.

"Silence!" said d'Artagnan, pressing her hand.

"Never mind," continued the man in the cloak. "You were a fool not to pretend to accept the mission. You would then be in present possession of the letter, the State, which is now threatened, would be safe, and you—"

"And I, Monsieur?"

"Well, you—the cardinal would probably have given you letters of nobility. In fact, I know that he meant to afford you that agreeable surprise."

"Don't worry," replied Bonacieux. "My wife adores me, and there is yet time for me to gain her secret."

"The ninny!" murmured Madame Bonacieux.

"Silence!" warned d'Artagnan, pressing her hand more firmly.

"How can there be still time?" asked the man in the cloak.

"I'll go to the Louvre. I'll ask for Madame Bonacieux. I'll say that I have thought the matter over. I'll renew the affair. I'll obtain the letter and run with it straight to the cardinal."

"Well, go quickly! I shall return soon to learn the result of your trip."

The unknown left the house.

"Infamous!" breathed Madame Bonacieux, addressing the remark to her husband.

"Silence!" said d'Artagnan, a third time, pressing her hand convulsively.

A fearful howling interrupted these whispered words in the room above. It was M. Bonacieux, who had just discovered the disappearance of his moneybag and was bawling, "Thieves!"

"Heavens," cried his wife, "he will rouse the whole quarter!"

Bonacieux kept up his clamor a long time. But, because such cries were a frequent matter in this quarter, nobody appeared in the Rue des Fossoyeurs to answer them. The mercer's house, too, had recently acquired a bad name in the neighborhood. Finding that nobody appeared, the mercer went outside, continuing to make the welkin ring. His voice gradually dulled away as he ran in the direction of the Rue du Bac.

A few seconds afterward d'Artagnan, enveloped in a large cloak, also left the house. The mantle, despite its size, ill-concealed the sheath of a long sword.

Madame Bonacieux followed him with her eyes—it was the look with which a woman accompanies the man she loves. But when he had turned the corner of the street, she fell upon her knees and, clasping her hands, she cried, "Merciful heaven, protect her Majesty and me!"

CHAPTER XVIII

PLAN OF THE CAMPAIGN

D'Artagnan went straight to M. de Tréville's.

He had reflected that his Eminence would be warned within a few minutes by this accursed unknown who appeared to be his agent. And the young Gascon judged with good reason that he had not a minute to waste.

The heart of the youngster overflowed with joy. An opportunity at last presented itself to him in which there was at the same time glory to be acquired and money to be gained. And, as a far higher encouragement than either, this chance brought him into close intimacy with the woman he adored. The occasion, then, did more for him at once than he would have ever dared ask of fate.

The captain of Musketeers was in his saloon with his habitual court of gentlemen. D'Artagnan, known to the retainers as an intimate of the house, went straight to M. de Tréville's office and sent word that he wished to see him on an affair of vital importance.

The youth had waited scarcely more than five minutes when the captain appeared. By the joy that was painted on his visitor's countenance the worthy Tréville plainly perceived that something new was afoot.

All the way to the mansion d'Artagnan had been consulting with himself as to whether he should place confidence in his patron or only beg him to grant his protégé free rein in a secret mission. But M. de Tréville had always been so thoroughly his friend, had always been so devoted to the king and queen, and hated the cardinal so cordially that the young Gascon determined to tell him everything.

"My business," said d'Artagnan without prelude, "concerns nothing less than the honor and perhaps the life of the queen. Chance has rendered me master of a secret—"

"Which you will guard, young man, as your life!"

"But which I must impart to you, Monsieur, for you alone can aid me in the mission I have just received from her Majesty."

"Is this secret your own?"

"No, Monsieur. It is the queen's."

"Did she authorize you to communicate it to me?"

"No, Monsieur. On the contrary, I am desired to preserve it as the profoundest mystery."

"Why, then, are you about to betray it to me?"

"Because, Monsieur, without you I cannot move a step. I fear you will refuse me the favor I have come to ask if you do not know for what purpose I ask it."

"Keep your secret, young sir, and tell me what it is you wish."

"I want you to obtain for me from M. d'Essart leave of absence for a fortnight."

"When does the furlough begin?"

"This very night."

"Are you leaving Paris?"

"I am off on a somewhat lengthy mission."

"Can you consistently tell me your objective?"

"London.'

"Is any one interested in preventing your arrival?"

"His Eminence would give the world to hinder my success."

"Are you going alone?"

"Yes, Monsieur."

"In that case, you will not get beyond Bondy. I tell you this on the word of Tréville."

"Why say you so, Monsieur?"

"Because you will be assassinated."

"Then I shall die in the performance of my duty."

"Humph! But your mission will be left unfulfilled."

"Why, that is true," said d'Artagnan.

"Take my word for it," continued Tréville. "In enterprises of this sort, in order that one rider may arrive, four must set out."

"Ah, you are right, Monsieur. And luckily I can dispose of the efforts of Athos, Porthos, and Aramis."

"Without confiding to them the secret which I am not willing to have you tell me?"

"Yes, Monsieur. For we are sworn, once for all, to implicit confidence in one another against the necessity of proof. You can tell them you yourself trust me fully and they will not be more incredulous than you."

"I shall send each of them leave of absence for two weeks. To Athos, whose wound still pains him, that he may take the waters at Forges. To Porthos and Aramis, that they may accompany their friend, whom they are not willing to abandon in so painful a condition. My sending their furloughs will be sufficient evidence that I authorize their journey."

"Monsieur, you are a hundred times too good to me."

"Begone then, sir! Find them instantly, and let all be done tonight. Ha! But first write your request to d'Essart. Perhaps you had a spy at your heels. Your visit, if it should ever be known to the cardinal, will seem legitimate."

D'Artagnan drew up the request. M. de Tréville, on receiving it, assured him that by two o'clock in the morning the four furloughs would be at the respective lodgings of the travelers.

"Have the goodness, Monsieur, to send mine to Athos' dwelling. I should dread some disagreeable adventure if I were to go home."

"Be easy. Adieu, and a prosperous voyage! By the way, have you any money."

The young Gascon tapped the bag he had in the pocket of his cloak. "Three hundred pistoles," he replied.

"Oh, plenty! That would carry you to the end of the world."

D'Artagnan saluted M. de Tréville, who held out his hand to him. The young guardsman pressed it with a respect mingled with gratitude. Since his first arrival in Paris he had had constant occasion to honor this excellent man, whom he had always found worthy, loyal, and great-spirited.

His first visit was to Aramis, at whose place of residence he had not been since the famous evening on which he had followed Madame Bonacieux. What is more, he had seldom seen the young musketeer. But every time he had met him he had noticed a deep sadness on his face.

This evening, especially, Aramis was melancholy and

thoughtful. D'Artagnan asked some questions about the source of this prolonged attack of the blues. Aramis pleaded as his excuse a commentary upon the eighteenth chapter of St. Augustine which he was forced to turn into Latin for the following week and which engaged his attention a good part of the time.

After the two friends had been chatting a few minutes a servant from M. de Tréville entered, bringing a sealed packet.

"What is that?" asked Aramis.

"The leave of absence Monsieur asked for," replied the lackey.

"For me! I have asked for no—"

"Hold your tongue and take it!" said d'Artagnan. "And you, my friend, there is a demi-pistole for your trouble. You will tell M. de Tréville that M. Aramis is very much obliged to him. Go."

The lackey bowed to the ground and departed.

"And what does all this mean?" demanded the musketeer.

"Pack up everything you will need for a journey of two weeks and come along with me."

"But I cannot leave Paris just now without knowing—"

"What has become of her?"

"Become of whom?" asked Aramis.

"Of the woman who was here—the lady of the embroidered kerchief."

"Who told you there was a woman here?" gasped the musketeer, growing as pale as death.

"I saw her."

"And you know who she is?"

"I can hazard a good guess, at least."

"Listen!" said Aramis. "Since you appear to know so much, can you also inform me what has become of that woman?"

"I believe she has returned to Tours."

"Yes, that may well be. I see that you do know her. But why did she go back to Tours without telling me anything?"

"Because she was afraid of being arrested."

"Then why has she not written to me?"

"Because she was afraid of compromising you."

"D'Artagnan, you restore me to life!" cried the musketeer. "I fancied myself despised, betrayed. I was so delighted to see her again! I could not have believed she would risk her liberty for me, and yet for what other cause could she have returned to Paris?"

"For the same cause which today takes us to England."

"And what may that be?"

"Oh, you'll know some day, Aramis. But at present I must imitate the discretion of 'the doctor's niece.'"

The musketeer grinned as he remembered the tale he had foisted on his friends on a certain evening.

"Well then, since she has left Paris and you are sure of it, d'Artagnan, nothing prevents me from joining you. Where do we go next?"

"To see Athos. I beg you to make haste, for we have lost much time already. Take your servant Bazin with us."

Aramis called Bazin and ordered him to meet them at Athos' residence. He took up his cloak, sword, and three pistols—and was ready. As they went out, Aramis placed his hand upon the arm of his friend and looked at him earnestly.

"You have not spoken of this lady?" he asked gently.

"To nobody in the world."

"Not even to Athos and Porthos?"

"I have not breathed a syllable to them."

"Good enough!"

Tranquil on this important point, Aramis continued his way with d'Artagnan and they soon arrived at Athos' dwelling. They found him holding his leave of absence in one hand and M. de Tréville's note in the other.

"Can you explain to me what these things mean? I have just this moment received them," said the astonished musketeer.

My dear Athos:

I wish, as your health absolutely requires it, that you should rest for a fortnight. Go, then, and take the waters of Forges, or any other that may be more agreeable to you. And recuperate yourself as quickly as possible.

Your affectionate

De Tréville

"Why, that's easy to explain, Athos," said the young Gascon. "The furlough and the letter simply signify that you must follow me."

"To the waters of Forges—eh?"

"There or—elsewhere, Monsieur."

"In the king's service?"

"Either the king's or the queen's, what matters it? Are we not their Majesties' servants?"

At that very moment Porthos entered.

"*Pardieu!*" he cried. "Here is a strange thing. Since when, I wonder, in the Musketeers, have they been granting leaves of absence that the men do not ask for?"

"Ever since those men have had friends to ask the furloughs for them," replied d'Artagnan jauntily.

"Aha, gentlemen! It seems there's something fresh here."

"Yes, we are traveling to—" said Aramis.

"What country?" demanded Porthos.

"My faith! To one that I do not know much about," asserted Athos. "You would better ask the young Gascon."

"To London, my dear sirs," said d'Artagnan.

"Whew! And what the devil are we going to do in London when we get there?" exclaimed Porthos.

"That is what I am not free to tell you, gentlemen."

"But in order to reach England, money is necessary," added Porthos, "and I have none."

"Nor I," said Aramis.

"Nor I," said Athos.

"But I have," replied the young guardsman, pulling his treasure from his pocket and placing it on the table. "There are in this bag three hundred pistoles. Let each take seventy-five. That is enough to take us to London and back. Besides, make yourselves easy—not all of us will arrive in England."

"Why so?"

"Because, in all probability, some of us will be left on the road."

"It is a campaign on which we are now entering?"

"One of a most dangerous kind, I give you due notice."

"If we are risking our necks," observed Porthos, "I should at least like to know what for."

"You would be a lot the wiser then!" said Athos.

"And yet," added Aramis, "I find myself somewhat of friend Porthos' opinion."

"Is the king accustomed to give you such reasons?" inquired the Gascon. "Not at all. He says to you offhand, 'Gentlemen, there's fighting going on in Flanders—go and fight.' And you go and fight. Why? You do not worry about that part of it."

"D'Artagnan is right," declared Athos. "Here are our three furloughs from M. de Tréville. Here are three hundred pistoles from I don't know where. So let us go quietly and get killed where we are told to. Is life worth the trouble of so many questions? D'Artagnan, I am ready to follow you."

"And I also," said Porthos.

"Count me in," said Aramis. "I'm not sorry to quit Paris for a while. I had need of distraction."

"Do not worry. You will have distractions enough."

"And now, when are we to start?" asked Athos.

"Immediately," replied d'Artagnan. "We have not a single minute to lose."

"Hello! Grimaud! Planchet! Mousqueton! Bazin!" The four young men were summoning their lackeys. "Clean my boots and fetch the horses from the hotel."

Each musketeer was accustomed to leave at the general hotel of his company, as at a barracks, his own horse and that of his lackey. Planchet, Grimaud, Mousqueton, and Bazin set off at full speed.

"Now let us lay down the plan of campaign," suggested Porthos. "Where do we go first?"

"To Calais," said d'Artagnan. "That is the most direct route to London, I am sure."

"Well," continued Porthos, "this is my advice—"

"Speak!"

"Four men traveling together would be suspected. D'Artagnan will give each of us his instructions. I shall go by way of Boulogne, to clear the way. Athos will set out two hours afterward, by the route of Amiens. Aramis will follow us by Noyon. As to d'Artagnan, he will go by the line he thinks best, in Planchet's clothes, while Planchet will follow us as d'Artagnan, in the uniform of the Guards."

"Gentlemen," said Athos, "my opinion is that it is not proper to allow servants to have anything to do with such an affair. A secret may by chance be betrayed by gentlemen—but it is always sold by lackeys."

"Porthos' plan appears to me impracticable," observed the young Gascon, "inasmuch as I am myself ignorant what instructions I can give you. I am the bearer of a letter, that is all. I cannot make three copies of that letter, because it is sealed. We must then, I believe, travel together. The letter is here in this pocket," and he pointed to the spot where the writing was concealed. "If I should be killed, one of you must take it and continue the route. If he be killed, it is another's turn, and so on. Provided a single one arrives, that is all that is necessary."

"Bravo, d'Artagnan, your opinion is mine!" cried Athos. "Besides, we must be consistent and stick to our

story. I am on my way to take the waters, you are bearing
me company. Instead of taking the waters of Forges I
go to those of the sea—the choice lies open to me. If
any one wishes to stop us, I shall show M. de Tréville's
letter. If we are attacked, we shall defend ourselves. If
we are tried in court, we shall stoutly maintain that we
were only anxious to dip ourselves a certain number of
times in the sea. Our enemies would have an easy bargain
of four isolated men—whereas four men together make a
troop. We shall arm our lackeys with pistols and musketoons. If the foe sends an army against us, we shall
give battle, and the survivor, as d'Artagnan says, will carry
the letter to its final destination."

"Well said!" cried Aramis. "You do not speak often,
but when you do, it's like St. John of the Golden Mouth."

"I agree to Athos' plan, too," said Porthos.

"Then everything is decided," said d'Artagnan, "and
off we go in half an hour."

Each one took seventy-five pistoles from the bag and
made his preparations to set out at the time appointed.

CHAPTER XIX

THE JOURNEY

At two o'clock in the morning our four adventurers left Paris by the Barrière St. Denis. As long as it stayed dark they remained silent. In spite of themselves they succumbed to the influence of the gloom about them and apprehended ambushes in every shadow.

With the first rays of day, however, their tongues were loosened. With the sun their gaiety revived. It was like the hour before a battle—the heart beat high, the eyes laughed, and the soldiers felt that the life which they perhaps were soon going to lay down was after all a mighty good thing.

The appearance of the caravan was formidable. The black horses of the musketeers, their martial carriage, the regimental pace of these noble companions to the soldier, would have betrayed the most strict incognito. The lackeys were armed to the teeth and followed in the rear

All went merrily as a marriage bell until they arrived at Chantilly, which they reached about eight o'clock in the morning. They were ripe for breakfast, and alighted at the door of an inn recommended by a sign that represented St. Martin giving half his cloak to a poor man. They ordered the lackeys not to unsaddle the horses, and to hold themselves in readiness to set off again immediately.

They entered the common hall of the inn and placed themselves at table. A gentleman who had just arrived by the route of Dammartin was seated at the same table and was breakfasting. He opened the conversation with talk about the weather; the travelers replied. He drank to their health, and the musketeers returned the courtesy.

But when Mousqueton came to announce that the horses were ready and they were arising from table, the stranger proposed to Porthos to drink the health of the cardinal. Porthos retorted that he asked no better, if the stranger in his turn would consent to drink the health of the king. The stranger cried that he acknowledged no other sovereign than his Eminence. Porthos called him drunk, and the stranger drew his sword.

"You have committed a piece of folly," said Athos chidingly. "But it can't be helped now. Kill the fellow, and rejoin us as soon as you can."

The three remounted their horses and set out at a good pace while Porthos was promising his adversary to perforate him with all the thrusts known to the fencing schools.

"There goes one of us!" cried Athos at the end of five hundred paces.

"But why did that man attack Porthos rather than any other one of us?" asked Aramis.

"Because," explained d'Artagnan, "as Porthos was talking louder than the rest of us, he took him to be the chief."

"I always said that this cadet from Gascony was a well of wisdom undefiled," murmured Athos, and the travelers continued their route.

At Beauvais they stopped two hours, as well to breathe

their horses a little as to wait for Porthos. At the end of the period, as Porthos did not come, nor any news of him, they resumed their journey.

About a league from Beauvais where the road was hemmed in by two high banks they fell in with eight or ten men who appeared to be employed in digging holes and filling up the ruts with mud.

Aramis, not liking to soil his boots with this artificial mortar, swore at the diggers rather sharply. Athos tried to restrain him, but it was too late. The laborers began to jeer at the travelers, and by their insolence they disturbed the equanimity even of the cool Athos, who urged on his horse against one of them.

Then each of the men retired as far as the ditch, from which he took a concealed musket. The result was that our seven travelers were outnumbered in weapons. Aramis received a ball which passed through his shoulder, and Mousqueton another bullet that lodged in the lower portion of his loins. Therefore Mousqueton alone fell from his horse, not because he was severely wounded, but, not being able to see his wound on account of his portliness, he judged it must be more serious than it really was.

"It is an ambuscade!" shouted d'Artagnan. "Don't waste a charge! Forward—gallop!"

Aramis, wounded as he was, seized the mane of his horse and was carried along with the others. Mousqueton's horse rejoined them and loped by the side of its companions.

"That animal will serve us for a relay," said Athos.

"I should rather have had another hat than a second horse," said d'Artagnan. "My bonnet was blown away by a ball. By my faith, it is very fortunate the letter was not in it."

"They'll kill poor Porthos when he comes up," said Aramis.

"If Porthos were on his two legs, he would have rejoined us by now," replied Athos. "My own idea is that when the drunken stranger reached the dueling ground, he was no longer intoxicated."

The travelers had chosen crossroads in the hope that they might meet with less interruption. But at Crèvecœur, after two more hours of hard galloping, Aramis declared he could proceed no farther. He grew paler every minute, and they were obliged to support him on his horse. They lifted him off at the door of a cabaret, left Bazin with him, and set forward again in the hope of sleeping at Amiens.

"*Morbleu!*" said Athos as soon as they were in motion. "We are now reduced to two masters and Grimaud and Planchet! I won't be the enemy's dupe, I take an oath on it. I shall neither open my mouth nor draw my sword between this and Calais. I swear by—"

"Don't waste time in swearing," said d'Artagnan. "Let us gallop if our jaded horses will consent."

And the travelers buried their rowels in the flanks of their horses, who thus vigorously stimulated recovered their waning energies. They arrived at Amiens at midnight and alighted at the inn of the Golden Lily.

The host wished to lodge the two travelers each in a charming chamber, but unfortunately these rooms were at opposite ends of the inn. D'Artagnan and Athos refused them. The host averred he had no other worthy of their Excellencies. But the travelers said they would sleep in the common chamber of the hotel, each on a mattress thrown upon the floor. The travelers were firm and the landlord was forced to comply with their wishes.

They had just prepared their beds and barricaded their door from within, when some one knocked at the yard shutter. It was Planchet and Grimaud. The former mounted by the window and installed himself to spend the night across the doorway, to make sure no one could reach his master. Grimaud said he was going to shut himself up in the stable, undertaking that by five o'clock in the morning he and the four horses would be ready to continue the journey.

The night was quiet enough. Toward two o'clock in the morning somebody endeavored to open the door. Planchet awoke in an instant and cried, "Who goes there?" The man outside replied that he had made a mistake and went away.

At four o'clock they heard a terrible riot in the stables. Grimaud had tried to waken the stableboys and they had beaten him. When the travelers opened the window, they saw the poor lad lying senseless with his head split open by a blow from a pitchfork.

Planchet went down into the yard and wished to saddle the horses, but the horses were all used up. Mousqueton's animal, which had traveled for five or six hours without a rider the day before, might have been able to pursue the journey, but by an inconceivable error it appeared that the veterinary surgeon who had been sent for to bleed one of the host's horses had bled Mousqueton's.

This began to be annoying. All these successive accidents were perhaps the result of chance, but they might be
fruits of a plot. Athos and d'Artagnan went out, while
Planchet was sent to inquire if there were not three horses
for sale in the neighborhood. At the door of the inn stood
two horses, fresh, strong, and fully equipped. These would
have just suited them.

The lackey asked where the owners of the horses were
and was informed that they had just passed the night in
the hotel and were then settling their bill with the host.

Athos went to pay the reckoning, while d'Artagnan
and Planchet stood at the street door. The host was downstairs in a back room to which Athos was requested to go.

He entered without the least mistrust and took out two
pistoles to settle the account. The host was alone, seated
before his desk, one of the drawers of which was partly
open. He took the money which Athos offered to him
and turned it over and over in his hands. Suddenly he
cried out that it was bad and that he would have him and
his two companions arrested as forgers.

"You blackguard!" cried Athos, going toward him,
"I'll cut your ears off!"

At the same instant four men, armed to the teeth, entered by side entrances and rushed upon the unsuspecting
musketeer.

"I am taken!" shouted Athos with all the power of his
lungs. "Go on, d'Artagnan, spur! spur!" And he fired
two pistols.

D'Artagnan did not require a second bidding. He and
Planchet untied the two horses that were waiting at the

door, leaped upon them, buried their spurs in their sides, and set off at a full gallop.

"Do you know what became of Athos?" asked d'Artagnan as they rode forward with terrible speed.

"Ah, Monsieur," called back Planchet, "I saw one fall at each of his two shots, and he appeared to me, through the glass door, to be fighting the others with his sword."

"Brave Athos!" murmured the young Gascon. "And to think that we are compelled to leave him! Maybe the same fate awaits us two paces hence. Meanwhile, forward with God! Planchet, you are a brave fellow!"

"As I told you, Monsieur," replied Planchet, "Picards are found out by being used. Besides, here I am in my native country, and that excites me."

At a hundred paces from the gates of Calais, d'Artagnan's horse gave out. He fell and could not be made to rise again, the blood flowing from his eyes and his nose. There still remained Planchet's animal, but he stopped short and could not be forced to move a step.

They left their two nags upon the highroad by the city gate and ran toward the quay. Planchet called his master's attention to a gentleman who had just arrived with his lackey and only preceded them by some fifty paces. They made all speed to come up to this gentleman, who appeared to be in great haste. His boots were covered with dust, and he inquired if he could not cross over to England instantly.

"Nothing would be easier," said the captain of a vessel ready to sail, "but this morning an order came from the cardinal to let no one leave port without his permission."

204 THE THREE MUSKETEERS

"I have that permission," said the gentleman, drawing a paper from his pocket, "and here it is."

"Have it examined by the governor of the port," said the shipmaster, "and give me the preference."

"Where shall I find the governor?"

"At his country house."

"And that is situated?"

"A quarter of a league from the city. Look, you can see it from here — at the foot of that little hill, that slated roof."

"Very well," said the gentleman. And with his lackey he took the road to the governor's country house.

D'Artagnan and Planchet followed them for a distance of five hundred paces. Once they were outside the city, the young Gascon overtook the gentleman as he was entering a little wood.

"Monsieur," he said, "you appear to be in very great haste."

"No one can be in any greater, Monsieur."

"I am sorry for that," continued d'Artagnan, "for, as I am much pressed for time also, I wished to beg you to render me a service."

"And what is that, please?"

"To let me sail first."

"That is impossible," replied the gentleman. "I have traveled sixty leagues in forty-four hours, and by tomorrow at midday I must be in London."

"I have performed the same distance in forty hours, Monsieur, and by tomorrow forenoon at ten o'clock I must be in London."

"I am very sorry, Monsieur, but I was here first and shall certainly not sail second."

"I am disconsolate, Monsieur, but I arrived second and really must sail first."

"The king's service!" said the gentleman.

"My own service!" replied d'Artagnan.

"But this is a needless quarrel you seek with me."

"Oh, not at all, Monsieur. For I want the order from the cardinal which you are carrying."

"My bantam, I shall blow out your brains. Holla, Lubin! My pistols, quick!"

"Planchet," called out d'Artagnan, "take care of the lackey. I am attending to his master."

Planchet, emboldened by his first exploit, sprang upon Lubin. And, as he was strong and vigorous, he soon got him on the broad of his back, and placed his knee upon his breast.

"Go on with your affair, Monsieur," Planchet called. "I have finished with mine."

Seeing this, the gentleman drew his sword and sprang upon d'Artagnan, but he had too excellent an adversary. In three seconds the young Gascon had wounded him three times, exclaiming at each thrust, "One for Athos! One for Porthos! And one for Aramis!"

At the third hit the gentleman fell like a log. D'Artagnan believed him dead, or at least insensible, and went toward him for the purpose of taking the order. But the moment he extended his hand to search for it, the wounded man, who had not dropped his sword, plunged the point of it into his breast, crying, "And one for you!"

"And one for me, you are right! The best for the last!" cried the guardsman, furious, nailing his antagonist to the earth with a fourth thrust through the body.

This time, the gentleman closed his eyes in good earnest and fainted. D'Artagnan searched his pockets, and took from one of them the order for the passage. It was issued in the name of the Comte de Wardes.

Meanwhile Planchet held his victim tightly by the throat.

"Monsieur," he said to his master, "as long as I hold this fool Lubin in this manner, he can't cry. But as soon as I let him go, he howls again. I know him for a Norman, and Normans are obstinate."

"Stay!" said d'Artagnan, taking out his handkerchief. And he gagged the lackey and bound him to a tree.

This being achieved, they drew the Comte de Wardes close to his servant. As the wounded man and the bound man were at some little distance within the wood, it was evident they were likely to remain there until the next day.

Then the two victors set forward as fast as they could toward the country house of the governor of the port.

The Comte de Wardes was introduced to that worthy functionary.

"You have an order signed by the cardinal?" he asked.

"Yes, Monsieur," replied d'Artagnan, "here it is."

"Ah, ah! It is quite regular and explicit."

"Quite likely," said the young Gascon. "I am one of the most faithful servants of his Eminence."

"It appears the cardinal is anxious to prevent some one from crossing to England?"

"Yes, a certain d'Artagnan, a Béarnese gentleman who left Paris in company with three friends with the intention of going to London."

"Do you know him personally?"

"Perfectly well."

"Describe him to me, then," asked the governor.

"Nothing more easy, Monsieur."

And d'Artagnan gave feature for feature a description of the Comte de Wardes.

"Is he alone or accompanied?"

"He has a lackey named Lubin."

"We shall keep a sharp lookout for them. And if we lay hands on them, his Eminence may be assured they will be conducted back to Paris under a good escort."

"By doing so, Monsieur the Governor," said d'Artagnan, "you will deserve well of the cardinal."

The governor countersigned the passport and delivered it to the young guardsman. The latter lost no time in useless compliments. He thanked the governor, bowed, and departed. Once outside, he and Planchet set off as fast as they could run. And by making a detour they avoided the wood and reëntered the city by another gate.

The vessel was quite ready to sail, and the captain was waiting on the wharf. "Well?" he said, on catching sight of d'Artagnan.

"Here is my pass countersigned," said the guardsman.

"And where is the other gentleman?"

"He will not go today. But, rest easy, captain—I'll pay you for us two."

"In that case, let us go," said the shipmaster.

In five minutes they were all on board. And it was high time they were! For they had sailed scarcely half a league when d'Artagnan saw a flash from shore and heard a detonation. It was the cannon which announced the closing of the port.

He now had leisure to examine his wound. Fortunately, as d'Artagnan had thought, it was not dangerous. The point of the sword had touched his rib and had been deflected by it. Still further, his shirt had stuck to the wound, and he had thus lost only a few drops of blood.

He was worn out with fatigue. A mattress was laid upon the deck for him. He threw himself upon it and fell asleep.

On the morrow at break of day they were still three or four leagues from England. The breeze had been so light all night they had made but little progress. At ten o'clock the vessel cast anchor in the harbor of Dover, and at half-past ten d'Artagnan placed his foot on English soil, crying, "Here I am at last!"

But that was not all—they must get to London. In England the post was well served. D'Artagnan and Planchet each took a post horse, and a postilion rode before them. In a few hours they were in the capital. The Gascon, of course, did not know London, nor did he know a word of English. But he wrote the name of Buckingham upon a piece of paper, and everyone pointed out to him the way to the duke's palace.

D'Artagnan inquired for the confidential valet of the duke, who, having accompanied him on all his voyages, spoke French perfectly. He told this man that he had come from Paris on a mission of life and death, and that he must speak with his master at once.

"Whom must I announce to my Lord Duke?" asked Patrick, for such was the name of this minister of the minister.

"The young man who one evening sought a quarrel with him on the Pont Neuf opposite the Samaritaine."

"A singular introduction!"

"You will find it as good as another."

The confidence with which d'Artagnan spoke convinced Patrick of the truth of his errand; so he went to the duke and announced to him in the terms directed that a messenger from Paris awaited him.

Buckingham at once remembered the circumstance, and, suspecting that something was going on in France of which he should be informed, he went immediately to the young Gascon.

"No misfortune has happened to the queen?" cried Buckingham, throwing all his fear and love into the question.

"I believe not. Still, she is endangered by some great peril from which your Grace alone can extricate her."

"What is it? I should be only too happy to be of any service to her. Speak, man, speak!"

"Take this letter. It is from her Majesty, I think."

"From her Majesty!" said Buckingham, becoming so pale that the young guardsman feared he would faint as he broke the seal.

"What is this rent in the paper?" he asked, showing d'Artagnan a place where it had been pierced through.

"Oho! I had not noticed that," said the Gascon. "It was the sword of the Comte de Wardes which made that hole when he gave me a good thrust in the breast."

"You are wounded?" asked Buckingham.

"Nothing but a scratch," answered d'Artagnan.

"Just heaven, what have I read!" cried the duke a moment later. "Come with me, Monsieur, come!"

CHAPTER XX

THE COMTESSE DE WINTER

The duke walked so fast that d'Artagnan had some trouble keeping up with him. He passed through several apartments of an elegance of which the greatest nobles in France had not even an idea. They arrived at last in a bedchamber which was at once a miracle of taste and sumptuousness. In the alcove of this chamber was a door concealed in the tapestry. This the duke opened with a small gold key that he wore suspended from his neck by a chain of the same metal. With discretion d'Artagnan remained behind. But just as Buckingham crossed the threshold, he turned around and, seeing the hesitation of the young soldier, he said, "Come in! And on your return to France, if you have the good fortune to be admitted to her Majesty's presence, tell her just what you have seen."

The two found themselves in a small chapel hung with a tapestry of Persian silk worked with gold and brilliantly lighted by a vast number of candles. Over a species of altar and beneath a canopy of blue velvet, surmounted by red and white plumes, was a full-length portrait of Anne of Austria. The figure was so perfect in its resemblance that d'Artagnan uttered a cry of surprise on beholding it. One might believe that the queen was about to speak. On the altar and beneath the portrait was the casket containing the diamond studs.

The duke approached the altar, knelt as might a priest before a holy relic, and opened the casket.

"There," he said, drawing from the shrine a large bow of blue ribbon all sparkling with diamonds—"there are the precious studs which I have taken an oath should be buried with me. The queen gave them, the queen requires them again. Her will, like that of God, be done in all things."

All at once he uttered a terrible cry. "All is lost!" cried Buckingham, becoming as pale as a corpse. "Two of the studs are missing. There are only ten."

"Lost or stolen, do you think, my Lord?"

"They have been stolen," replied the duke, "and it is the cardinal who has dealt the blow. Look! The ribbons which held them have been cut with scissors."

"Perhaps the thief still has them in his hands."

"Wait!" said the duke. "The one time I have worn these studs was at a ball given by the king at Windsor. The Comtesse de Winter, with whom I had quarreled, became reconciled to me at that ball. That reconciliation was nothing but the vengeance of a jealous woman. I have never seen her from that day to this. The woman is an agent of the cardinal."

"He has agents, then, throughout the world?"

"Oh, yes," said Buckingham, gritting his teeth with rage. "Yes, he is a terrible antagonist. But when is this Paris fête to take place?"

"Monday next."

"Monday next! Then we still have five days before us. Patrick!" called the duke, opening the door of the chapel. His confidential valet appeared.

"My jeweler and my secretary."

The valet went out with a mute promptitude which showed him accustomed to obey blindly and without reply. The secretary lived in the duke's palace and therefore made his appearance quickly. He found Buckingham seated at a table in his chamber, writing orders with his own hand.

"Mr. Jackson," he said, "go instantly to the Lord Chancellor and tell him that I charge him with the execution of these commands. I wish them to be carried out immediately."

The secretary bowed and retired.

"And now we are safe on that side," said Buckingham, turning to d'Artagnan. "If the studs have not yet gone to Paris, they will not arrive there until after you."

"How so, my Lord?"

"I have placed an embargo on all vessels at present in his Majesty's ports and, without particular permission, no one dare lift anchor."

D'Artagnan looked with stupefaction at a man who thus employed, in the prosecution of his private intrigues, the unlimited power with which he was clothed by the confidence of a king. The Gascon was amazed to note by what fragile and unsuspected threads the lives of men and the destinies of nations were suspended. He was lost in these reflections when the goldsmith entered.

The jeweler was an Irishman, one of the most skillful of his craft. He himself confessed that he gained a hundred thousand livres a year by the patronage of the Duke of Buckingham.

"Mr. O'Reilly," said the duke, leading him into the

chapel, "look at these diamond studs and tell me what they are worth."

The goldsmith cast a glance at the elegant manner in which they were set, calculated, one with another, what the diamonds were worth, and without hesitation said, "Fifteen hundred pistoles each, my Lord."

"How many days will it take to make two studs exactly like them? You see there are two wanting."

"Eight days, my Lord."

"I shall give you three thousand pistoles apiece if I can have them day after tomorrow."

"They shall be yours, my Lord."

"You are a jewel of a man, Mr. O'Reilly. But that is not all. These studs cannot be trusted to anybody. They must be done here in the palace."

Impossible, your Grace! No one but me can so execute them that they cannot be told from the original."

"Therefore, my dear Mr. O'Reilly, you are my prisoner —so make the best of it. Name to me such of your workmen as you need, and point out the tools they must bring."

The goldsmith knew the duke. He knew all objections would be useless, so he yielded with a good grace. Buckingham conducted him to the chamber destined for him. This, at the end of half an hour, had been transformed into a workshop. The jeweler's most skillful apprentice, an assortment of diamonds, and necessary tools were there.

Then the duke placed a sentinel at each door of the shop with an order to admit, on any pretext, nobody except his valet Patrick. We need hardly add that O'Reilly and his assistant were likewise prohibited from going out under any pretext. This point settled, Buckingham turned to d'Artagnan.

"Now, my young friend," he said, "England belongs to you. For what do you wish?"

"A bed, my Lord," replied d'Artagnan.

The duke assigned the young Gascon to a chamber adjoining his own. He wished to have him near at hand for the sake of a companion to whom he could talk of the queen.

On the day after the morrow, by eleven o'clock, the two diamond studs were finished. And they were copied so exactly, were so perfectly alike, that Buckingham could not tell the new from the old. Even the most well versed in such matters would have been deceived as he was.

He immediately called d'Artagnan. "Here," he said, "are the diamond studs you came to get. Be my witness that I have done all that lay in human power to do."

"Be satisfied as to that, your Grace. But shall I take the studs without the casket?"

"The box would but encumber you. Besides, it is more precious to me from being all that is left. You will say that I retain it. And now, sir, how shall I ever acquit myself of the debt I owe you?"

D'Artagnan blushed to the whites of his eyes. "Let us understand each other, my Lord," he replied. "I am in the service of the King and Queen of France. What I have done springs from my particular attachment to one of them, and not at all for your Grace."

"That is true, sir. We say 'proud as Scotchmen,'" murmured the Duke of Buckingham.

"And we say 'proud as Gascons,' for they are the Scots of France," replied d'Artagnan. Whereupon he saluted and was retiring.

"Well, and are you going away so, without 'by your leave'? Where and how do you travel?"

"That's true!"

"Before gad! These Frenchmen have no foresight."

"I had only forgotten that England was an island, Monsieur Duke, and you the king of it."

"Go to the riverside, ask for the brig 'Sund,' and give this letter to the captain. He will convey you to St. Valery, a small port on the French coast, where you certainly are not expected, and which ordinarily is frequented only by fishermen. When you have arrived there, go to a mean tavern—you cannot be mistaken, there is only one. Ask for the host and repeat to him the words *en avant*. They are the password."

"Afterward?"

"He will give you a horse all saddled and will point out the way you are to take. You will find in the same way four relays on your route. If you will give at each relay your address in Paris, the four horses that you ride will be forwarded to you there. These are noble animals, sir, and will reach you equipped for the field. However proud you may be, you will not refuse to accept one of these horses for yourself, and request your three companions to accept the others. I wish them thus to know that I have heard the story of their brave help to you when you were serving the queen. And now your hand, young man."

D'Artagnan offered his hand. Then he bowed to the

duke and made his way to the waterside. Opposite the Tower of London he found his vessel waiting, delivered his letter to the shipmaster, who after having it examined by the governor of the port made immediate preparations to sail.

Fifty ships were waiting to set out. Passing alongside one of them, d'Artagnan fancied he perceived on board of it the woman of Meung—the same whom the unknown had called Milady and whom the Gascon had thought so beautiful. But, thanks to the current of the stream and to a fair wind, his vessel passed so quickly that he got only a cursory glance at her.

The next day about nine o'clock in the morning he landed at St. Valery. D'Artagnan went instantly in search of the inn and easily discovered it by the riotous noise which issued from it. War between England and France was talked of as near and certain, and the jolly sailors were having a carousal.

The young Gascon made his way through the crowd, advanced toward his host, and pronounced the words *en avant*. The landlord instantly made him a sign to follow, went out with him by a door that opened into a yard, led him to the stable where a saddled horse awaited him, and asked him if he stood in need of anything else.

"Tell me only the route I have to follow."

"Go from hence to Blangy, from there to Neufchâtel. At this place go to the tavern of the Golden Harrow, give the password to the landlord, and you will find another horse ready saddled."

"Have I anything to pay?" demanded d'Artagnan.

"Everything is paid, and liberally, Monsieur. Begone, and may the good God guide you!"

Four hours later the young man was in Neufchâtel. He followed strictly the instructions he had received. He was about to remove the pistols from the saddle he had quitted to one he was about to fill, but he found the holsters furnished with weapons exactly like the others.

"Your address in Paris, Monsieur?"

"Hotel of the Guards, company of d'Essart."

"Enough!" replied the landlord.

"Which route must I take?"

"That of Rouen, Monsieur, but you should leave the city on your right and not rest there. You must stop at the little village of Écouis, in which there is but one tavern, the Shield of France. Do not judge it by its outward appearance. You will find a horse in the stable quite as good as this."

"Same password?"

"Exactly."

D'Artagnan again set off at full speed. At Écouis the same scene was repeated; he found as provident a host and a fresh horse. He left his address as he had before and set off again at the same pace for Pontoise. There he changed his horse for the last time, and at nine o'clock galloped into the yard of Tréville's mansion. He had made nearly sixty leagues in little more than twelve hours.

M. de Tréville received him as if he had met him that very morning. Only, when pressing his hand a bit more warmly than usual, he informed the young man that the company of d'Essart was on duty at the Louvre, and that he might repair at once to his post.

CHAPTER XXI

THE BALLET OF LA MERLAISON

On the morrow nothing was talked of in Paris but the ball which the aldermen of the city were to give to the king and queen. At the ball their Majesties were to dance the famous La Merlaison—the favorite ballet of the king.

At midnight great cries and loud acclamations were heard. It was Louis XIII, who was passing through the streets which led from the Louvre to the Hôtel de Ville, and which were all illuminated with colored lanterns.

Immediately the aldermen, clothed in the vestments of their office and preceded by six sergeants each holding a flambeau in his hand, went to attend upon the king. They met his Majesty on the steps, where the provost of the merchants made him the speech of welcome—a compliment to which the king replied with an apology for coming so late, laying the blame for his delay upon the cardinal, who had detained him until eleven o'clock talking over affairs of state. Everybody noticed that the king looked dull and preoccupied.

A private room had been prepared for the king, another for Monsieur the Prince Royal. In each of these rooms were placed masquerade dresses. The same arrangements had been made for the queen and for Madame the wife of the President. The nobles and ladies of their Majesties' suites were to dress, two by two, in chambers prepared for the purpose. Before entering his closet the king desired to be informed the moment the cardinal arrived.

Half an hour after the entrance of the king fresh acclamations were heard; these announced the arrival of the queen. The aldermen did as they had done before and, preceded by their sergeants, advanced to receive their illustrious guest. Her Majesty entered the great hall, and it was at once remarked that, like the king, she looked dull and even weary.

At the moment of her entrance the curtain of a small gallery which up to that time had been closed was drawn, and the face of the cardinal appeared. He was dressed as a Spanish cavalier. His eyes were fixed upon those of the queen, and a smile of terrible joy swept over his lips—the queen was not wearing her diamond studs.

The queen remained for a short time to receive the compliments of the city dignitaries and to reply to the salutations of their ladies. All at once the king appeared with the cardinal at one of the doors of the hall. Richelieu was speaking to him in a low voice, and the king was very pale.

His Majesty made his way through the crowd without a mask and with the ribbons of his doublet scarcely tied. He went straight up to the queen and in an altered voice said, "Why, Madame, have you not thought it proper to wear your diamond studs, when you knew it would give me so much gratification?"

Anne of Austria cast a glance around her and saw the cardinal behind with a diabolical smile on his countenance.

"Sire," replied the queen in a faltering voice, "because in the midst of so great a throng as this, I feared some accident might happen to them."

"And you were wrong, Madame. If I made you that present, it was that you might adorn yourself with it. I say again you were wrong."

"Sire," said Anne, "I can send for them to the Louvre, where they are, and thus your Majesty's wishes will be complied with."

"Do so, Madame, and that at once. For within an hour the ballet will commence."

The queen bent her head in token of submission and followed the ladies who were to conduct her to her room. On his part the king returned to his apartment.

There was a moment of trouble and confusion in the assembly. Everyone had noticed that something had passed between their Majesties. But both of them had spoken in such low tones that people near them, out of respect, had withdrawn several paces; so nobody was sure just what had been said. The violins began to sound with all their might, but no one paid the least attention to them.

Louis XIII came out first from his room. He was clad in a most elegant hunting costume; the Prince Royal and the other nobles were dressed like him. This was the costume that best became the king. When clad in this fashion he really appeared to be the first gentleman of France.

The cardinal drew near to the king and placed in his hand a small casket. The king opened the box and found within it two diamond studs.

"What does this signify?" he asked the cardinal.

"Nothing," replied Richelieu. "Only, if the queen has the studs at all, which I very much doubt, count them, sire. And if you find only ten, ask her Majesty who can have stolen from her the two that are in your possession."

The king glanced at the cardinal as if to interrogate him further, but he had not time for the question—a cry of admiration burst from every throat. If the king appeared to be the first gentleman of his kingdom, the queen was without doubt the most beautiful woman in all France.

It is true that the habit of a huntress became her admirably. She wore a beaver hat with blue feathers, a surtout of pearl gray velvet fastened with diamond clasps, and a petticoat of blue satin embroidered with silver. On her left shoulder sparkled the diamond studs on a bow of the same color as the plumes and the petticoat.

The king trembled with joy, and the cardinal with vexation. Distant as they were from Anne of Austria, neither could count the number of studs. The queen had them. The only question was, did she have ten or twelve?

At this instant the violins sounded the signal for the ballet. The king advanced toward Madame the wife of the President, with whom he was to dance, and the prince royal toward the queen. They took their places and the ballet began.

The king danced facing the queen, and every time he passed by her, he devoured with his eyes those studs of which he could not ascertain the number. A cold sweat covered the brow of his Eminence.

The ballet lasted an hour and had sixteen entrées. The

dance ended amid the applause of the whole assemblage, and everyone conducted his lady back to her place. But the king took advantage of the privilege he had of leaving his lady to advance eagerly in the direction of Anne of Austria.

"I thank you, Madame," he said, "for the deference you have shown to my wishes, but I think two of your studs are missing, and I am bringing them back to you."

"How, sire?" cried the young queen, affecting surprise. "You are giving me, then, two more? I shall now have fourteen."

In fact, the king counted them. And the twelve studs were all there on her Majesty's shoulder.

Louis XIII summoned the cardinal.

"What does this mean, Monsieur Cardinal?" asked his Majesty in a severe tone.

"It signifies, sire, that I was desirous of presenting two studs to her Majesty. And, as I did not dare to offer them myself, I adopted this means of inducing her to accept them."

"And I am the more grateful to your Eminence," replied Anne of Austria with a smile which proved she was not the dupe of this ingenious gallantry, "because I feel sure these two studs alone have cost you as much as all the others did his Majesty."

Then, saluting the king and the cardinal, the queen resumed her way to the chamber in which she had dressed, and where she was to take off her costume. . . . .

While the above scene was being enacted, d'Artagnan, to whom Anne of Austria owed the extraordinary triumph she had obtained over the cardinal, was standing lost in the crowd gathered at one of the doors of the Hôtel de Ville.

The queen had just gained her tiring-room, and the young Gascon was about to withdraw from his post of observation when he felt his shoulder lightly touched. He turned and saw a young woman who made him a sign to follow her. The face of the woman was covered with a black velvet mask, but notwithstanding this precaution he at once recognized his usual guide, the bright and intelligent Madame Bonacieux.

On the evening before, they had seen each other for scarcely a moment in the apartment of the Swiss guard, Germain, whither d'Artagnan had summoned her. The young woman's haste to convey to her queen the joyful news of the happy return of her messenger prevented the two lovers from exchanging more than a few words.

And now, light and quick as a bird, she was leading him down half-deserted corridors. But when he wished to speak to her, she placed her finger upon her mouth with a little imperative gesture full of grace, reminding him that he was under the command of a power which he must blindly obey and which forbade him to utter even the slightest complaint. At length, after winding about for a minute or two, Madame Bonacieux opened the door of a closet which was entirely dark and led d'Artagnan into it. There she made a fresh sign of silence and opened a second door concealed by tapestry. The opening of this door disclosed a brilliant light, and she disappeared.

The young Gascon remained a moment without moving,

asking himself where he could possibly be.   And then a
hand and an arm, surpassingly adorable in their form and
whiteness, glided through the tapestry.   D'Artagnan at
once comprehended that this was to be his recompense.   He
cast himself upon his knees, seized the hand and touched
it respectfully to his lips.   Then the hand was withdrawn,
but not before leaving in his palm an object which he
perceived to be a ring.   The door immediately closed, and
the young guardsman again found himself in the most
complete obscurity.

CHAPTER XXII

THE RENDEZVOUS

D'Artagnan ran home immediately. And though it was but three o'clock in the morning, and he had some of the worst quarters of Paris to traverse, he met with no misadventures.

He found the door of his passage open, sprang up the stairs, and knocked softly in a manner agreed upon between him and his lackey. Planchet, whom he had sent home two hours before from the Hôtel de Ville, telling him to wait up for him, opened the door.

("But how is this?" you will ask, dear reader. "How came Planchet in Paris? Did we not leave him stiff as a rush and lifted from his tired horse before the home of the Duke of Buckingham in London?"

Well, you are right. The attention we have been obliged to give recently to illustrious personages has diverted us from stating that the lackey was returned to Paris by the duke, reaching there with the promised four horses. And now, forward!)

"A letter has come for you, Monsieur," announced Planchet. "It is on the green table cover in your bedroom."

The letter was from Madame Bonacieux and couched in the following terms:

There are some thanks to be offered to you by me. About ten o'clock this evening will you be at St. Cloud, in front of the pavilion which stands at the corner of the house of M. d'Estrées?

C. B.

It was the first billet he had received from the lady he loved. His heart swelled in the intoxication of joy. Planchet, who had observed his master growing pale and red successively, knew the letter was satisfying to the young guardsman, for he was given a crown with which to drink his health.

"And may I profit by Monsieur's happiness?" he asked. "I should much like to sleep a while in my own bed."

"Go, and may the blessings of heaven lighten your slumbers!"

Left alone, d'Artagnan read his billet through twenty times. He kissed the lines written by the hand of the beautiful woman he adored. At length he sought his couch, fell asleep, and had golden dreams.

At seven o'clock in the morning he arose and called Planchet.

"My lad," the Gascon said, "I am going out for all day perhaps. You are therefore your own master until seven o'clock tonight. But at that hour you must hold yourself in readiness, with two horses."

"There!" said the lackey. "We are going again to have our hides pierced in all sorts of ways."

"You will take a musketoon and two pistols."

"Didn't I say so?" cried Planchet.

"Don't be afraid, you idiot. There is nothing on hand but a pleasure party."

"Like the charming excursion the other day, when it rained bullets and produced a crop of steel traps."

"You are afraid, eh? Did you wear out all your courage on your little trip to London?"

"At the appointed hour I shall be ready, Monsieur."

As d'Artagnan went out of his chamber he found M. Bonacieux at the door. His intention was to pass by without speaking to the worthy mercer, but the latter made him so friendly a salutation that the tenant felt obliged to enter into some conversation with him. So the young guardsman approached him with the most amiable air he could assume.

"You," cried M. Bonacieux in a tone of perfect goodfellowship, "what has become of you all these days? I have seen neither you nor your friends. And I don't believe you could gather all that dust I saw Planchet brush from your boots yesterday from the pavements of Paris."

"You are right, my dear M. Bonacieux. My friends and I have been on a little outing."

"Far from here, Monsieur Guardsman?"

"Oh, Lord, no! Some forty leagues only. We went to take M. Athos to the waters of Forges, where my friends stayed on after me."

"But you were impatient to return, weren't you?" grinned the mercer, giving his countenance a most sly air. "A handsome young fellow like you does not obtain long furloughs from his lady. We were most impatiently awaited in Paris, eh?"

"My faith!" replied the young guardsman, laughing. "I see there is no use trying to hide anything from you. Yes, I was expected by a lady, and very impatiently, egad!"

D'Artagnan departed, laughing at his joke, which he felt quite sure he alone could comprehend. He took his way toward the residence of M. de Tréville. His visit of the day before, it may be remembered, had been extremely short and had explained little.

He found the captain of Musketeers in a merry mood.

"Now," said Tréville, lowering his voice and looking into every corner of his apartment to see whether they were alone—"now let us talk about you, my friend. For it is evident that your happy return has something to do with the joy of the king, the triumph of the queen, and the humiliation of his Eminence. You must look out for yourself, however!"

"Why, what have I to fear?" asked d'Artagnan. "At least, as long as I have the luck to enjoy the favor of their Majesties?"

"Everything, believe me. The cardinal is not one to forget a mystification until he has settled accounts with the mystifier. And that mystifier looks a lot like a certain young Gascon of my acquaintance."

"Do you think the cardinal is as well posted as yourself and knows that I have been to London?"

"The devil! Was it from London you brought that beautiful diamond that glitters on your finger?"

"This jewel does not come from an English enemy, Monsieur," replied d'Artagnan. "It comes from the queen."

"Oh, oh!" exclaimed M. de Tréville. "Why, it is indeed a royal gem, worth a thousand pistoles if it is worth a farthing. By whom did the queen send you the bauble?"

"She gave it to me herself," said the Gascon. And he related to M. de Tréville how the whole affair came to pass.

"Oh, the women, the women!" cried the old soldier. "Everything that savors of mystery charms their romantic imagination. So you have kissed the hand and seen the arm—that is all. You would meet the queen and not know her. She might meet you and not recognize you."

"No, unless it were by the diamond, Monsieur."

"Let me give you a little good counsel, youngster! Go to the nearest goldsmith's and sell that diamond for the highest price you can get for it. He will have to give you at least eight hundred pistoles. Money has no name, young man, but that ring has a terrible one and may betray him who wears it."

"Sell it? When it comes from my sovereign? Never! You think I have something to dread, then, Monsieur?"

"I mean to say, young man, that he who sleeps over a mine, the match of which is already lighted, may consider himself in safety in comparison to you."

"The devil!" said d'Artagnan, whom the positive tone of M. de Tréville was beginning to disquiet. "What must I do?"

"Above all things, be on your guard. The cardinal has a long arm and a tenacious memory."

"But what sort of ill turn will he do me?"

"Eh! How can I tell? Has he not all the tricks of the demon at his command? See enemies in all directions. If any one seeks a quarrel with you, shun it, even though it be with a child but ten years old. If you are attacked by day or by night, fight, but retreat without shame. If you cross a bridge, feel every plank of it with your foot, lest one give way beneath you. If you pass before a house that is being built, look up, for fear a stone fall upon your head. If you stay out late, be always followed by your lackey, and let him be armed—that is to say, if you can be sure of your lackey!"

D'Artagnan began to feel a shiver along his spine.

"But, by the way," resumed M. de Tréville, "what has become of your three companions?"

"I was about to ask you, Monsieur, if you had had no news."

"Not a word."

"Well, I left them on my route—Porthos at Chantilly, with a duel on his hands; Aramis at Crèvecœur, with a musket ball in his shoulder; and Athos at Amiens, detained by an accusation of coining."

"See there now?" asked M. de Tréville. "And how in the name of all the saints in the calendar did you escape?"

"By a miracle, Monsieur, and with a sword thrust in my breast. Also by nailing the Comte de Wardes on the byroad to Calais like a butterfly on a curtain."

"There again! De Wardes, one of the cardinal's men, a cousin of Rochefort! In your place, son, I should do just one thing."

"And what is that?"

"While his Eminence was seeking for me in Paris, I should take without sound of drum or trumpet the road to Picardy. I should make some inquiries regarding my three companions. They richly merit that attention on your part."

"The advice is good; tomorrow I shall set out."

"Why not this evening?"

"Monsieur, I am unavoidably detained in town by important business."

"Some flirtation, eh? Have you given your word to stay?"

"Yes, Monsieur."

"Ah, then that's quite another thing. But promise me that if you are not killed tonight you will leave tomorrow."

"I promise it."

"A pleasant journey, then!"

"Thanks, Monsieur."

D'Artagnan left M. de Tréville and called successively at the abodes of Athos, Porthos, and Aramis. None of them had returned. Their lackeys were likewise absent.

As he passed the Hôtel des Gardes he took a glance into the stables. Planchet had just finished grooming two horses.

"Monsieur," asked the lackey, "I have a question to ask you. Do you place confidence in our landlord?"

"Not the least in the world. But why do you speak of this at this moment?"

"Because while you were talking with him I saw his color alter two or three times. And as soon as Monsieur had left, M. Bonacieux seized his hat, slammed his door, and set off at a quick pace in an opposite direction from the one you had taken."

"It seems you are right, Planchet, this does appear to be a trifle mysterious. Be assured that we shall not pay him our rent until this matter is categorically explained to us."

"Monsieur jests, but Monsieur will see."

"What would you have me do, my dear fellow?"

"Monsieur does not then renounce his excursion for this evening?"

"Quite the contrary, Planchet. The more ill will I bear M. Bonacieux, the more punctual I shall be in keeping the appointment made by the letter that came in my absence."

Planchet, seeing there was no hope of making his master renounce his project, set to work to groom the third horse.

As to d'Artagnan, being at bottom a prudent youth, he did not return to his apartment. Instead, he went and dined with the Gascon priest who, at the time of famine among the four friends, had given them a breakfast of chocolate.

CHAPTER XXIII

THE PAVILION

At nine o'clock d'Artagnan was at the Hôtel des Gardes. He found Planchet all ready.

The lackey was armed with a musketoon and a pistol. The master had his sword and placed two pistols in his belt. Then both mounted and departed quietly. It was very dark and no one saw them go out. Planchet took his place behind his master and kept at a distance of ten paces from him.

D'Artagnan crossed the quays, went out by the gate of La Conférence, and followed the road which led to St. Cloud.

As long as he was in the city Planchet maintained the respectful distance he had imposed upon himself. But as soon as the road began to be more lonely and dark, he drew softly nearer, so that when they entered the Bois de Boulogne he found himself riding quite naturally side by side with the young guardsman. In fact, we have to admit that the swaying of the tall trees and the reflection of the moon in the dark underbrush gave him serious uneasiness.

"Monsieur, is that not the barrel of a musket which glitters yonder?" demanded Planchet suddenly. "Had we better not lower our heads?"

"Decidedly, this animal will end by making me afraid," murmured d'Artagnan, to whom M. de Tréville's admonitions now recurred. And he put his horse to the trot. Planchet followed the movements of his master as if he had been his shadow.

"Are we going to continue this pace all night?" asked the lackey after a few more minutes had sped by.

"No, you are at your journey's end. I am going a few steps farther. You are afraid to be left alone, Planchet?"

"No. I only beg leave to remind Monsieur that the night bids fair to be very cold. And chills bring on rheumatism. And a lackey with the rheumatism makes but a poor servant."

"Well, if you are cold, my dear fellow, you can go into one of those cabarets that you see yonder and be in waiting for me two hours from now. Here's half a pistole for your refreshment."

D'Artagnan sprang from his horse, threw the bridle to Planchet, and departed at a quick pace, folding his cloak around him. He plunged into a bypath, continued his route, and reached St. Cloud. But instead of following the main street, he turned behind the château, reached a sort of lonely lane, and soon found himself in front of the pavilion he sought.

It was situated in a very deserted spot. A high wall, at the angle of which was the pavilion, ran along one side of this lane, and on the other was a little garden connected with a poor cottage which was protected by a hedge from the view of passers-by.

He gained the place appointed, and, as he had not been told to announce his presence by any signal, he waited.

Not the slightest noise was to be heard—it might be imagined that he was a hundred miles from the capital. D'Artagnan leaned against the hedge after having cast a glance behind it. A dark mist enveloped with its folds that immensity where Paris slept—a vast void from which glittered a few luminous points, the funeral stars of that human hell!

Wrapped in his sweet reflections, the young Gascon waited a long time without the least impatience, his eyes fixed upon that charming abode of which he could perceive a part of the ceiling with its gilded moldings, attesting the elegance of the remainder of the apartment where love awaited him.

The brazen voice of the clock in the belfry of St. Cloud sounded the hour of half-past ten.

Without knowing why, D'Artagnan felt a cold shiver run through his veins. Perhaps the cold was beginning to affect him and he was mistaking a purely physical sensation for a moral impression.

Eleven o'clock sounded.

The young guardsman now really began to fear that something had happened to Madame Bonacieux. He clapped his hands three times, the usual signal of lovers. But nothing replied to him, not even an echo.

It then occurred to him that perhaps the young woman had fallen asleep while waiting for him. At that moment he thought of the trees upon whose leaves the light from the chamber within still shone. As one of them drooped over the road, he believed that from its branches he might get a glimpse of the interior of the pavilion.

The tree was easy to climb. Besides, the Gascon was but twenty years old, and consequently had not yet quite forgotten his schoolboy habits. In an instant he was among the leafy boughs of the tree, and his keen eyes pierced through the transparent panes into the chamber of the pavilion.

It was a strange thing, and one that made d'Artagnan tremble from the soles of his feet to the roots of his hair, to note that this soft light, this calm lamp, illumined a scene of the wildest disorder.

One of the windows was broken, the door of the chamber had been beaten in and, split in two, was hanging on its hinges. A table, which had been spread with an elegant supper, was overturned. The decanters, broken in pieces, and the fruits, crushed, strewed the floor. Everything in the apartment gave evidence of a violent and desperate struggle. The young guardsman even fancied that he could recognize amid this strange disorder fragments of garments and some bloody spots staining the cloth and the curtains. He hastened to descend into the street, his heart beating frightfully. He wished to see whether he could find other traces of violence.

He then perceived a thing he had not before remarked — for nothing had prompted him to the examination — that the ground was trampled and hoof-marked here and there. It showed confused traces of men and horses. Besides, the wheels of a carriage, which appeared to have come from Paris, had made deep ruts in the soft earth. The ruts did not extend beyond the pavilion, but turned back again toward Paris.

At length d'Artagnan, in pursuing his researches, found near the wall a woman's torn glove. As he continued his investigations a more abundant and icy sweat rolled in large drops from his forehead. His heart was oppressed by a terrible anguish, and he kept saying, to reassure himself, that the appointment had been made with him before the pavilion and not in it, that Madame Bonacieux might have been detained in the city by her duties or perhaps by the jealousy of her husband.

But all this reasoning was overthrown by that feeling of exquisite pain which on certain occasions takes possession of our being. This feeling cries to us in unmistakable terms that some great misfortune is hanging over us.

Then it was that the Gascon became almost wild. He ran along the highroad, retook the path he had traveled before, and interrogated the boatman at the ferry.

The skipper told him that at about seven o'clock in the evening he had ferried across a young woman wrapped in a black mantle who seemed very anxious not to be recognized. But, just because of her precautions, the boatman had paid more than usual attention to her, and discovered she was amazingly pretty.

Thereupon d'Artagnan ran back to the château. It appeared to him that something might have happened at the pavilion during his absence and that fresh information awaited him. The lane was still deserted and the same calm, soft light shone through the window.

He then recollected that cottage, silent and obscure, which had no doubt witnessed all and could tell the tale of it. The gate of the inclosure was shut, but he leaped

over the hedge. And, in spite of the frenzied barking of
a chained dog, he approached the house.

No one answered to the first knocking. A silence as
of death reigned in the cottage, as it did in the pavilion.
But as this place was his last resource he knocked again.
After this second summons it seemed to him that he heard
a slight stirring within—a timid noise which seemed to
tremble lest it should be heard.

Then the guardsman ceased his pounding on the door
and begged for an answer in an accent so full of anxiety
and promises, terror and cajolery, that his voice would have
reassured the most fearful soul alive. At length an old
worm-eaten shutter was opened. But it closed again with
a slam as soon as the light from a wretched lamp shone
upon the baldric, sword-belt, and pistol pommels of
d'Artagnan. Rapid as the movement had been, the Gascon
had time to descry the head of an old man.

"Listen!" he cried. "I've been dying with anxiety,
waiting for somebody who did not come. Has anything
happened in this neighborhood? Speak!"

The window was again opened slowly and the same
face appeared. Only it was now, if possible, paler than
before.

Oh, Monsieur!" said the old man. "Ask me nothing.
For, if I dared tell you what I have seen, no good would
befall me."

D'Artagnan threw the miserable ancient a pistole.
"Tell me," he promised, "what you have seen, and I pledge
you the word of a gentleman that not one of your words
shall escape from my heart."

The scared old man read so much truth and grief in the face of the guardsman that he said in a low voice, "Three men brought a carriage quietly up to the pavilion. They took out of it a small man—stout, short, elderly—who was dressed in common clothes of a dark color. He ascended a ladder very carefully, looked suspiciously in at the lighted window of the pavilion, and said, 'It is she!' One of the three men, a great cavalier by his swaggering gait, walked up to the door of the pavilion. He opened it with a key, closed it, and disappeared. At the same time the other two men ascended the ladder.

"All at once great cries resounded from within the pavilion, and a woman came to the window as if to throw herself out. But as soon as she perceived the other two men, she fell back and they climbed from the top of the ladder into the chamber.

"Then I saw no more, but I heard the noise of breaking furniture. The woman screamed and cried for help. But her cries were soon stifled. Two of the men appeared, carrying the woman in their arms. She was thrust into the carriage—the little old man got in after her. They all disappeared at a quick pace, and from that moment I have neither seen nor heard anything."

D'Artagnan, entirely overcome by this terrible story, remained motionless and mute, while all the demons of anger and jealousy were howling in his heart.

"But, my good gentleman," resumed the old man, upon whom this silent despair certainly produced a greater effect than cries and tears would have done, "do not take on so! They did not kill her and that's a comfort."

"Can you guess," asked the Gascon, "who the man was who headed this infernal expedition?"

"I don't know him. But, if it's a description you want, he was a tall, dark man, with black mustaches, dark eyes, and the air of a gentleman."

"That's the man!" cried d'Artagnan. "Again he, forever he! He is my demon, apparently."

With a heavy heart the young guardsman again bent his way toward the ferry. Sometimes he hoped it could not be Madame Bonacieux, and that he should find her next day at the Louvre. At other times he feared that she had had an intrigue with another man, who, in a fit of jealousy, had surprised her and carried her off. His mind was torn by doubt, grief, and despair.

"Oh, if I had my three friends here!" he cried. "Then I should have at least some hope of finding her. But who knows what has become of the Inseparables?"

Where and how he came to find Planchet again, he could never remember. But, when he emerged from his melancholy and came to look about him, the first thing he saw in the damp gray mist before him was the faithful lackey. The servant, with the two horses in hand, awaited him at the door of a small cabaret that one might have passed a dozen times before suspecting its existence.

CHAPTER XXIV

THE LADYLOVE OF PORTHOS

That morning, as soon as it was in any way possible, d'Artagnan reached the door of M. de Tréville and ran quickly up the stairs. This time he decided to tell everything that had happened. The great captain would doubtless give him good advice as to the whole affair. Besides, as M. de Tréville saw the queen almost daily, he might be able to draw from her Majesty some information regarding the young woman whom the cardinal's people were making pay so dearly for her devotedness to her royal mistress.

M. de Tréville listened to the young man's account with a seriousness which proved that he saw something else in the adventure than a mere love affair. When d'Artagnan had finished, he said, "Hum! This savors of his Eminence a league off."

"But what is to be done, Monsieur?"

"Absolutely nothing, at present, except to quit Paris as soon as possible. I shall see the queen and relate to her the details of the disappearance of this poor young woman, of which she surely is ignorant. These facts will guide her actions, and on your return I shall perhaps have some good news to tell you. Rely upon me."

Full of gratitude for the past and the future, d'Artagnan bowed to M. de Tréville and resolved to put his advice into practice immediately. So he directed his course toward the Rue des Fossoyeurs in order to superintend the packing of his valise.

On approaching the house he perceived M. Bonacieux in morning costume standing at his threshold. The possibly sinister character of the old man recurred to the mind of the young guardsman, who looked at him with more attention than he had previously done. In addition to the yellow, sickly pallor of Bonacieux's skin, which indicates the infusion of bile into the blood, d'Artagnan remarked something perfidiously significant in the play of the wrinkled features of the mercer's face.

A rogue does not laugh in the same way that an honest man does, nor does a hypocrite shed the tears of a man of good faith. All falsehood is a mask and, however well made the disguise may be, with careful study we may always succeed in distinguishing it from the true countenance. Because of his feeling of repugnance, d'Artagnan was about to pass without speaking to his landlord, but, as he had done the day before, Bonacieux accosted him.

"Well, young man!" he said. "We appear to pass rather gay nights. Coming home at seven o'clock in the morning, *peste!* You seem determined to reverse ordinary customs."

"No one can reproach you for anything of the kind, M. Bonacieux," replied the young man. "You are a model for regularity. It is true that when one possesses a young and pretty wife he has no need to seek happiness elsewhere."

Bonacieux became as pale as death and grinned a ghastly smile.

"Where the devil were you gadding last night, my young master?" he countered. "It does not appear to be very clean in the country crossroads."

D'Artagnan looked down at his boots all covered with mud. But that same glance fell upon the shoes and stockings of the mercer, and it might have been said that they had been dipped in the same compound of filth. For both were stained with mud of the identical sort. At that a sudden idea flashed into the brain of the Gascon. That small stout man of the evening before—short and elderly, a kind of lackey, dressed in dark clothes, and treated without ceremony by the men wearing swords who composed the escort! That man was no other than Bonacieux himself! The husband had presided at the abduction of his wife.

A terrible inclination seized hold of d'Artagnan to grasp the mercer by the throat and strangle him. But, as we have said, he was a prudent youth, and he restrained himself. However, the resolution which appeared upon his countenance was so visible to Bonacieux that he was terrified at it, and he endeavored to draw back a step or two. But, as the mercer was standing before the half of the door which was shut, the obstacle compelled him to keep his place.

"Ah, but you are joking, my honorable fellow!" said d'Artagnan. "For it seems to me that if my boots need a sponge, your shoes and stockings stand in equal need of a brush. Perhaps you were philandering a bit, too, M. Bonacieux? What the devil! That is unpardonable in a man of your age, who has such a pretty wife."

"Heavens, no!" replied the mercer. "Yesterday I went to St. Mandé to see if I could possibly find a servant. And the roads were so vile I brought back all this mud which I have not yet had a chance to scrape off."

The place named by Bonacieux as his objective point was fresh proof to d'Artagnan in support of the suspicions he had conceived. The mercer had mentioned Mandé because it was a spot in an exactly opposite direction from St. Cloud. This probability afforded the Gascon his first consolation. For if Bonacieux knew where his wife was, one might by extreme means force him to open his mouth and let his secret escape.

"Pardon me, my dear fellow," said d'Artagnan, "but I am parched with thirst. I'll get a glass of water in your apartment."

And, without waiting for the permission of his landlord, the young man went quickly into the house and cast a rapid glance at the bed. It had not been used. Bonacieux had not been abed. He had been back only an hour or two—he had then accompanied his wife to the place of her confinement or at least to the first relay.

"Thanks, my friend," said d'Artagnan, emptying his glass, "that is all that I wanted. I'll run up to my rooms and have Planchet brush my boots."

At the top of the stairs he found Planchet in a great fright.

"Ah, Monsieur!" cried the lackey. "I thought you would never come. Here is some more trouble. M. de Cavois, the captain of the cardinal's Guards, has been here while you were at M. de Tréville's."

"Did he come to arrest me?"

"I could not tell; he was as sweet as honey, Monsieur. He said he came from his Eminence, who wished you well. He said you were to call upon the cardinal at the Palais-Royal during the course of the day, and that your fortune might depend upon the interview."

"I thought the cardinal could set a better snare than that," remarked the young man, smiling.

"Oh, I saw the trap fast enough, Monsieur. So I answered that you would be in despair at missing M. de Cavois, but that you had gone to Troyes in Champagne and I did not know the hour of your return."

"Planchet, you are really a precious fellow."

"You see, Monsieur, I thought there would still be time, if you wished, to contradict me and say you were not yet gone. The falsehood would then lie at my door. And, as I am not a gentleman, I of course can tell lies as I wish."

"Be of good heart, Planchet, you shall preserve your reputation as a veracious man. We set off almost at once."

"May I ask, without seeming too curious, where we are going?"

"*Pardieu!* In the direction exactly opposite to that of your tale to M. de Cavois. You must be as anxious to learn what has become of Grimaud, Mousqueton, and Bazin as I am to discover the fate of Athos, Porthos, and Aramis."

"Certainly, Monsieur. And I think provincial air will suit our lungs just now much better than that of Paris."

"Well, then, pack our luggage, Planchet. I shall go out with my hands in my pockets so that my departure shall not be suspected. You may join me at the Hôtel des Gardes."

Now that this was agreed upon, d'Artagnan visited the residences of his three friends. No news had been received of them. But a letter, highly perfumed and addressed in an elegant writing of small characters, had come for Aramis. The young Gascon took charge of this.

Ten minutes afterward Planchet met him at the Hôtel des Gardes. In order that there might be no loss of time, d'Artagnan had saddled his own horse.

"All right," he said to his lackey when the latter added the portmanteau to the equipment. "Now saddle the other three horses."

"Do you then think, Monsieur, that we shall travel faster with two animals apiece?" asked Planchet with his shrewd air.

"No, Monsieur Jester," replied the master, "but with our four horses we may bring back our three friends in case we have the good fortune to find them still living."

"Which is a slim chance," observed Planchet solemnly, "but we must not despair of the mercy of God."

"Amen to that!" said d'Artagnan, vaulting into his saddle.

Our two travelers arrived at Chantilly without any accident or misadventure. They alighted at the tavern of Great St. Martin, the same one at which they had stopped on their first journey.

The host, on seeing a young man followed by a lackey with two extra horses, advanced respectfully to the door. Now, as they had ridden eleven leagues already, the

Gascon thought it good to stop, no matter whether Porthos was at the inn or not. Perhaps it might not be prudent to ask the landlord at once what had become of the musketeer. So the young Gascon, without seeking information of any kind, dismounted, commended the horses to the care of the lackey, and entered a small room designed for privacy. He asked the landlord to bring him a bottle of his best wine and as good a breakfast as possible. These desires of the new arrival further corroborated the high opinion the innkeeper had at first sight formed of him.

"Faith, my good host," said d'Artagnan, "if you have deceived me in the quality of your wine, you will be punished for your sin. I hate to drink alone, therefore you shall drink with me. I raise my glass and drink, sir, to the prosperity of your establishment."

"Your Lordship does me much honor," replied the host, bowing and sipping his own glass. "And I thank you sincerely for your kind wishes. It seems to me this is not the first time I have had the privilege of seeing your Worship."

"Bah, I have passed perhaps ten times through Chantilly, and of these ten times I have stopped at your house three or four. Why, now that I think of it, I was here only ten or twelve days ago. I was conducting some friends, musketeers—one of whom, by the way, had a dispute of some sort with a stranger."

"I remember the event perfectly, Monsieur. Is it not M. Porthos that your Lordship means? He has done us the honor to remain with us since. And we are even a little uneasy—"

"On what account?"

"Because of certain expenses he has contracted."

"He is surely in a condition to pay whatever he owes. But may I see this Porthos?"

"Why, of course, Monsieur. Go up the first flight of stairs and knock at the door of No. 1. But warn him it is you."

"And why is that necessary?"

"Otherwise M. Porthos may imagine you belong to the house and in a fit of passion run his sword through you or blow out your brains."

"What have you done to incur his enmity?"

"We asked him to pay for his room and board."

"The devil you did! That is a demand my friend takes very ill when he is out of funds. But he will pay you."

"Hum!" said the host in a doubtful tone.

"The favorite of a great lady will not be allowed to inconvenience himself for such a paltry sum as he owes you."

"But, your Lordship, if I durst say what I believe on that head—I should say that I know this great lady."

"You!"

"Well, Monsieur, you understand that uneasiness makes us do all sorts of things. M. Porthos gave us a note for his duchess, ordering us to put it in the post. Instead of mailing it, which is never safe, I gave the billet to a lad of mine who was setting out for Paris, and bade him convey it to this duchess himself. This was fulfilling the intentions of M. Porthos, was it not, your Lordship?"

"Nearly so, at least."

"Well, Monsieur, do you know who this pretended duchess is? Why, she is the old wife of a procurator of the Châtelet, named Madame Coquenard. Although she is at least fifty, she still gives herself jealous airs. It struck me as very odd that a princess should live in the Rue aux Ours."

"But how do you know all this?"

"Because she flew into a great passion on receiving the letter, saying M. Porthos was a weathercock, and she was sure it was for some woman he had received his wound."

"Has he been wounded, then?"

"Oh, good Lord! What have I said?"

"You remarked that Porthos had received a sword cut."

"But he forbade me strictly to say so."

"Why should he do that?"

"Zounds, Monsieur! Because he had boasted that he would perforate the stranger with whom you left him in dispute. Whereas, in spite of his rodomontades, the stranger quickly threw him on his back. As M. Porthos is a very boastful man, he insists that nobody shall know he has received this wound except the duchess, whom he endeavored to interest by an account of his adventure."

"Is he confined to his bed?"

"Yes, for it was a master stroke that downed him, I assure your Lordship. Your friend's soul must be stuck fast to his body not to fly loose at such a time."

"Were you there, then?"

"I spied on the affair through curiosity, Monsieur. I saw them without their seeing me."

"And what happened?"

"Oh, the business was not a long one! They placed themselves on guard. The stranger made a feint and a lunge so rapidly that when M. Porthos came to the *parade* he already had three inches of steel in his chest. He at once fell backward. The stranger placed the point of his weapon at M. Porthos' throat and asked his name. When he learned that it was Porthos and not d'Artagnan, he assisted your friend to rise, brought him back to the hotel, mounted a horse, and disappeared like the wind."

"Thank you, my host, I know everything I wish to. Porthos' chamber, you say, is on the first story, No. 1?"

"Yes, Monsieur, the handsomest the inn contains. I could have rented it ten times over."

"Bah! Be satisfied," said d'Artagnan, laughing. "Porthos will repay you with the money of the Duchess Coquenard."

Saying these words, the Gascon mounted the stairs. Upon the most conspicuous door of the corridor was traced in black a gigantic "No. 1." The young man knocked, and upon the bidding to enter he walked into the apartment.

Porthos was in bed playing a game of lansquenet with Mousqueton. A spit loaded with partridges was turning before the fire. And on each side of a large chimney piece over two chafing dishes were boiling two stewpans, which exhaled a double odor of rabbit and fish stews most attractive to the sense of smell. In addition to this, d'Artagnan noticed that on top of a wardrobe were rows of empty bottles.

At sight of his friend, Porthos uttered a loud cry of

joy. And Mousqueton, rising respectfully, yielded his place to the young Gascon. He went over to give an eye to the two stewpans, of which he appeared to have the particular oversight.

"Ah, *pardieu,* is that you!" cried Porthos. "You are as welcome as flowers in spring. Excuse me if I do not go to meet you halfway. But," he added, looking at his friend uneasily, "you know what happened to me?"

"How could I know that?" asked d'Artagnan.

Porthos seemed to breathe more freely.

"I must tell you, then. You see, on making a thrust at my adversary, whom I had already hit three times, I slipped on a stone and sprained my knee."

"Truly?"

"Honor! Luckily for the rascal, I assure you!"

"And what became of him?"

"Oh, he had had enough, and set off without waiting for the rest I had in store for him."

"So this sprain in your knee keeps you in bed, my dear Porthos?"

"Surely. I shall be about again in a few days."

"But why did you not have yourself brought to Paris? You must be cruelly bored here."

"Just because I was bored, in order to amuse myself, I invited a gentleman who was traveling past to come up to see me. I proposed a cast of dice. He accepted my challenge. And, my faith, the seventy-five pistoles you had given me passed quickly from my pocket to his, without reckoning my horse, which he won into the bargain. But how has the world been treating you, d'Artagnan?"

"Oh, I am so-so. But, then, you are fortunate, Porthos. What do you care for the reverses of the gaming table? Happy rogue that you are! When you are out of funds, have you not your duchess who cannot fail to come to your aid?"

"Well, my dear d'Artagnan, just to show you in what hard luck I am playing," replied Porthos with the most careless air in the world, "I wrote to her to send me fifty louis or so."

"And—"

"She must be at her countryseat, for she has not answered me."

"But your host certainly behaves very well toward you, that's one comfort, at least," said d'Artagnan, directing the sick man's attention to the full stewpans and the empty bottles.

"On the contrary. Only three or four days ago the impertinent jackanapes presented his bill, and I was forced to turn him out of the door. So I am here something in the fashion of a conqueror who holds his position by right of conquest."

"And yet from time to time you must make *sorties*." Again the Gascon indicated the pans and the bottles.

"Not I, unfortunately!" said Porthos. "This miserable sprain confines me to my bed, but Mousqueton forages and brings in provisions. Friend Mousqueton, you see that we have a reinforcement, and so we must have an increase of supplies."

While Porthos and Mousqueton were breakfasting with the appetites of convalescents and with that brotherly cordiality which unites men in misfortune, d'Artagnan related how Aramis, being wounded, was obliged to stop at Crèvecœur; and how he had left Athos fighting at Amiens with four men who accused him of being a coiner; and how he, d'Artagnan, had been compelled to run the Comte de Wardes through the body in order to reach England.

But at that point the confidence of d'Artagnan stopped. He only added that on his return from Great Britain he had brought back four magnificent horses—one for himself and one for each of his companions. Then he informed Porthos that the animal intended for him was already installed in the stable of the tavern.

At this moment Planchet entered to inform his master that the horses were sufficiently rested and that it would be possible to sleep at Clermont.

As the young guardsman was tolerably reassured with regard to Porthos, and as he was anxious to obtain news of his other two friends, he held out his hand to the wounded man and told him he was about to resume the road to continue his search. As he reckoned upon returning by the same route in seven or eight days, if Porthos was still at the Great St. Martin he would call in for him on the way.

CHAPTER XXV

THE THESIS OF ARAMIS

D'Artagnan had said nothing to Porthos of his wound or of the wife of the procurator. Our Béarnais was a prudent lad, young as he was. Consequently he had appeared to believe all that the vainglorious musketeer had told him, for he was convinced that no friendship will hold out against a surprised secret, particularly if pride is interested in that secret.

As he journeyed along a profound sadness weighed upon his soul. He thought of the young and pretty Madame Bonacieux, who was to have paid him the price of his devotedness. He had no doubt but that she was a victim of the cardinal's vengeance, and everybody knew that the anger of his Eminence was terrible.

Nothing makes time pass more quickly than a thought which absorbs all the faculties of the one who is doing the thinking. External existence at such a time resembles a sleep of which this thought is a dream. Under its influence the passage of the hours has no longer a measure, space has no longer a distance. D'Artagnan traveled the six or eight leagues which separated Chantilly from Crèvecœur without being able later to remember any of the things he had met on the road.

There only his memory returned to him. He shook his head, the better to appreciate the reality of his situation. He perceived the cabaret at which he had left Aramis,

255

and, putting his horse to a trot, he shortly pulled up at the door.

This time it was not a host but a hostess who received him. His eye took in at a glance the plump, cheerful countenance of the mistress of the inn. And he at once perceived there was no occasion for dissembling with her, or of fearing anything from one blessed with such a joyous face.

"My good dame," d'Artagnan asked, "can you tell me what has become of one of my friends whom we were obliged to abandon here about a dozen days ago?"

"A handsome young man, four and twenty years old, mild, amiable, and well built?"

"That is he—wounded in the shoulder."

"Just so. Well, Monsieur, he is still here."

"Ah, *pardieu!* My dear dame," said the Gascon, springing from his horse and throwing the bridle to Planchet, "you restore me to life. Where is this dear Aramis? Let me embrace him. I am in a tearing hurry to see him again."

"Pardon, Monsieur, but I doubt if he can receive you just now."

"Why so? Has he a lady with him?"

"Saints alive! What do you mean by that? Poor lad! No, Monsieur, he has no feminine company."

"With whom is he, then?"

"With the curate of Montdidier and the superior of the Jesuits of Amiens."

"Good heavens!" cried the young guardsman. "Is he worse? Does he need the sacraments of holy church?"

"Quite the contrary, Monsieur. But divine grace touched him after his illness, and he determined to take orders."

"I see," said d'Artagnan. "I had forgotten that he was a musketeer only for the passing season."

"Monsieur still insists on seeing him?"

"More than ever, my good dame."

"Well, in that case, Monsieur has only to take the right-hand staircase in the courtyard and knock on No. 5 on the second floor."

D'Artagnan quickly gained the proper corridor, but there he found Bazin stationed before the door of his master barring his further passage. It had long been the dream of Bazin's life to serve a churchman, and he awaited with impatience the moment when Aramis should throw aside the uniform and assume the cassock. It may easily be understood that in the present disposition of his master nothing could be more disagreeable to Bazin than the arrival of d'Artagnan, which might cast Aramis back into that vortex of mundane affairs that so long and so successfully carried him away.

He resolved, therefore, to defend the door bravely. Betrayed by the mistress of the inn, he could not say that Aramis was absent, but he endeavored to persuade the newcomer that it would be the height of indiscretion to disturb his master in his pious conference.

But d'Artagnan took small heed of the eloquent discourse of M. Bazin. He simply moved him out of the way with one hand, and with the other turned the handle of the door to No. 5.

At the noise made by the guardsman in entering, Aramis lifted up his head and beheld his friend. But, to the great astonishment of the young man, the sight of him did not produce much effect upon the musketeer, so completely was his mind detached from the things of this world.

"Good day, dear d'Artagnan," said Aramis calmly. "Believe me, I am glad to see you."

"The same here, exactly!" replied the Gascon. "Although I am not yet sure it is Aramis to whom I am speaking."

"Why, what makes you doubt it, old fellow?"

"I was afraid I had made a mistake in the number of the room and had found my way into the apartment of some churchman. Then I thought you might be dangerously ill."

The superior of the Jesuits and the curate of Montdidier, two men in black, guessed the guardsman's meaning. They darted at him a glance which might have been thought threatening, but d'Artagnan took not the least heed of it.

"I disturb you, perhaps, my dear Aramis," continued the Gascon. "For, by what I see, I am led to believe that you are confessing to these two somber gentlemen."

Aramis colored imperceptibly. "You disturb me? On the contrary, dear friend, I swear. And, as a proof of what I say, permit me to declare I am rejoiced to see you safe and sound."

"That's not so bad!" thought d'Artagnan. "He'll come around."

"You arrive in good time, my dear fellow," said Aramis. 'And by taking part in our discussion you may assist us with your intelligence. Monsieur the Principal of Amiens, Monsieur the Curate of Montdidier, and I are arguing certain theological questions in which we are much interested. I shall be delighted to have your opinion."

"The opinion of a swordsman can have very little weight," replied the guardsman, who began to be uneasy at the turn things were taking. "You had better be satisfied with the knowledge of these two gentlemen."

The two men in black bowed in their turn.

"Oh, quite the contrary," asserted Aramis. "Your judgment will be very valuable to me. The question is this: Monsieur the Principal thinks my thesis ought to be dogmatic and didactic."

"Your thesis! Are you making one?"

"Without doubt," answered the Jesuit. "For the examination which precedes ordination a thesis is always requisite."

"Ordination!" cried d'Artagnan, who had not believed what the landlady and Bazin successively had told him. Half stupefied, he gazed upon the three persons before him.

Aramis cast a glance at d'Artagnan to see what effect this whole scene had produced, and found his friend gaping enough to split his jaws.

"Now," continued Aramis, taking the same graceful position in his easy-chair that he would have assumed in bed, "Monsieur the Principal is desirous my thesis should be dogmatic, while I, for my part, prefer that it should be ideal."

"Then," cried the Jesuit, "you persist in continuing that thesis which argues that verse is the proper vehicle for theology?"

"Yes, Father. I feel called upon to treat it and no other. I shall see you about the continuation of it, and tomorrow I hope you will be satisfied with the corrections I shall have made in consequence of your advice."

"Work slowly," said the curate. "We leave you in an excellent frame of mind."

"Yes, the ground is all sown," said the Jesuit.

"Farewell, my son," said the curate. "Till tomorrow."

"Till tomorrow, rash youth," said the Jesuit.

The two men in black arose, bowed to Aramis and d'Artagnan, and advanced toward the door. Aramis conducted them to the foot of the stairs and then immediately returned to the young Gascon, whose senses were still in a state of confusion.

When left alone, the two friends at first maintained an embarrassed silence. It became necessary, however, for one of them to break it sooner or later, and as d'Artagnan appeared determined to leave that honor to his companion, Aramis said, "You see that I have returned to my fundamental ideas."

"And so, Aramis, you are really going into the church? What will our two friends say? What will M. de Tréville say? They will treat you as a deserter, I warn you."

"I do not enter the church, dear d'Artagnan, I reënter it. For before I ever met you I had deserted the true life for the world."

"But why are you moved to go back to the religious

life today rather than yesterday or tomorrow? What has happened to you today to raise all these melancholy ideas?"

"This wound, my dear fellow, has been a warning from heaven."

"This wound! Bah, it is now nearly healed. And I am sure it is not that which gives you the most pain."

"What else could it be?" asked Aramis, blushing.

"It is a deeper and more terrible wound in your heart, Aramis, which is laying you low. And it was made by a woman."

The eye of Aramis kindled in spite of him.

"Ah," he smiled, dissembling his emotion under a feigned carelessness, "do not speak of such vain things! I think of such silliness and suffer love pains! According to your idea, then, my brain is turned. And for whom, perchance—for some grisette, some chambermaid with whom I have trifled by the roadside? Fie!"

"Pardon, my dear Aramis, but I thought you carried your ambitions much higher."

"Higher? And who am I to nourish such ambition? A poor musketeer, a beggar, an unknown, who hates slavery and finds himself ill-placed in the world."

"Aramis, Aramis!" cried d'Artagnan, looking at his friend with doubting air.

"Dust I am, and to dust I return. Life is full of humiliations and sorrows," he continued, becoming still more melancholy. "All the ties which attach a man to life break in his hand, particularly the golden ties. Oh, my dear d'Artagnan, trust my experience! Conceal your wounds when you have any—silence is the last joy of the unhappy. Beware of giving any one the clue to your griefs—the curious suck our tears as flies suck the blood of a wounded deer."

"Alas, Aramis," said d'Artagnan, in his turn heaving a profound sigh, "that is my history you are relating!"

"In what way?"

"Yes, a woman whom I love, whom I adore, has just been torn from me by force. I do not know where she is or whither they have conducted her. She is perhaps a prisoner or—dead!"

"But you have, no doubt, this consolation, at least— you can say that she did not quit you voluntarily. You can know that if you have no news of her, it is because all communication between you is interdicted, whereas I—"

"What?'

"Nothing," replied Aramis, "nothing."

"So you renounce the world, then, forever! It is a settled thing—an unalterable decision."

"Forever! You are my friend today; tomorrow you will be no more to me than a shadow, or rather, you will no longer even exist. As for the world, it is a sepulcher and nothing else."

"Well, then, let us say no more about it," suggested d'Artagnan. "And let us burn this letter which, no doubt, announces to you some fresh infidelity of your grisette or your chambermaid."

"What letter?" cried Aramis eagerly.

"A billet which was sent to your apartment in your absence and which was handed to me to bring to you."

"Oh, from whom is that letter?"

"From some heartbroken waiting woman, some desponding grisette. From Madame de Chevreuse's chambermaid, perhaps, who was obliged to return with her mistress to Tours and who, in order to appear smart and attractive, stole some perfumed paper and sealed her letter with a duchess' coronet."

"What do you say?"

"Hold! I must have lost it," said the young man maliciously, pretending to search for it. "But, fortunately, the world is a sepulcher. Man and consequently woman are shadows. And love is a sentiment to which you cry, 'Fie, fie!'"

"D'Artagnan," cried Aramis, "you are killing me!"

"Well, here it is at last!" said the Gascon as he drew the writing from his pocket.

Aramis made a bound, seized the dainty epistle, and read it—or rather, he devoured it, with a radiant countenance.

"This same waiting-maid seems to have an agreeable style," said the messenger carelessly.

"Thanks, d'Artagnan, thanks!" cried the musketeer, almost in a state of delirium. "She was forced to return to Tours, but she is not faithless, she still loves me! Come, my friend, let me embrace you. My happiness almost stifles me."

The two friends began to do a war dance around the statuette of St. Chrysostom, kicking the sheets of the thesis, which had been swept to the floor, here, there, and anywhere.

At that inopportune moment Bazin made his appearance with a lean repast consisting chiefly of spinach and an omelet.

"Be off with you, wretch!" threatened Aramis, throwing his skullcap in the face of the amazed servitor. "Return whence you came. Take back those horrible vegetables and that poor kickshaw! Order a larded hare, a fat capon, a leg of mutton dressed with garlic, and four bottles of old Burgundy."

Bazin, who looked at his master without comprehending the cause of this alteration, grew vastly melancholy. He allowed the omelet to slip into the spinach and the spinach to slide to the carpet.

"Now is the instant to consecrate yourself to the King of Kings," suggested d'Artagnan, "if you persist in offering him a civility. *Non inutile desiderium oblatione.*"

"Go to the devil with your Latin! Let us drink, my dear young Gascon, *morbleu!* Let us drink while the wine is newly opened, and heartily, famously! And while we are doing this, you may tell me, my chosen comrade, a little of what has been going on in the world yonder."

CHAPTER XXVI

THE WIFE OF ATHOS

"We have now to search for Athos," said d'Artagnan to the vivacious Aramis, when he had informed him of all that had passed since their departure from Paris. An excellent dinner had made them forget, one his thesis, the other his fatigue.

"Do you really believe that any harm can have come to him?" asked the musketeer. "Athos is so cool, so brave, and handles his sword so skillfully."

"No doubt. And nobody has a higher opinion of his courage and his cleverness than I have. Still, I like better to hear my blade clang against lances than against staves. I fear lest Athos may have been beaten down by serving-men. Those fellows strike hard and don't leave off in a hurry. That is why I wish to set off at the first possible moment."

"I shall try to accompany you," promised Aramis, "though I scarcely feel in a condition to mount on horse-back. Yesterday I undertook to use that whip you see hanging against the wall, but pain prevented my continuing the pious exercise."

"That's the first time I ever heard of anybody's trying to cure gunshot wounds with cat-o'-nine-tails. But you were ill, and sickness renders the brain weak; therefore you may be excused."

"When do you mean to set out?"

"Tomorrow at daybreak. Sleep as soundly as you can tonight."

"Until morning, then!" said Aramis. "For iron-nerved as you are, d'Artagnan, you must need repose."

The next morning when the Gascon entered the musketeer's chamber, he found him at the window.

"What are you looking at?" asked d'Artagnan.

"My faith! I am admiring three magnificent horses which the stable boys are leading about. It would be a princely pleasure to travel upon such steeds."

"Well, Monsieur, that joy is yours. Choose which one of the three animals you prefer."

"And the rich caparison, that will be mine too, eh?"

"Of course."

"You are mocking me, d'Artagnan."

"Oh, no, I have ceased laughing at you, now that you speak French instead of the Latin of the Jesuits."

"You mean to say that those rich holsters, that velvet housing, that saddle studded with silver are all for me?"

"For you and nobody else, *mon ami*. Just as surely as that the animal pawing the ground yonder is mine, and that other horse which is caracoling belongs to Athos."

"*Peste!* They are three superb creatures. It must have been the king himself who made you such a present."

"Certainly it was not the cardinal. But don't trouble yourself whence they come. Think only that one of the three is your property."

"I choose the one the red-haired boy is leading."

"It is yours."

"Good heaven! That is enough to drive away the last

traces of my dolor. I could mount such a steed with thirty musket balls in my body! On my soul, those are handsome stirrups, too! Holla, Bazin, come here this moment!"

Bazin appeared on the threshold, dull and spiritless.

"Furbish my sword, put my hat to rights, brush my cloak, and load my pistols!" said Aramis.

"That last order is unnecessary," d'Artagnan intervened. "There are loaded pistols in your holsters."

Bazin sighed like an expiring ox.

"Oh, come, M. Bazin!" counseled d'Artagnan. "Do not take things so hard. People of all conditions gain the kingdom of heaven."

"Monsieur was already such a good theologian," said Bazin, almost weeping. "He would have become a bishop certainly, and perhaps a cardinal in a red robe."

"Well, but just reflect a little, you. Of what use is it nowadays to be a churchman, pray? You do not avoid going to war by that means. You see, Richelieu is about to make the next campaign, helm on head and partisan in hand. And M. de Nogaret de la Valette, what do they say of him? He is a cardinal likewise. Ask his lackey how often he has had to prepare lint for him."

"Alas!" groaned Bazin. "I know it, Monsieur. Everything is turning topsy-turvy in the world now."

While this dialogue was going on, the two young men and the poor lackey went downstairs.

"Hold my stirrup, Bazin," said Aramis. And he sprang into the saddle with his customary grace and agility. But after a few vaults and curvets of the noble animal, his rider felt his pains come on so insupportably that he turned pale and became unsteady in his seat. D'Artagnan had foreseen such an event and had kept a watchful eye upon him. He sprang therefore quickly to Aramis, caught him in his arms, and assisted him up to his chamber.

"That's all right, my dear Aramis, take care of yourself," he consoled the musketeer. "I'll find Athos without your help."

"You are a man of bronze," replied Aramis.

"Nonsense. I have good luck, that's all. But how do you mean to spend your time until I come back? No more theses, mind you!"

Aramis smiled. "I shall make verses," he said.

"Yes, I dare say you will. Verses perfumed with the odor of the billet from the attendant of Madame de Chevreuse. Teach Bazin the rules of meter and rhyme—that will console him. As to the horse, ride a little each day, and that will accustom you to his maneuvers."

"Oh, make yourself easy on that head," observed Aramis. "You will find me ready to follow you on your return."

They took leave of each other. D'Artagnan commended his friend to the especial care of his landlady and his servant. Ten minutes later the young guardsman was trotting along in the direction of Amiens.

How was he going to find Athos? Should he find him at all? The situation in which he had left his friend was most critical—he probably had succumbed. This idea, while darkening his brow, drew several sighs from him and caused him to formulate to himself a few vows of vengeance.

"Well," said d'Artagnan aloud, "poor Athos is perhaps at this moment dead, and all through my fault. For it was I who dragged him into the affair of the studs. He did not know the beginning of the quest, is ignorant of the result, and from it can derive no possible advantage."

"Without reckoning, Monsieur," added Planchet, "that we undoubtedly owe our lives to him. Do you remember how he cried, 'On, d'Artagnan, on! I am taken'? And when he had discharged his two pistols, what a terrible noise he made with his sword! One might have thought that twenty men, or rather twenty devils, were fighting."

These words redoubled the eagerness of the guardsman, who urged his horse, though the animal stood in need of no incitement, and they proceeded at a rapid pace. About eleven o'clock in the morning they came in sight of Amiens, and at half-past eleven they were at the door of the accursed inn.

D'Artagnan had often meditated against the perfidious host one of those hearty vengeances which offer consolation by merely thinking of them. He entered the hostelry with his hat drawn down over his eyes, his left hand on the pommel of his sword, and cracking his whip with his right hand.

"Do you remember me?" he asked the landlord, who was advancing to meet him.

"I have not that honor, Monseigneur," replied the latter, his eyes fairly dazzled by the brilliant style in which d'Artagnan was traveling.

"Well, two words will refresh your memory. What have you done with that gentleman against whom you had

the audacity, about twelve days ago, to make an accusation
of passing false money?"

The host became as pale as death. For the Gascon had
assumed a truculent attitude, and Planchet modeled himself
after his master.

"Deign to listen to me, Monseigneur, and be merciful!"

D'Artagnan, mute with anger and anxiety, took a seat
with the attitude of a suspicious judge. Planchet glared
fiercely over the back of his armchair.

"I had been warned," began the innkeeper, "by the
authorities that a celebrated coiner of bad money would
arrive at my tavern, together with several of his companions, all disguised as guards or musketeers. I was
furnished with a description of your horses, Monseigneur,
of your lackeys, and of yourselves—nothing at all was
omitted."

"Proceed," said the young Gascon, who understood
quickly enough the source of so exact a description.

"In conformance with the orders of the authorities,
who sent me a reinforcement of six men, I then took such
measures as I thought necessary to seize the persons of
the pretended coiners."

"Again that word!" said d'Artagnan, whose ears
chafed terribly at the repetition of this word *coiners*.

"Patience, Monseigneur! There happened then that
which you already know. Your friend defended himself
desperately. He disabled two men with his pistols, retreated fighting with his sword, put one of my men out
of business, and stunned me with a blow of the flat side
of it."

"You villain, will you finish the tale?" cried the guards-man. "What became of Athos?"

"While fighting and retreating, he found the cellar stairs behind him. As the door was open, he took out the key and barricaded himself inside. As the authorities were sure of finding him there they left him alone."

"Oh, I see! You did not really wish to kill him. You only wanted to imprison him."

"Heavens above us! To imprison him, Monseigneur? Why, he imprisoned himself. I swear to you he did. And he made rough work of it—one man was killed on the spot, and two others severely wounded. And when I ran to Monsieur the Governor and told him what had happened, he informed me that if I had the audacity to mention his name as being concerned in the disturbance, he would have me hanged."

"But where is Athos now?"

"In the cellar, Monsieur."

"Scoundrel! Have you kept him there all this time?"

"We keep him in the cellar? Merciful heavens, no! You do not know what he is up to down there. Ah, if you could only persuade him to come out, Monsieur, I should adore you as my patron saint."

"Then I shall find him in this dungeon?"

"Without doubt, Monsieur. He persists in remaining there. Every day we pass him through the air hole some bread at the end of a fork. We give him meat when he wishes it. But, alas, it is not of meat and bread that he makes the greatest consumption."

"How do you know?"

"One day I endeavored to go down with two of my servants. He flew into a terrible rage. I heard the noise he made in loading his pistols and the servant in loading his musketoon. Then, when we asked what their intentions were, your friend replied that he had forty charges to fire. And he said he and his lackey would use up their entire stock of ammunition before he would allow a single soul of us to set foot below the ground. Upon this, I went and complained to the governor, who answered that I had only received my just deserts, and that this occurrence might perhaps teach me not to insult honorable gentlemen who took up their abode with me."

"So that since that time—" replied d'Artagnan, totally unable to refrain from laughter at the pitiable face of the host.

"From that time, Monsieur, we have led the most deplorable existence imaginable. For you must know, Monsieur, that all our provisions are in the cellar. There is our wine in bottles, and our wine in casks. The beer, the oil, the spices, the bacon, the sausages are stored there. And as we are prevented from descending, we are forced to refuse food and drink to travelers, so our hostelry is daily going to ruin. If your friend remains one more week, I shall be a ruined man."

"And nothing more than what you deserve, you ass! Could you not tell by our appearance that we were people of quality?"

"Yes, Monsieur, you are right," said the host. "But, my prophetic soul! Hark, hark! What is that? Oh, there he goes again!"

"Somebody has disturbed him, no doubt," suggested d'Artagnan.

"But he must be disturbed," cried the host in anguish. "Here are two English gentlemen just arrived."

"Well, what of that?"

"Well, the English like good wine, as you know, Monsieur. These gentlemen have asked for our best. My wife has perhaps requested permission of M. Athos to go into the cellar to satisfy the thirst of these cavaliers, and he as usual has refused. Ah, good heavens! The hullabaloo is growing louder than ever."

The young Gascon, in fact, heard a great noise from the direction of the cellar. He rose and, preceded by the landlord wringing his hands, and followed by Planchet with his musketoon ready for use, he approached the scene of action.

The two gentlemen were exasperated. They had had a long ride and were dying of hunger and thirst.

"But this is tyranny!" cried one of them in very good French, although with a foreign accent. "To think that this madman will not permit these good people access to their own wine! Let us break open the door, and if he is too far gone in his madness to be safe, we shall kill him."

"Softly, gentlemen!" said d'Artagnan, drawing his pistols from his belt, "you will kill nobody, if you please."

"Good, good!" called the calm voice of Athos from the other side of the door. "Just let them enter, these devourers of little children, and we shall see."

Brave as they appeared to be, the English gentlemen looked at each other hesitatingly. One might have thought there was in that underground room one of those famished ogres—the gigantic heroes of popular legend—into whose cavern nobody could force his way with impunity.

There was a tense moment of silence. But at length the two Englishmen were ashamed to draw back, and the angrier one descended the five or six steps that led down to the cellar, giving the door a kick stout enough to split an ordinary wall.

"Planchet," said d'Artagnan, cocking his pistols, "I shall take charge of the one at the top. You look to the one below. Ah, sirs, you want battle. And you shall have it."

"Good Lord!" cried the hollow voice of Athos. "I can hear my friend d'Artagnan, I think."

"Yes," called the Gascon, who in turn raised his voice, "I am here, old fellow."

"That is good," replied the musketeer. "We shall teach them a lesson, these wretched breakers of doors."

The Englishmen had drawn their swords, but found themselves caught between two fires. They still hesitated an instant. But, as before, pride prevailed, and a second kick split the door from top to bottom.

"Stand one side, d'Artagnan," shouted Athos, "I am going to fire."

"Gentlemen," exclaimed the young guardsman, whom prudence but rarely abandoned, "think of what you are about! Be patient, Athos. You are running your heads into a very silly affair. You will be riddled. My lackey and I have three shots at you, and you will receive as many from the cellar. You will then have our swords to face, and I assure you bluntly, my friend and I can play with them tolerably well. Let me conduct your business and my own. You shall soon have something to drink, I give you my word."

"If there is anything left," mumbled the jeering voice of the concealed Athos.

The landlord felt a cold sweat creep down his back.

"What the devil! There must be plenty left," replied the Gascon. "Be satisfied of that—these two cannot have drunk the whole cellar. Gentlemen, replace your swords in their scabbards."

"Provided you return your pistols to your belt."

"Willingly."

And d'Artagnan set the example of disarmament. Then, turning toward Planchet, he made him a sign to uncock his musketoon.

The Englishmen, convinced by these peaceful proceedings, sheathed their swords grumblingly. The history of Athos' imprisonment was then related to them by the guardsman. And as they really were of gentle birth and breeding the Britishers pronounced the landlord to be in the wrong.

"Now, gentlemen," urged d'Artagnan, "go up to your room again. And in ten minutes, I shall answer for it, you shall have all you desire."

The Englishmen bowed and went upstairs.

"And now, Athos, I am alone," said the Gascon. "Open the door, I beg of you."

"Instanter," said Athos.

Then was heard a great noise of fagots being removed

and of the groaning of posts. These were the counter-
scarps and bastions of Athos, which the besieged himself
was demolishing.

A moment later the broken door was removed, and the
pale face of Athos appeared. D'Artagnan threw himself
on his friend's neck and embraced him tenderly. He then
tried to draw him from his moist abode, but to his surprise
he noticed that Athos staggered.

"You are wounded," he cried.

"Not at all. I am simply very drunk, and no wonder,
for, my good host, I must have consumed at least one
hundred and fifty flasks."

"Mercy!" shouted the host. "If the lackey has drunk
only half as much as his master, I am a ruined man."

"Grimaud is a well-bred servant. He would never
think of faring in the same fashion as his employer—he
drank entirely from the cask. Mark you, I do not think
he troubled to replace the spigot! Do you hear? It is
running full-head now."

D'Artagnan burst into a laugh which changed the
chills of the landlord into a burning fever.

In the meantime Grimaud appeared in his turn behind
his master, with his musketoon on his shoulder and his
head shaking like one of those drunken satyrs in the pic-
tures of Rubens. He was moistened behind and before
with a greasy liquid which the frenzied landlord recognized
as his best olive oil.

Beyond the fortifications through which Athos had
made a breach in order to get out, they found, swimming
in puddles of oil and wine, the bones and fragments of

the hams that had been eaten. While a heap of broken bottles filled the whole left-hand corner of the cellar, a tun, the cock of which was left open, was yielding its last drop of blood. Of fifty large sausages suspended from the joists, but ten or twelve remained.

Then the lamentations of the host and hostess pierced the vault of the ceiling. To grief succeeded rage. The landlord armed himself with a spit and rushed into the chamber now occupied by the two friends.

"Some wine!" ordered Athos, on perceiving the landlord.

"Some wine, did you say?" cried the stupefied host. "Why, man, you have drunk more than a hundred pistoles' worth!"

"Bah!" retorted Athos, "we were always dry."

"If you had only been contented with drinking, Monsieur! But you went and broke all the bottles."

"You pushed me upon a pile of them and they rolled down. That was your fault."

"All my oil is lost!"

"Oil is a sovereign balm for wounds. And my poor Grimaud here was obliged to dress those you had inflicted upon him."

"All my sausages are gnawed."

"There is an enormous quantity of rats in that cellar."

The host drew back and burst into tears.

"This will teach you," said d'Artagnan, "to treat the guests God sends you in a more courteous manner."

"God? Say the devil, rather, Monsieur."

"My dear friend," threatened the Gascon, "if you

annoy us further, we shall all four shut ourselves up in that cellar, and we shall see whether the mischief is as great as you say."

"Oh, gentlemen," sobbed the host, "I have been wrong and I confess it. But there is pardon for every sin. You are gentlemen and I am a poor innkeeper. Won't you have pity on me?"

"Ah, if you speak in that way," said Athos, "you will break my heart, and the tears will flow from my eyes as the wine flowed from the cask. Come hither. Let us talk."

The landlord approached with hesitation.

"Come hither, I say, and do not be afraid," continued the musketeer. "At the very moment when I was about to pay you, some twelve days ago, I placed my purse on the table."

"Yes, Monsieur."

"That bag contained sixty pistoles—where is it?"

"Deposited with the justice, Monsieur. They swore it was counterfeit money."

"Very well. Get me the purse back and keep the sixty pistoles."

"But Monseigneur knows very well that justice never lets go of anything it once gets hold of. If it were bad money, there might be some slight hope, but unfortunately the money is good."

"Manage the matter as best you can, my good man. It does not concern me, the more so as I have not a livre left."

"Come," said d'Artagnan, "let us inquire further. Where is the horse of Monsieur Athos?"

"In the stable."

"How much is it worth?"

"Fifty pistoles at most."

"It is worth eighty. Take it, and that ends the matter."

"What!" cried Athos, "you are selling my horse—my Bajazet? And pray upon what shall I make my campaign —upon Grimaud?"

"I have brought you another," said the Gascon.

"A magnificent one it is!" exclaimed the host.

"Well, since there is another finer and younger, why, you may take the old one. And let us drink."

"What do you desire?" asked the host, quite cheerful again.

"Six of the bottles at the bottom, near the laths. There are twenty-five bottles of that sort left, all the rest were broken by my fall."

"And don't forget," d'Artagnan reminded the landlord, "to take four bottles of the same label to the two Englishmen."

"And now," said Athos, "while they are bringing the wine, tell me, d'Artagnan, what has become of the others."

The young guardsman related how he had found Porthos in bed with a sprained knee, and Aramis at a table between two theologians. As he finished his story, the host entered with the wine they had ordered and a ham which, fortunately for him, had been left out of the cellar.

"All right!" said the musketeer, filling his glass and that of his friend. "Here's to the other two Inseparables! But you, my dear d'Artagnan, what has happened to you personally? I must say, you wear a sad expression."

10

Thus encouraged, the Gascon related his adventures with Madame Bonacieux. Athos listened to him without a frown, but when he had finished, said, "Trifles, only trifles!" This was his favorite word.

"You always say *trifles,* my dear Athos!" objected d'Artagnan. "And that comes very ill from you who have never loved."

The deadened eye of Athos flashed, but only for an instant. It became dull and lifeless as before.

"Your misfortune in the matter of Madame Bonacieux is laughable," continued Athos, shrugging his shoulders. "I should like to know what you would say if I were to spin you a real yarn about love!"

"Something that happened to you?"

"Or to one of my friends—what matters it?"

"Tell it to me, Athos."

"I'll do it better if my lips are wet."

"Drink all you please, but do not keep me waiting."

"Not a bad idea of yours about drinking all I please!" remarked Athos, emptying and refilling his glass several times. "Drink and talk seem to agree marvelously well."

"I am all attention," d'Artagnan reminded him.

Athos collected himself, and in proportion as he did so, the Gascon perceived that he became pale. He was at that period of intoxication where vulgar drinkers fall down and sleep. He kept himself upright and dreamed without sleeping. This somnambulism of inebriety had something frightful in it.

"One of my friends, a count of the province of Berry, noble as a Dandolo or a Montmorency, at twenty-five years of age fell in love with a girl of sixteen. She was as beautiful as fancy can paint. Through the ingenuousness of her age beamed an ardent mind, not of the woman, but of the poet. She did not please, she intoxicated.

"She lived in a small town with her brother, a curate— both had recently come into the country. Nobody knew whence they came, and on seeing her so lovely, and her brother so pious, no one thought of making inquiry. They were said, however, to be of good extraction. My friend, who was seigneur of the country, might have taken the girl by force if he had wished—for he was the master. Unfortunately, he was an honest man; he married her. Oh, the fool, the ass, the idiot!"

"Why, how so, if he loved her?" asked d'Artagnan.

"Wait!" said Athos. "He took her to his château and made her the first lady of the province. And, in justice, it must be allowed that she supported her rank becomingly."

"Well?" asked d'Artagnan.

"Well, one day when she was hunting with her husband," continued Athos in a low voice and speaking very quickly, "she fell from her horse and fainted. The count flew to her help, and as she appeared to be oppressed by her clothes, he ripped them open with his poniard and in so doing laid bare her shoulder. D'Artagnan," demanded Athos, with a maniacal burst of laughter, "guess what she had on her shoulder."

"How can I tell?" said the Gascon.

"A fleur-de-lis," said Athos. "She was branded."

The musketeer emptied at a single draught the glass he was holding in his hand.

"Horrors!" cried the guardsman.

"Truth, my friend. The angel was a demon. The poor young girl had stolen the sacred vessels from a church."

"And what did the count do?"

"He was of the highest nobility. He had on his estates the right of high and low tribunals. He tore the dress of the countess to pieces. He tied her hands behind her and hanged her to a tree."

"Heavens, Athos, a murder!"

"No less," answered the musketeer, as pale as a corpse. "But methinks I need wine!" And he seized by the neck the last bottle, placed it to his lips, and emptied it at a single draught as he would have emptied a single glass.

Then he let his head sink upon his two hands while the Gascon stood before him, stupefied.

"That has cured me of beautiful and loving women," said Athos after a considerable pause. He raised his head, forgetting to continue the fiction of the count. "God grant you as much! Let us drink."

"Then she is dead?" stammered d'Artagnan.

"*Parbleu!*" said Athos. "But hold out your glass. Some ham, my boy, or we can't continue to drink."

"And her brother?" added d'Artagnan timidly.

"Oh, I inquired after him for the purpose of hanging him, too. But he was beforehand with me. He had quitted the curacy the night previous."

"Was it ever known who this miserable fellow was?"

"He was doubtless the first lover and the accomplice of the fair lady. A worthy man who had pretended to be a curate for the purpose of getting his mistress married and securing her a position. He has been hanged and quartered, I hope."

D'Artagnan was quite stunned by the relation of this horrible adventure.

"Taste some of this ham, my boy. It is exquisite," said Athos, cutting a slice and putting it on the young man's plate. "I could drink fifty bottles more."

The guardsman could no longer endure the conversation, which had entirely saddened and bewildered him. Allowing his head to sink on his two hands, he pretended to fall asleep.

"These young fellows can none of them drink properly," observed Athos, looking at his friend in pity. "And yet this lad is one of the best of them, at that!"

CHAPTER XXVII

THE RETURN

D'Artagnan went into his friend's chamber the next morning with a fixed determination to renew the talk of the preceding evening. But he found Athos quite himself again, that is to say, the most shrewd and impenetrable of men. So the musketeer, after having exchanged a hearty shake of the hand with the Gascon, broached the matter first.

"I had drunk more or less wine yesterday, d'Artagnan," he said. "I can tell that by my tongue, which is slightly swollen and hot this morning, and by my pulse, which is the least bit tremulous. I'll wager that I uttered a thousand extravagances."

While saying this, Athos looked at his friend with an earnestness that embarrassed him.

"No," replied the guardsman, "if I recollect well what you said, it was nothing out of the common way."

"You surprise me. I thought I had related to you a most lamentable history." And he looked at the young man as if he would probe to the bottom of his heart.

"My faith," said d'Artagnan innocently, "I must have been more bemused than you, since I recall nothing of the kind."

Athos did not trust this reply; so he resumed: "You cannot have failed to remark, my dear friend, that every one has his particular kind of wine mood, grave or gay.

My mood, after wine, is always sad. And when I have been really imbibing, it is my mania to relate all the lugubrious histories which, in impressionable childhood, my foolish nurse implanted in my brain. This is a failing, I admit. But, with that sole exception, I am a fairly successful drinker."

Athos spoke all this in so natural a manner that d'Artagnan was somewhat shaken in his conviction that Athos had really given him a terrible confidence.

"I remember as if in a dream," said the young guardsman, "that we were speaking of hanging."

"Ah, you see how it is," observed Athos, becoming still paler, but still attempting to laugh. "I was sure I had got going on my hobby—the hanging of people is my nightmare."

D'Artagnan remained silent. And then, changing the conversation all at once, Athos said, "By the way, thank you for the horse you brought me."

"Is it to your mind?"

"Quite. But it is not a horse for hard work."

"You are mistaken. I rode it nearly ten leagues in less than an hour and a half and it appeared no more blown or distressed than if it had only made the tour of the Place St. Sulpice."

"Ah, you begin to awaken my regret."

"Regret, did you say?"

"Yes. I parted with it some time ago."

"How?"

"Why, here is the simple fact. This morning I awoke at six oclock. You were still fast asleep and I did not know what to do with myself. I was still stupid from our yesterday's drinking bout. Now, as I came into the public room downstairs, I saw one of our Englishmen bargaining with a dealer for a horse, his having died yesterday from bleeding. I drew near and found he was bidding a hundred pistoles for a fine chestnut nag."

"I am afraid of what you are about to tell me, Athos."

"*Pardieu,* my boy, there is nothing to fear. I told the Englishman I had a fine horse for sale. He said he had seen my lackey leading it and wished to know if I would take a hundred pistoles for it. I said no, but that I would play at dice for the beast. No sooner said than done. And I lost the horse. Ah, ah, but please observe that I won back the equipage."

D'Artagnan looked much disconcerted.

"That vexes you?" asked Athos.

"Well, I must confess it does," replied the guardsman. "That horse was to have identified us in the day of battle. It was a pledge, a remembrance. Athos, you have done wrong."

"But, my dear friend, put yourself in my place," said the musketeer. "I was bored stiff, and what is more, on my honor, I don't fancy English horses. If it is a question only of being recognized in battle, why, the saddle will suffice for that! It is quite remarkable enough. And, as to the horse, we can easily find some excuse for its disappearance. What the devil! A horse is mortal, and perhaps mine had the glanders or the farcy, anyway."

D'Artagnan did not smile.

"It makes me unhappy that you attach so much importance to the horses," continued Athos, "for I am not at the end of my story."

"What else have you done?"

"After having lost my own horse, nine against ten— see how near a thing it was?—I formed the idea of staking yours."

"But you stopped at the idea, I hope?"

"No, for I put the plan into immediate execution."

"And with what result?" asked d'Artagnan anxiously.

"I threw the dice and I lost."

"What! My horse?"

"Your horse, seven against eight—just one point short."

"Athos, you are not in your right senses, I swear."

"My dear lad, you could have told me that yesterday when I was manufacturing silly stories, but not this morning. I lost your horse with all its appointments."

"Really, this is hair-raising!"

"Stop a moment, you don't know all yet. I should make an excellent gambler, if I only were not so hot-headed."

"Well, but what else could you play for? You had nothing left."

"Yes I did, my friend. There was still that diamond that sparkles on your finger and which I noticed yesterday."

"This jewel!" cried the horrified d'Artagnan, placing his hand quickly over his ring.

"And as I am a connoisseur of such things, having had a few of my own once, I estimated its value at a thousand pistoles."

"Athos, you make me tremble!" exclaimed the Gascon.

"My adversary had likewise remarked the stone. What the devil! My dear fellow, do you think you can wear a star from heaven on your finger and nobody observe it? Well, we divided this diamond into ten parts of one hundred pistoles each—in ten throws, without revenge. In thirteen throws I had lost all—in thirteen throws, mind you! The number thirteen was always fatal to me. It was on July 13—"

"*Ventrebleu!*" cried d'Artagnan, rising from the table.

"Patience!" said Athos. "I had a plan. The Englishman was an original fellow. I had seen him conversing that morning with Grimaud, making the lackey proposals to enter into his service. I therefore staked Grimaud, the silent Grimaud, divided into ten portions."

"Well, what next?" demanded d'Artagnan, laughing in spite of himself.

"Why, with the ten parts of Grimaud, which are not worth a picayune, I regained the diamond. Tell me, now, if persistence is not a virtue?"

"My faith, but this is droll!" cried the guardsman, consoled and holding his sides in laughter.

"You may guess that, finding the luck turned, I again staked the diamond ring."

"The devil you did!" exclaimed the Gascon, becoming angry again.

"I won back your harness, then your horse, then my harness, then my horse, and then I lost again. In brief, I finally regained your harness and mine. That's where we are. The last was so superb a throw that I left off right there."

D'Artagnan breathed as if the whole hostelry had been removed from his chest.

"Then the diamond is safe?" he inquired timidly.

"Intact, my dear friend, besides the harness of your Bucephalus and mine."

"But what is the use of harnesses without horses?"

"I have an idea regarding them."

"Athos, you make me shudder again."

"Listen to me. You have not played for a long time, d'Artagnan?"

"No. And I have no inclination to do so."

"Make no promises to yourself! You have not played for a long time, I said. You ought then to have a lucky hand."

"Well, what of it?"

"Just this: the Englishman and his companion are still here. I notice that he regretted losing the horse trappings exceedingly. You appear to think a great deal of your horse. In your place I should stake the trappings against the horse."

"But he would not care for only one harness."

"Stake them both, *pardieu!* I am not selfish, as you are."

"You would do so if you were I?" asked the Gascon, undecided.

"On my honor. Everything on a single throw of the dice."

Athos went in quest of the Englishman, whom he found in the stable examining the trappings with a greedy eye. The opportunity was good. The musketeer proposed the conditions—the two harnesses against either one horse or one hundred pistoles. The Englishman consented.

D'Artagnan threw the dice with a trembling hand, and turned up the number three. His paleness terrified Athos, who, however, contented himself with saying, "That's a sad fall of the dice, comrade. You will have your horses fully equipped, Monsieur."

The triumphant Englishman did not even take the trouble to shake the dice. He threw them on the table without glancing at them, so sure was he of victory. D'Artagnan turned aside to conceal his gloom.

"Hold!" said Athos in his quiet voice. "That throw of yours, Monsieur, is extraordinary. I have not seen such a one but four times in my life. Two aces!"

The Englishman looked and was overcome with astonishment. "Then Monsieur d'Artagnan takes his horse back again," he said.

"One moment!" said Athos. "With your permission, Monsieur, I wish to speak a word aside with my friend."

"Tempter! What do you want with me now?" inquired the Gascon.

"I only wish you to reflect, my lad. If I were you, I should take the hundred pistoles."

"But I prefer to take the horse, Athos."

"In which decision you are wrong, little man. Of what use is one animal for two of us? I could not ride behind. You cannot think of humiliating me by prancing along at my side on that magnificent charger. And we want money for our return to Paris."

"I am greatly attached to that horse, Athos."

"A master must feed his horse, d'Artagnan, but the hundred pistoles will feed the master."

"But how shall we get back, then?"

"Upon our lackey's nags, *pardieu!* Anybody can see by our bearing that we are people of circumstance. With the hundred pistoles we can live well to the end of the month. We have undergone a great deal of fatigue, remember, and a little rest will do us no harm."

"I rest? Oh, no, Athos. Once in Paris, I shall prosecute my search for Madame Bonacieux very vigorously."

"For that end your horse will not be half so serviceable as good golden louis. Take the hundred pistoles, friend."

D'Artagnan never required two reasons where one was sufficient. He acquiesced, and the Englishman paid the money on the spot.

They then determined to depart. Peace with the landlord cost, in addition to Athos' old horse, six pistoles. The two soldiers took the nags of Planchet and Grimaud, and the lackeys started off on foot, carrying the saddles on their heads.

However badly our two friends were mounted, they were soon far in advance of the servants and arrived at Crèvecœur. From a distance they beheld Aramis seated in a melancholy pose at his window, looking out, like Sister Anne, at the dust on the horizon.

"Hello! What the devil are you doing there?" cried the friends.

"I am reflecting upon the rapidity with which the blessings of this world take wings and fly away," answered Aramis. "My English horse, which has just disappeared amid a cloud of dust, has furnished me a living example of the fragility of earthly things."

"Which means—" said d'Artagnan, who began to suspect the truth.

"That I have just been duped. Sixty louis for a horse which by the manner of his gait can do at least five leagues an hour."

D'Artagnan and Athos laughed aloud.

"Don't be too angry with me," pleaded Aramis. "Necessity knows no law. Besides, I am the person punished, as that rascally horse dealer has robbed me of fifty louis at least. Ah, you fellows are good managers! You ride on your lackeys' horses, and have your own gallant steeds led along carefully by hand, by short stages."

At the same instant a market cart, which some minutes before had appeared on the Amiens road, pulled up at the inn, and Planchet and Grimaud came out of it with the saddles on their heads. The cart was returning empty to Paris, and the two servants had agreed, in return for their transportation, to slake the wagoner's thirst along the way.

"What is this?" asked Aramis, on seeing them arrive. "Is nothing left but the saddles?"

"Now you understand," remarked Athos.

"My friends, that is exactly like me. I retained my harness by instinct. Hello, Bazin! Bring my new saddle and carry it along with those of these gentlemen."

"And so, my friends, we are now ready to march upon Porthos," said the young Gascon.

"Bravo! You cannot think how I have missed him, the great simpleton," continued Aramis. "To see him so self-satisfied reconciles me with myself. He would not sell his horse, not for a kingdom. I think I can see him now mounted upon his superb animal. I am sure he will look like the Great Mogul."

They made a halt of an hour to refresh their horses. Aramis paid his bill, placed Bazin in the cart with his comrades, and they set out to join Porthos.

They found him up from bed, less pale than when d'Artagnan left him after his first visit, and seated at a table on which, though he was alone, was spread enough for four persons. This dinner consisted of meats nicely dressed, choice wines, and wonderful fruit.

"Ah, *pardieu!*" he said, rising, "you have come in the nick of time, gentlemen. I was just beginning the soup, and you will dine with me."

"But this lordly dinner was not intended for you alone, Porthos?" asked Aramis.

"No," said Porthos, "I expected some gentlemen of the neighborhood who have just sent me word they could not come. You will take their places, and I shall not lose by the exchange. Here you, Mousqueton, seats, and order double the number of bottles!"

"Do you know what we are eating?" inquired Athos at the end of ten minutes.

"*Peste!*" replied d'Artagnan, "for my part, I am devouring veal garnished with shrimps and vegetables."

"And I some lamb chops," said Porthos.

"And I a plain chicken," said Aramis.

"You are all mistaken, Messieurs," answered Athos gravely. "You are eating horse."

"Eating what?" said d'Artagnan.

"Horse!" cried Aramis. "Good heavens!"

"Yes, horse," persisted Athos, "are we not, mine host? Horse and perhaps his saddle therewith."

"Not the saddle, gentlemen, I have kept the harness," asserted Porthos.

"Faith! we are all alike," said Aramis. "One would think we had tipped our friend the wink."

"What could I do?" demanded Porthos. "This English horse made my visitors ashamed of theirs, and I do not like to humiliate people."

"Then your duchess is still taking the waters?" asked the Gascon.

"Still," replied Porthos. "And, on my honor, the governor of the province—one of the expected guests today—seemed to have such a wish for the animal that I gave it to him."

"Made him a present of it?" cried d'Artagnan.

"My God, that's just the phrase for it," retorted Porthos. "For the beast was worth at least a hundred and fifty louis, and the stingy fellow would give me only eighty."

"Without the saddle?" said Aramis.

"Yes, without the saddle."

"You will observe, Messieurs," said Athos, "that Porthos has made the best bargain of any of us."

"There is one comfort, we are all in cash," said d'Artagnan.

"Well, as to that," began Athos, "I found Aramis' Spanish wine so good that I sent on a hamper of sixty bottles of it in the wagon with the lackeys. That weakened my purse."

"And I," confessed Aramis, "—just imagine it—I have given almost my last sou to the church at Montdidier and the Jesuits of Amiens, with whom I made engagements which I ought to have kept. I ordered masses for my soul and for yours, gentlemen. I have no doubt you will be marvelously benefited."

"And I," said Porthos, "do you think my sprain cost me nothing—without reckoning Mousqueton's wound, for which I had to have the surgeon twice a day?"

"Ay, ay!" said Athos, exchanging a smile with d'Artagnan and Aramis, "it is very clear you acted nobly with regard to the poor lad. That is like a good master."

"In short," resumed Porthos, "when all my expenses are paid, I shall have at the most thirty crowns left."

"And I about ten pistoles," said Aramis ruefully.

"Well, then," remarked Athos, "it appears that we are the Croesuses of the society, d'Artagnan. How much have you left of the hundred pistoles?"

"Why, in the first place, I gave you fifty, Athos."

"You think so?"

"*Pardieu,* of course!"

"Ah, that is true. I recollect now."

"Then I paid the landlord six."

"Brute of a host! Why did you give him six pistoles?"

"Because you told me to give them to him."

"It is true. I am too good-natured. In brief, how much remains?"

"Twenty-five pistoles," said d'Artagnan.

"And I," said Athos, taking some small change from his pocket, "I seem to have—"

"You? Nothing!"

"My faith! At least so little that it is not worth reckoning in the general fund."

"Now then, let us calculate how much we possess in all."

"Porthos?"

"Thirty crowns."

"Aramis?"

"Ten pistoles."

"You, d'Artagnan?"

"Twenty-five."

"And that makes altogether?"

"Four hundred and seventy-five livres," said d'Artagnan, who could reckon like Archimedes.

"On our arrival in Paris we shall still have four hundred, in addition to the harnesses," said Porthos.

"But our troop horses?" inquired Aramis.

"Well, we can sell the four horses of our lackeys and buy two for ourselves with the proceeds. For these we shall draw lots. With the four hundred we'll have half enough for one horse without a saddle. And then we will give the sweepings of our pockets to d'Artagnan, who has a lucky hand, and will go and play in the first gaming house we come to."

"There! That's all settled, then," said Porthos. "Let's continue to eat; the meal is growing cold."

At ease with regard to the future, the friends did honor to the repast, the remains of which were abandoned to Bazin, Mousqueton, Planchet, and Grimaud.

On arriving in Paris, d'Artagnan found a letter from M. de Tréville which informed him that, at the captain's own request, the king had promised he should enter the company of Musketeers.

As this was the height of d'Artagnan's worldly ambition, apart of course from the finding of Madame Bonacieux, he ran full of joy to seek his comrades, whom he had left only half an hour before but whom he found very sad and deeply preoccupied.

They were assembled in council at the residence of Athos, which always indicated an event of some gravity. M. de Tréville had intimated to them his Majesty's fixed intention to open the campaign on the first of May, and they must immediately prepare their outfits.

The four philosophers looked at one another in a state of bewilderment. M. de Tréville never jested in matters pertaining to discipline.

"And what do you reckon your outfit will cost?" said d'Artagnan.

"Oh, that's hard to tell. We have made our calculations with Spartan economy, and we each need fifteen hundred livres."

"It seems to me," replied d'Artagnan, "with a thousand livres each—I do not speak as a Spartan but as a procurator—"

The word *procurator* roused Porthos from his lethargy. "Stop!" he cried, "I have an idea."

"Well, that's something, anyway, for I have not the shadow of one," said Athos coolly. "But as to the young Gascon here, the idea of belonging to our company has driven him out of his senses. A thousand livres indeed! For my part, I declare I want two thousand."

"Four times two makes eight," groaned Aramis. "It is eight thousand that we need to complete our outfits, toward which, it is true, we already have the saddles."

"Besides," said Athos, waiting until d'Artagnan had gone to thank M. de Tréville, "there is that beautiful ring which beams from the finger of our friend. What the devil! D'Artagnan is too good a comrade to leave his brothers in distress when he wears the ransom of a king on his hand."

CHAPTER XXVIII

A SEARCH FOR EQUIPMENTS

The most preoccupied of the four friends was certainly d'Artagnan. For, notwithstanding all his inquiries respecting Madame Bonacieux, he could obtain no news of her. M. de Tréville had spoken of her to the queen, but her Majesty was ignorant of the whereabouts of the young wife of the mercer. She had promised to have her sought for, but sovereigns' promises are apt to be a bit vague and did not especially reassure the young Gascon.

Athos had not left his chamber for some time. He made up his mind not to take a single step toward equipping himself.

"We have still fifteen days before us," he reminded his friends. "Well, if at the end of a fortnight I have found nothing (or rather, if nothing has come to me), I shall move in the matter. Now, I am too good a Catholic to kill myself with a pistol bullet, so I shall seek a good quarrel with four of his Eminence's guards or with eight Englishmen. And then I shall fight until one of them has killed me, which—considering the number—cannot fail to happen. It will then be said of me that I died for the king. Thus I shall have performed my duty without the expense of an outfit."

Porthos continued to walk about with his hands behind him, tossing his head and repeating, "I shall follow up my idea."

Aramis, anxious and negligently dressed, said nothing.

From these melancholy details it may be seen that desolation prevailed in the community.

The lackeys, not to be outdone, shared the sadness of their masters. Mousqueton collected a store of crusts (against future need). Bazin, who had always been inclined to devotion, never quitted the churches. Planchet watched the flight of flies. Grimaud, whom the common distress could not induce to break the silence imposed by his master, heaved sighs enough to soften stones.

Porthos had been the first to find an idea. He was the first to act. D'Artagnan one day perceived him walking toward the Church of St. Leu, and followed him instinctively.

Porthos twisted his mustache and elongated his imperial, a sign that always announced he had reached a triumphant resolve. Then he entered the church. D'Artagnan took such precautions to remain hidden that Porthos believed he had not been seen. The guardsman entered behind the musketeer. Porthos leaned against the side of a pillar. D'Artagnan, still unperceived, supported himself against the other side.

The audience room was full of people. Porthos took advantage of this fact to ogle the women. Thanks to the exceeding care of Mousqueton, his exterior was far from announcing the distress of his pocketbook and his soul. His hat may have been a little napless, his feather a trifle faded, his gold lace slightly tarnished, his facings the least frayed. But in the obscurity of the church these things were not seen, and Porthos was still the handsome Porthos.

D'Artagnan observed, on the bench nearest to the pillar against which Porthos was leaning, a ripe beauty. She was a bit yellow and rather weazened, but still erect and haughty under her black hood. The eyes of Porthos were furtively cast toward this lady, but thereafter they roamed about at large across the nave.

On her part, the lady of the black hood, who from time to time blushed, darted with the rapidity of lightning a glance at the inconstant Porthos. And at such a moment the eyes of Porthos would wander aimlessly. It was plain that this mode of procedure piqued the lady in the black hood, for she bit her lips until they bled, scratched the tip of her nose, and could not sit still in her seat.

Porthos, on seeing this, twisted his mustache, elongated his imperial, and began to make signals to a beautiful lady who was near the choir of the church. She was, quite evidently, not only a beautiful woman, but also a great person of some sort, for she had behind her a negro boy who had brought the cushion on which she knelt, and a female servant who held the emblazoned bag in which was placed the book from which she read the Mass.

Through all their rovings the lady in the black hood followed the looks of Porthos, and she soon enough remarked that they rested with particular pleasure upon the lady with the velvet cushion, the little negro, and the serving maid.

During this time Porthos stuck close to his objective. It was the almost imperceptible motions of his eyes, the fingers placed upon lips, the quick, killing smiles, which really did plague the disdained beauty in the black hood.

Then she cried, "Ahem!" (under cover of the Mea Culpa). And she beat her breast so vigorously that everybody, even the lady with the red cushion, turned around to look in her direction. Porthos seemed to pay no attention to all this. Nevertheless, he understood it all.

The lady with the red cushion produced a great impression. She was very handsome—a fact not lost upon the lady in the black hood, who saw in her a rival terribly to be dreaded. She had a great effect likewise upon Porthos, who thought her much prettier than the lady in the black hood. She struck particularly the attention of d'Artagnan, who recognized in her the lady of Meung, of Calais, and of Dover, whom his persecutor, the man with the scar, had called Milady.

The young guardsman, without losing sight of the lady with the red cushion, continued to watch the proceedings of Porthos, which amused him mightily. He guessed that the lady in the black hood was the wife of the procurator of the Rue aux Ours, which was the more likely because the Church of St. Leu was not far from that locality.

He also guessed, by induction, that Porthos was taking revenge for his defeat at Chantilly when the procurator's wife had proved so refractory in the matter of opening up her purse.

During all this period d'Artagnan observed also that not one countenance responded to the gallantries of Porthos. There were no real facts, therefore, upon which to base a sensible jealousy—only chimeras and illusions. But for real love, for true jealousy, is there any reality except chimeras and illusions?

The sermon over, the procurator's wife advanced to the holy font. Porthos anticipated her and, instead of a finger, he dipped his whole hand in the basin. The procurator's wife smiled, for she thought it was in her interest that Porthos put himself to this trouble. She was promptly and cruelly undeceived.

When she was only about three steps from him, he turned his head around and fixed his eyes steadfastly upon the lady with the red cushion. She had risen and was approaching, followed by her black boy and her woman attendant.

When the lady of the red cushion had come close to Porthos, he drew his dripping hand from the font. The fair worshiper touched the great paw of Porthos with her delicate fingers, smiled, made the sign of the cross, and left the church.

This was too strong for the procurator's wife. She doubted not from that moment that there was an understanding between this lady and the musketeer. If she had been a noble lady, she would have swooned, but as she was only a procurator's wife, she contented herself with saying to Porthos with concentrated fury, "You do not offer me any holy water, M. Porthos, eh?"

At the sound of that voice the musketeer started like a man who had just been awakened from a hundred years' sleep.

"Mad—Madame!" he cried. "Is it you! How is your husband, our worthy M. Coquenard? Is he still as stingy as ever? Where can my eyes have been, not to have seen you during the two hours of the sermon?"

"I was within two steps of you, Monsieur," replied the procurator's wife. "But you did not notice me, since you had no eyes but for the pretty lady to whom you just now gave holy water."

Porthos worked hard to appear confused. "Ah," he said, "you have seen—"

"I must have been blind not to have noticed it."

"Yes," replied Porthos, "that is a duchess of my acquaintance whom I have great trouble in meeting on account of the jealousy of her husband. She sent me word she would come today to this poor church, buried in this vile quarter of the city, solely for the purpose of seeing me."

"M. Porthos," pleaded the procurator's wife, "won't you have the kindness to offer me your arm for five minutes? I have something to say to you."

"Certainly, Madame," replied Porthos, winking to himself as a gambler does who laughs at the dupe he is about to pluck.

At that moment d'Artagnan passed the couple in his pursuit of Milady. He cast a fugitive glance at his friend and beheld his triumphant look. "Eh, eh!" he said to himself, reasoning in accord with the strangely easy manners of that period, "there is a musketeer who will have his troop equipment before very long."

Porthos, yielding to the pressure of the arm of the procurator's wife as a bark answers to its rudder, arrived at the cloister St. Magloire — a seldom-frequented passage entered at either end by a turnstile. In the daytime nobody ever was seen there but children at play and beggars munching their crusts.

"Ah, M. Porthos," cried the procurator's wife when she was assured that no one could either see or hear her, "you are a great flirt, it would seem."

"I, Madame?" retorted Porthos, drawing his great frame up proudly. "Why, what do you mean?"

"Your signals a short while ago, and the incident of the holy water. She must be a princess, at least—that lady with the negro boy and her maid."

"Madame, you are frightfully deceived," said Porthos, "she is nothing more than a duchess."

"Then how about that footman waiting at the church door and the equipage with a coachman in grand livery who sat waiting on his high seat?"

Porthos had seen neither of the two men, but with the discerning eye of the jealous woman Madame Coquenard had missed nothing.

Porthos regretted that he had not at once made the lady of the red cushion at least a foreign sovereign.

"Ah, you are quite the pet of the ladies, M. Porthos!" resumed the procurator's wife with a sigh.

"Well," Porthos acknowledged grudgingly, "what with the physique with which nature endowed me, you may imagine that I have to fight against my own good luck."

"Good Lord, how quickly fickle men forget!" cried the procurator's wife, raising her eyes toward the sky.

"Less quickly than inconstant women, it seems to me," replied Porthos. "For I, Madame, may say I was your victim, when wounded and dying I was abandoned by the surgeons. I, the offspring of a noble family, who placed reliance upon your friendship! I was near to death of my wounds at first and of hunger afterward in a beggarly inn at Chantilly. And you never once deigned to reply to the burning letters I addressed to you."

"But, M. Porthos," murmured the procurator's wife, who began to feel that, judged by the standards of the great ladies of the town, she was indeed wrong.

"I who had sacrificed for you the Baroness of—"

"Oh, I know you did."

"To say nothing of the Countess of—"

"You overwhelm me, M. Porthos!"

"And the unforgettable Duchess of—"

"I beg of you, Monsieur, be generous!"

"You are right, Madame. I have finished my complaint."

"But it was my husband who simply would not hear of my lending you money."

"Madame Coquenard," Porthos reminded her, "do you recall the first letter you wrote me, and which I preserve graven on the tablets of my soul?"

The procurator's wife emitted a groan. "But," she explained, "the sum you wished to borrow was so large."

"Madame Coquenard, I gave you the preference. I had but to write the Duchess—no, I shall not repeat her name, for I am incapable of compromising a woman. But this I know—I had but to write to her and she would have sent me fifteen hundred."

The procurator's wife shed a tardy tear.

"M. Porthos," she said, "I can assure you I am sufficiently punished. And if, in time to come, you should find yourself in a similar situation, you have but to apply to me."

"Fie, Madame, fie!" said Porthos, as if disgusted. "Let us not talk about money, if you please. It is too humiliating."

"Then you no longer love me?" asked the procurator's wife sadly and slowly.

Porthos maintained a majestic silence.

"And is this reticence of yours the only reply I am to have? Alas, I understand only too well!"

"Think of the crime you have committed against me, Madame! It sticks fast—here!" said Porthos, placing his hand on the region of his heart and pressing it strongly.

"I shall repair my fault, indeed I shall, my dear Porthos!"

"Besides, what did I ask of you?" resumed Porthos. "A few paltry crowns! Ah, if you were a duchess, a marchioness, or a countess, it would be quite a different thing. Then it would be unpardonable."

The procurator's wife was piqued.

"Please to know, M. Porthos," she said, "my strong box is better filled than those of your affected minxes."

"That just doubles the offense," remarked Porthos severely, disengaging his arm from that of the procurator's wife, "for if you are rich, Madame Coquenard, then there is no excuse for your refusal."

"When I said rich," replied the harassed woman, who saw that she had gone too far, "you must not take me too literally."

"Hold, Madame," interjected Porthos, "let us say no more upon the subject. You have grossly misunderstood me. All friendship between us is at an end."

"Ingrate that you are!"

"You are a fine one to complain!"

"Begone to your beautiful duchess. I shall not detain you."

"Yet she is not to be despised, in my opinion."

"M. Porthos, for the last time—do you love me still?"

"Alas, Madame," grieved Porthos in his best melancholy manner, "when we are just on the point of entering a campaign—one in which my presentiments tell me I am to be killed—"

"Oh, don't talk of such things!" cried the procurator's wife, bursting into tears.

"Something whispers the message to me," continued Porthos.

"Rather say that you have a new love."

"Not so. I speak frankly to you. Nothing concerns me now but my outfitting for war. I must at once journey to see my family in the lower part of Brittany to obtain the sum necessary for my departure."

Porthos was now witness of a last struggle between love and avarice.

"And as," he went on to say, "the duchess whom you saw in church has estates near those of my people, we mean to make the journey together. Traveling, you know, seems much shorter when we travel two in company."

"Have you no friends in Paris, then, M. Porthos?" demanded the procurator's wife.

"I thought I had," replied Porthos, resuming his melancholy air, "but I have been taught my mistake somewhat sharply."

"Still you have some, Monsieur!" cried the jealous woman, in a transport that surprised even herself. "Come to our house tomorrow. You are the son of my aunt, remember? Consequently, you are my cousin—don't forget that. You come from Noyon in Picardy. You have several lawsuits and no attorney. Can you keep all this in mind?"

"Perfectly, Madame."

"Come at dinner time."

"Very well."

"And be upon your guard before my husband, who is rather shrewd, despite his seventy-six years."

"Seventy-six years! *Peste!* That is a fine age!" replied Porthos.

"A great age, you mean. Yes, the poor man may be expected to leave me a widow almost any hour," she continued, throwing a significant glance at the musketeer. "And fortunately, by our marriage contract, the survivor takes everything."

"All, without restriction?"

"Yes, all."

"You are a woman of precaution, I see, my dear Madame Coquenard," said Porthos, squeezing the hand of the procurator's wife tenderly.

"We are then reconciled?" she asked, simpering.

"For life!" replied the soldier hardily.

"Till we meet again! Dear traitor!"

"Till we meet again! Forgetful charmer!"

"Tomorrow, my angel!"

"Tomorrow, flame of my existence!"

CHAPTER XXIX

MILADY

D'Artagnan followed Milady without being noticed by her. He saw her enter her carriage and heard her order the coachman to drive to St. Germain.

It was useless to try to keep pace with a carriage drawn by two powerful horses. D'Artagnan therefore returned to the Rue Férou. In tl e Rue de Seine he met Planchet, who had stopped before the shop of a pastry cook and was contemplating with ecstasy a cake of the most appetizing appearance.

The young Gascon told his servant to go to M. de Tréville's stables and saddle two horses, then to bring them to the house of Athos. Once for all, the captain of Musketeers had placed his stable at the guardsman's service.

Athos was at home sadly emptying a bottle of the famous Spanish wine he had sent back from Picardy. He made a sign for Grimaud to fetch a glass for d'Artagnan.

The young visitor then related to his host all that had passed at the church between Porthos and the procurator's wife, and how their comrade was in a fair way to being equipped.

"As for me," was Athos' comment to this recital, "I am quite at my ease. It will not be women who defray the expense of my outfit."

"Handsome, well-bred, noble lord that you are, my dear

Athos, neither princesses nor queens would be secure from your solicitations if you should see fit to try them out."

"How young this guardsman is!" said Athos, shrugging his shoulders. And he made a sign to Grimaud to bring another bottle.

Then the visitor described the meeting which he had had at the church, and how he had found that lady who, with the seigneur in the black cloak and with the scar near his temple, filled his mind constantly.

"Which is to say, you are in love with this lady as you were with Madame Bonacieux," said Athos, shrugging his shoulders contemptuously, as if he pitied human weakness.

"Not at all!" replied the guardsman. "I am only curious to unravel the mystery in which she is involved. I do not know why, but I imagine that this woman, wholly unknown to me though she is, has an influence over my life."

"Well, perhaps you are right," said Athos. "I do not know a woman who is worth the trouble of being sought for when she is once lost. Madame Bonacieux is lost—so much the worse for her if she is found."

"Ah, my friend, you are mistaken," asserted d'Artagnan. "I love my poor Constance more than ever. If I knew where she was, were it at the end of the world, I should go to free her from the hands of her enemies. But I am ignorant. All my searching has been useless. I must divert my attention somehow."

"Amuse yourself with Milady, d'Artagnan. I wish you success with all my heart."

At that moment Planchet thrust his head modestly in at the half-open door and told his master that the horses were ready. D'Artagnan and his lackey mounted and took the road to St. Germain.

All along the road, what Athos had said respecting Madame Bonacieux recurred to the mind of the young man. Although d'Artagnan was not of a very sentimental character, the mercer's pretty wife had made a real impression on his heart. As he said, he was ready to go to the end of the world to seek her. But the world, being round, has many ends; so he did not know which way to turn.

Meantime he was going to try to find Milady. Milady had spoken to the man in the black cloak—therefore she knew him. Now, in the opinion of d'Artagnan, it was certainly this man of the black cloak who had carried Madame Bonacieux off a second time as he had the first. The young guardsman, then, was only telling half a lie when he said to himself that by going in search of Milady he at the same time would be in search of Constance.

Thinking of all this and from time to time giving the spur to his horse, the Gascon completed his short journey and arrived at St. Germain. He rode up a very quiet street, looking to the right and the left to see whether he could find any vestige of his beautiful Englishwoman. Finally, from the ground floor of a pretty house, he saw a face peep out with which he thought himself acquainted. But Planchet was the first to recognize it.

"Eh, Monsieur!" he asked, "don't you remember that visage that is blinking at us over yonder?"

"No," said d'Artagnan, "and yet I am sure it is not the first time I have seen it."

"Why, Monsieur, it is Lubin, the lackey of the Comte de Wardes—he whom you took such good care of a month ago at Calais on the road to the governor's country house."

"So it is! Do you think he would recollect you, Planchet?"

"My faith, Monsieur, he was in such trouble that I doubt if he can have retained a very clear recollection of me."

"Well, then, go and talk with the boy," said d'Artagnan, "and find out from his conversation whether his master is dead or not."

Planchet dismounted and went straight up to Lubin, who did not remember him at all. The two lackeys began to chat with the best understanding possible.

After an instant's observation d'Artagnan heard the noise of an approaching vehicle and saw Milady's carriage stop opposite to him. He could not be mistaken, for the charming person herself was in it. The Gascon, who had ridden behind a hedge of filberts, leaned upon the neck of his horse in order that he might see without being seen.

Milady put her dainty head out of the carriage window and gave her orders to her maid.

The latter was a pretty girl of about twenty years of age, active and lively, the true soubrette of a great lady. She jumped from the step upon which, according to the custom of the time, she was seated, and took her way toward the terrace upon which d'Artagnan had first caught sight of Lubin.

The Gascon followed the soubrette with his eyes. Now it happened that some one in the house called Lubin; so Planchet remained alone, looking in every direction to discover where his master might have disappeared. The maid approached Planchet, whom she mistook for Lubin, and, holding out a billet, said, "Give this to your master, please."

"To my master!" exclaimed the astonished lackey.

"Yes, and it is important, too. Be quick about it."

Thereupon she ran back to the carriage—which had turned around to face the way it came—jumped upon the step, and was driven off.

At first Planchet turned the billet over and over mechanically. But he was accustomed to unquestioning obedience; so he jumped down from the terrace, ran toward the lane, and at the end of twenty paces met d'Artagnan, who, having seen the whole episode, was coming in his direction.

"For you, Monsieur," said Planchet, presenting the billet to the young man.

"For me!" ejaculated d'Artagnan. "Are you sure?"

"The soubrette said it was for my master, Monsieur. I have no other master but you."

The Gascon opened the letter and read:

A person who takes more interest in you than she is willing to confess wishes to know on what day it will suit you to walk in the forest. Tomorrow, at the Hotel Field of the Cloth of Gold, a lackey in black and red will await your reply.

"Aha!" said d'Artagnan. "It appears that Milady and I are both anxious about the health of the same person. The good M. de Wardes is not dead, then, Planchet?"

"No, Monsieur. He is as much alive as a man can be
with four sword wounds in his body. He is still quite
weak, having lost almost all his blood. Lubin did not
recognize me, Monsieur, and so he told me our adventure
from one end to the other."

"Well done, Planchet! You are the king of lackeys.
Now jump on your horse and we will overtake the
carriage."

This did not take long. At the end of five minutes they
beheld the equipage drawn up by the roadside. A cavalier,
richly dressed, was standing near the door.

The conversation between Milady and the seigneur took
place in English, a tongue which d'Artagnan could not
understand. But by the accent the young man plainly saw
that the beautiful Englishwoman was in a great rage. She
terminated the talk by an action which left no doubt as to
her humor—this was by a blow of her fan, applied with
such force that the small feminine weapon flew into a
hundred pieces.

The cavalier laughed aloud, which seemed to exas-
perate the lady still more.

D'Artagnan considered this was the moment to
interfere. He stepped up to the other door and, taking
off his hat respectfully, said, "Madame, will you permit
me to offer my services? It appears to me that this gentleman has made you very angry. Speak but one word,
Madame, and I take it upon myself to punish him for his
lack of courtesy."

At the first word of the Gascon's, Milady turned and
looked at him in astonishment. And when he had finished

she said in most excellent French, "Monsieur, I should
place myself under your protection with every confidence,
but the person with whom I am quarreling is my brother."

"Excuse me, please," said d'Artagnan. "I was
ignorant of that important fact, Madame."

It might be thought that Milady, timid as women are
in general, would have interposed to prevent a quarrel
between her brother and an intrusive cavalier. But, on
the contrary, she threw herself back in her carriage and
called out coolly to the coachman, "Go on—home!"

The carriage started away and left the two men facing
each other.

The brother of Milady made a movement as if to follow
the retreating equipage, but d'Artagnan's anger had by
this time increased. He recognized in this fellow the
Englishman of Amiens who had won his horse from Athos
and was very near winning his diamond. So he caught
at the bridle of the cavalier's horse and stopped him.

"Well, Monsieur," he said, "you appear to forget there
is a small quarrel to arrange between us two."

"You see plainly that I have no sword," the Englishman
replied. "Do you wish to play the braggart with an
unarmed man?"

"Very well, my worthy sir," agreed d'Artagnan. "Pick
out the longest blade you can find at your home and come
and show it to me this evening."

"Where, if you please?"

"Behind the Luxembourg."

"A charming and convenient spot! I shall be there."

"Your hour?"

"Six o'clock."

"A propos, you probably have one or two friends?"

"I have exactly three in Paris who would be honored by joining in the sport with me."

"That falls out oddly! Three is just my number, too."

"Tell me your name, please."

"I am M. d'Artagnan, a Gascon gentleman, serving now in the Guards, M. d'Essart's company. And you, sir?"

"I am Lord de Winter, Baron Sheffield."

"I am your servant, Monsieur Baron!"

And, touching his horse with the spur, the young man cantered back to Paris. As he was accustomed to do in all cases of any consequence, d'Artagnan went straight to the residence of Athos.

He found that gentleman reclining upon a large sofa, where he was waiting (so he said) for his outfit to come and find him. The young soldier related to Athos all that had happened except the letter to M. de Wardes.

Athos was delighted to find that he was going to fight an Englishman. One might say that was his chosen dream. They immediately sent their lackeys to Porthos and Aramis. When the other Inseparables arrived, in answer to their summons, they too were made acquainted with the situation.

Porthos drew his sword from its scabbard and made passes at the wall, springing back from time to time and engaging in contortions that would have done credit to a dancer.

Aramis, who was writing a poem on which he was constantly at work, shut himself up in Athos' closet and begged not to be disturbed before the very moment of drawing swords.

Athos, by signs, indicated to Grimaud that he wished another bottle of Spanish wine.

D'Artagnan employed his time in arranging a simple plan, of which we shall hear more anon. His scheme promised him some agreeable adventure, as might be seen by the smiles which from time to time passed across his face, whose thoughtfulness they animated.

CHAPTER XXX

ENGLISH AND FRENCH

When the appointed hour came, they went with their four lackeys to the spot behind the Luxembourg devoted to the grazing of goats. Athos threw a piece of money to the goat keeper to induce him to withdraw.

A silent party soon drew near the same inclosure, entered, and joined the musketeers. Then, according to the English custom, presentations took place. The Englishmen were all men of rank. Consequently the odd names of their opponents were for them a source of surprise and even of annoyance.

"You played very willingly with us without knowing our names," objected Athos. "By the same token, you won our horses."

"True," answered Lord de Winter, "but we then only risked our pistoles, now we are staking our blood. One games with anybody, one fights only with equals."

"That is justly spoken," remarked Athos. And he took aside the one of the four Englishmen with whom he was to fight and communicated his name in a low voice.

Porthos and Aramis did the same.

"You would have acted much more wisely," said Athos to his adversary, "if you had not required me to make my rank known."

"Why so, Monsieur?"

"Because I am believed to be dead and have reasons

for wishing nobody to know I am alive. I shall now be obliged to kill you to prevent my secret from roaming over the fields."

The Englishman looked at Athos, thinking he jested.

"On guard!" cried d'Artagnan.

Immediately eight swords flashed in the rays of the setting sun. The combat began with the animosity very natural between men who are twice enemies.

Athos killed his antagonist first. He hit him but once. As he had foretold, however, that thrust was a mortal one. The sword pierced the heart.

Porthos stretched his man upon the grass with a wound through the thigh. As the Englishman, without making further resistance, then surrendered his sword, Porthos took him up in his arms and bore him off to his carriage.

Aramis, who had the third canto of his poem to finish, behaved like a man in haste. He pressed his opponent so vigorously that after going back fifty paces the man finally took to his heels and disappeared, amid the hooting of the lackeys, who were standing at one side as sentinels.

D'Artagnan fought purely on the defensive. And when he noted that his man was fairly well fatigued, with a vigorous side thrust he sent Lord de Winter's sword flying. The latter, finding himself disarmed, took two or three steps back. His foot slipped and he fell.

The Gascon was over him at a single bound. He pointed his blade at the baron's throat and said, "You are completely in my hands, my Lord. I could kill you, but I spare your life for the sake of your sister."

The young man was at the pinnacle of joy. He had

realized the plan he had plotted out beforehand, the pic-
turing of which had caused the smiles we observed upon his
face.

The Englishman, naturally, was delighted at having to
do with a gentleman of so kindly a disposition. He pressed
d'Artagnan in his arms, and paid a thousand compliments
to the three musketeers.

Meanwhile, Porthos and Aramis were undressing the
dead man in the vain hope of finding that his wound was
not mortal, when a large purse dropped from his clothes.
D'Artagnan picked it up and handed it to Lord de Winter.

"What the devil would you have me do with it?" asked
the baron.

"Restore it to his family," replied d'Artagnan.

"His family will inherit fifteen thousand louis a year
from him, so keep the purse for your lackeys," said Lord
de Winter.

"Yes," chimed in Athos, taking the purse from his
friend's hand and throwing it to the coachman, "let us
give the money to the lackeys, but to the English ones."

This greatness of spirit in a man who was quite desti-
tute was highly applauded by the baron. Everyone was
pleasantly struck by it, in fact, except MM. Grimaud,
Bazin, Mousqueton, and Planchet.

On quitting d'Artagnan, Lord de Winter gave him his
sister's address. She lived in the Place Royale at No. 6.
And he agreed to call and take d'Artagnan with him, in
order to present him to Milady Clarik. The Gascon appointed eight o'clock at Athos' residence as the time and
place of meeting.

Shortly before this hour d'Artagnan in his most splendid toilet went to Athos' house and, according to custom, related everything to him.

"What!" cried Athos. "You have just lost one woman whom you term charming and perfect. Here you are, headlong after another."

D'Artagnan could not but feel the truth of this reproach.

"I loved Madame Bonacieux with my heart," he said, stammering a little, "while I love Milady with my head. In getting introduced to her I am chiefly actuated to learn what part she plays at court."

"It is not difficult to divine that, my lad, after what you have told me. She is an emissary of the cardinal. She will draw you into a snare in which you will leave your head."

"The devil, my dear Athos! You view things on the dark side."

"I mistrust all women, especially fair ones."

Lord de Winter arrived at the appointed time, but Athos, warned of his coming, went into his other chamber. He found the young Gascon alone, therefore, and as it was nearly eight o'clock he took the new friend off with him.

An elegant carriage waited below. It was drawn by two magnificent horses, so they were soon at the Place Royale.

Milady Clarik received d'Artagnan ceremoniously. Her residence was sumptuous, Milady having just expended much money upon it. This proved that the general war measure which was driving the English out of France did not affect her.

"You behold," said Lord de Winter as he presented d'Artagnan to his sister, "a young gentleman who held my life in his hands but did not abuse his advantage, although we are twice enemies, although it was I who insulted him, and I who am an Englishman. Thank him, Madame, for me."

Milady frowned slightly. So peculiar a smile appeared upon her lips that the young man almost shuddered at it.

"You are welcome, Monsieur," she said in a voice whose singular sweetness contrasted with the symptoms of ill humor which d'Artagnan had just remarked. "You have today acquired eternal rights to my gratitude."

The Englishman then turned to his sister and described the duel without omitting a single detail. When he had finished, he went to a table on which was a salver with Spanish wine and glasses. He filled two goblets and by a sign invited the Gascon to drink.

D'Artagnan knew it was considered disobliging to refuse to pledge the Englishman, so he drew near to the table and took up his glass. He did not, however, lose sight of Milady and in a mirror he beheld the change that came over her face. Now that she believed herself to be unobserved, a sentiment resembling ferocity animated her countenance. She bit her handkerchief with her beautiful teeth.

The pretty little soubrette whom d'Artagnan had already noticed then came in. She spoke some words in English to Lord de Winter, who thereupon requested his guest's permission to retire. He excused himself on account of the urgency of the business that called him away and charged his sister to obtain his pardon for him.

The Gascon exchanged a handshake with Lord de Winter and then returned to Milady. Her face, with surprising mobility, had recovered its gracious expression. But some small red stains on her handkerchief indicated that she had bitten her lips until the blood came. Those lips were magnificent. They might be said to be of coral.

The conversation took a cheerful turn. Milady appeared to have entirely recovered. She told d'Artagnan that Lord de Winter was her brother-in-law, and not her real brother. She had married a younger scion of the family, who had left her a widow with one child. This youngster was the only heir to Lord de Winter in case he did not marry.

D'Artagnan was profuse in gallant speeches and protestations of devotion. Milady replied to all his sallies with a smile of kindness. The hour came for him to retire. D'Artagnan took leave of his hostess and left the drawing-room the happiest of men.

D'Artagnan came again on the morrow and the day after that, and each time Milady accorded him a more gracious reception.

Every evening, in the antechamber, in the corridor, or on the stairs, he met the pretty soubrette. But, as one might imagine, the Gascon paid no attention to this persistence on the part of poor Kitty.

CHAPTER XXXI

SOUBRETTE AND MISTRESS

Despite the cries of his own conscience and the wise counsels of Athos, d'Artagnan became hourly more enamored of Milady.

One day when he arrived with his head in the air and as light of heart as a man who awaits a shower of gold, he found the soubrette under the gateway of the hotel. But this time Kitty was not content merely to touch him as he passed; she took him gently by the hand.

"Good!" thought d'Artagnan. "She is charged with some message for me from her mistress. Milady is about to appoint some meeting of which she had not the courage to speak."

"I wish to say three words to you, Monsieur Chevalier," stammered the soubrette.

"I am listening, my child," said d'Artagnan.

"That which I have to say is too long and too secret to tell here. If Monsieur Chevalier would follow me?" said Kitty timidly.

"Where you please."

And Kitty, who had not let go the hand of d'Artagnan, led him up a dark, winding staircase. After ascending about fifteen steps she opened a door.

D'Artagnan cast a glance around him. The small apartment was charming for its taste and neatness. But in spite of himself his eyes were directed to the door which led to the next room, which he guessed to be Milady's chamber.

Kitty guessed what was passing in the mind of the young man and heaved a deep sigh.

"You love my mistress, then, very dearly, Monsieur Chevalier?" she asked.

"Much more than I can say, Kitty."

"That is too bad, Monsieur," she said.

"What the devil do you see so bad in it?" inquired d'Artagnan.

"Because, Monsieur," stated the soubrette, "my mistress loves you not at all."

"What is that? Did she charge you to tell me so?"

"Oh, no, Monsieur. But because of the regard I have for you, I made up my mind to tell you."

"I am much obliged for your intention, my dear Kitty. The information, you will acknowledge, is not likely to be agreeable to me.

"Which means that you don't believe what I have told you."

"I confess that unless you see fit to give me some proof of what you assert—"

Kitty drew a small note from her bosom. "And what does Monsieur think of this?" she asked.

"For me?" said d'Artagnan, seizing the billet.

"No, for another."

"His name!" cried the young Gascon.

"M. le Comte de Wardes."

The remembrance of the scene at St. Germain flashed into the mind of d'Artagnan. He tore open the letter in spite of the cry that the soubrette uttered on seeing what he was about to do. He read:

You have not answered my first note. Are you indisposed, or have you forgotten the glances with which you favored me at the ball of Madame de Guise? You have an opportunity now, my dear Count. Do not allow it to escape.

The soldier became very pale. He was wounded in his vanity. He imagined that it was his love which was hurt.

"Poor dear M. d'Artagnan," said the soubrette in a voice full of compassion.

"Instead of pitying me," said the Gascon, "you would do much better to assist me in avenging myself upon your mistress."

"I shall never help you in that, Monsieur Chevalier," stated Kitty warmly.

"And why not?" demanded d'Artagnan.

"For two reasons."

"And what are they?"

"The first is, that my mistress will never love you."

"You don't know that, Kitty. But let me know your second reason, just the same."

"The other one, Monsieur Chevalier," replied the soubrette, "is that, in love, every one for herself!"

Not until this moment did d'Artagnan remember the languishing glances of the maid, her constant meeting of him in the antechamber, in the corridor, and on the stairs. He recalled the fact that she touched his hand every time she passed him; he recollected her deep sighs.

The Gascon saw at once all the advantages to be derived

from the love which Kitty confessed so boldly: the intercepting of letters addressed to the Comte de Wardes, news on the spot, entrance at any hour into Kitty's chamber, which was next to her mistress'.

Midnight sounded. And almost at the same instant the bell was rung in Milady's apartment.

"Heavens! There is my mistress calling me," cried the soubrette. "Go—go directly!"

D'Artagnan rose, took his hat, as if it were his intention to obey. Then, opening quickly the door of a large closet instead of that leading to the staircase, he buried himself amid the robes and dressing gowns of Milady.

"Well," cried Milady in a sharp voice, "are you asleep that you don't answer when I ring?"

And the Gascon heard the door between the rooms thrown violently open.

"Here I am, Milady," answered Kitty, springing forward to meet her mistress.

Both went into the bedroom, and as the door of communication remained open, for some time d'Artagnan could hear Milady scolding her maid. She was at length appeased, and while Kitty was assisting her mistress to disrobe, the conversation turned upon the Gascon.

"Well," said Milady, "I have not seen our young knight this evening."

"Can he be inconstant?" asked Kitty innocently.

"Oh, no. He must have been prevented by M. de Tréville or M. d'Essart. I have this one safe enough!"

"What do you want of him, Madame?"

"Kitty, there is something between that man and me

that he is quite ignorant of. He nearly made me lose my
credit with his Eminence."

"I thought that Madame loved him."

"Love him? I detest him! An idiot who held the life
of Lord de Winter in his hands and did not kill him, by
which I missed three hundred thousand livres' income."

"That is true," said Kitty. "Your son is the only heir
of his uncle, and until his coming of age you would have
had the enjoyment of his income."

D'Artagnan shuddered at hearing this suave creature
reproach him for not having killed a man whom he had seen
load her with kindness.

"For all this," continued Milady, "I should have long
ago revenged myself upon him, but for some reason or
other the cardinal requested me to conciliate him."

"Madame, however, did not try to conciliate the little
woman he was so fond of."

"You mean the mercer's wife of the Rue des Fossoyeurs? Why, he has forgotten she ever existed! That
was not much of a vengeance, on my faith!"

A cold sweat broke from d'Artagnan's brow. Oh, this
woman was a monster! He resumed his listening, but,
unfortunately for his purpose, the toilet was finished.

"That will do tonight," said Milady. "Go into your
own room, and tomorrow try again to get me an answer to
the letter I gave you."

"For M. de Wardes?" asked the soubrette.

"To be sure—for M. de Wardes."

"Now, there is one," said Kitty, "who appears to me
quite a different sort of man from poor d'Artagnan."

"When I want your comments, Mademoiselle, I shall ask for them," said Milady.

D'Artagnan heard the door close, then the noise of two bolts by which Milady fastened herself in. On her side, but as softly as possible, Kitty turned the key of the lock. And then the young Gascon opened the closet door.

"Oh, good Lord!" said Kitty in a low voice, "what is the matter with you? How pale you are!"

"The abominable creature!" murmured d'Artagnan.

"Silence, and begone!" said the soubrette.

"I shall go, but later." He drew Kitty to him.

Kitty blushed and surrendered to his embrace.

The first use that d'Artagnan made of his influence over the maid was to try to discover what had become of Madame Bonacieux. But the poor girl swore upon the crucifix that she was entirely ignorant in this matter, her mistress never admitting her into half her secrets. The one thing she believed he could be sure of was that the mercer's wife was not dead.

As to the cause which came near making Milady lose her credit with the cardinal, Kitty knew nothing at all. But this time d'Artagnan was better informed than she was. Since he had seen Milady on board a vessel at the moment he was leaving England, he suspected that it was on account of the diamond studs.

But what was clearest of all was that the profound hatred of Milady was increased by his not having killed her brother-in-law when the chance lay in his hands.

The young Gascon came the next day to Milady's, and, finding her in an ill humor, had no doubt that it was lack of an answer from M. de Wardes that provoked her thus. Kitty entered, but Milady was very cross with her. The poor soubrette ventured a glance at d'Artagnan which said, "See how I suffer on your account!"

Toward the end of the evening, however, the beautiful lioness became milder. She smilingly listened to the soft speeches of d'Artagnan, and even gave him her hand to kiss.

The young man departed, scarcely knowing what to think. But as he was a youth who did not easily lose his head, while continuing to pay court to Milady he had framed a plan in his mind.

He found Kitty at the gate and, as on the preceding evening, went up to her chamber. The soubrette had been accused of negligence and severely scolded. Milady could not at all comprehend the silence of the Comte de Wardes, and she ordered Kitty to come at nine o'clock in the morning to take a third letter.

D'Artagnan made the girl promise to bring him the billet as soon as she had received it. The poor thing promised all that her lover asked—she was madly infatuated.

At eleven o'clock next day the soubrette came to him with the letter. D'Artagnan opened it and read as follows:

This is the third time I have written to you to tell you that I love you. Beware that I do not write to you a fourth time to tell you that I detest you.

If you repent of the manner in which you have acted toward me, the young girl who brings you this will tell you how a man of spirit may obtain his pardon.

D'Artagnan colored and turned pale several times while he was reading this message.

"Oh, you love her still," said Kitty, who had not taken her eyes off the young man's face for an instant.

"No, my dear girl, you are mistaken. I do not love her, but I shall avenge myself for her contempt."

"Oh, yes, I know what sort of vengeance you will take!"

"What matters that to you, Kitty? It is you alone whom I love."

"How can I know that is true?"

"By the scorn that I shall cast upon her."

D'Artagnan took a pen and wrote:

MADAME:

Until the present moment I could not believe that it was to me your first two letters were addressed, so unworthy did I feel myself of such an honor. Besides, I was so seriously indisposed that I could not in any case have replied to them.

But now I am forced to believe in the excess of your kindness, since not only your letter but your servant assures me that I have the good fortune to be beloved by you.

She has no occasion to teach me the way in which a man of spirit may obtain his pardon. I shall come and ask mine at eleven o'clock in the evening.

To delay my pardon for but a single day would be in my eyes now to commit a fresh offense.

From him whom you have rendered the happiest of men,

COMTE DE WARDES.

In the first place, this note was a forgery—it was likewise an indelicacy. It was even, according to our present manners, something of an infamous action. But at that period people did not manage affairs as they do today. Besides, from her own admission, d'Artagnan knew Milady guilty of treachery in matters more important and could entertain no respect for her.

D'Artagnan's plan was simplicity itself. Through
Kitty's chamber he would gain access to that of her
mistress. He would take advantage of the first moment
of surprise and terror to triumph over her. He might fail,
of course, but something must be left to chance. In eight
days the campaign would open and he would be compelled
to leave Paris. D'Artagnan had thus no time for a prolonged love siege.

"There," said the young man, handing Kitty the letter
sealed, "give that to Milady. It is the count's reply."

Poor Kitty became as pale as death. She suspected
what the letter contained. "Ah, you do not love me," she
cried, "and I am very wretched."

To this reproach there is always one response which
deludes women. D'Artagnan replied in such a manner
that Kitty remained in her delusion.

CHAPTER XXXII

THE OUTFITS OF ARAMIS AND PORTHOS

Since the four friends had each been in search of his equipment, there had been no fixed meeting between them. They dined apart from one another, wherever they might happen to be, or, rather, where they could. Duty, likewise, took a portion of that precious time which was gliding away so rapidly. But they had agreed to meet once a week about one o'clock at the residence of Athos, seeing that he, in accordance with the vow he had taken, did not cross the threshold of his door.

This day of reunion happened to be the same one as that on which Kitty came to find d'Artagnan. So as soon as the soubrette had left his lodgings the young Gascon directed his steps toward the Rue Férou.

He found Athos and Aramis philosophizing. Aramis, it seems, had some slight inclination to resume his cassock. Athos, as was his custom, neither encouraged nor dissuaded him.

"In general," he said, "people only ask advice in order not to follow it. Or if they do follow it, it is only for the sake of having some one to blame for having given it."

Porthos arrived a minute after d'Artagnan.

At the end of a moment's conversation, in which Porthos hinted that a lady of elevated rank had condescended to relieve him of his financial embarrassment, Mousqueton entered. He came to request his master to return to his lodgings, where his presence was urgent, as he piteously said.

"Is it something about my equipment?"

"Yes and no," replied Mousqueton.

"Well, then, can't you speak straight out?"

"I can only beg you to come at once, Monsieur."

Porthos rose, took leave of his friends, and followed Mousqueton. An instant later Bazin made his appearance.

"What do you want with me, my friend?" inquired Aramis with that mildness of accent which was observable in him every time that his ideas were directed to the church.

"A mendicant wishes to see Monsieur in his home."

"Give him alms, Bazin, and bid him pray for a poor sinner."

"This mendicant pretends, Monsieur, that you will be very glad to see him. He said that, if you refused to come, I should say he was from Tours."

"From Tours!" cried Aramis joyfully. "A thousand pardons, gentlemen, but no doubt this man brings me the news I hoped for." He rose and went off at a quick pace.

"I believe these fellows have managed their business. What do you think, d'Artagnan?" asked Athos.

"I have never been seriously uneasy on their account," returned the Gascon. "But you, my dear Athos, who so generously tossed away the Englishman's pistoles which were your legitimate property, what are you going to do?"

"I am satisfied with having killed the fellow, my boy. It is blessed bread to kill an Englishman. But if I had weighted my pockets with his gold, they would have burdened me like remorse. Let it pass. But, see here, M. de Tréville tells me you are associating with the suspected English, whom the cardinal protects."

"That is to say, I visit an Englishwoman. I have acquired certain knowledge that she was concerned in the abduction of Madame Bonacieux."

"Yes, I understand now. To find one woman you are paying court to another. It is the longest way to go about it, but certainly the most amusing road."

D'Artagnan was on the point of telling his friend all, but one consideration restrained him. Athos was a gentleman, punctilious in points of honor, and there were in the plan which our young lover had devised for Milady, he was sure, certain things that would not meet the approval of this Puritan. He therefore was silent. And, as Athos was the least inquisitive man on earth, d'Artagnan's confidence stopped there. We shall therefore leave the two friends, who had nothing important to say to each other, and follow Aramis.

This musketeer ran without stopping to his home in the Rue Vaugirard. On entering his apartment he found a man of short stature and intelligent eyes, but covered with rags.

"I wish to speak to M. Aramis," the stranger said. "Is that your name, Monsieur?"

"My very own. You have brought me something?"

"Yes, if you show me a certain embroidered handkerchief."

Aramis made his lackey a sign to retire, and the curious Bazin was forced to obey. Then the musketeer opened a small ebony box inlaid with mother-of-pearl. "Here is the token," he said. "Look!"

Bazin gone, the mendicant cast a rapid glance around him in order to make sure that no one could either hear or see him. Then he opened his ragged vest, badly held together by a leather strap, and began to rip the upper part of his doublet, from which he drew a letter.

Aramis uttered a cry of joy at the sight of the seal, kissed the superscription with an almost religious fervor, and opened the epistle, which contained the following:

MY FRIEND:

It is the will of fate that for some time we should still be separated. But the delightful days of yore are not lost beyond return. Perform your duty in camp. I shall do mine elsewhere. Accept that which the bearer brings you. Go through the campaign like the handsome and true gentleman you are. And think of me who kiss tenderly your black eyes. Adieu, or rather, au revoir.

The mendicant continued to rip his garments and drew from amid his rags a hundred and fifty Spanish double pistoles, which he laid down upon the table. Then he opened the door, bowed, and went out before the young man, stupefied by the letter, had ventured to address a word to him.

Aramis kissed the letter with passion, without ever vouchsafing a look at the heap of gold that sparkled on the table. Bazin scratched at the door, and as Aramis no longer had any reason to exclude him, he bade him enter.

At sight of the gold Bazin forgot to announce d'Artagnan. Now, as the young Gascon wasted no ceremony with Aramis, he made his presence known with his own lips.

"The devil!" he exclaimed. "If these are the prunes that are sent you from Tours, I beg you will offer my compliments to the gardener who gathers them."

"You are in error, friend d'Artagnan," said Aramis, who was always on his guard. "This money is from my publisher, who has just sent me the pay for that poem I told you I was writing."

"Ah," said d'Artagnan with a smile, "you sell your productions for their weight in gold. You are very fortunate, my friend. But take care, or you will lose that letter which is peeping from your doublet, and which also comes, no doubt, from your publisher."

Aramis blushed to the eyes, crammed in the letter, and re-buttoned his doublet. He put three or four double pistoles into his pocket, and the friends then started out to fortify themselves with a good dinner and a few good glasses of old Burgundy.

They repaired to the apartment of Athos. And he, faithful to his vow of not going out, undertook to order dinner brought to them. As he was perfectly acquainted with the details of gastronomy, d'Artagnan and Aramis made no objection to abandoning this important office to him.

They set out to find Porthos, and at the corner of the Rue Bac they met Mousqueton, who with a most pitiable air was driving before him a mule and a horse.

D'Artagnan uttered a cry of surprise which was not quite free from joy. "Ah, my yellow horse!" he cried. "Aramis, just cast a glance at the beast."

"Oh, the frightful brute!" exclaimed the musketeer.

"Not so, my dear chap!" replied d'Artagnan. "Upon that very animal I rode to Paris."

"Pray you, gentlemen," begged the lackey, "say nothing about it. It is a scurvy trick of the husband of our duchess."

"How so, Mousqueton?"

"Why, we are looked upon with rather a favorable eye, Messieurs, by a lady of quality. She forced us to accept a small souvenir of her regard—a magnificent Spanish *genêt* and an Andalusian mule—they were beautiful to look upon. The husband heard of the affair. On their way to us he confiscated the beasts and substituted for them these horrible animals."

"Which you are taking back to him?"

"Exactly, Monsieur."

"That is a pity, Mousqueton, for I should have liked to view Porthos on my yellow horse. But don't let us hinder you, my lad. Go and perform your master's orders. Is he at home?"

"Yes, Monsieur, but he is in a very ill humor. Get up, you!"

The two friends went to ring at the bell of the unfortunate Porthos. But he had seen them crossing the yard and took care not to answer. So they rang in vain.

Meanwhile Mousqueton continued his way toward the Quai des Grands Augustins. He crossed the Pont Neuf, still driving the two sorry animals before him, and reached the Rue aux Ours. According to the orders of his master, he fastened both horse and mule to the knocker of the procurator's door. Then, without further thought for

their future, he returned to Porthos and informed him that
his commission was done.

In a short time the two unfortunate beasts, who had
not had a bite to eat since breakfast, made such a noise by
raising and letting fall the knocker that the procurator
ordered his errand boy to go around the neighborhood and
inquire to whom this horse and mule might belong.

Madame Coquenard recognized her present and could
not at first understand this restitution, but the visit of
Porthos soon enlightened her.   The anger which fired the
eyes of the musketeer, in spite of his efforts to suppress
it, terrified his sensitive inamorata.   In fact, Mousqueton
had not concealed from his master that d'Artagnan had
recognized in the yellow horse the Béarnese pony upon
which he had ridden into Paris and which he had sold for
three crowns.

All that a man wounded in his self-love could utter in
the shape of imprecations and reproaches, Porthos let fall
upon the bowed head of the procurator's wife.

"Alas!" she whined.   "I did it for the best!   One of our
clients is a horse dealer.   He owes money to the office and
is backward in his payment.   I took the horse and the mule
in payment of what he owed us.   He assured me that they
were two noble steeds."

"Well, Madame," said Porthos, "if he owed you more
than five crowns, your horse dealer is a thief."

"There is no harm in trying to buy things cheap, M.
Porthos," said the procurator's wife, seeking to excuse
herself.

"Not at all, Madame.   But they who so assiduously try

to purchase cheap objects should permit others to seek more generous friends."

And Porthos, turning on his heel, made a step to depart.

"I have been wrong, I see it," sobbed the procurator's wife. "I ought not have driven a bargain when it was to equip a cavalier like you, M. Porthos."

The musketeer without reply retreated a second step. His companion fancied that she saw him in a brilliant cloud, all surrounded by duchesses and marchionesses, who cast bags of money at his feet.

"Stop, in the name of heaven!" she cried. "Stop, M. Porthos, and let us talk."

"Talking with you only brings me misfortune," objected Porthos.

"But tell me, what do you ask?"

"Nothing, for that amounts to the same thing as if I asked you for something."

The procurator's wife clung to the arm of Porthos, and in the violence of her grief she cried out, "M. Porthos, I am ignorant of all such matters. How should I know what a horse is? How should I know good horse-trappings when I see them?"

"You should have left it to me, then, Madame, who know what they are. But you wished to be frugal, and consequently to lend at usury."

"It was wrong of me, M. Porthos. But I shall repair the wrong, upon my word of honor."

"How so?" asked the musketeer.

"Listen. This evening M. Coquenard is going to the home of the Duc de Chaulnes for a consultation that will

last at least three hours.   We shall be alone and can make
up our accounts."

"Now you are talking, my dear."

"You pardon me?"

"We shall see," answered Porthos majestically.   And
the two separated, saying, "Until this evening."

"The devil!" thought Porthos as he strode away.   "It
appears that I am getting somewhat nearer to M. Coquenard's strong box."

CHAPTER XXXIII

THE SAPPHIRE RING

The evening so impatiently awaited by Porthos and by d'Artagnan at last arrived.

As was his custom, d'Artagnan presented himself at Milady's about nine o'clock. He found her in a charming humor. Never had he been so well received. By the first glance that he cast at his hostess the Gascon knew that his billet had been delivered and that its contents had had their effect.

At ten o'clock Milady began to grow restless. D'Artagnan knew very well what she wanted. She looked at the clock, rose, reseated herself, and smiled at the young soldier with an air that said, "You are very nice, no doubt, but you would be a most charming fellow if you would only take your hat and go."

D'Artagnan rose and took his hat. Milady gave him her hand to kiss. The young man felt her press his hand, and comprehended that this was a sentiment, not of coquetry, but of gratitude because of his departure.

"She loves him terribly," he murmured. Then he went out.

This time Kitty was nowhere waiting for him, neither in the antechamber, nor in the corridor, nor beneath the great door. D'Artagnan had to find the staircase and the small chamber by himself. She heard him enter, but she did not raise her head.

As little sensitive as was the heart of d'Artagnan, he was touched by this mute sorrow. But he held too tenaciously to his projects, above all to this one, to change the program which he had laid out in advance. He therefore did not allow the soubrette any hope that he would flinch — only, to her he represented his action as one of simple vengeance.

And this vengeance turned out to be easy of accomplishment, for Milady, doubtless to conceal her blushes from her lover, had ordered Kitty to extinguish all the lights in her apartment. It was arranged that M. de Wardes would not only arrive but take his departure in obscurity.

Presently they heard Milady retire to her chamber. D'Artagnan slipped into the wardrobe of Kitty's room. Hardly was he concealed when the little bell sounded. The soubrette went to her mistress and did not leave the door open. But the partition between the two chambers was so thin that one could hear nearly all the talk that passed between the two women.

Finally, as the hour for her interview with the count approached, Milady had everything about her darkened, and ordered Kitty to return to her own chamber and to bring up de Wardes whenever he presented himself.

Kitty's detention was not long. Hardly had d'Artagnan made sure, through a crevice in his closet, that the whole apartment was in obscurity, when he slipped out of his concealment at the very moment when the soubrette reclosed the door of communication.

"What noise is that?" demanded Milady.

"It is I," answered d'Artagnan in a subdued voice. "It is the Comte de Wardes."

"Well," said Milady in a trembling voice, "why do you not enter? You know that I am waiting for you."

At this appeal the young Gascon drew Kitty quietly away and slipped into the chamber.

"Yes, Count," continued Milady in her softest voice and pressing his hand in her own, "I am happy because of what your looks and your words have expressed to me every time we have met. I also—I love you. Oh, tomorrow I must have some pledge from you that will prove that you think of me. And that you may not forget me, take this!"

She slipped a ring from her finger and thrust it upon d'Artagnan's. He remembered having seen this jewel on the hand of Milady. It was a magnificent sapphire encircled with brilliants.

The first impulse of d'Artagnan was to return it, but Milady added, "No, no! Keep that ring as a symbol of our affection. Besides, in accepting it," she went on to say in a voice full of emotion, "you are rendering me a far greater service than you imagine."

"This woman is full of mysteries," murmured the Gascon to himself. At that moment he felt ready to reveal all. He even opened his mouth to inform Milady who he was, and with what a revengeful purpose he had come. But she added, "My poor angel, whom that monster of a Gascon almost succeeded in slaying!"

D'Artagnan felt uncomfortable when he reflected that the monster spoken of was himself.

"Oh," continued Milady, "do your wounds still make you suffer? Be tranquil. I shall avenge you—and cruelly."

"*Peste!*" said d'Artagnan to himself. "The moment for confidences has apparently not yet come."

All the ideas of vengeance which the young Gascon had brought with him seemed to have vanished completely. This woman exercised over him an unaccountable power— he hated and adored her at the same time. He would not have believed that two sentiments so opposite could dwell in the same heart and by their union constitute a passion so strange and diabolical.

It was soon necessary for the two to separate. At the moment of quitting Milady, d'Artagnan felt only the keenest regret at the parting. And as they addressed each other in a reciprocally passionate adieu, another interview was arranged for the following week.

The next morning d'Artagnan ran to find Athos. He was engaged in an adventure so singular that he wished for advice. He therefore told the older musketeer everything.

"Your Milady," asserted Athos, "appears to be an infamous creature. But none the less you have done wrong to deceive her. In one way and another you have a terrible enemy on your hands."

While thus speaking Athos regarded with attention the sapphire set with diamonds. This had taken the position on d'Artagnan's finger which had previously been occupied by the queen's ring, now carefully kept in a casket.

"You are noticing my ring?" said the Gascon, proud to display so rich a gift before the eyes of his friend.

"Yes," replied Athos. "It reminds me of a family jewel. Did you trade it for your diamond?"

"No. It is a gift from my beautiful Englishwoman— or rather Frenchwoman—for I am convinced she was born in France, although I have not questioned her regarding it."

"That ring comes from Milady?" cried Athos with a voice in which it was easy to detect strong emotion.

"Her very self—she gave it to me last night. Here it is," returned d'Artagnan, taking it from his finger.

Athos examined the bijou and became very pale. He tried it on his left hand. It fitted his finger as if made for it. A shade of anger passed across the usually calm brow of this gentleman.

"It is impossible it can be she," he muttered. "How could this ring come into the possession of Milady Clarik? And yet it is difficult to suppose that such a resemblance should exist between two gems."

"Do you know this ring?" asked the Gascon.

"I thought I did," replied Athos, "but no doubt I was mistaken."

He returned the ring to d'Artagnan without, however, ceasing to stare at it with a puzzled air.

"Pray, my dear friend," Athos continued after a moment, "either take off that ring or turn the setting inside. It recalls such cruel memories that I shall have no head to converse with you. Don't ask me for advice. But stop! Let me look at that sapphire again—the one I mentioned to you had one of its faces scratched by accident."

D'Artagnan took off the ring, giving it to Athos.

Athos started. "Look!" he said. "Is it not strange?" And he pointed out to his friend the scratch he had remembered.

"But from whom did this ring come to you, Athos?"

"From my mother, who inherited it from her mother. It is an old family jewel."

"And you sold it?"

"No," replied Athos with a singular smile. "I gave it away in a night of love, as it has been given to you."

D'Artagnan became pensive in his turn. It appeared there were abysses in Milady's soul whose depths were dark and unknown. He took back the ring, but did not put it on his finger. He thrust it in his pocket.

"My friend," said Athos, taking his hand, "you know my feeling for you. If I had a son, I could not love him better. Take my advice, renounce this woman. I do not know her, but a sort of intuition tells me she is a lost creature and that there is something fatal about her."

And Athos bowed to d'Artagnan like a man who wishes it understood he would not be sorry to be left alone with his own thoughts.

On reaching home the young Gascon found Kitty awaiting him. A month of fever could not have changed her more than this one night of sleeplessness and sorrow.

The soubrette had been sent by her mistress to the false de Wardes. She wished to know when her lover would meet her a second time. Poor Kitty, pale and trembling, awaited d'Artagnan's reply. The counsels of Athos, joined to the cries of his own heart, made the Gascon determine, now his pride was saved and his vengeance satisfied, not to see Milady again. As a reply to Kitty's message, therefore, he composed the following:

Do not depend upon me, Madame, for the next meeting. Since my convalescence I have so many affairs of this kind on my hands that I am forced to regulate them a little. When your turn comes, I shall have the honor to inform you of it. I kiss your hands.

COMTE DE WARDES.

D'Artagnan gave the open letter to Kitty, who at first was unable to comprehend it. But on reading it a second time she became almost wild with joy. She could scarcely believe in her happiness. And negligent of the danger that she ran in giving such a letter to her mistress, she flew back to the Place Royale as fast as her feet would carry her.

Milady opened the billet with eagerness equal to Kitty's in bringing it. But at the first words she read she became livid. She crushed the paper in her hand and, turning with flashing eyes upon the soubrette, she cried, "What letter is this which you have brought?"

"The answer to Madame's note," stammered Kitty.

"Impossible!" declared Milady. She ground her teeth; she was the color of ashes. She tried to approach the window for air, but her limbs failed her and she sank helplessly into an armchair.

"Oh, Madame, are you ill? May I help?" asked the maid, frightened at the terrible expression which had come over her mistress' face.

"Do you take me for half a woman?" retorted Milady. "When I am insulted I do not swoon away, I avenge myself."

And she made a sign for Kitty to leave the room.

CHAPTER XXXIV

DREAM OF VENGEANCE

That evening Milady gave orders that when M. d'Artagnan came as usual, he should be at once admitted. But he did not come.

The next day Kitty went to see the young man again and related to him what had passed on the preceding evening. D'Artagnan smiled—this jealous anger of Milady was his revenge.

That evening Milady was still more impatient than on the preceding night. She renewed the order relative to the Gascon. But, as before, she awaited him in vain.

The next morning when Kitty presented herself at the Gascon's she was no longer joyous and alert as on the two previous days. She gave d'Artagnan a letter in Milady's handwriting, only this time it was really addressed to him and not to M. de Wardes. He opened it and read as follows:

DEAR M. D'ARTAGNAN:

It is wrong thus to neglect your friends, particularly at a moment when you are about to leave them for so long a time. My brother-in-law and I expected you yesterday and the day before, but in vain. Will it be the same tonight?

Your ever grateful

MILADY CLARIK.

"That's all very simple," said d'Artagnan, "I expected this letter. My credit rises by the fall of that of the Comte de Wardes."

"And will you go?" asked Kitty.

"Listen," said the Gascon, who sought for an excuse in his own eyes for breaking the promise he had made Athos, "it would be impolitic for me not to accept such a positive invitation. Milady would not be able to understand what could cause the interruption of my visits and might suspect something. Who can say how far the vengeance of such a woman might go?"

D'Artagnan went on to reassure Kitty as well as he could, promising to remain insensible to the seductions of Milady. He desired the soubrette to inform her mistress that he would be gratefully obedient to her orders.

As nine o'clock sounded d'Artagnan was at the Place Royale. It was evident that the servants who waited in the antechamber were aware of his expected arrival. For as soon as the Gascon appeared one of them ran to announce him.

"Show him in," said Milady in a tone so penetrating that d'Artagnan heard her in the antechamber.

He was brought in.

"I am at home to nobody," said Milady. "Do you hear? To nobody!"

The servant left the room.

D'Artagnan cast an inquiring glance at Milady. She was pale and looked fatigued, either from tears or from want of sleep. The number of lights in the saloon had been intentionally diminished, but still the young woman could not conceal the traces of the fever which had devoured her for two days.

Her guest approached with his usual gallantry. She

made an extraordinary effort to receive him, but never did a more distressed countenance give the lie to a lovelier smile.

To the questions which the visitor put concerning her health, she replied, "Bad, very bad."

"Then," remarked d'Artagnan, "my visit is ill-timed. You are no doubt sadly in need of repose, and I shall withdraw."

"On the contrary, stay, M. d'Artagnan. Your agreeable company will divert me."

"She has never been so kind to me before," thought d'Artagnan. "Be on your guard, my boy."

By degrees Milady became quite communicative. She asked the young Gascon if he were in love with any woman.

"Alas!" said the young man with the most sentimental air he could assume, "can you be cruel enough to ask such a question of me? Of me, who, from the first moment I saw you, have breathed and sighed only through you and for you?"

Milady favored him with a strange smile.

"Then you love me?" she said.

"Have you not perceived it?"

"It may be I have. But you know the more worth while hearts are to capture, the more difficult they are to be won."

"Difficulties do not affright me, Milady. I shrink from nothing except impossibilities."

"Nothing is impossible," replied Milady, "to true love."

"Nothing, Madame?"

"Not a thing in the world, Monsieur."

"The devil!" thought d'Artagnan to himself. "The note is changed. Is she going to fall in love with me by any chance? And will this fair, inconstant creature show herself disposed to give me another sapphire like the one she gave me for de Wardes?"

The young Gascon rapidly drew his seat nearer to Milady's.

"Come now," Milady said, "let us see what you would do to prove this love of which you speak so glibly."

"Command me for any service. I am ready."

"Ready for anything?"

"Yes!" cried d'Artagnan, who knew beforehand that he had not much to risk in engaging himself thus. "I am all attention, Madame. Just tell me what you need."

Milady remained thoughtful and undecided for a moment. Then, as if appearing to have formed a resolution, she said, "I have an enemy, Monsieur."

"You, Madame!" said d'Artagnan, affecting surprise. "Is it possible that can be? You are so good and beautiful."

"A mortal enemy, Monsieur."

"Indeed!"

"An enemy who has insulted me so cruelly that between him and me it is war to the death. May I reckon on you as an auxiliary?"

D'Artagnan at once perceived the goal which the vindictive woman wished to gain.

"You may, Madame," he said with emphasis. "My arm and my life belong to you, like my love."

"Then," said Milady, "since you are as generous as you are loving—" She stopped.

"Well?" demanded d'Artagnan.

"Well," replied Milady after a moment of silence, "from now on you must cease to talk of impossibilities where love is concerned."

"Do not overwhelm me with happiness," cried the Gascon, throwing himself on his knees and covering with kisses the hand abandoned to him.

"Avenge me on that infamous de Wardes," said Milady under her breath, "and I shall soon know how to get rid of you—you double idiot, you animated sword blade!"

"Fall voluntarily into my arms, hypocritical and dangerous woman," said d'Artagnan, likewise to himself, "after having abused me with such effrontery! And afterward I shall laugh at you with him whom you wished me to kill."

The young soldier lifted up his head. "I am ready," he said.

"You have understood me then, dear M. d'Artagnan?"

"I could interpret a look of yours, Milady."

"Then you would employ in my service your arm which has already acquired so much renown?"

"Instantly."

"But how shall I repay such a service?" asked Milady.

"You know the only payment that I desire," said d'Artagnan, and he drew her unresisting form nearer.

"Selfish creature!" she cried, smiling.

"Ah," replied the soldier, really carried away by the passion this woman had the power to kindle in his heart— "ah, that is because my happiness appears so impossible to me."

"Well, merit this pretended happiness then!"

"I am at your orders, Milady."

"Quite certain of it, Monsieur?"

"Just name to me the base man who has brought tears to your beautiful eyes!"

"Who said I had been weeping?"

"Come, tell me the name of this man. Do I know him?"

"Yes."

"Surely it cannot be one of my friends?" suggested d'Artagnan, affecting hesitation in order to convince her of his ignorance.

"If it were one of your friends, would you hesitate, then?" demanded Milady, and a threatening glance darted from her eyes.

"Not if it were my own brother!" cried the Gascon, as if carried away by his enthusiasm.

Our hero promised this without risk, for he knew in advance just what and who were meant.

"I love your devotedness," said the woman.

"Alas, and do you love nothing else in me?" queried d'Artagnan.

"I love you also—you!" she said, taking his hand in hers.

"You love me!" he cried. "Oh, if that were true, I should lose my reason."

And he folded her in his arms. She made no effort to remove her lips from his kisses, only she did not respond to them. If de Wardes at that moment had been under his hand, d'Artagnan would have killed him. Milady seized the occasion.

"His name is—" she said

"De Wardes—I know it," completed d'Artagnan.

"And how do you know that?" asked Milady, seizing both his hands and endeavoring to read with her eyes to the bottom of his heart.

D'Artagnan felt that he had permitted himself to be carried away and that he had committed a gross error.

"How do I know it?" stuttered the Gascon. "Why, I know it because in a drawing-room where I happened to be yesterday M. de Wardes showed a ring which he said he had received from you."

"Wretch!" cried Milady.

"Well, I shall avenge you on this wretch," replied d'Artagnan, giving himself a mighty air.

"Thanks, my brave friend! And when?"

"Whenever you please."

Milady was about to exclaim, "Now—at once!" But she reflected that such precipitation would not be very gracious to her champion.

"Tomorrow," the latter said, "you will be avenged or I shall be dead. But would it be just on your part to allow me to face possible death without giving me at least something more than hope?"

"I assure you, Monsieur, that you may rely on my tenderness."

"I cannot wait until tomorrow."

"Silence! I hear my brother. It would be unfortunate for him to find you here."

She rang the bell and Kitty appeared. Milady held out her hand to him. He kissed it devotedly and went.

CHAPTER XXXV

MILADY'S SECRET

D'Artagnan had been given permission to return to the residence of Milady Clarik at eleven o'clock that evening.

What was most clear in the matter was that the Gascon loved this strange woman like a madman and that she did not care for him at all. In an instant of clarity, d'Artagnan perceived that the most honest way in which he could act would be to go home and write Milady a long letter. In this writing he would confess to her that he and de Wardes were, up to the present moment, absolutely the same person. Consequently he could not undertake to kill the Comte de Wardes without committing suicide.

But the young man was also spurred on by a ferocious desire for vengeance. He wished to subdue this Milady in his own name. And as this vengeance appeared to him to have a certain sweetness in it, he could not make up his mind to renounce it.

He walked six or seven times around the Place Royale, turning at every ten steps to look at the light in Milady's apartment, which was to be seen through the blinds. At length the light disappeared. With a beating heart the young soldier promptly reëntered the house and gained Milady's chamber through Kitty's room.

D'Artagnan had gained the summit of all his wishes. It was no longer a rival who was beloved, it was he himself who was the object of Milady's tenderness. To be sure, a secret voice still whispered to him that he was but an instrument of vengeance, that he was being caressed only until he had given death. But pride and self-love silenced this still small voice of conscience and of reason and stifled its murmurs.

He was absorbed entirely by the sensations of the moment. But Milady, who had not the same motives for forgetfulness that d'Artagnan had, was the first to return to reality. And she asked him if the means which were on the morrow to bring on the encounter between him and de Wardes were already arranged in his mind.

Now, the young Gascon, whose ideas in the transports of his love had taken quite another course, forgot himself like a fool. And he responded gallantly that it was too late to think of duels and sword-thrusts. This coldness toward the only interests that occupied her mind naturally terrified Milady, whose questions thereafter became more pressing.

Then d'Artagnan, who had never seriously considered the matter of this impossible duel, endeavored to turn the subject of the conversation, but he could not succeed. Milady kept him within the limits she had traced beforehand with her irresistible spirit and her iron will.

The young soldier fancied himself very cunning when advising Milady to renounce, by pardoning de Wardes, the furious projects she had formed. But at the first word he spoke the young woman started and exclaimed in a fierce, bantering tone which sounded strange in the darkness, "Are you afraid, dear M. d'Artagnan?"

"De Wardes shall die, since you condemn him!" answered d'Artagnan, in so firm a tone that it appeared to Milady an undoubted proof of devotion. This reassured her.

Again, a long time afterward, when the Gascon was about to leave Milady, she recalled his promise to avenge her on the count.

"I am quite ready," said d'Artagnan. "But in the first place I should like to be certain of one thing."

"What is that?" asked Milady.

"Whether you really love me or not."

"I have given you proof enough of that, Monsieur."

"And I am yours, body and soul, Madame."

"Thanks, my brave lover. But now you must satisfy me of your love, that is only fair."

"Assuredly," replied d'Artagnan. "Still, if you care for me as much as you say, do you not entertain a little fear on my account?"

"What have I to fear?"

"Why, that I may be dangerously wounded—killed, even."

"Impossible, sir! You are such an expert swordsman."

"You would not, then," resumed d'Artagnan, "prefer a method which would equally avenge you while rendering the combat useless?"

Milady looked at her lover in silence. A pale light in the room gave to her clear eyes a strangely frightful expression.

"*Peste!* I do not hesitate about the duel," declared the Gascon. "But I really pity this poor de Wardes, since you have ceased to love him. I think a man must be so severely punished by the loss of your love that he stands in need of no other chastisement."

"Who told you I loved him?" asked Milady sharply.

"At least, I am now at liberty to believe, without too much conceit, that you love another," said the young man, in a caressing tone. "And I repeat that I am actually interested for the count."

"You?" asked Milady.

"Yes, I, Madame."

"And why just you?"

"Because I alone know—"

"What?"

"That he is far from being so guilty toward you as he appears."

"Indeed!" exclaimed Milady in an anxious tone. "Explain yourself, please, as I've no notion what you mean."

And she looked at d'Artagnan, who embraced her tenderly, with eyes which seemed to consume themselves in fire.

"Yes, I am a man of honor," said d'Artagnan, determined to come to an end, "and since your love is mine and I am satisfied I possess it, a confession weighs upon my mind."

"A confession?"

"If I had the least doubt of your love, I should not make it."

"My love is yours, without doubt. Proceed, Monsieur."

"Then if through excess of affection for you I have rendered myself guilty, you will pardon me?"

"Perhaps."

With his sweetest smile d'Artagnan tried to touch his lips to Milady's, but she evaded him. "This confession," she said, growing paler, "what is this confession?"

"You had a rendezvous with de Wardes on Thursday last in this very room, did you not?"

"No, no! It is not true," answered Milady in a tone of voice so firm and with a face so unchanged that d'Artagnan would have doubted had he not been in such perfect possession of the fact.

"Do not lie, my angel," said the Gascon, smiling. "For denial would be useless."

"What do you mean? Speak! You are killing me."

"Simply this: de Wardes cannot boast of your favors."

"How is that? You told me yourself that the ring—"

"That ring I have! The Comte de Wardes of Thursday and the d'Artagnan of today are one and the same person."

The imprudent young man expected a surprise, mixed with shame—a slight storm which would resolve itself into tears. But he was strangely deceived, and his error was not of long duration.

Pale and trembling, Milady repulsed d'Artagnan with a violent blow on the chest. The young Gascon tried to detain her in order to implore her pardon. With a strong and unexpected movement she attempted to free herself from his despairing clutch. As a result, her dress was torn away from one of her shoulders. And on this lovely shoulder, round and white, d'Artagnan recognized to his ineffable astonishment the fleur-de-lis—that indelible brand which the ignominious hand of some executioner had imprinted.

The young lover loosed his hold of Milady's dress, and remained where he stood—mute, motionless, and frozen.

Not so, Milady. She turned upon him, no longer like a furious woman but like a wounded panther.

"Wretch!" she cried. "You have my secret. You shall die."

And she flew to a small inlaid casket which stood upon the dressing table, opened it with a feverish and trembling hand, and drew from it a small poniard with a golden haft and a long thin blade. She threw herself upon d'Artagnan with a bound.

He was terrified at that wild countenance, those terribly dilated eyes, those pale cheeks and bleeding lips. He recoiled to the other side of the room as he would have done from a serpent. He drew his blade from its scabbard and presented its point sometimes at her eyes and sometimes at her breast. Thus he compelled her to glide behind the bedstead, while he endeavored to make his retreat by the door that led to Kitty's apartment.

"Scoundrel, infamous scoundrel!" cried Milady.

At this moment Kitty, disturbed by the noise they were making, opened the door. D'Artagnan was through it like a flash. He slammed the panel shut and placed all his weight against it, while the soubrette shot the bolts.

"Quick, Kitty!" cried the young man. "Get me out of the house. If we give her time to turn around, she will have me killed by the servants."

The maid conducted him hurriedly down the stairs.

And it was time, indeed! For Milady had already rung her bell and roused the whole household. The porter was drawing the cord for the lower entrance gate at the second Milady shrieked from the upper window, "Don't open!"

But the young man had fled through the opening while the demented creature was still threatening him with an impotent gesture. The moment Milady lost sight of him in the shadows of the street below, she tumbled back fainting into her chamber.

CHAPTER XXXVI

THE OUTFIT OF ATHOS

Without taking any heed of what might become of Kitty, d'Artagnan ran at full speed half across Paris, and did not stop until he had come to Athos' door. He knocked upon this hard enough to break it down.

The musketeer recognized his young friend at once, although the light in the corridor was dim and d'Artagnan still looked very much like an escaped inmate of the Bastille.

"Whatever you do, don't laugh at me!" cried d'Artagnan. "For, upon my soul, it's no laughing matter."

And he pronounced these words with such a solemn air and with so real an appearance of terror that Athos eagerly seized his hand, crying, "Are you wounded, my lad? How shockingly pale you are!"

"No, but I have just met with an awful adventure."

"Come, speak out!" continued Athos, closing the hall door and bolting it that they might not be disturbed. "Is the king dead? Have you slain the cardinal?"

"Prepare, Monsieur, to hear an incredible story."

"I am prepared, d'Artagnan."

The young Gascon bent his mouth to Athos' ear and lowered his voice. "Milady is branded with a fleur-de-lis on her shoulder!"

"Ah!" cried the musketeer as if he had received a bullet in his heart.

"Are you sure the other woman is dead?"

"The other?" whispered Athos in so stifled a voice that d'Artagnan scarcely heard him.

"Yes. She of whom you told me that day at Amiens."

Athos uttered a groan at this remark and allowed his head to sink slowly into his hands.

"This is a woman of twenty-six or twenty-eight years."

"Fair," said Athos, "is she not?"

"Extremely so."

"Blue and clear eyes of a strange brilliancy, with black eyelashes and brows?"

"Exactly."

"Tall, well formed? She has lost a tooth next to the eyetooth on the left side?"

"Just so!"

"The brand of the fleur-de-lis is small, rosy in color, and looks as if efforts had been made to efface it?"

"Right you are."

"But you say she is English?"

"She is called Milady, and yet she may be French. Lord de Winter is only her brother-in-law."

"I shall see her, d'Artagnan."

"Beware, Athos! You tried to kill her. She is a woman to return you the like, and not to fail."

"She would not dare to say anything, for that would be to denounce herself."

"On the contrary, she is capable of anything or everything. Did you ever see her in a rage?"

"Never," answered Athos.

"A tigress, I tell you, a panther! Ah, my dear friend,

I am greatly afraid I have drawn down a terrible vengeance on both of us."

"You are right," said Athos after d'Artagnan had related all to him—Milady's mad passion and her threats of death. "And upon my soul, our lives seem to hang by a thread. Fortunately, the day after tomorrow we are leaving Paris. We are probably going to La Rochelle, and once we are gone—"

"She will follow you to the end of the earth, Athos, if she recognizes you. Let her exhaust her vengeance on me alone, I beg!"

"My dear friend, who cares a sou if she kills me? Do you think I set any great store by life?"

"There is something mysteriously sinister under all this, Athos. This woman is one of the cardinal's spies, I am sure."

"In that case, take care! If the cardinal does not hold you in high admiration for the affair of London, he hates you terribly. Now, as he dare not accuse you openly, and as a hatred must be satisfied, particularly if it is a cardinal's hate, take care of yourself. Mistrust everything and everybody, even your own shadow."

"Once with the army," said d'Artagnan, "we shall have only men to dread."

"In the meantime," said Athos, "I renounce my plan of seclusion and walk with you wherever you go. But all this will not advance your outfit unless you make use of your sapphire."

"The jewel is yours, Athos. Did you not tell me it was a family heirloom?"

"Yes. My grandfather gave two thousand crowns for it, he once told me. It formed part of the nuptial present he gave his wife, and it is magnificent. My mother gave it to me. And I, fool that I was, instead of keeping the ring as a holy relic, handed it to this wretch."

"Take it back, my friend."

"Not after it has passed through the hands of that infamous creature—that ring is defiled, d'Artagnan."

"Sell it, then."

"Sell a jewel that came from my mother! To my eyes that would be profanation."

"Pledge it, then."

"Good! Pledge the ring we shall, but on one condition —that there shall be five hundred crowns for you and the like amount for me."

"Don't dream of that, Athos. I don't need a quarter of such a sum—I, who am still only in the Guards, and by selling my saddle I shall procure it. What do I want after all? A horse for Planchet. Besides, you forget that I, too, have a ring."

"To which you attach more value, it seems, than I do to mine."

"Yes. For in any extreme circumstance it might not only extricate us from great embarrassment, but even a great danger. It is an enchanted talisman."

"Either you take half the sum advanced upon my ring, d'Artagnan, or I shall throw the thing into the Seine."

"Well, I shall take it then," responded the Gascon.

When d'Artagnan and Athos were ready to go out, the latter made Grimaud the sign of a man taking aim, and the lackey immediately took down his musketoon and prepared to follow his master.

They arrived without accident at the Rue des Fossoyeurs. Bonacieux was standing at the door and looked at the Gascon hatefully.

"Make haste, dear lodger," he said. "There is a very pretty girl waiting for you upstairs, and women don't like to be kept waiting."

"That's Kitty!" said d'Artagnan to himself. And he darted into the passage.

"Oh, it is you, Monsieur!" cried Kitty. "After you had gone the lackeys were brought by the cries she made—she was mad with passion. There are no curses that she did not call down upon your head. I knew she would remember it was through my chamber you had penetrated into hers. So I took what little money I had and the best of my things, and I got away."

"Poor dear girl! But what can I do with you?"

"Whatever you please, Monsieur Chevalier. Help me out of Paris, out of France."

"But I cannot take you to the siege of La Rochelle, where I am bound day after tomorrow," said d'Artagnan.

"I don't care where I live," said Kitty, "provided I am well concealed and nobody knows where I am."

"Now, Kitty, that we are about to separate, and you are no longer jealous of me—"

"Monsieur Chevalier, far off or near, I shall always love you."

"Where the devil will constancy hide itself next?" murmured Athos.

"And I also," said d'Artagnan, "shall love you—be sure of that. But now, answer me. I attach great importance to the question I am about to put to you. Did you ever hear talk of a young woman who was carried off one night?"

"There, now! Oh, Monsieur Chevalier, do you love that woman still?"

"No, no. It is one of my friends who loves her—Monsieur Athos, this gentleman here."

"I!" cried Athos, with an accent like that of a man who perceives he is about to tread upon an adder.

"You, to be sure!" said d'Artagnan, pressing Athos' hand. "You know the interest we both take in poor little Madame Bonacieux. Besides, Kitty will say nothing, will you, Kitty? You understand, my dear girl," continued d'Artagnan, "she is the wife of that frightful baboon you saw at the door as you came in."

"Heavens above! You remind me of my fright! If he should have known me again!"

"Know you again? Did you ever see him before?"

"That awful man came twice to Milady's."

"Now we're talking! About what time?"

"Why, about sixteen or eighteen days ago."

"Exactly so."

"And yesterday evening he came again."

"Yesterday evening?"

"Yes, just before you came."

"My dear Athos, we are enveloped in a network of spies. And do you believe that he recognized you again, Kitty?"

"I pulled down my hood as soon as I saw **him**, but perhaps it was too late."

"Go down, Athos — he mistrusts you less than me — and see if he is still at the door."

Athos went down and returned immediately. "He is gone," he said, "and the house door is shut."

"He has gone to make his report and to say that all the pigeons are at this moment in the dovecote."

"Well, then, let us fly," counseled Athos, "and leave nobody here but Planchet to bring us news later."

At that moment, by good fortune, Aramis entered.

The whole matter was explained to him swiftly, and he was given to understand that among all his high connections he must find a place for Kitty.

Aramis reflected for a moment, and then said, coloring, "Will it really be rendering you a service, d'Artagnan?"

"I shall be grateful to you all my life."

"Very well. Madame de Bois-Tracy asked me, for one of her friends who resides in the provinces, I believe, for a trustworthy maid. If you can answer for Mademoiselle—"

"Oh, Monsieur," declared Kitty, "be assured that I shall be entirely devoted to the person who gives me the means of quitting Paris."

"Then," said Aramis, "this falls out very well."

He placed himself at the table and wrote a short note which he sealed with a ring. He then gave the billet to Kitty.

"And now, my dear girl," said d'Artagnan, "you know

it is not good for any of us to be here. Therefore let us separate at once. We shall meet again in happier days."

"And whenever and wherever we find each other again," said Kitty, "you will find me loving you as I love you today."

"Dicers' oaths!" grinned Athos, while d'Artagnan went to conduct the soubrette downstairs.

An instant afterward the three young men separated, agreeing to meet again at four o'clock with Athos, and leaving Planchet on guard in d'Artagnan's rooms. Athos and the young Gascon busied themselves about pledging the sapphire.

As they had foreseen, they easily obtained three hundred pistoles on the ring. Furthermore, the broker told them that if they would sell it to him, he would give them five hundred pistoles for it since it would make a magnificent pendant for an earring.

Athos and d'Artagnan, with the activity of two soldiers and the knowledge of two connoisseurs, hardly required three hours to purchase the entire equipment of the musketeers. Athos met with a superb Andalusian horse, black as jet, nostrils of fire, legs clean and elegant, rising six years. He examined him and found him to be sound and without blemish. The dealer asked a thousand livres for him.

Grimaud had a stout Picard cob which cost three hundred livres. But when the saddle and arms for Grimaud were purchased, Athos had not a sou left of his hundred and fifty pistoles. D'Artagnan offered his friend part of his share, which he could return when convenient.

But Athos only replied to this proposal by shrugging his shoulders.

"How much did the Jew say he would give us for the sapphire if he purchased it?" asked Athos.

"Five hundred pistoles."

"That is to say, two hundred more—one hundred pistoles for you and one hundred for me. Well, now, that would be a real fortune for us, my boy. So let's go back to the broker's again."

"What! Will you—"

"This ring would certainly only recall very bitter remembrances. Besides, we shall never be masters of three hundred pistoles to redeem it. Go and tell him the ring is his, d'Artagnan, and bring the two hundred pistoles back with you."

A half hour later the young Gascon came back with the two thousand livres and without having met with any accident.

It was thus that Athos had found at home resources which he did not expect.

CHAPTER XXXVII

A VISION

At four o'clock the friends were all assembled with Athos. Their anxiety about their outfits had disappeared and each countenance was placid in the extreme.

Suddenly Planchet entered, bringing two letters for d'Artagnan. One was a small billet, genteelly folded, with a pretty seal in green wax on which was impressed a dove bearing a green branch. The other was a large square epistle resplendent with the terrible arms of his Eminence, the cardinal duke.

At sight of the little note the heart of d'Artagnan bounded, for he believed he recognized the handwriting. And although he had seen those characters but once, the memory of them remained at the bottom of his heart. He therefore seized the small epistle and opened it eagerly. The words were:

On Thursday next, between six and seven o'clock in the evening, be on the road to Chaillot, and look carefully into the carriages that pass. But if you have any consideration for your own life or that of those who love you, do not speak a single word. Do not make a movement which may lead any one to believe you have recognized her who exposes herself to everything for the sake of seeing you but for an instant.

There was no signature.

"It is a snare," said Athos. "Do not go, d'Artagnan."

"And yet," replied the Gascon, "I think I know the handwriting."

"It may be counterfeit," persisted the musketeer. "Between six and seven o'clock the road to Chaillot is quite deserted. You might as well go ride in the forest of Bondy."

"But suppose we all go," suggested d'Artagnan. "What the devil! They won't devour all four of us, four lackeys, horses, arms, and all."

"And besides, it will be a chance to display our new equipments," said Porthos.

"Still, if it is a woman who writes," declared Aramis, "and that woman desires not to be seen, remember, you compromise her, d'Artagnan, which is not the part of a gentleman."

"We can remain in the background," said Porthos, "and he will advance alone."

"Yes, but a pistol shot is easily fired from a carriage that is passing at full gallop."

"Bah!" put in d'Artagnan, "they will miss me most probably. And if they should fire, we shall ride after the carriage and exterminate any one in it who looks like an enemy."

"He is right," asserted Porthos stoutly. "Battle—that's the word for us. We must try out our new arms."

"That would be fun, rather," said Aramis with his mild and careless manner.

"As you please," agreed Athos.

"Gentlemen," said d'Artagnan, "it is half-past four. We have scarcely time to be on the road of Chaillot by six."

"Besides, if we are too late, nobody will see us, and that

would be a pity," asserted Porthos. "Let us get ready at once."

"But this second letter," said Athos, "you forget that. And it appears to me that the seal denotes it deserves to be opened. For my part, d'Artagnan, I declare it's of more consequence than the small wisp of waste paper which you have so cunningly thrust into your bosom."

"Well," said the young Gascon, "let us see what are his Eminence's commands." He unsealed the letter and read:

M. d'Artagnan, of the king's Guards, company d'Essart, is expected at the Palais-Cardinal this evening, at eight o'clock.

LA HOUDINIÉRE, Captain of the Guards.

"The devil!" cried Athos. 'Here is a rendezvous much more serious than the other."

"I shall go to the second after attending the first," observed d'Artagnan. "One is for seven o'clock at latest, and the other for eight. There will be ample time for both."

"Hum! I should not go at all," advised Aramis. "A gallant knight cannot refuse a rendezvous with a lady. But a prudent gentleman may excuse himself from waiting on his Eminence, particularly when he has reason to suspect he is not invited to make his compliments."

"I am of Aramis' opinion," said Porthos.

"Messieurs," retorted the Gascon, "I have already received from M. de Cavois a similar invitation from his Eminence. I neglected it, and on the morrow a serious misfortune happened to me—Constance disappeared. Whatever may ensue, I shall go."

"If you are determined to go, do so," said Athos.

"But how about the Bastille?" queried Aramis.

"Bah! You would get me out of there, even if they put me in," said d'Artagnan.

"Let us do better than that," remarked Athos. "Let each one of us wait at a gate of the palace with three musketeers behind him. Then, if we see a closed carriage come out which looks the least mite suspicious, we can fall upon it."

"At any rate," said Porthos, "I shall run to the hotel and engage our comrades to hold themselves in readiness by eight o'clock—our objective to be the Place du Palais-Cardinal. Meanwhile, you see that the lackeys saddle the horses."

"I have no horse," said d'Artagnan, "but that is of no consequence, I can take one of M. de Tréville's."

"You can have one of mine," suggested Aramis.

"How many animals have you, then?" asked d'Artagnan.

"Three," replied Aramis, smiling.

"Certes," cried Athos, "you are the best mounted poet in France."

"But, my dear Aramis, I cannot comprehend what induced you to buy three. You don't need three horses."

"Therefore I only purchased two," said Aramis.

"The third one fell from the clouds, eh?"

"No. The third was brought to me this morning by a groom out of livery, who would not tell me in whose service he was, and who said he had received orders from his master to place the horse in my stable without informing me whence it came."

"From his master, eh? Or from his mistress?"

"It is only to poets that such things happen," said Athos.

"Well, in that case we can manage famously," agreed d'Artagnan. "Which of the two horses will you ride— that which you bought or the one which was given you?"

"The one given me, assuredly. You cannot for a moment imagine, d'Artagnan, that I should commit such an offense against—"

"The unknown giver," interrupted the Gascon.

"The mysterious benefactress," added Athos.

"The one you bought will then become useless to you?"

"Practically so."

"And you selected it yourself?"

"With the greatest care."

"Well, transfer it to me at the price it cost you?"

"I was about to make you the offer, my dear d'Artagnan. Take all the time you wish to repay the trifling obligation."

"How much did you give for the animal?"

"Eight hundred livres."

"Here are forty double pistoles, my friend," said the Gascon, taking the sum from his pocket. "I know that is the coin in which you were paid for your—poems."

"You are rich, then?" asked Aramis, surprised.

"Richer than that, dear fellow!"

And d'Artagnan chinked the remainder of his pistoles which were in his pocket.

"Send your saddle to the hotel of the Musketeers and your horse can be brought back with the others."

"Good! But it is five o'clock; so make haste."

A quarter of an hour afterward Porthos appeared at the end of the Rue Férou on a very handsome *genêt*. Mousqueton followed him on an Auvergne horse, small but very splendid. Porthos' face shone with joy and satisfied pride.

At the same moment Aramis made his appearance at the other end of the street upon a superb English charger. Bazin followed on a roan and held by the halter a vigorous Mecklenburg horse—this last was d'Artagnan's mount.

Planchet and Grimaud appeared in their turn, leading their masters' steeds. D'Artagnan and Athos mounted and the four Inseparables set forth.

As Porthos had foreseen, the cavalcade produced a good effect. If Madame Coquenard had met her champion and seen what a magnificent appearance he made upon his Spanish *genêt,* she would not have regretted the bleeding she had inflicted upon the strong box of her husband.

Near the Louvre the four friends met M. d Tréville, who was returning from St. Germain. He stopped them to offer his compliments upon their appointments, which in an instant drew around them a hundred gapers. At this moment the clock of La Samaritaine struck six. The four friends pleaded an engagement and took their leave.

A short gallop brought them to the road of Chaillot. The day began to decline; carriages were passing and repassing. D'Artagnan, keeping at some distance from his friends, darted a scrutinizing glance into every vehicle that appeared, but he saw no face with which he was acquainted.

At length, after they had waited a quarter of an hour, and just as twilight was beginning to thicken, a carriage appeared, coming at a fast pace on the road to Sèvres. A presentiment instantly told d'Artagnan that this equipage contained the person who had appointed the rendezvous. The young man was himself astonished to find his heart beat so violently. Almost instantly a woman's head was put out of the window with two fingers placed upon her mouth, either to enjoin silence or to send him a kiss. D'Artagnan uttered a slight cry of joy. For this woman was Madame Bonacieux.

In spite of the injunctions given in the letter, the Gascon put his horse to a gallop and in a few leaps had overtaken the carriage, but the window was now hermetically closed; the vision had disappeared. D'Artagnan remembered the words, "If you value the life of those who love you, remain motionless, as if you had seen nothing." And so he was forced to rein in his horse and stop.

His three companions joined him. All had plainly seen the woman's head at the window, but none of them, except Athos, knew Madame Bonacieux. Athos felt sure it was she, but he had fancied he saw a second head—that of a man—inside the carriage.

"If that be the case," said the guardsman, "they are doubtless transporting her from one prison to another. What can they intend to do with the poor creature, and how shall I ever meet her again?"

"Friend," said Athos gravely, "it is the dead alone whom we are not likely to meet again on this earth. And perhaps," he added with that misanthropic tone that was peculiar to him, "perhaps you may see her again sooner than you wish."

Half-past seven had sounded; the carriage was twenty minutes behind the time appointed. D'Artagnan's friends reminded him that he had a second visit to pay, but at the same time bade him observe that there was yet time to retract.

But the young guardsman was both impetuous and curious. He had made up his mind that he would go to the Palais-Cardinal and that he would learn what his Eminence had to say to him. Nothing could turn him from this purpose.

They reached the Rue St. Honoré, and in the Place du Palais-Cardinal they found the twelve invited musketeers walking about and waiting for the Inseparables to arrive. First the matter in hand was explained to them, and then Athos divided them into three groups, assuming the command of one, giving the second to Aramis, and the third to Porthos. Each group then went to take its watch near an entrance.

"If de Wardes has related our affair to the cardinal," d'Artagnan said to himself as he boldly entered the principal gate of the palace, "I may practically consider myself a condemned man. But why has his Eminence, then, waited until now to send for me? Oh, I imagine that's plain enough! Milady must have laid her complaints against me with that hypocritical grief that renders her so interesting, and this last offense has made my cup overflow. D'Artagnan, my friend, you are brave, you are at times prudent, you have other excellent qualities—but the women will ruin you!"

He came to this melancholy conclusion as he entered the antechamber. An usher appeared and made a sign to the young Gascon to follow him. He traversed a corridor, crossed a grand saloon, entered a library, and found himself in the presence of a man who was seated at a desk writing.

D'Artagnan at first believed he had to do with some judge examining his papers, but he soon perceived that the man at the desk was correcting lines of unequal length, scanning the words on his fingers. He saw then that the man was a poet. At the end of a minute or two the poet closed his manuscript, on the cover of which was written "Mirame, a Tragedy in Five Acts," and raised his head.

D'Artagnan recognized the cardinal.

CHAPTER XXXVIII

A STRANGE INTERVIEW

The cardinal leaned his elbow upon his manuscript, his cheek on his hand, and looked intently at the young man for a moment. No one had a more searching eye than the Cardinal de Richelieu, and the Gascon felt this glance run through his veins like a fever.

He, however, kept a good countenance, holding his hat in his hand and awaiting the good pleasure of his Eminence without too much assurance but also without too much humility.

"Monsieur," said the cardinal, "are you d'Artagnan of Béarn?"

"Yes, Monseigneur," replied the young man.

"To which branch do you belong?"

"I am the son of him who served in the Religious Wars under the great King Henry, the father of his Majesty."

"It is you who set out some eight months ago to seek your fortune in the capital?"

"Yes, Monseigneur."

"The letter to M. de Tréville was lost at Meung, where something befell you," resumed the cardinal, with a smile that indicated he knew very well just what had happened. "But, despite the loss, M. de Tréville, who is a skilled student of character, placed you in the company of his brother-in-law, M. d'Essart, leading you to hope that some day you should enter the Musketeers."

"Monseigneur is correctly informed," said d'Artagnan.

"Since that time many things have occurred. You were walking one day behind the Chartreux, when it would have been better for you to be elsewhere. Then with your friends you took a journey to the waters of Forges. They stopped on the road, but you continued the trip. That is all very simple—you had business in England."

"Monseigneur," said d'Artagnan quite confused, "I went—"

"I know—because it is my office to know everything. On your return you were received by an august personage, and I note with pleasure that you preserve the souvenir she gave you."

D'Artagnan placed his hand upon the queen's diamond which he wore, and quickly turned the stone inward, but it was too late.

"The day after that you received a visit from Cavois," continued the cardinal. "He went to request you to come to the palace. You have not paid that visit, and you did wrong."

"Monseigneur, I feared I had incurred disgrace with your Eminence."

"How could that be? Could you incur my displeasure, Monsieur, by following the orders of your superiors with more courage and intelligence than another would have done? It is the people who do not obey that I punish, and not those who, like yourself, obey too well. As a proof, remember the date of the day on which I had you bidden to come to me and seek in your memory for what happened that very night."

D'Artagnan trembled. For that was the very evening when the abduction of Madame Bonacieux took place. And he likewise recollected that during the past half hour the poor woman had passed close to him, without doubt carried away by the same power which had caused her earlier disappearance.

"In short," went on the cardinal, "as I have heard nothing of you for some time past, I wished to know what you were doing. Besides, you owe me some thanks. You must yourself have remarked how much you have been spared in all the circumstances."

D'Artagnan bowed with respect.

"That," continued the cardinal, "arose not only from a natural sense of justice, but also from a plan I have worked out concerning you."

D'Artagnan became more and more astonished.

"I wished to explain this plan to you on the day you received my first invitation. But you did not come. Fortunately, nothing is lost through this delay, and you are now about to hear the proposal. Sit down there before me, M. d'Artagnan. You are gentleman enough not to listen standing."

And the cardinal pointed with his finger to a chair for the young man, who was so astonished at what was passing that he awaited a second sign from his interlocutor before he obeyed.

"You are brave, M. d'Artagnan," said his Eminence, "and you are prudent, which is better. I like men of head and heart. Don't be afraid," he said, smiling. "By men of heart I mean men of courage. But young as you are, and scarcely entering into the great world, you have powerful enemies. If you do not take great heed, they will destroy you."

"Alas, Monseigneur!" replied the young man. "Very easily, no doubt, for they are strong and well supported, while I am alone."

"Yes, that is true. But, alone as you are, you have done much already, and will do still more, I don't doubt."

"I am at the age of extravagant hopes, Monseigneur."

"There are no extravagant hopes but for fools, Monsieur. Now, what would you say to an ensign's commission in my Guards, and a company after the campaign?"

"Ah, Monseigneur!"

"You accept, do you not?"

"Monseigneur," replied d'Artagnan with an embarrassed air.

"What! You refuse?" cried the cardinal with astonishment.

"I am in his Majesty's Guards, Monseigneur, and I have no reason to be dissatisfied."

"But it appears to me that my Guards—mine—are also those of his Majesty. And whoever serves in a French corps serves the king."

"Monseigneur, your Eminence has ill understood my words."

"You wish a pretext? I comprehend. Well, you have this excuse: advancement, the opening campaign, the opportunity I offer you—so much for the world. As regards yourself, the need of protection, for it is fit that you should know, M. d'Artagnan, I have received heavy and serious complaints against you. You do not consecrate your days and nights wholly to the king's service."

D'Artagnan colored.

"In fact," said the cardinal, placing his hand upon a roll of papers, "I have a whole bundle of reports concerning you. Come, reflect and make your decision."

"Your goodness confounds me, Monseigneur," replied d'Artagnan, "and I am conscious of a greatness of soul in your Eminence that makes me mean as an earthworm. But since Monseigneur permits me—"

D'Artagnan paused.

"Speak freely, Monsieur."

"Then I shall presume to say that all my friends are in the king's Musketeers and Guards, and that by an inconceivable fatality my enemies are in the service of your Eminence. I should, therefore, be ill received here and ill regarded there if I accepted what Monseigneur offers me."

"Do you happen to entertain the haughty idea that I have not yet made you an offer equal to your value?" asked the cardinal with a smile of disdain.

"Monseigneur, your Eminence is a hundred times too kind to me. On the contrary, I think I have not proved myself worthy of your goodness."

"Which is to say, you refuse to serve me, Monsieur," said the cardinal with a tone of vexation, in which, however, might be heard a sort of esteem. "Remain free, then, and keep your hatreds and your friendships."

"Monseigneur—"

"Well, well," said the cardinal, "I do not wish you any ill. But take care of yourself, M. d'Artagnan, for from

the moment I withdraw my hand from behind you I should
not give a penny for your life."

"I shall try to guard my safety, Monseigneur," replied the Gascon with a noble confidence.

"Well, let it be then as you have said, M. d'Artagnan.
We shall see each other after the campaign. And on our
return from La Rochelle we shall settle our account."

"Ah, Monseigneur," cried d'Artagnan, "spare me the
weight of your displeasure. Remain neutral, your Eminence, if you find that I am acting as becomes a gallant
man."

"If I shall be able to say to you at another time what I
have said to you today, Monsieur, I shall do so."

This last expression of Richelieu's conveyed a terrible
doubt. It alarmed d'Artagnan more than an open threat
would have done, for it was a warning. The cardinal,
then, was seeking to preserve him from some misfortune
which menaced him. He opened his mouth to reply, but
with a haughty gesture the cardinal dismissed him.

D'Artagnan went out, but at the door his heart almost
failed him and he felt inclined to return. Then the noble
and severe face of Athos crossed his mind. If he made
this compact with the cardinal, Athos would no longer
give him his hand—Athos would denounce him. It was
this fear that restrained the young guardsman, so powerful
is the influence of a truly great character on all that sur-
rounds it.

D'Artagnan descended by the staircase at which he had
entered and found Athos and four musketeers awaiting
his appearance and beginning to grow uneasy. With a

word the young guardsman reassured them, and Planchet
ran to inform the other sentinels that it was needless to
keep watch longer, as his master had come out safe from
the Palais-Cardinal.

Returned home with the three Inseparables, d'Artagnan confined himself to telling them that M. de Richelieu
had sent for him to propose he enter his Guards with the
rank of ensign, and that he had refused.

"And you were right," cried Aramis and Porthos with
one voice.

Athos fell into a profound reverie and said nothing.

At the first sound of the morning trumpet the friends
separated, the musketeers hastening to the residence of
M. de Tréville, the guardsman to that of M. d'Essart.
Each of the captains then led his company to the Louvre,
where Louis XIII held his review.

The review over, the Guards set forward alone on their
march, the Musketeers waiting for the king, which fact
allowed Porthos time to go and take a turn in the Rue
aux Ours.

The procurator's wife saw him pass in his new uniform
and on his fine horse. She loved Porthos too dearly to
allow him to depart thus—she made him a sign to dismount
and come to her. Porthos was magnificent. His spurs
jingled, his cuirass glittered, his sword knocked proudly
against his ample limbs. This time the clerks in the counting room evinced no desire to laugh, such a real ear-clipper
did Porthos appear to be.

The musketeer was introduced to M. Coquenard, whose
small gray eyes sparkled with anger at seeing his wife's

"cousin" all blazing new. Nevertheless, one thing afforded
him inward consolation: It was expected by everyone that
the campaign would be a severe one. He whispered a
hope to himself that this beloved friend might be killed
on the field of battle.

But the real adieux were made in Madame Coquenard's
chamber—they were heart-rending.

As long as the procurator's wife could follow Porthos
with her eyes, she waved her handkerchief to him, leaning
so far out of the window that passers-by believed she
wished to hurl herself down. Porthos received all these
attentions like a man accustomed to demonstrations of
love.

On his part, Aramis wrote a long letter. To whom?
Nobody knew. Kitty, who was to set out that evening
for Tours, was waiting in the next chamber.

Athos sipped the last bottle of his Spanish wine.

In the meantime d'Artagnan was marching away with
his company. Arrived at the Faubourg St. Antoine, he
turned gaily around to look at the Bastille. But, as it was
the gloomy prison alone he was looking at, he did not observe Milady. Mounted upon a light chestnut horse, she
was designating d'Artagnan with her finger to two evil-
looking men who came close up to the ranks to study him.
Then, certain that there could be no mistake in the execution
of her orders, Milady started her horse and disappeared.

The two men followed the company of the Guards, and
on leaving the Faubourg St. Antoine mounted two horses,
properly equipped, which a servant without livery had been
guarding for them.

CHAPTER XXXIX

THE SIEGE OF LA ROCHELLE

Now, whenever the king halted, the Musketeers halted. Thus it followed that d'Artagnan, who was as yet purely and simply in the Guards, found himself for the time at least separated from his good friends—Athos, Porthos, and Aramis. This separation, which was no more than an unpleasant circumstance, would surely have become a cause of serious uneasiness to him if he had been able to guess to what unknown dangers he was subjected.

The Guards, under the command of M. d'Essart, took up their quarters with the Minimes. But d'Artagnan, possessed with ambitions to enter the Musketeers, had formed but few friendships among his comrades, and so he found himself isolated and abandoned to his own reflections.

These were not particularly cheerful. From the time of his arrival in Paris he had been mixed up with public affairs. But his own private affairs had made no great progress, either in love or in fortune. As to love, Madame Bonacieux had disappeared without his being able to discover what had become of her. As to fortune, he had made an enemy of the cardinal—that is to say, of a man before whom trembled the greatest men of the realm, beginning with the king.

And then there was Milady to be reckoned with.

What he had clearly gained in the scramble was the

diamond, worth five or six thousand livres, which he wore on his finger. But, since he did not feel that he could safely part with it, the jewel had no more present value to him than the gravel which he trod beneath his feet.

We say than the gravel he trod beneath his feet, for d'Artagnan was reflecting thus while walking in solitude along a pretty little road which led from the camp to the village of Angoutin. Now, these dark thoughts of his had led him farther afield than he intended, and the day was beginning to decline. In the last rays of the setting sun he thought he saw the barrel of a musket glitter from behind a hedge.

D'Artagnan had a quick eye and a keen mind. He comprehended that the musket had not come there of itself. He also knew that the one who bore the weapon had not concealed himself behind a bush with any friendly intentions. He determined, therefore, to direct his course as clear of the hedge as he could, when on the opposite side of the road behind a rock he perceived the end of another musket. Clearly this was an ambuscade.

The young man cast a glance at the first musket and saw, with a certain degree of disquietude, that it was leveled in his direction. But the moment he saw that the orifice of the barrel was motionless, he threw himself upon the ground. At the same instant the gun was fired, and he heard the whistling of a ball passing over his head.

No time was to be lost. D'Artagnan sprang up with a bound, and at just that second the ball from the other musket tore up the gravel on the very spot of the road where he had thrown himself with his face to the ground.

D'Artagnan was not one of those foolhardy men who seek a ridiculous death in order that it might be said of them that they did not retreat a single step. Besides, courage was out of the question here. D'Artagnan had fallen into an ambush.

"If there is a third shot," he said to himself, "I am a gone goose."

He immediately took to his heels and ran toward the camp with the swiftness of the young men of his country, so renowned for their sprightliness of foot. But, whatever might be his speed, he was still well within range of a bullet when another shot was fired, and this time so well aimed that it struck his hat and carried it ten paces before him. As he had no other covering for his head, he picked up this as he ran, and arrived at his quarters very pale and out of breath. Without saying a word to anybody, he sat down and proceeded to consider.

The event might have any one of three causes.

The first and most natural was that it might be an ambuscade of the Rochellais, who would not be sorry to kill one of his Majesty's Guards, because that would be one enemy the less. Also, this enemy might have a well-lined purse in his pocket.

D'Artagnan took his hat, examined the hole made by the bullet, and shook his head. The bullet was not a musket ball—it was that of an arquebuse. The accuracy of the aim had first given him the idea that a special weapon had been employed. This could not, then, be a military ambuscade, as the bullet was not of the regular calibre.

This might, of course, be a kind remembrance of Mon-

sieur the Cardinal. But here again the Gascon shook his
head. For people toward whom his Eminence had but
to put forth his hand, he scarcely would resort to such
means.

Third? Aha! It might be a vengeance of Milady.
And this was most probable. D'Artagnan tried in vain to
remember the faces or the dress of the assassins, but he
had escaped so rapidly that he had not had leisure to
notice anything.

He passed a very bad night. Three or four times he
started up, imagining that a man was approaching his
bed for the purpose of stabbing him. Day dawned, nevertheless, without darkness having brought any accident.
D'Artagnan suspected that evil deferred did not mean evil .
abandoned. He remained all day in his quarters, saying
to himself as an excuse that the weather was bad.

At nine o'clock next morning the drums beat to arms.
The Duc d'Orléans visited the posts. The Guards were
drawn up in battle formation, and d'Artagnan took his
place in the midst of his comrades. Monsieur passed along
the front of the line. Then all the superior officers approached him to pay their respects, M. d'Essart, captain of
the Guards, as well as the others.

At the expiration of a minute or two it seemed to our
Gascon that M. d'Essart made him a sign to approach. He
waited for a fresh gesture on the part of his superior for
fear he might be mistaken. But when the signal was
repeated, he left the ranks and advanced to receive orders.

"Monsieur is about to ask for some men of good will
for a dangerous mission. It is one which will do honor

to those who shall accomplish it. And I made you a sign that you might hold yourself in readiness."

"Thanks, my captain!" replied d'Artagnan, who wished for nothing better than an opportunity to distinguish himself under the eye of the lieutenant general.

In fact, the Rochellais had made a sortie during the night and had retaken a bastion of which the royal army had gained possession two days before. The matter was to ascertain by reconnoitering how strongly the enemy guarded the bastion.

At the end of a few minutes Monsieur raised his voice and said, "I want for this mission three or four volunteers led by a man who can be depended upon."

"As to that dependable man, Monsieur, I have him right here," responded M. d'Essart, pointing to d'Artagnan. "And as to the four or five volunteers, Monsieur has but to make his intentions known and the men shall not be wanting."

"Four men of good will who will risk being killed with me!" cried d'Artagnan, raising his sword.

Two of his comrades of the Guards immediately sprang forward. Two other soldiers having joined them, the number was deemed sufficient. The young Gascon declined all other volunteers, being unwilling to take the first chance away from those who had the priority.

It was not known whether, after the taking of the bastion, the Rochellais had evacuated it or left a garrison in it. The object of the volunteer party was, then, to examine the spot at a range close enough to verify the reports.

D'Artagnan set out with his four companions and followed the trench. The two guards marched abreast with him and the other two soldiers trailed behind.

Screened by the lining of the trench, they arrived within a hundred paces of the bastion. There, on turning around, d'Artagnan noticed that the two soldiers had disappeared. He thought that, becoming afraid, they had stayed behind, and he continued to advance.

After rounding the counterscarp they found themselves within about sixty paces of the bastion. They saw no one, and the bastion seemed deserted. The three composing our forlorn hope were deliberating whether they should proceed any farther or not, when all at once a circle of smoke enveloped the giant of stone and a dozen musket balls came whistling around d'Artagnan and his comrades.

They knew everything they had set out to discover— the bastion was guarded. A longer stay in this dangerous spot would have been useless imprudence. D'Artagnan and his two companions turned their backs and commenced a retreat that resembled a flight.

On arriving at the corner of the trench which was to serve them as a rampart, one of the guardsmen fell. A bullet had passed through his breast. The other, who was safe and sound, continued his way toward the camp.

D'Artagnan was not willing to abandon his comrade thus. He stooped to raise him and to assist him in regaining the lines—but at this moment two shots were fired. One ball struck the head of the already wounded guard, and the other flattened itself against a rock after having passed within two inches of d'Artagnan.

The young man wheeled rapidly about, for this attack could not come from the bastion, which was hidden by the angle of the trench. The two soldiers who had abandoned the expedition occurred to his mind, and at once he remembered the assassins of two evenings before. He resolved this time to know with whom he had to deal and fell upon the body of his comrade as if he were dead.

He quickly saw two heads appear above an abandoned outwork within thirty paces of him—they were the heads of the two soldiers. D'Artagnan had not been deceived. These two soldiers had followed for tne purpose of assassinating him, hoping that the young victim's death would be placed to the account of the enemy.

As he might be only wounded and thus able to denounce their crime, they came up to him with the purpose of making sure of their fell intent. Fortunately, deceived by d'Artagnan's trick of playing dead, they neglected to reload their guns. When they were within some ten paces of him, d'Artagnan, who in falling had taken care not to let go his sword, sprang upon them.

This placed the assassins in a dilemma. They comprehended that if they fled toward the camp without having killed their man, they would be accused by him. Therefore their first idea was to join the enemy. One of them grasped his gun by the barrel and used it as he would a club. He aimed a terrible blow at the Gascon, who avoided it by springing to one side—but by this movement he left a passage free to the ruffian, who darted off toward the bastion. As the Rochellais who guarded the bastion were ignorant as to the intentions of the man they saw running toward them, they fired upon him. He fell, hit by a ball which broke his shoulder.

Meantime, d'Artagnan had thrown himself upon the other soldier, attacking him with his sword. The conflict was not long—the wretch had nothing with which to defend himself but the discharged arquebuse. The sword of the guardsman slipped along the barrel of the now useless weapon and passed through the thigh of the assassin. He fell.

D'Artagnan immediately placed the point of his sword at the culprit's throat.

"Oh, do not kill me!" cried the bandit. "Pardon, officer, and I will tell you all."

"I wonder if your secret is important enough for me to spare your life to hear it?" asked the Gascon, withholding his arm.

"Yes, if you think existence worth anything to a brave man of twenty who may hope for everything."

"Wretch," cried d'Artagnan, "speak quickly! Who employed you to do away with me?"

"A woman called Milady."

"How do you know this woman?"

"I do not, but my comrade does. He made the bargain with her and has a letter in his pocket you might like to see."

"How did you get mixed up in this villainous affair?"

"My comrade offered me a hundred louis to help him in it."

"Very fine, indeed!" said the young guardsman, laughing. "Milady thinks I am worth something. A hundred louis? That's a temptation for two wretches like you. I grant you pardon on one condition: that you will fetch me the letter from your comrade's pocket."

"But," whined the bandit, "that's only another way of killing me. I'll be right under fire from the bastion."

"Get it, or I swear you shall die by my hand."

"Pardon, Monsieur, pity! In the name of that young lady you love, and whom you perhaps believe dead, but who is not!" panted the ruffian, throwing himself upon his knees and leaning upon his hand, for his strength was oozing away with his blood.

"And how do you know there is a young woman whom I love, and that I believed this woman dead?" asked d'Artagnan.

"By that letter my comrade has in his pocket."

D'Artagnan took the soldier's arquebuse, made him go on before him, and urged him toward his companion by pricking him behind with his sword. It was a frightful thing to see this wretch, leaving a long trail of blood on the ground he passed over, pale with approaching death, try to drag himself along without being seen, to the body of his accomplice which lay twenty paces away. Terror was so strongly painted on the ruffian's face, covered with a cold sweat, that d'Artagnan took pity upon him. He cast at him a look of contempt.

"Stop!" he said. "I shall show you the difference between a man of courage and a coward like yourself. Stay where you are. I go."

And with a light step, an eye on the watch, observing the movements of the enemy and taking advantage of every unevenness of the ground, d'Artagnan succeeded in reaching the second soldier.

There were two means of gaining his object—to search him on the spot, or to carry him away, making a buckler of his body, and search him in the trench. D'Artagnan preferred the second way. He lifted the assassin onto his shoulders at the moment the enemy fired. A slight shock, the dull noise of three balls penetrating the flesh, a last cry, a convulsion of agony, proved to the young Gascon that the would-be assassin had saved his life. The guardsman regained the trench and threw down the corpse beside the wounded man, who was himself as pale as death.

Then he began to search. A leather pocketbook, a purse in which was evidently a part of the sum which the bandit had received for blood money, with a dicebox and dice, completed the possessions of the dead man.

D'Artagnan left the box and the dice where they fell, threw the purse to the wounded man, and eagerly opened the pocketbook. Among some unimportant papers he found the following letter—that which he had sought at the risk of his life:

Since you have lost sight of that woman and since she is now in safety in the convent, which you should never have allowed her to reach, try, at least, not to miss the man. If you do, you know that my hand stretches far and that you shall pay very dearly for the hundred louis that you received from me.

No signature. Nevertheless it was plain as day that the letter came from Milady.

Consequently d'Artagnan kept it as a piece of evidence, and, being in safety behind the corner of the trench, he began to interrogate the wounded man. The bandit confessed that he had undertaken, with his comrade—the same who was killed—to carry off a young woman who was to leave Paris by the Barrière de la Villette. But, having stopped for a drink at a cabaret, they had missed the carriage by ten minutes.

"But what were you to have done with that woman?" demanded the guardsman in anguish.

"We were to take her to a house in the Place Royale," answered the wounded man.

"To Milady's own residence!" murmured d'Artagnan.

Then the trembling Gascon comprehended what a terrible thirst for vengeance urged Milady on to destroy him as well as all who loved him. And he marveled at how well she must be acquainted with the affairs of the court, since she had discovered all. There could be no doubt that she owed this information to the cardinal.

But amid all this he perceived, with a feeling of real joy, that Anne of Austria must have discovered the prison in which poor Madame Bonacieux was expiating her devotion and that the queen had freed her from that prison. And now were explained the letter he had received from the young woman and her passage along the road of Chaillot.

Then also, as Athos had predicted, it became possible to find Madame Bonacieux, and a convent was not impregnable.

This idea completely restored clemency to his heart. He turned to the wounded man, who had watched with intense anxiety all the various expressions of his face, and, holding out his arm to him, said, "Come. I shall not abandon you thus. Lean upon me and let us return to the camp."

"I suppose you are saving me only to have me hanged," said the bandit, who could scarcely believe in such magnanimity.

"You have my word," replied d'Artagnan; "for the second time I give you your life."

The wounded man sank upon his knees to kiss the feet of his preserver. But the guardsman, who no longer had a motive for staying so near the enemy, cut short the testimonials of gratitude.

D'Artagnan explained the sword wound of his companion by a sortie which he pretended to have made. He described the death of the soldier and the perils they had encountered. This recital was for him the occasion for a veritable triumph. For a day the whole army talked of his expedition, and Monsieur paid him his compliments upon it. Besides this, as every great action brings its own reward, this brave exploit of d'Artagnan resulted in giving him back the peace of mind he had lost. In fact, the young Gascon really believed he could afford to be tranquil, since one of his two enemies was killed and the other devoted to his interests.

But this calm state of mind proved one thing—that d'Artagnan did not yet know Milady.

CHAPTER XL

THE ANJOU WINE

D'Artagnan felt he had nothing to worry him except that he was without tidings of his friends, the Inseparables. But one morning at the beginning of the month of November, everything was explained to him by this letter, dated from Villeroy:

MM. Athos, Porthos, and Aramis, after having had an entertainment at my house and greatly enjoying themselves, created such a disturbance that the provost of the castle, a very rigid man, ordered them to be confined for some days. But I am carrying out the command they gave me by forwarding you a dozen bottles of my Anjou wine, with which they are much delighted. They wish you to drink to their health in their favorite wine.

With great respect, I am

M. d'Artagnan's very humble and obedient servant,

GODEAU, Purveyor of the Musketeers.

"Ha-ha!" cried d'Artagnan. "So they think of me in their pleasures as I thought of them in my troubles. Well, I certainly shall drink to their health with all my heart and soul, but I shall not drink alone."

And the Gascon visited those guardsmen with whom he was on terms of special intimacy, to invite them to enjoy with him this present of delicious Anjou wine which had been sent from Villeroy. One of the two guardsmen he called upon was engaged that evening, another one the next, so the meeting was fixed for the day after that.

The hour of the banquet having arrived, the two guests

arrived and took their places at the table. One of the guardsmen had brought his lackey, Fourreau, to aid Planchet with the service.

Planchet waited, napkin on arm, as if he were a dignified steward attending important personages. Fourreau uncorked the bottles. Brisemont, which was the name of the convalescent bandit, poured the wine carefully into decanters, for it had been a little shaken by its journey. The first bottle of Anjou was a bit muddy at the bottom, so Brisemont poured the lees into a glass. D'Artagnan desired him to drink it, as the poor devil had not yet recovered his strength.

The guests had eaten their soup and were about to lift the first glass of wine to their lips, when all at once the cannon sounded from Fort Louis and Fort Neuf. The guardsmen naturally imagined this firing of ordnance was caused by some unexpected attack either of the besieged Rochellais or of their English allies, and therefore sprang to their swords. D'Artagnan, not less nimble than his guests, ran from the table to repair to his post.

But scarcely were the three out of the room ere they were made aware of the cause of the disturbance. Cries of "Long live the king!" "Long live the cardinal!" resounded on every side, and the drums were beaten in all parts of the camp.

In short, the king had grown impatient of delays and had come by forced marches, arriving at that moment with all his household and a reinforcement of ten thousand troops. His Musketeers preceded and followed him. D'Artagnan, placed in the receiving line with his company, saluted with an expressive gesture his three friends, whose eyes soon discovered him, and M. de Tréville, who detected him at once.

The ceremony of reception over, the four friends were soon in one another's arms.

"*Pardieu!*" cried d'Artagnan. "You could not have come at a better time. The dinner has hardly had time to grow cold, has it, gentlemen?" he added, turning to the two guardsmen, whom he introduced to his friends.

"Oh, oh!" said Porthos. "It appears we are feasting!"

"I hope there are no ladies present," observed Aramis.

"Is there drinkable wine in your tavern?" asked Athos.

"There is your very own, my dear friend," replied d'Artagnan.

"Our wine!" cried Athos, astonished.

"The identical bottles you sent me."

"We send you wine?"

"You know very well that you did—from the hills of Anjou."

"Oh, I know very well the brand you mean."

"The kind you especially favor."

"Perhaps—when I have neither champagne nor Chambertin."

"Well, in the absence of those two, you must put up with the noble juice of Anjou grapes."

"And so, connoisseurs of wine that we are, we seem to have sent you a basket of Anjou wine?" inquired Porthos.

"At least, it was sent by your order."

"On our order?" said the three musketeers.

"Did you arrange for any wine, Aramis?" asked Athos.

"No. And you, Porthos?"

"No. And you, Athos?"

"Absolutely not."

"Ah, then! If it was not one of you, it was at least your purveyor," said d'Artagnan, suspecting a hoax.

"It seems now that we have a purveyor."

"Yes, Godeau—the purveyor of the Musketeers."

"My faith! Never mind where this gift of the gods comes from," cried Porthos, "let us taste it. If it's good, let us drink it."

"No," answered Athos. "Do not let us, on any account, drink wine which comes from an unknown source."

"You are right, Athos," said d'Artagnan. "You are not hoaxing me about Godeau?"

"Really not. He sent you wine as from us?"

"Here is his letter," said the Gascon, and he presented the note to his comrades.

"That is not his writing!" declared Athos. "I am acquainted with it. Before we left Villeroy I audited the accounts of the regiment."

"A false letter altogether," said Porthos. "We have not been in any way disciplined."

"D'Artagnan," asked Aramis in a reproachful tone, "how could you believe we had made a disturbance?"

The Gascon grew pale. A convulsive trembling shook his limbs.

"Thou alarmest me!" said Athos, who never used the familiar *thee* and *thou* except on very particular occasions.

"Look you!" exclaimed d'Artagnan. "A horrible suspicion comes to my mind. Is this another vengeance of that woman?"

It was now Athos' turn to grow pale.

D'Artagnan rushed toward the refreshment room, the three musketeers and the two guards following on his heels.

The first object to meet their eyes was Brisemont, stretched upon the ground and rolling in horrible convulsions. Planchet and Fourreau were trying to give him succor. But it was plain that all assistance was vain; the features of the dying man were distorted with agony of the most fearful sort.

"Curse you!" groaned Brisemont, on perceiving the Gascon. "You pretend to pardon, only to poison me."

"Wretch!" shouted d'Artagnan. "What are you saying?"

"You gave me the wine. You told me to drink it. You have your horrible vengeance now!"

"Not so, Brisemont! I swear to you, I protest—"

"God will punish you! God grant you suffer some day what I am suffering now!"

"Upon the holy gospels I swear," said d'Artagnan, throwing himself down by the dying man, "I was going to drink the wine myself."

"I do not believe you!" screamed the soldier. And he expired in the midst of horrible tortures.

"Frightful!" murmured Athos, while Porthos broke the bottles, and Aramis gave orders (a little late in the day) that a confessor be sent for.

"My friends," said d'Artagnan, "you come once again

to save my life, and that of these gentlemen, too. And you, Messieurs," he continued, addressing the guardsmen, "I earnestly beg you will be silent regarding this adventure. Great personages have doubtless had a hand in what you have seen, and, if talked about, the evil will only recoil upon us."

"Ah, Monsieur," stammered Planchet, more dead than alive, "what a narrow escape I have had!"

"How, sirrah! You were going to drink my wine?"

"To the health of the king, Monsieur. I was going to drink a small glass of it, when Fourreau told me I had been called."

"Alas!" confessed Fourreau, whose teeth were chattering with fright. "I wanted him out of the way so I might drink by myself."

"Gentlemen," said d'Artagnan, addressing the guardsmen, "you will realize a feast cannot but be dull after what has taken place. Accept my excuses and put off our party until another day, I beg."

The two guardsmen courteously accepted the Gascon's excuses and, perceiving that the four friends wished to be alone, departed.

When the young guardsman and the three musketeers were without witnesses, they looked at one another with an air which expressed the fact that each one of them was acquainted with the gravity of the situation.

"Planchet," said d'Artagnan, "I commit to your care the corpse of this poor devil. Let him be interred in holy ground. He committed a crime, it is true, but he repented of it." And the four friends quitted the room, leaving to

Planchet and Fourreau the duty of paying mortuary honors
to Brisemont.

The landlord gave them another chamber and served
them with soft-boiled eggs and some water which Athos
himself went to draw at the well. In a few words Porthos
and Aramis were posted as to the situation and the reasons
for believing Milady responsible for it.

"You see, my dear friend," said d'Artagnan to Athos,
"that this is to be war to the death."

"I perceive that plainly, dear fellow," replied Athos,
shaking his head sadly; "but do you really believe it is
she?"

"I am sure of it."

"Nevertheless, I confess I still harbor doubt."

"But the fleur-de-lis on her shoulder?"

"She is some Englishwoman who has committed a crime
in France and been branded in consequence."

"Athos, she is your wife, I tell you. Don't you remember how perfectly the two descriptions agree?"

"Still, I should think the other must be dead, for I
hanged her very effectually."

"But in either case, what is to be done?"

"The fact is, one cannot remain forever thus with a
sword suspended by a thread over one's head. We must
extricate ourselves from this position."

"But how?"

"See her. Say to her: 'Peace or war! I'll give you
my word of honor never to speak of you, never to do anything against you. On your side, give me your solemn
oath to remain neutral with regard to me. If not, I shall

apply to the chancellor, to the king, to the hangman. I shall move the courts against you, denounce you as branded, bring you to trial. And if you are acquitted, well, by the faith of a gentleman, I shall kill you at the corner of some wall as I should a mad dog.' "

"I like the means well enough," said d'Artagnan, "but where and how to meet her?"

"Time, dear friend, brings with it opportunity, and opportunity is the martingale of man. The more we have ventured, the more we gain, if we but know how to wait."

"It's hard waiting when one is surrounded by assassins and poisoners."

"Bah!" said Athos. "God has preserved us hitherto, He will continue to do so."

"Oh, we shall get along all right. Besides, we are men; it is our lot to put our lives into the balance. But how about her?" the Gascon added in an undertone.

"Whom do you mean?" asked Athos.

"Constance."

"Madame Bonacieux! I had forgotten you were in love," said Athos.

"Well," asked Aramis, "but have you not learned by the letter that you found upon the dead bandit that she is in a convent? One may be very comfortable in a convent. And as soon as the siege of La Rochelle is terminated, I promise you, on my part—"

"Good!" cried Athos. "We all know, Aramis, that your views have a religious tendency."

"I am only temporarily a musketeer," replied Aramis humbly.

"It is some time since d'Artagnan heard from his lady-love," explained Athos in a low voice.

"Well," said Porthos, "it appears to me that the means of correcting that are very simple."

"What are they?" asked d'Artagnan.

"You say she is in a convent?"

"Yes."

"Very well. As soon as the siege is over, we shall carry her off from that convent."

"But we must first learn what convent she is in."

"Why, that's true," acknowledged Porthos.

"I think I have the solution," said Athos. "Did you not say that the queen chose the convent for her?"

"I believe so, at least."

"In that case Porthos will assist us."

"And how so, if you please?"

"Why, through your marchioness, your duchess, your princess. She must have a long arm."

"Hush!" warned Porthos, placing a finger on his lips. "I believe her to be a cardinalist. She must know nothing of the matter."

"Then," said Aramis, "I take it upon myself to obtain intelligence of her."

"You, Aramis?" cried the three friends. "And how?"

"By the queen's almoner, with whom I am very intimately allied," answered Aramis, blushing.

And upon this assurance the four friends, who had finished their modest repast, separated with the promise to meet again that evening. D'Artagnan returned to less important affairs, and the three musketeers repaired to the king's quarters, where they had to prepare their lodging.

CHAPTER XLI

THE INN OF THE RED DOVECOTE

It is no part of our intention to give a journal of the siege of La Rochelle, but on the contrary only to describe such events as are connected with the history we are relating.

So we shall content ourselves with saying in two words that the French expedition against the English succeeded, to the great astonishment of the king and the great glory of the cardinal.

The English army, repulsed foot by foot, beaten in all encounters, and defeated in the passage of the Isle of Loie, was obliged to reëmbark, leaving on the field of battle two thousand men.

Te Deums were chanted in camp, and afterward throughout France.

The cardinal was left free to carry on the siege, without having, at least for the present, anything to fear from without.

But it must be acknowledged this repose was only momentary. An envoy of the Duke of Buckingham, Montague by name, was taken. And proof was obtained of a league between the German Empire, Spain, England, and Lorraine. This confederation was directed against France.

It was upon the cardinal that all the responsibility for the further conduct of the siege fell, for one is not a despotic minister without responsibility. Therefore, all of the vast resources of his genius were at work night and day, engaged in listening to the least rumor heard in any of the great kingdoms of Europe.

Couriers, becoming every instant more numerous, succeeded one another throughout the twenty-four hours in the little house of the bridge of La Pierre in which the cardinal had established his residence.

There were monks who wore the frock with such ill grace that it was easy to perceive they belonged to the church militant. There were women, a little inconvenienced by their costume as pages, whose large breeches could not entirely conceal their rounded forms. There were peasants with blackened hands but with fine limbs, savoring of the man of quality a league off.

There were also less agreeable visits, for two or three times reports were spread that his Eminence had nearly been assassinated. These attempts did not prevent the cardinal, to whom his most inveterate detractors never denied personal bravery, from making nocturnal excursions. Sometimes he wished to communicate important secret orders to the Duc d'Angoulême, sometimes to confer with the king, and often to have an interview with a messenger whom he did not care to admit to his house.

On their part, the Musketeers, who had not very much to do with the siege itself, were not under very strict orders and led a joyous life. This was the more easy for our three companions in particular, for, being friends of M. de Tréville, they obtained from him special permission to be absent after the closing of the camp.

Now, one evening when d'Artagnan, who was in the trenches, was unable to accompany them, Athos, Porthos, and Aramis had ridden off in search of a good glass of wine. Mounted on their battle steeds, enveloped in their war cloaks, with their hands on their pistol butts, they were returning from a tavern called the Red Dovecote, which Athos had discovered two days before upon the route to Jarrie. Following the road that led to camp, and quite on their guard for fear of an ambuscade, they were about a quarter of a league from the village of Boisnau when they fancied they heard horses approaching them.

All three immediately halted, closed in, and waited in the middle of the road. An instant later, as the moon broke from behind a cloud, they saw two horsemen at the turning of the road. The latter perceived them at the same moment, stopped, and appeared to deliberate as to whether they should continue their route or go back. This hesitation seemed suspicious to the three friends, and Athos, advancing a few paces in front of the others, cried in a firm voice, "Who goes there?"

"Who goes there, yourselves!" replied one of the horsemen.

"Answer or we charge!" warned Athos.

"Beware of what you are about, gentlemen!" said a clear voice which seemed accustomed to command.

"It is some superior officer making his night rounds," conjectured Athos. In a louder voice he said, "What do you wish, gentlemen?"

"Who are you?" demanded the same commanding voice. "Answer, or you may repent your disobedience."

"King's musketeers," returned Athos, by this time quite convinced that their questioner had the right to an answer.

"What company?"

"Company of Tréville."

"Advance and explain your presence here at this hour."

The three companions advanced rather humbly—for all were now persuaded that they had to do with some one more powerful than themselves—leaving Athos the post of speaker.

One of the two riders, he who had spoken second, was ten paces in advance of his companion. Athos made a sign to Porthos and Aramis also to remain in the rear, and went forward alone.

"Your pardon, my officer," said Athos, "but we were ignorant with whom we had to do, and you may see that we were keeping good guard."

"Your name?" said the officer, who had covered a part of his face with his cloak.

"But what of yourself, Monsieur?" continued Athos, who began to be irritated at this inquisition. "Give me, I beg of you, the proof that you have the right to question me."

"Your name?" repeated the cavalier a second time, letting his cloak fall and leaving his face uncovered.

"Monsieur the Cardinal!" cried the stupefied musketeer.

"Your name?" demanded his Eminence for the third time.

"Athos," said the musketeer.

The cardinal made a sign to his attendant, who drew near. "These three musketeers shall follow us," he said in an undertone. "I am not willing it should be known I have left the camp. If they follow us, we shall be certain they will tell nobody."

"We are gentlemen, Monseigneur," retorted Athos. "Ask for our word of honor and give yourself no uneasiness. Thank God, we can keep a secret."

Richelieu fixed his piercing eyes on this courageous speaker.

"You have a quick ear, M. Athos," he said. "But now listen to this: it is not from mistrust that I request you to follow me, but for my security. Your companions are, no doubt, MM. Porthos and Aramis."

"Yes, your Eminence," answered Athos, while the two musketeers who had remained behind advanced, hat in hand.

"I know you, gentlemen," said the cardinal. "You are not quite my friends, and I am sorry you are not. But you are brave and loyal gentlemen and I feel that confidence may be reposed in you. Do me the honor, Messieurs, to accompany me, and then I shall have an escort to excite envy in his Majesty if we should meet him."

The three musketeers bowed to the necks of their horses.

"Well, upon my honor," said Athos, "your Eminence is right in taking us with you. We have seen several evil-looking faces on the road, and we have even had a quarrel at the Red Dovecote with four of these faces."

"A quarrel, and why, gentlemen?" said the cardinal. "You know I do not like brawlers."

"And that is the reason why I have the honor to inform

your Eminence of what has happened. For you might learn it from others and, hearing a false account, believe us to be at fault."

"What were the results of your scuffle?" asked Richelieu, knitting his brow.

"My friend Aramis here received a slight sword wound in the arm, but not enough to prevent his mounting to the assault tomorrow if your Eminence should order an escalade."

"But you are not the men to allow sword wounds to be inflicted upon you thus," said the cardinal. "Come, be frank, gentlemen. You have settled accounts with somebody! Confess—you know I have the right of giving absolution."

"I, Monseigneur?" asked Athos. "I did not even draw my sword, but I took him who offended me around the body and threw him out of the window. It appears that in falling," added Athos with some hesitation, "the rascal broke his thigh."

"Ah, ah!" murmured the cardinal. "And you, M. Porthos?"

"I, Monseigneur, knowing that dueling is prohibited, seized a bench and gave one of these brigands such a blow that I believe his shoulder is broken."

"Very well," said Richelieu. "And you, M. Aramis?"

"Monseigneur, being of a mild disposition, and likewise about to enter into orders, I endeavored to appease my comrades. At that juncture one of the wretches treacherously gave me a wound with a sword, across my left arm. Then, I admit, my patience deserted me. I drew my sword in my turn, and as he came back to the charge, I fancied I felt that in throwing himself upon me he let the blade pass through his body. I only know for a certainty that he fell. And it seemed to me that he was carried away with his two comrades."

"The devil, gentlemen!" said the cardinal. "Three men placed *hors de combat* in a cabaret squabble! You do not do your work by halves. And pray, what was this quarrel about?"

"These fellows were drunk," declared Athos. "And knowing there was a lady who had arrived at the cabaret this evening, they wanted to force her door."

"Force her door!" cried the cardinal. "And why?"

"To do her violence, without doubt," said Athos. "I have had the honor to inform your Eminence that these men were drunk."

"And was this lady young and pretty?" asked Richelieu with a certain degree of anxiety.

"We did not see her, Monseigneur," replied Athos.

"Ah, very well," remarked the cardinal quickly. "You did well to defend the honor of a woman. And as I am going to the Red Dovecote myself, I shall know if you have told me the truth."

"Monseigneur," observed Athos haughtily, "we are gentlemen, and to save our heads we would not be guilty of a falsehood."

"Therefore I do not doubt for a single instant what you say, M. Athos. But," he added, "to change the conversation, was this lady unattended?"

"The lady had a cavalier shut up with her," said Athos.

"But as, notwithstanding the noise, this cavalier did not show himself, it is to be presumed that he is a coward."

" 'Judge not rashly,' says the Gospel," replied the cardinal.

Athos bowed.

"And now, gentlemen, that's that," continued his Eminence. "I know what I wish to know. Follow me."

The three musketeers passed behind the cardinal, who again enveloped his face in his cloak and put his horse in motion, keeping from eight to ten paces ahead of his four companions.

They soon arrived at the silent, solitary inn. No doubt the host knew what illustrious visitor was expected and had consequently sent all intruders on their way.

Ten paces from the door the cardinal made a sign to his esquire and the three musketeers to halt. A saddled horse was fastened to the window shutter. The cardinal knocked three times in a peculiar manner.

A man enveloped in a cloak came out immediately and exchanged some rapid words with Richelieu. After this he mounted his horse and set off in the direction of Surgères, which was likewise the way to Paris.

"Advance, gentlemen," said the cardinal.

"You have told me the truth, Messieurs," he said, addressing the musketeers, "and it will not be my fault if our encounter this evening be not advantageous to you. In the meantime, follow me."

Richelieu alighted; the three musketeers did likewise. The cardinal threw the bridle of his horse to his esquire. The musketeers fastened their steeds to the shutters.

The host stood at the door. For him the cardinal was only an officer coming to visit a lady.

"Have you any chamber on the ground floor where these gentlemen can wait near a good fire?" asked Richelieu.

The landlord opened the door of a large room in which an old stove had just been replaced by a large and excellent fireplace.

"I have this," he said.

"That will do," replied the cardinal. "Enter, gentlemen, and be kind enough to wait for me. I shall not be more than half an hour."

And while the musketeers entered the room on the ground floor Richelieu, without asking further information, ascended the staircase like a man who has no need of having his way pointed out to him.

CHAPTER XLII

THE UTILITY OF STOVEPIPES

It was evident that, without suspecting it, and actuated solely by their chivalric and adventurous characters, our three friends had just rendered a service to some one the cardinal honored with his special protection.

Now, who was that some one? This was the first question the three musketeers asked one another. Then, seeing that none of their replies could throw any light upon it, they dismissed the subject. Porthos called the host and asked for dice.

Porthos and Aramis placed themselves at the table and began to play. Athos walked about in a contemplative mood.

While thinking and strolling to and fro, Athos kept repassing the pipe of the stove, which was broken in halves, one end of it reaching into the chamber above. And every time he went by the stove he heard a murmur of words, which at last attracted his attention. Athos walked over close to the stove and distinguished some words that seemed to merit his interest so greatly that he made a sign to his friends to be silent. He himself remained bent over, his ear placed just as high as the opening of the lower orifice.

"Listen, Milady," the cardinal was saying, "the affair is important. Sit down and let us talk it over."

"Milady!" muttered Athos.

"I am listening to your Eminence with the greatest at-

tention," responded a feminine voice that made the musketeer start.

"A small vessel with an English crew, whose captain
is one of my men, awaits you at the mouth of the Charente,
at Fort of the Point. He will set sail tomorrow evening."

"I must go there tonight?"

"At once! That is to say, when you have received my
instructions. Two men whom you will find at the door on
going out will serve as your escort. You will allow me
to depart first. Then, after half an hour's time, you may
leave."

"I understand, Monseigneur. And now let us discuss
the mission with which you wish to charge me. And, as
it is my hope to continue to enjoy the confidence of your
Eminence, deign to inform me of my duty in terms clear
and precise, that I may commit no error."

There was an instant of deep silence between the two.
It was plain that the cardinal was weighing carefully the
terms in which he was about to speak. It was equally
evident that Milady was concentrating all her mind so
as to understand whatever he was going to say and to
engrave it on her memory.

Athos took advantage of this pause to whisper to his
two companions to lock the door from inside. He also
made them a signal to come over and listen with him.

"You will go to London," the cardinal finally said. "On
your arrival there seek out Buckingham."

"I beg your Eminence not to forget that since the business of the diamond studs his Grace suspects me."

"But this time, Madame, it will not be necessary to

steal into his confidence.   You are to present yourself
frankly and openly as a negotiator."

"Frankly and openly," repeated Milady with an indescribable tone of duplicity.

"You will go to Buckingham in my behalf and tell him
I am acquainted with all the preparations he has made, but
that these give me not a moment's uneasiness because at
the first step he takes I shall ruin the queen."

"I must be able to prove that your Eminence is in a
position to accomplish the threat."

"Certainly.   Tell him I shall publish the interview
which the duke had with the queen on the evening Madame
the Constable gave a masquerade.   Tell him I know he came
there in the costume of the Great Mogul, which the
Chevalier de Guise was to have worn, and that he purchased this exchange of mask for three thousand pistoles."

"I shall remember, Monseigneur."

"All the details of the night he introduced himself in
the character of an Italian fortune teller must also be
told him.   He had under his cloak a large white robe dotted
with black tears, death's heads, and crossbones, because in
case of a surprise he was to pass himself off as the phantom
of the White Lady who is supposed to appear in the Louvre
every time a great event is impending."

"Is that all, Monseigneur?"

"Tell Buckingham likewise that I am informed as to
all the details of the adventure at Amiens.   Tell him I shall
have a pretty romance made of the theme, wittily pointed,
with a plan of the garden and portraits of the main actors
in that nocturnal scene."

"I shall not forget a word of this."

"Tell him further that Montague is in the Bastille, and that torture may make him speak much of what he knows, and even of what he does not know."

"Precisely."

"Then add that his Grace left behind him on the Isle of Ré a letter from Madame de Chevreuse which singularly compromises the queen. You recollect perfectly all that I have told you?"

"I have an excellent memory, Monseigneur. But if, in spite of all these reasons, the duke does not yield and continues to menace France, what then?"

"The duke is in love to the point of madness," replied Richelieu with great bitterness. "If he is once persuaded that this war will cost the honor and perhaps the liberty of his ladylove, I shall answer for his decision."

"And yet, if he should after all persist —"

"Why, then," said his Eminence slowly, "I shall hope for one of those events which change the destiny of nations."

"Would your Eminence be good enough to quote me one such historical event?" asked Milady.

"Well, here, for example," replied Richelieu. "In the year 1610 Henry IV was about to invade Flanders and Italy in order to attack Austria on both flanks. Did there not happen an event which saved Austria?"

"Monseigneur means the knife stab in the Rue de la Feronnerie?"

"Exactly."

"Does not your Eminence fear that the punishment

meted out to the assassin Revaillac may deter any one from imitating him?"

"There are at all times and in all countries fanatics who ask nothing better than a chance to become martyrs. Ay, and it just occurs to me that the Puritans are furious against Buckingham, and their preachers denominate him the Antichrist."

"Well?" said Milady.

"Well," resumed the cardinal in an indifferent voice, "the only thing to be sought for at this moment is some woman, handsome, youn␣, and clever, who has cause of quarrel with the duke. Buckingham has had many affairs of gallantry, and he must have sown the seeds of hatred broadcast by his constant infidelities. We must find such a woman who is desirous of avenging herself upon him."

"She is found," said Milady.

"Thereafter the wretched fanatic must be discovered who will serve as an instrument of divine justice."

"He will be discovered," said Milady. "And now let me recite my orders to see if I am letter-perfect. I announce to his Grace that you are acquainted with the various disguises by means of which he succeeded in reaching the queen at the fête of Madame the Constable. You have proofs of the interview granted by the queen to an Italian astrologer. You have ordered a satirical romance written upon the adventure at Amiens, with a plan of the gardens in which this episode occurred and portraits of the actors concerned in it. Montague is in the Bastille, and torture may make him say things he remembers, and even things he has forgotten. You have a letter from

Madame de Chevreuse, found in his Grace's lodging, which is compromising to both writer and recipient. Then if, notwithstanding all these facts, he persists in his plans, I shall have nothing to do but to pray God to work a miracle for the salvation of France."

"That is it," answered the cardinal drily.

"And now, Monseigneur, that I have received your instructions regarding your enemies, will your Eminence permit me to speak a few words to him about mine?"

"Who are they?" asked Richelieu.

"First, there is a little intrigante named Bonacieux."

"She is in the prison at Mantes."

"No longer," replied Milady. "The queen obtained from the king an order for her transfer to a convent."

"To which one?"

"I do not know. The secret has been well preserved."

"But I shall learn, Madame."

"Your Eminence will then tell me the name of the convent?"

"I really do not see why not," said the cardinal.

"And then I have another enemy much more to be feared than this little Madame Bonacieux."

"What is his name?"

"Your Eminence knows him pretty thoroughly," cried Milady, carried away by her anger. "He is the evil genius of both of us. In an encounter with your Eminence's Guards he turned the victory in favor of the king's Musketeers. He thrice wounded de Wardes, your emissary, and caused the fiasco of the diamond studs. And, knowing it was I who had Madame Bonacieux abducted, he has

sworn my death. I am referring to this miserable
d'Artagnan."

"He is a bold villain," remarked the cardinal. "But I
must have proof of his connection with Buckingham."

"A proof?" said Milady. "I shall get you ten."

"Get me the evidence and I shall send him to the
Bastille."

"So far, so good, Monseigneur. But afterward?"

"Once in the Bastille, there is no afterward!" declared
the cardinal dully.

"Monseigneur," replied Milady, "fair exchange is no
robbery. A life for a life—a man for a man. Give me
one; I shall promise you the other."

"I do not know what you mean, nor do I wish to," said
Richelieu. "But I see nothing out of the way in granting
your demand with respect to so infamous a creature, particularly as you tell me this paltry d'Artagnan is a wanton,
a duelist, and a traitor."

"An unheard-of scoundrel, Monseigneur."

"Give me some paper, then, a quill and ink, and I shall
write you the order you require—one that shall ratify
beforehand all that you think proper to do for the greatest
good of France."

There was an interval of silence during which the cardinal was employed in hunting for terms in which to write
the note. Athos, who had lost no word of the conversation,
led his two comrades to the other end of the room.

"Why don't you let us hear the rest of the talk?" asked
Porthos.

"Hush!" whispered Athos. "We have heard enough

for our purpose. Besides, I don't forbid your listening, but I must be gone."

"Gone!" said Porthos. "Suppose the cardinal asks for you, what answer can we make?"

"Don't wait for him to question you. Tell him I have gone on ahead because certain expressions of our landlord have caused me to suspect the road is unsafe. I shall say two words about it to the esquire of the cardinal, too."

"Look out for yourself, Athos," cautioned Aramis.

"Be easy, my friend. You know I am cool enough."

Porthos and Aramis resumed their places by the stovepipe. Athos went out openly and took his horse, which was tied with those of his friends to the fastenings of the shutters. In a sentence or two he convinced the esquire of the need for a vanguard during the return trip. Then he carefully examined the priming of his pistols, drew his sword, and started on the road that led to camp.

CHAPTER XLIII

A CONJUGAL SCENE

As Athos had suspected, it was not long before the cardinal descended the stairs. He opened the door of the room in which he had left the musketeers and found Porthos earnestly engaged in shaking dice with Aramis. He cast a quick glance about the chamber and noted the absence of one of his men.

"What has become of M. Athos?" he asked.

"He has ridden on ahead, Monseigneur," replied Porthos, "because of some words of the landlord which made him think the road was not safe."

"And what have you been doing meanwhile, M. Porthos?"

"I have won five pistoles from Aramis."

"Are you now ready to return to camp with me?"

"We are at your Eminence's service."

"To horse then, Messieurs, for it is growing late."

The esquire was at the door holding the cardinal's horse by the bridle. Farther off, two men and three horses were standing in the shadows. These were the two men who were to escort Milady to the Fort of the Point and be responsible for her embarkation.

The esquire confirmed what the two musketeers had already said regarding the actions of Athos. The cardinal made a sign of approval and retraced the route to camp with the same precautions that he had used in coming.

And now, as to Athos.

For a hundred yards or so he maintained the speed at which he had started away from the Red Dovecote. But once out of sight of the inn he turned his horse to the right, made a wide detour, and came back within twenty paces of a high hedge to watch the departure of the little troop. After he had recognized the laced hats of his companions and the gold fringe of the cardinal's cloak, he waited until the cavaliers had turned the angle of the road and were lost to sight. Then he tore back to the inn at a gallop. The door was opened to him without the slightest hesitation.

"My officer," said Athos to the host, "has forgotten to give the lady an important piece of information, and I have been sent back to repair the omission."

"Go right up," answered the landlord; "she is still in her room."

A few seconds later Athos was standing before the open door of Milady's chamber, enveloped in his cloak, with his hat drawn deep down over his eyes. On beholding this mute and immovable statue, Milady was seized with fright.

"Who are you and what do you wish?" she cried.

"Aha," muttered Athos, "it is most certainly she!"

He let fall his cloak and raised his hat. He stepped toward the trembling woman. "Do you know me, Madame?" he asked.

Milady took a step forward, and then suddenly started back as if she had seen a snake.

"I see that you remember me," observed Athos.

"The Comte de la Fère!" breathed Milady, growing exceedingly pale and shrinking back until the wall of the room stopped her further progress.

"Yes, Milady," responded Athos, "it is the Comte de la Fère in person. He has come from the other world expressly to pay you a visit. Sit down, Madame, and let us talk—as the cardinal said."

Under the influence of indescribable terror, Milady sank upon a chair without uttering a syllable.

"You are a veritable demon sent to this earth!" began Athos. "You threw yourself in my path once before. I thought I had crushed you, Madame, but either I was deceived or hell has brought you back to life."

At these words, which recalled terrible remembrances, Milady hung her head and gave vent to a groan.

"Yes," continued Athos, "hell has made you rich, hell has given you another name, and almost another face, but it has not wiped the stains from your soul nor the brand from your body."

Milady started up as if moved by a powerful spring, and her eyes flashed lightning. Athos remained seated.

"You thought me dead, eh, as I believed you to be? The name Athos hid the Comte de la Fère as well as Milady Clarik concealed Anne de Brueil. Did you not so call yourself when your honored brother performed our marriage?"

Rigid, motionless, the woman made no reply.

"Our position is truly an odd one," resumed Athos with a laugh. "We have lived as long as we have only because each believed the other dead."

"What brings you back to me?" asked Milady in a faint and hollow voice. "What do you want of me?"

"Merely to tell you that, though invisible to your eyes, I never lost sight of you."

"You know what I have done?"

"I can relate to you day by day what you have done from the time you entered the cardinal's service up to now."

A smile of disbelief swept across the pallid lips of Milady.

"Listen. It was you who cut the diamond studs from the shoulder of the Duke of Buckingham. It was you who had Madame Bonacieux carried off; you who, in love with de Wardes, opened the door of your chamber to d'Artagnan; you who, believing de Wardes had betrayed you, tried to have him murdered by his rival; you who, when your infamous secret was discovered, sent two assassins in pursuit of this rival."

Milady was livid with fear and rage.

"It was you, Madame," continued the inexorable nobleman, "who, finding that bullets had missed their mark, sent a forged letter to convince your victim that poisoned wine came from his friends. In short, it was you who have but a few moments since, in this room, seated in the very chair I now occupy, made an engagement with Richelieu to secure the murder of the Duke of Buckingham in return for the permission he gave you to assassinate d'Artagnan."

"You must be Satan!" cried Milady.

"Perhaps," said Athos. "But listen well to what I now say. Kill Buckingham for aught I care—he is an Englishman and not known to me. But touch with the tip of your finger a single hair of d'Artagnan, and I swear to you, by the head of my father, that act shall be your last one."

"M. d'Artagnan cruelly insulted me," said Milady in a muffled voice, "and he shall die."

"Oho!" cried Athos, laughing loudly. "It is then possible to insult you, Madame?"

"He shall die," repeated Milady. "She first, and he afterward."

Athos was seized with a kind of dizziness. His desire for blood came strongly back upon him, racking him like a fever. He got up from his chair, drew forth a pistol, and cocked it.

Milady, pale as a corpse, tried to cry out, but her tongue could only make hoarse sounds that resembled the rattlings of a wild beast. She cringed against the dark tapestry, her hair in disorder, appearing some horrid image of fright.

Athos stretched out his arm so that the pistol almost touched Milady's forehead. "Madame," he said, "deliver to me this instant the paper the cardinal signed or I shall blow out your brains."

Milady might have doubted the will of another man, but she knew this Athos. Nevertheless, she did not move.

"You have one second to decide," he said.

The woman saw by the contraction of the muscles of his face that the trigger was about to be pulled. She thrust her hand quickly into her bosom, drew forth a paper, and held it out to Athos.

"Take it," she snarled, "and be forever damned!"

Athos seized the writing, returned the pistol to his belt, drew near the lamp that he might make sure the billet was the one he sought, unfolded it, and read:

December 3, 1627.

It is by my order and for the good of the State that the bearer of this note has done what has been done.

RICHELIEU.

Athos resumed his cloak and put his hat upon his head. "And now, viper, that I have drawn your teeth, bite if you can."

Thereupon he immediately left the room without glancing once behind him. At the entrance door of the Red Dovecote he found the two men and the spare horse they held.

"Gentlemen," he said, "Monseigneur's orders are to conduct the woman without loss of time to the Fort of the Point, and not to leave her until she is on board."

As these words agreed entirely with the command they had been given, they bowed their heads in token of assent. As for Athos, he vaulted lightly into his saddle and set off at full gallop. Only, instead of following the road, he struck across fields, urging his horse to the utmost and frequently stopping to listen.

Finally, in such a pause, he heard the hoof beats of several horses on the road and was sure it was the cardinal and his escort. He at once struck out on a new diagonal, and when he had reached a new point in advance about two hundred yards from the camp, he rubbed his sweating horse down with grass and foliage, and placed himself across the road.

"Who goes there?" he called as soon as he caught sight of the company of horsemen.

"That is our brave musketeer, I think," the cardinal answered.

"Yes, Monseigneur," said Porthos, "it is he."

"M. Athos," said Richelieu, "pray accept my thanks for the good guard you have kept. Messieurs, we have arrived; take the gate on the left. The password is 'King and Ré.'"

So saying, the cardinal saluted the three friends with a nod of his head and, followed by his esquire, took the right-hand gate, for that night he slept in camp.

"Did you know," asked Porthos, the moment the cardinal was out of hearing, "that Richelieu signed the paper she required?"

"I did," returned Athos, coolly, "for here it is."

Not another word did the friends speak until they reached their quarters, except to give the countersign to the sentinels. But without delay they sent Mousqueton to inform Planchet that his master was wanted the instant he could leave the trenches.

As Athos had thought, on finding the two men who awaited her, Milady did not object to following them. She was for a moment terribly tempted to be taken to the cardinal and tell him what had happened after his departure from the inn. But if she should lay bare the acts of Athos, he in turn would make revelations about her. If she said Athos had hanged her, he would tell of the executioner's brand. Under all the circumstances, therefore, it seemed best to preserve a discreet silence and to accomplish her difficult mission successfully. When once Richelieu was satisfied with her work, she could come to him and claim her vengeance.

Thus, after a whole night of riding, at seven o'clock she was at the Fort of the Point. At eight she had embarked. At nine the ship, which with letters of marque from the cardinal was supposed to be sailing for Bayonne, raised anchor and steered for the coast of England.

CHAPTER XLIV

THE BASTION ST. GERVAIS

When he reached the quarters of his three friends, d'Artagnan found them together in the same room. Athos was buried in his thoughts. Porthos was twisting his mustaches. Aramis was reciting his prayers with the aid of a charming book of hours bound in blue velvet.

"*Pardieu,* gentlemen," said the Gascon, "I hope your message repays my efforts, for I need a short rest after a night spent in taking and dismantling a bastion. It was warm work."

"We were where it was not exactly cold," replied Porthos.

"Hush!" warned Athos.

"Aha," said d'Artagnan, "it seems there is some new business demanding our attention."

"Aramis," asked Athos, "day before yesterday you breakfasted at the inn of the Parpaillot, did you not?"

"Yes."

"How did they treat you?"

"For my part, I ate but little. Day before yesterday was a fish day, and they were serving only meat."

"That is odd," remarked Athos, "no fish at a seaport."

"They claim," answered Aramis, turning back to his pious reading, "that the sea wall the cardinal is building drives the fish all out into the open water."

"But what I really wish to discover, Aramis, is whether

you were left to your own devices and not interrupted by any one."

"Why, I do not remember that there was any disturbance. I think, Athos, that we shall do very comfortably at the Parpaillot."

"Let us go there for our talk, then, for here the walls are like thin sheets of paper."

On their way to the Parpaillot the four friends met Grimaud. Athos waved to him to come with them. According to his habit, Grimaud obeyed his master's sign in silence. The poor chap had nearly reached the pass where he had forgotten how to speak.

They arrived at the bar of the inn. It was seven o'clock in the morning, and daylight began to appear. They ordered breakfast and entered a room where the landlord promised they should not be disturbed.

But the hour was badly chosen for a private conference. Reveille had just been sounded; everyone was shaking off the drowsiness incident to the hour. Soldiers of all sorts were dropping in at the bar for a morning drop to dispel the wet cold of the autumnal air. Dragoons, Swiss, guardsmen, musketeers, light-horse cavalrymen followed one another in a way that promised well for the pecuniary profit of the landlord but agreed badly with the purposes of the four Inseparables. They replied almost brusquely to the constant succession of greetings, healths, and jokes of their boisterous comrades.

"I see how it will turn out," commented Athos. "We shall get caught in some petty quarrel or other, and we can get along without one just now. D'Artagnan, we shall have to waste a little time in idle talk. So, tell us what sort of experience you underwent last night, and we'll describe ours later."

"Ah, yes," observed a light-horseman, raising a glass of brandy to his lips and sipping at it slowly. "I hear you gentlemen of the Guards were in the trenches last night. You did not get much the best of the scuffle with the Rochellais, did you?"

D'Artagnan glanced at Athos, wondering if he should reply to this tactless intruder who had mixed unasked in their conversation.

"My friend," said Athos to the young guardsman, "don't you hear M. de Busigny, who does you the honor of asking you a question?"

"I hear you took a bastion, or something of the sort," said a Swiss, who was drinking rum out of a beer glass.

"Yes, Monsieur," replied d'Artagnan with a bow. "We introduced a keg of powder under one of the corners of the bastion and blew a very pretty breach in it."

"What bastion was it?" asked a dragoon, who was carrying on his saber the stolen goose he was bringing to the kitchen to be cooked.

"St. Gervais," replied d'Artagnan, "from behind which the Rochellais had been annoying our workmen."

"Was it a hot affair?"

"Moderately so. The Rochellais lost eight or ten men; our killed numbered five."

"*Balzampleu!*" cried the Swiss. Notwithstanding the excellent collection of oaths ready for use in the German tongue, he had acquired the habit of cursing in French.

"But don't you think it likely that the Rochellais will send sappers and pioneers this morning to mend the bastion?" asked the light-horseman.

"Yes, that's very probable," agreed d'Artagnan.

"Gentlemen," said Athos, "let's make a bet!"

"Ah, woo-ee! A pet!" cried the Swiss.

"What's the wager?" asked the light-horseman.

"Wait a minute," said the dragoon, placing his saber with the spitted goose upon the two great andirons that held the firewood in the hearth. "Not so fast, I'm in on that! Here, you damned landlord! Bring a dripping pan in a hurry. I don't want to lose a drop of the fat of this honorable fowl."

"You was ride," stated the Swiss. "Koose krease is kood mit preat and basdry."

"And now for the wager," said the dragoon.

"Yes, let's have it, M. Athos," chimed in the light-horseman.

"Well, M. de Busigny," said Athos, "I shall bet you that my three companions here and I will take breakfast in the bastion St. Gervais. And we agree to remain there an hour by the clock, no matter how much the enemy tries to dislodge us."

Porthos and Aramis looked at each other—they began to understand the idea.

"I take the bet," stated M. de Busigny. "What are the stakes?"

"There are four of you gentlemen and four of us," said Athos. "How about an unlimited dinner for eight, paid by the losers?"

"Capital!" replied M. de Busigny.

"Fine idea!" chimed in the dragoon.

"Dat zoots me," said the Swiss.

The fourth auditor, who had nothing to say during all this colloquy, nodded his head to signify his acquiescence.

"Breakfast is ready for these gentlemen," said the landlord.

"Bring it right along," ordered Athos.

The host did as he was bidden. Athos summoned Grimaud, pointed to a large hamper that stood in a corner, and signed to him to wrap the food up in the napkins.

Grimaud understood it was to be a picnic breakfast in the open air, took the hamper, packed the victuals in it, added the bottles, and slung the basket on his arm.

"But where are you going with the meal?" asked the landlord.

"What do you care so long as you get your pay for it?" demanded Athos, as he threw two pistoles carelessly upon the table.

"Shall I bring the change right now?" asked the host.

"Don't bother. Just add two bottles of champagne, and the difference will pay for the napkins."

The host did not make so good a profit as he had hoped to, but he saved himself a fair amount by slipping in two bottles of Anjou wine instead of the champagne.

"M. de Busigny," suggested Athos, "will you be kind enough to set your watch by mine, or let me regulate my own with yours?"

"Whichever you wish, Monsieur," assented the light-horseman. "My watch says half-past seven."

"And mine thirty-five minutes after," said Athos. "So you see I am just five minutes faster than you."

With polite bows to all the persons present, the four young men walked up the road that led to the bastion St. Gervais. Grimaud followed them, carrying the hamper. He was ignorant of their destination, but, as usual, so passively obedient to Athos' instructions that he never thought to inquire.

As long as they were within the limits of the camp inclosure, the four friends had nothing to say one to the other. But when they had passed beyond the outer walls of fortification and found themselves in the open country, d'Artagnan thought it was time to demand an explanation of Athos.

"Do me the kindness to tell me whither we are bound, Athos?"

"We are going to the bastion, of course."

"What are we going to do when we get there?"

"We are to breakfast there, of course."

"Why not at the Parpaillot?"

"Since we have some very important things to talk about, and at the inn it is a sheer impossibility to talk five minutes on end without being annoyed by all kinds of bothersome people. They will not follow us out here with their idle chatter," said Athos, pointing to the bastion which they were approaching.

"But could we not quite as easily have found some spot on the downs or by the seashore that is equally retired?"

"There all four of us would have been observed. And at the end of fifteen minutes it would have been reported

to the cardinal by some one of his spies that we were holding a conference."

"But in the bastion we shall indubitably attract bul·
lets," said d'Artagnan.

"For such an expedition we surely ought to have
brought our muskets along," added Porthos.

"You are stupid, my dears," replied Athos. "Why
should we burden ourselves with such a useless load? Have
I not been told that in the attack of last night eight or ten
Frenchmen were killed, and as many Rochellais?"

"Well, what then?"

"The bodies were not plundered, were they?"

"Again, what of that?"

"Only that we shall find their muskets, cartridges, and
powder flasks. And instead of the four musketoons and
the twelve balls that we should have dragged with us, we
shall find fifteen guns and a hundred charges on the ground
awaiting us."

"Oh, Athos!" cried Aramis, "truly, of all living men,
thou alone art great." Porthos nodded in token of agree-
ment. D'Artagnan, somehow, did not seem entirely convinced.

Grimaud apparently shared the misgivings of the young
Gascon, for as he saw that they continued to advance
toward the bastion he tugged at the skirt of his master's
cloak.

"Where are we going?" he asked (by a gesture).

Athos pointed at the bastion.

"But," continued Grimaud (in the same silent dialect),
"we are like to leave our skins there."

Athos raised his eyes and looked toward heaven.

Grimaud set his hamper down on the ground and shook his head.

Athos drew a pistol from his belt, examined its priming, cocked it, and placed the muzzle close to Grimaud's ear.

The valet, who had squatted down on the ground, was on his legs again like a jack-in-the-box. Athos signed to him to pick up his basket and walk on ahead. The valet obeyed. The only advantage Grimaud gained by the silent skirmish was to be advanced from the rear guard to the van.

Arrived safely at the bastion, the four friends turned and looked back.

More than three hundred soldiers of all kinds were assembled at the gate of the camp. And in a separate group might be distinguished M. de Busigny, the dragoon, the Swiss, and the fourth better.

Athos took off his hat, placed it upon the tip of his sword, and waved it in the air. All the spectators returned his salute, uttering a loud hurrah which was distinctly audible to the four friends. After which, the Inseparables disappeared into the bastion whither Grimaud had preceded them.

CHAPTER XLV

THE COUNCIL OF THE MUSKETEERS

The bastion was occupied by a dozen corpses, French and Rochellais.

"Messieurs," proposed Athos, who had assumed the command of the expedition, "let us begin collecting the guns and cartridges while Grimaud is setting the table. There is no reason why we should not say what we wish, for these gentlemen," he added, pointing to the dead bodies strewn about, "can't hear us."

"We might throw them into the ditch," suggested Porthos, "after having gone through their pockets."

"Heaven forbid!" replied Athos. "These corpses may yet be of use to us. How many muskets have you gathered, gentlemen?"

"Twelve," said Aramis, saluting.

"How many rounds of cartridges?"

"One hundred, nearly."

"That is all we need. Let's load the guns."

The four musketeers set to work, and as they were loading the last guns Grimaud announced that breakfast was ready.

"As there is no longer any danger of being overheard," said d'Artagnan, "I hope you're going to let me in on the secret."

"The secret is," replied Athos, "that I saw Milady last night."

D'Artagnan was lifting a glass to his lips. But at the name of Milady his hand trembled so that he was obliged to set the glass down again for fear of spilling its contents.

"You saw your wi—"

"Silence!" interrupted Athos. "You are forgetting that these gentlemen are not as familiar with my private affairs as you are."

"Where did you see Milady?" demanded d'Artagnan.

"Not more than two leagues away at the inn of the Red Dovecote."

"In which case," said d'Artagnan, "we are lost."

"I don't know about that," responded Athos, "for by this time she must have left the shores of France behind her."

"But when all is said and done," asked Porthos, "who is this Milady?"

"A charming woman," replied Athos, "who was very kind to our friend d'Artagnan. He, on his part, has given her some cause for offense, so she tried, a month ago, to have him killed by bullets. A week ago she endeavored to have him poisoned. And yesterday she demanded his head of the cardinal."

"What!" exclaimed d'Artagnan. "She demanded my head?"

"Yes, that is as true as gospel," answered Porthos. "I heard her with these very ears."

"So did I," chimed in Aramis.

"In that case," said d'Artagnan, "there is no use struggling any longer. I may as well blow out my brains now as later."

"That folly should always be left to the last," commented Athos, "for that is the only one that has no remedy."

"But," continued the young Gascon, "I can never escape from such enemies. First my unknown man of Meung. Then de Wardes, to whom I have given three sword wounds. Next Milady, whose secret I have found out. Finally the cardinal, with whose act of vengeance I have interfered."

"After all," Athos comforted him, "that only makes four of them. And there are four of us. *Pardieu!* If there is any meaning in the signals Grimaud is making, we are about to have to engage with a much larger number of people. What is it, Grimaud? Because of the gravity of the situation, I permit you to speak out loud. But be terse, my friend. What is it you see?"

"A troop."

"How many in it?"

"Twenty."

"What kind of people?"

"Sixteen pioneers, four soldiers."

"How far distant are they?"

"Five hundred yards."

"Ah! Then we have just time to finish this fowl and to drink a last glass of wine to your health, d'Artagnan."

"To your health!" repeated Porthos and Aramis.

"Just as you say, to my health, then! But I fear your good wishes will not prove of any great value to me."

"Pah!" replied Athos. "God is great, as the Mohammedans say, and the future is in His hands."

He downed the contents of his wineglass and then arose carelessly, picked up the musket nearest to him, and approached one of the loopholes. Porthos, Aramis, and d'Artagnan followed suit. Grimaud received orders to place himself behind the four friends and reload the discharged muskets.

After a minute or two of waiting, the troop appeared. They advanced along a sort of narrow channel of the trench which afforded a means of communication between the town and the bastion.

"*Peste!*" cried Athos. "It was scarcely necessary for us to station ourselves for twenty soldiers armed with pickaxes, mattocks, and spades. Grimaud had only to make them a sign to depart and I am sure they would have left us in peace."

"I doubt if they would," returned d'Artagnan, "for they are advancing quite doggedly. Besides, in addition to the pioneers, there are four soldiers and a brigadier, armed with guns."

"That is because they do not see us," said Athos.

"Faith," declared Aramis, "I must confess I don't at all fancy opening fire on these poor defenseless civilians."

"You are a bad priest," said Porthos, "if you have pity on heretics."

"On the other hand," observed Athos, "Aramis is right. I'll give them a warning."

"What the devil are you doing?" cried d'Artagnan. "You will be shot for your pains!"

Athos, however, did not heed the advice. He mounted to the top of the breach, musket in one hand and hat in

the other. He bowed courteously to the approaching troop,
who were so astonished by this apparition that they halted
fifty yards from the bastion.

"Gentlemen," said Athos to the soldiers and pioneers,
"a few friends and I are about to breakfast in this bastion.
Now you will realize that nothing is more disagreeable
than to be disturbed at one's morning meal. We ask,
therefore, in case you have business here, that you defer it
until we have finished our repast. Perhaps you will decide
to go away and return after a while. Or, better still, why
not resolve to quit the side of the rebels, and come in and
drink the health of the king of France?"

"Look out!" cried d'Artagnan. "They are aiming at
you, Athos."

"But they are only civilians," replied the musketeer,
"and sure to be bad marksmen."

At that very moment four shots were fired. The bullets flattened themselves against the wall on both sides of
Athos, but not one grazed him.

Four shots made instantaneous reply, but these were
much better aimed than those of the attacking party.
Three of the soldiers fell dead, and one of the pioneers was
wounded.

"Grimaud," called Athos, who was still standing in the
breach, "hand me another musket."

The lackey obeyed at once. The three friends had re-
loaded their arms—a second discharge followed the first.
The brigadier and two pioneers bit the dust. The remainder of the troop took to their heels.

"Now, gentlemen," cried Athos, "up and after them!"

The four Inseparables rushed out of the fort, gained the field of battle, and picked up the four muskets of the privates and the half-pike of the brigadier. Convinced that the fugitives would not stop until they reached the city, the four friends turned back toward the bastion, carrying their plunder with them.

"Reload the weapons, Grimaud," commanded Athos. "And we, Messieurs, will proceed with our breakfast and our conversation. What were we saying?"

"You were saying," d'Artagnan recalled without effort, "that after having demanded my head of the cardinal, Milady left the shores of France. Where was she bound?"

"Off to England," returned Athos.

"With what in view?"

"To assassinate the Duke of Buckingham or at least to have it done."

D'Artagnan uttered an exclamation of surprise and anger. "But that is infamous!" he said.

"Oh, I don't bother much about that, my dear lad. Now, Grimaud, that you have finished reloading, take the brigadier's half-pike, fasten a napkin to it, and plant the thing at the top of the bastion in order that these rebels of La Rochelle may see they have to deal with brave and loyal soldiers of the king."

Grimaud obeyed without replying. A moment later the white flag was floating above the heads of the four friends. A thunder of applause saluted its appearance. By this time half the camp was crowded at the barrier.

"You will understand, d'Artagnan," resumed Athos, "that I was chiefly occupied in getting away from this woman a sort of *carte blanche* which she had extorted from the cardinal, and by means of which she could with impunity get rid of you and even of us."

"And did this *carte blanche* remain in her hands?" asked d'Artagnan.

"No, it passed into mine, but not without a certain amount of trouble on my part, I must confess."

"Then it was to go to Milady that you left us?" said Aramis.

"Exactly."

"And you have that letter from Richelieu with you?"

"Here it is," said Athos. And he took the invaluable paper from the pocket of his uniform. D'Artagnan unfolded it with hands whose trembling he did not attempt to conceal, and read:

December 3, 1627.

It is by my order and for the good of the State that the bearer of this note has done what has been done.

RICHELIEU.

"It is, in fact, an absolution, according to rule," said Aramis.

"That paper must be torn into scraps," exclaimed d'Artagnan, who regarded it as a sentence of death.

"Not at all," replied Athos. "Rather let us preserve it carefully. I would not sell this paper for gold enough to cover it."

"What do you suppose her next move will be?" asked the Gascon.

"Oh," answered Athos indifferently, "she will probably write his Eminence that a damned musketeer named Athos has stolen her safe-conduct. She will advise the cardinal to get rid of the two friends, Porthos and Aramis, at the same time. Richelieu will recall that these are the three men who have so often crossed his path. And some fine morning he will arrest d'Artagnan and, for fear that he should feel lonely, he will send us to keep him company in the Bastille."

"Shut up!" growled Porthos. "It seems to me that you are making some very dull jokes, my dear fellow."

"I am not jesting," replied Athos.

"Do you know," Porthos suddenly broke out, "it would be a much smaller sin to twist Milady's neck than to kill those poor devils of Huguenots whose only crime is that they sing in French the psalms we sing in Latin?"

"What does the abbé say to that?" asked Athos quietly.

"I say amen to it," replied Aramis.

"And I likewise," said d'Artagnan.

"Fortunately she has gone away," observed Porthos. "I confess she would worry me if she were near at hand."

"She worries me as much in England as she does in France," acknowledged Athos.

"She worries me everywhere," declared d'Artagnan.

"But when you had her in your power, Athos, why the devil did you not drown her, strangle her, hang her?" asked Porthos. "It is only dead people who do not come back."

"Do you think so?" replied the musketeer, with a sad smile which d'Artagnan alone could understand.

"I have an idea," said d'Artagnan.

"Out with it," cried Porthos.

"To arms, Messieurs!" called Grimaud at just that juncture.

The young men sprang up and seized their muskets. A small troop was advancing upon them, consisting this time of from twenty to twenty-five men. But they were not pioneers, they were soldiers of the garrison.

"Shall we return to camp?" demanded Porthos. "I don't believe this could be called an equal combat."

"Impossible to retreat for three reasons," replied Athos. "In the first place, we are not through breakfast. Second, there are still some important things left to talk about. Third, it still lacks ten minutes of the hour our wager calls for."

"Then let's form a plan of battle," suggested Aramis.

"Nothing is simpler," said Athos. "As soon as the enemy is within range, we shall open fire upon them. If they continue to advance, we shall fire again. We must fire as long as we have loaded muskets. If what is left of the troop persists in making an assault, we shall allow them to get as far as that trench, and then we shall push down upon their heads that strip of wall which is maintaining its upright position only by a miracle."

"Bravo!" cried Porthos. "Athos, old man, you were born a great general. The cardinal is nothing compared to you."

"No divided attention now!" commanded Athos. "Each one of you pick his man."

"I've got mine covered," said d'Artagnan.

"Me too," called Porthos.

"I've drawn a bead on my target," said Aramis.

"Fire!" ordered Athos.

The four muskets made but one report. Four assailants fell. The drum immediately beat for the charge. The small troop advanced at sling trot.

Thereafter there was no regularity about the shooting, but the Inseparables continued to aim with the same accuracy. And yet, as if the Rochellais had been from the first aware of the numerical weakness of the four friends, the enemy continued to advance at a charging pace.

At least two men fell for every three shots fired, but the assault of the remainder did not waver. Arrived at the foot of the bastion, a dozen of the enemy were still upon their feet. A last discharge met them, but they did not flinch. They jumped into the trench and made ready to scale the breach.

"Now, my friends," shouted Athos, "finish them at a single stroke! To the wall with you!"

The four Inseparables, ably seconded by Grimaud, thrust the barrels of their muskets against a large section of the wall. This bent as if struck by a strong wind, detached itself from its foundation, and fell with a loud crash into the trench. Fearful cries were heard. A vast cloud of dust ascended skyward—and all was over.

"I wonder whether we have blotted them all out," said Athos.

"Faith! That's the way it looks!" responded d'Artagnan.

"Hello! There go three or four of them limping away," said Porthos.

Covered with dirt and blood, several of the unfortunate

assailants were fleeing along the hollow trench toward the city. These were the sole survivors of the small troop.

Athos, with his accustomed phlegm, reseated himself at the breakfast table and said, "D'Artagnan has not yet confided to us his idea."

"My idea?" repeated the Gascon uncertainly.

"Yes. You said you had an idea of some sort."

"Oh, I remember now! It is that I go a second time to England and seek out Buckingham."

"Absurd!" answered Athos coolly. "The first time you went we were not at war Such a trip would now amount to treason."

The young guardsman could not but recognize the force of this reasoning. He subsided and was silent.

"It would be much better to inform the queen," resumed Athos. "But how can that be done? Have we relations with the royal court? Could we send a messenger to Paris without the facts being known in camp? Before our letter was ten leagues away we should be cooling our heels in a dungeon."

"As to transmitting a letter with safety to her Majesty," suggested Aramis, flushing, "I might undertake that myself. I know a clever person at Tours—"

"I wish to remind Aramis," intervened Athos, "that he cannot quit the camp, and that no one but ourselves is trustworthy. Two hours after the messenger had started, all the capuchins, the black caps, and the police of the cardinal would know the contents of the letter by heart. And you and your clever person would be arrested."

"Without mentioning," stated Porthos, "that the queen

would save M. de Buckingham, but would take no notice of our fate."

"What Porthos says has sense," agreed d'Artagnan.

"Listen! What's going on in the city yonder?" said Athos.

"They are beating the general alarm."

The Inseparables listened with all their ears. The continuous rolling of the drums reached them plainly.

"Hang me, if they're not sending a whole regiment against us," laughed Athos.

"Surely you don't think of holding the bastion against a whole regiment?" asked Porthos.

"I am quite in the humor for it," confessed Athos. "I'd hold out against an entire army if we had only taken the precaution to bring along another dozen bottles of Anjou wine."

"Upon my word, the drums are approaching," said d'Artagnan.

"Let 'em come," said Athos with a yawn. "It's a quarter of an hour's journey for them from town. That gives us more than ample time to evolve a plan. Aha! I have the right idea. Allow me, please, to issue to Grimaud some necessary orders."

Athos beckoned to the lackey.

"Grimaud," said Athos, pointing at the dead bodies which lay beneath the wall of the bastion, "take those gentlemen, lean them against the ramparts, put their hats on their heads and their muskets in their hands."

The faithful lackey made a sign that he understood directions.

"Now for my idea," continued Athos. "This demon Milady has a brother-in-law, has she not, d'Artagnan?"

"Yes, but he has no great love for her."

"The more he detests her the better," replied Athos.

"In that case you may be quite content."

"Where is this Lord de Winter now?"

"He returned to London at the first sign of war."

"Well, there's just the man we want," said Athos. "Tell him his sister-in-law is on the point of having a great personage assassinated. He will lock up Milady in some establishment like that of the Magdalens or the Repentant Daughters, and we shall have peace."

"Yes," answered d'Artagnan—"until she gets out."

"Would it not be better," suggested Aramis, "to inform the queen and de Winter at the same time?"

"Who will carry the news to Tours and to London?"

"If we cannot leave camp, our lackeys may," replied Aramis. "I'll answer for Bazin."

"And I for Planchet," said d'Artagnan.

"Look out!" cried Porthos. "I see black points and red dots moving over there. Why, it's not a regiment—it's an army!"

"Faith!" said Athos. "There they are. See how they sneak along without trumpet or drum. Have you finished, Grimaud?"

Grimaud pointed silently at a dozen bodies which he had set up in the most picturesque attitudes. Some carried weapons, others appeared to be taking aim.

"Bravo!" said Athos. "That does credit to your imagination."

"Aha!" said Aramis. "The black and red dots are visibly enlarging. We have no time to lose in regaining camp."

"I have nothing more to say against a retreat," replied Athos. "Grimaud has cleared away the breakfast. We bet we should stay one hour, and we have already been here an hour and a half."

Grimaud was already ahead with the hamper and the scraps. The four friends followed ten paces behind him.

"*Morbleu!*" cried Athos. "We have forgotten the white flag. And we must not abandon a flag to the enemy, even though it be only a napkin."

And he ran back to the bastion, ascended the platform, and took down the pennant. But as the Rochellais had now come within range, they opened a scathing fire upon him. Athos might be said to bear a charmed life. The musket balls thudded and whistled all around him, but not one found its mark. He waved the flag high above his head, turning his back upon the Rochellais and saluting the watchers in the royal camp. On both sides shouts arose—cries of anger, cries of enthusiastic applause.

A second salvo of musketry followed the first. Three bullets passing through the napkin made it really a battle flag. Loud calls issued from the camp: "Come down! Come down!"

Athos descended. His friends who were anxiously awaiting him greeted his return with joy.

"Hurry up, Athos!" called d'Artagnan. "Now that we have everything except money to send our lackeys off with, it would be stupid to be killed."

But Athos kept to his majestic stride, no matter how his friends might chafe and rage. Finding their remarks of no avail, they regulated their pace to his. Grimaud and his hamper, of course, were by now far in advance, out of range of musket fire.

At the end of another minute a violent fusillade was heard.

"They are firing at the corpses," explained Athos.

"But the dead cannot return their fire," said Porthos.

"Certainly not. But the Rochellais will believe it is an ambuscade, and they will halt to deliberate. By the time they have solved our little joke, we shall be out of reach of their balls. So there is no use getting heart disease by hurrying overmuch."

At length a fresh discharge occurred. This time the bullets came rattling among the stones near the Insepa-rables and whistled sharply past their ears. The Rochellais had finally taken possession of the bastion.

"Those are bungling fellows," said Athos. "How many of them did we kill, I wonder—a dozen?"

"Nearer fifteen, I reckon."

"And how many did we crush beneath the wall?"

"At least eight or ten."

"And in return we did not even suffer a scratch! Ah—but what is wrong with your hand, d'Artagnan? It is bleeding!"

"Oh, it's nothing at all," answered the Gascon.

"A spent bullet?"

"Not even that."

"What is it, then?"

"Only grazed a trifle," replied the young guardsman. "My fingers were caught between two stones—one in the wall and one in my ring."

"That's what comes from wearing diamonds, young sir," remarked Athos with a slight sneer.

"Why, there we are! We have a diamond," said Porthos. "Why the deuce are we worrying as to where our money to send the lackeys to Tours and London is coming from? We'll sell the stone."

"But," objected d'Artagnan, "it's the queen's diamond."

"All the more reason for selling it," observed Athos. "Nothing could be more just than for the queen to save M. de Buckingham, her lover. Nothing more proper than for her to save us, her friends. What does Monsieur the Abbé think about it?"

"My idea," said Aramis, blushing as usual, "is that since his ring does not come from a ladylove, and is therefore not a token of intimate personal affection, d'Artagnan may sell it."

"Very well, then," cried the Gascon gaily, "let us dispose of the gem and never say another word about it."

The fusillade continued, but by this time the friends were out of range. The citizens of La Rochelle kept on firing only to save their faces.

As the Inseparables approached the camp they saw that it was all in motion. More than two thousand people had been present, as it were, at a theatrical performance given by the four friends. Nothing could be heard but "Long live the Musketeers!" "Long live the Guards!"

M. de Busigny was the very first to shake Athos by

the hand and acknowledge he had won the wager. There
was nothing but congratulations, huzzas, hand-shakings,
and embraces. There was no end to the inextinguishable
laughter at the Rochellais. The tumult at last grew to
such proportions that the cardinal imagined there must be
some sort of mutiny afoot, and he sent La Houdinière, his
captain of Guards, to discover what mischief was forward.
The affair was related to him with a bubbling enthusiasm.

"Well, sir," demanded his Eminence on La Houdinière's return, "what was the trouble?"

"Monseigneur," replied the latter, "three musketeers
and a guardsman laid a wager with M. de Busigny that
they would breakfast in the bastion St. Gervais. They
held the position for two hours against the enemy and
killed no one knows just how many Rochellais."

"Did you discover the names of the three musketeers?"

"Yes, Monseigneur."

"What were the names?"

"MM. Athos, Porthos, and Aramis."

"Again those three brave rascals!" murmured the
cardinal, admiringly. "And the guardsman?"

"D'Artagnan."

"Again that irrepressible scapegrace! These four men
must positively be in my service."

That same evening Richelieu spoke with M. de Tréville
regarding the wild exploit, which was still the talk of the
whole camp. Tréville, who had received the story of the
adventure from the lips of the actors in it, told it with
much detail to the cardinal, not omitting the episode of
the napkin.

"Excellent!" said his Eminence. "Pray have that napkin sent to me, Monsieur, and I shall have three fleur-de-lis embroidered on it in gold. I shall present it to your company as a standard."

"Monseigneur," said the captain of Musketeers, "that would be unfair to the Guardsmen. M. d'Artagnan is not in my troop — he serves under M. d'Essart."

"Well, then, enroll him with you," said the cardinal. "When four soldiers are so much attached to one another, it is but fair that they should serve in the same company."

When he heard this news, d'Artagnan was beside himself with joy. The three friends were likewise greatly delighted.

"My faith," d'Artagnan said to Athos, "that was one grand idea of yours! We not only had our talk which was of the highest importance, but we acquired great glory too."

"We can now go on talking without being suspected," grinned Athos. "For from now on, with luck, we shall pass as cardinalists."

That evening d'Artagnan went to present his respects to M. d'Essart and inform him of his promotion. His commander, who esteemed the young Gascon highly, placed himself at his service, as the change of regiment would entail expenses for new equipment. D'Artagnan refused the captain's kindly offer, but he thought the opportunity a good one to turn the diamond into cash. And so he begged M. d'Essart to have the stone valued for him.

Next day at two o'clock M. d'Essart's valet came to d'Artagnan's quarters and gave him a bag containing seven thousand livres. This was the price of the queen's diamond.

CHAPTER XLVI

A FAMILY AFFAIR

Athos invented the phrase "family affair." Such an affair was outside the jurisdiction of the cardinal. Such an affair concerned nobody not immediately involved. People could employ themselves in settling a family affair without being subject to investigation by the outer world.

M. de Tréville gave the four friends a festival breakfast, and the occasion was as gay and merry as it is possible to imagine. D'Artagnan was already in his new uniform. For he was nearly identical in size with Aramis, and the would-be abbé was so liberally paid (by the publisher who purchased his poem?) that he had bought two suits of everything. So he sold his friend a complete outfit.

After breakfast d'Artagnan passed the day in exhibiting his musketeer's uniform in every corner of the camp.

That evening the four friends met in Athos' lodging to finish their plans for sending the lackeys. There remained but three things to settle: what should be written to Milady's brother-in-law; what should be said to the clever person in Tours; which of the lackeys should carry the letters.

Each musketeer offered his own servant.

Athos called attention to the discretion of Grimaud, who never opened his mouth except when his master unlocked it.

Porthos boasted of the strength of Mousqueton, who was big enough to thrash four ordinary men.

Aramis delivered himself of a fulsome eulogy on his candidate, and praised especially Bazin's address.

D'Artagnan reminded his friends of the brave manner in which Planchet had handled the ticklish affair of Boulogne.

"Unfortunately," observed Athos, "the one we send must possess in himself alone the four qualities we have extolled."

"But where on earth is such a lackey to be found?"

"Nowhere!" declared Athos. "So take Grimaud."

"Take Mousqueton."

"Take Bazin."

"Take Planchet."

"Gentlemen," suggested Aramis, "the main thing is not to know which of the four lackeys is the most discreet, strong, clever, or brave. The main thing is to discover which one loves money best."

"Sensibly spoken," commented Athos. "We should speculate about the faults of servants and not about their virtues. Monsieur Abbé, you are really a great philosopher."

"Surely," acknowledged Aramis, "we must be well served not only in order to succeed, but also that we may not fail. For in case of failure our lackeys' heads will sit securely on their shoulders, but our own will not. Are our servants sufficiently devoted to us to risk their lives in our service? No."

"I would almost answer for Planchet," ventured d'Artagnan.

"Well, then, my dear friend, add to Planchet's natural

devotedness a whacking sum of money. And instead
of answering for him once, you can answer for him
twice."

"You will be fooled if you do," said Athos sourly. He
was an optimist about things and a pessimist about men.
"What the devil! Why, to reach England, all France must
be crossed. And it is covered with the spies and the creatures of the cardinal. A passport for embarkation must
be secured. Really, the affair seems to me to be beset
with insurmountable difficulties."

"Ah, it might be," said d'Artagnan, "if in our letter
we should openly write to Lord de Winter about state
affairs of vast importance, about all kinds of enormities
of the cardinal, about intrigues and secrets. But you seem
to forget, Athos, that we shall write to him only regarding
a family affair. We write to him only to beg that the
moment Milady arrives in London he will put it out of
her power to injure us. I shall couch my message, Athos,
in almost these very terms."

"No, my dear fellow, content yourself to handle the
musket and the sword—you succeed splendidly at both
these games. But when it comes to double meanings
and the speech of folderol, pass the pen to Monsieur the
Abbé. That is his special province."

"Ay, ay!" chimed in Porthos, "pass the goosequill to
Aramis. He can write theses in Latin."

"I am willing," offered Aramis with that ingenuous air
of confidence that every poet has in his own powers. "But
first let me be properly acquainted with the subject of my
theme. I have heard it hinted here and there that the

sister-in-law was a hussy, but the details of her crimes have escaped me."

"Me, too," said Porthos.

D'Artagnan and Athos regarded each other for some time in silence. At length the older musketeer, after serious meditation and with paler face than ordinary, made a sign of assent to the young Gascon that he was at liberty to speak.

"Well, the following is about the content of your note, I should imagine," said d'Artagnan:

"My Lord:

Your sister-in-law is an infamous woman who wishes to have you killed that she may inherit your wealth. Understand, however, that her marriage to your brother was illegal, for she already had a husband in France. And she was—"

"Repudiated by her French husband," completed Athos.

"Because she wore the executioner's brand," added d'Artagnan.

"Nonsense!" cried Porthos. "What are you two romancing about? You mean to say she wanted her brother-in-law murdered?"

"Absolutely."

"She was married?" asked Porthos.

"Exactly."

"And her husband discovered the fleur-de-lis on her shoulder!" exclaimed Porthos.

"He did."

These three affirmations had been uttered by Athos, each with a sadder intonation than the preceding.

"Why, who saw this brand?" demanded Aramis.

"D'Artagnan and I. Or, rather, to speak in chronological sequence, I and d'Artagnan," responded Athos.

"And does the original husband of this creature still live?"

"He still lives."

"You are quite convinced of the fact?"

"I am that husband."

Then there was a moment of cold silence! During this uncomfortable pause each of the four friends was affected according to his nature and experience.

"The letter must be written at once," said Athos, who was the first to break the uncanny stillness.

"Your are right," agreed Aramis. "The billet will prove rather a difficult matter, I fear. Never mind! Be silent. I shall write."

Accordingly Aramis took up the quill, considered for a few moments, and then wrote ten or twelve lines in a dainty, almost feminine, hand:

My Lord:

The person who writes you had the honor of crossing swords with you in the small inclosure of the Rue d'Enfer. As you have several times since stated that you are the friend of this person, he thinks it his duty to send you important information. Twice you have nearly been the victim of a near relative, whom you believe to be your heir. This is because you are ignorant that she had already contracted a marriage in France before she was married in England. The third time she tries to get you out of the way (which is right now) she may succeed. Your relative left La Rochelle for England during the night. Watch her arrival, because she is entertaining great and terrible projects. If you wish to know definitely to what bounds she may go, read her past history as it is written on her left shoulder.

"That will answer finely," said Athos when he heard the letter read aloud. "If this word reaches him, de Winter will now be on his guard. Even if it should fall into the claws of the cardinal, we should not be compromised. But as the lackey who goes may swear he has been to London, while he has only gone as far as Chatellerault, I suggest that we give him only half the promised sum when he is handed the letter. We shall agree to hand him the other half in exchange for the reply. Have you the diamond, d'Artagnan?"

"No, but I have the price of it."

The Gascon threw the bag of money upon the table. At the clink of the gold Aramis raised his eyebrows and Porthos fairly started up from his chair. Athos alone remained unmoved.

"How much is in the sack?"

"Seven thousand livres in louis of twelve francs."

"Gadzooks!" cried Porthos, staring at the sack, round-eyed. "That scrawny little diamond worth seven thousand livres?"

"So it seems," replied Athos, "for I don't suppose our friend d'Artagnan has added any funds from his own store."

"But, gentlemen," the Gascon reminded them, "we are not thinking of her Majesty in all this. Let us pay some heed to the fate of her beloved Buckingham. That is the least we owe her."

"True," said Athos, "but that is Aramis' job."

Aramis blushed and resumed his quill. He reflected a little as to what he should say to "the clever person who lives in Tours" and then wrote the following lines, which he at once submitted to the criticism of his friends:

MY DEAR COUSIN:

His Eminence—whom God preserve for the happiness of France and the humiliation of her enemies!—is on the point of putting an end to the heretic rebellion of La Rochelle. It is probable that the English fleet, sent for their rescue, will never even come in sight of the Rochellais. I even venture to predict that M. de Buckingham will be prevented by some great event from setting out. His Eminence is the most illustrious politician of all times—he would extinguish the sun if this planet incommoded him. Give these joyful tidings to your sister, my dear Cousin. I dreamt the unlucky Englishman was dead—I cannot recollect whether by steel or by poison. Only I am sure I dreamt he was dead, and you know my dreams never deceive me. Be assured, therefore, that you will shortly see me return.

"Capital!" cried Athos. "You speak like the Book of Revelations, my dear Aramis, and yet you are as true as the Gospel. Nothing remains but to put the address to this letter."

"That is easily done," replied Aramis. He folded the paper into a fanciful form and wrote, "To Mademoiselle Michon, seamstress, Tours." The three friends looked at one another and laughed. Their curiosity had been outwitted.

"And now," continued Aramis, "you will please to understand, gentlemen, that Bazin alone can carry this letter to Tours. My cousin would place confidence only in him; any other messenger would fail to convince her."

"Very well," agreed d'Artagnan, "I consent to Bazin with all my heart, but you must let me have Planchet. Milady had him turned out of doors one day with vigorous blows from a thick stick to accelerate his going. Now, Planchet has a good memory, and I know that, sooner than relinquish any possible means of vengeance upon her, he will gladly allow himself to be beaten to death."

"In that case," observed Athos, "Planchet must receive seven hundred livres for going and seven hundred livres for the return trip. Bazin shall have three hundred livres for the outbound journey and three hundred for coming back. These subtractions will reduce the jewel fund to five thousand livres. We shall each take one thousand to employ as we think best. And we'll leave a sum of one thousand livres in the hands of Monsieur the Abbé here for extraordinary occasions or common wants. What do you say?"

"Athos," cried Aramis, "you speak like Nestor, who was the wisest man among the ancient Greeks!"

"Agreed, then," said Athos. "Everything considered, I am not sorry to retain Grimaud at home. He is accustomed to my ways and I am somewhat particular. Yesterday's affair at the bastion must have shaken him a bit. This voyage would upset him quite."

Planchet was summoned and instructions given him.

"I shall carry the letter in the lining of my coat," said the lackey. "And if I am taken, I shall swallow it."

"But then you won't be able to carry out your commission," objected d'Artagnan.

"You can give me a copy of the message this evening, Monsieur, and I shall have it memorized by tomorrow."

D'Artagnan looked at his friends quizzically, as if to say, "Well, what did I tell you about this fellow?"

"And now," he continued, addressing himself to Planchet, "you have eight days to get your interview with Lord de Winter and eight for your return. If, on the sixteenth day after your departure, you are not here by eight o'clock in the evening—no money, even if you turn up only five minutes after that hour!"

"Then, Monsieur," announced Planchet, "you must buy me a watch."

"Take this one," said Athos, with his usual carefree generosity giving Planchet his own, "and be a good boy! Remember, if you babble, if you get drunk, you are risking your master's head. Recall likewise that if by your fault any trouble comes to d'Artagnan, I shall hunt you down, no matter where you may be concealed, for the purpose of cutting your heart out."

"And I," chimed in Porthos, rolling his large eyes, "I I shall skin you alive."

"And I," said Aramis, with his soft, melodious voice, "I shall roast you at a slow fire, like mutton."

Planchet, overcome, began to weep. We shall not venture to say whether it was from shame at the unjust suspicions, from terror created by the threats, or from tenderness at seeing the four friends united in so close a bond.

In the morning, as Planchet was mounting his horse preparatory to starting forth, d'Artagnan, who at the bottom of his heart had a soft spot for the duke, took the lackey aside.

"Listen!" he whispered. "When you have given the billet to Lord de Winter and he has read it, say to him further, 'Watch over his Grace Lord Buckingham, for they wish to assassinate him.' These words, Planchet, are so serious and important that I have not told my friends that I am intrusting this secret to you. And I would not write this message down, not in exchange for a captain's commission."

"Don't worry, Monsieur," answered Planchet. "You shall soon see whether I have deserved your confidence."

Mounted on an excellent horse, which he was to abandon after twenty leagues in order to ride by post, Planchet set off at a gallop. His spirits were slightly depressed by the treble menace of the musketeers, but otherwise he was as light-hearted as one could wish.

Bazin set out the next day for Tours. He was allowed eight days to finish his business satisfactorily.

During the interval of the lackeys' absence the nerves of the Inseparables were on edge. They passed their days in trying to catch everything that was said or even hinted at. They had their weather eye open for all the couriers who arrived in camp, and observed narrowly the comings and goings of the cardinal. They trembled involuntarily if called upon for some unexpected service. They had their own safety to consider. Milady was a phantom which, once it had appeared to a person, did not thereafter permit him to sleep very quietly.

On the morning of the eighth day Bazin, smiling and fresh as a dewy daisy, entered the cabaret of the Parpaillot just as the four friends were sitting down to breakfast. He spoke the phrase agreed upon in advance, "M. Aramis, the answer from your cousin."

The Inseparables exchanged a joyful glance, for half
of the work was done. It is true, however, that it was the
shortest and easiest part of it. Aramis, blushing in spite
of himself, took the letter, which was written in a large,
coarse hand and one not particular for its correctness in
the spelling of words:

My Cousin:

Sister and I are skillful in interpreting dreams and I may even
say that we feel a great terror of them. But I hope that your
vision may turn out to be an illusion. Adieu! Take care of yourself, and so comport yourself that we may from time to time hear
your name spoken.

Marie Michon.

Of course, Bazin's lucky return removed only part of
the uneasiness that weighed upon the friends. Days of
waiting are long periods of time. D'Artagnan, in particular, would willingly have bet that each day contained not
less than forty-eight hours.

He forgot the necessary delays in navigation. He exaggerated to himself the powers of Milady. He credited
this woman, whom he considered a sort of demon, with
possessing agents as supernatural as herself. Further still,
his confidence in the worthy Picard valet lessened from
hour to hour. His anxiety became so contagious that it
spread to Aramis and Porthos. Of the four friends, Athos
alone remained impassive, as if no danger hovered over
him, as if he was breathing his accustomed atmosphere.

On the last day of the term agreed upon, in particular,
d'Artagnan and his two friends could not stay for any
length of time in one place, but wandered about like uneasy

ghosts along the road by which Planchet was expected to return.

"Really, you know," said Athos to them, "you are perfect children to permit a woman to terrify you so. And what, after all, is the very worst thing that can happen to you? To be imprisoned. Well, but after a while we should be taken out of the prison—Madame Bonacieux was released, was she not?"

Finding that this well-meant reasoning was of no avail in raising the spirits of his comrades, Athos tried another tack.

"Do you fear you will be decapitated?" he inquired. "Suppose you are — there are other things just as bad or worse. Why, every day a bullet may break our legs in the trenches. And I am sure that a surgeon would cause more pain in amputating a thigh than an executioner would in cutting off one's head. Have faith in Planchet. He is sure to arrive before long."

"But if he does not come?" sighed d'Artagnan.

"He will arrive all right, slightly delayed, maybe. Perhaps he has fallen from his horse or come a cropper on a sloping deck. He may have galloped so fast against head winds as to have brought on a violent attack of catarrh. Life is a chaplet of minor miseries which the philosopher regards with a patient smile. Be philosophic, Messieurs! Sit down to the table and let us drink. Survey the future through the rose-hued spectacles of a bottle of Chambertin."

The sixteenth day finally drew to a close. The taverns were filled with thirsty and half-drunken soldiers. Athos was spending his share of the diamond at the Parpaillot, which he rarely quitted. He had discovered in M. de Busigny (who, by the way, had given the Inseparables a magnificent dinner) a partner worthy of him when it came to the surrounding of spirituous refreshment. They were playing together, as usual, when seven o'clock sounded— the patrol was heard passing to double the outposts. At half-past seven the retreat was sounded.

"We are lost," d'Artagnan whispered to Athos.

"You mean to say we have lost," Athos quietly corrected him. "But the affair, after all, is but a single hazard."

He quietly drew four pistoles from his pocket and threw them upon the table. "Come, gentlemen," he said, "they are beating the tattoo. Off to quarters!"

As the four stumbled out of the Parpaillot, all at once a shadow appeared before them. Its outlines were familiar to d'Artagnan, and a well-known voice was addressing him:

"Monsieur, I have brought your cloak. It is chilly this evening."

"Planchet!" cried the Gascon, beside himself with joy.

"Why, of course, Planchet—to be sure," said Athos. "But what is there so amazing about that? He promised to be back by eight o'clock, and that hour is just striking. He is a lad of his word."

D'Artagnan felt a strong temptation to hug Planchet, but he was afraid so unusual a mark of affection bestowed upon his lackey in the open street might appear strange to the passers-by. So he restrained himself.

"Planchet has given me the note," he said to Athos.

"That's good," replied Athos. "Let's go home and read it."

The letter that the lackey had handed him burned in the Gascon's clenched fist. But at length they reached their tent, lit a lamp, and stationed Planchet at the door so they might not be surprised. With trembling hand d'Artagnan broke the seal of the letter and read to his friends the following line: "Thank you. Be easy."

D'Artagnan translated this British statement to his friends. Then he drew near the lamp, set fire to the paper, and did not let it fall to the ground until it was reduced to a black cinder.

Then he summoned Planchet and said, "Here, my lad, are the seven hundred livres. Tell us all about your trip."

"*Dame!* That will be a long business, Monsieur."

"Right you are, Planchet," commented Athos. "Besides, the tattoo has sounded, and we should be specially observed if we kept our light going much longer than the others."

"So be it," said d'Artagnan. "Go to bed, Planchet, and sleep soundly. Tomorrow we shall hear the yarn."

"My faith, Monsieur!" fairly whimpered the lackey. "Tonight will be the first real rest for me in sixteen days."

"And me, too!" said d'Artagnan.

"And me, too!" said Porthos.

"And me, too!" said Aramis.

"Well, if you must have the truth—and me, too!" said Athos.

CHAPTER XLVII

LEAVE OF ABSENCE

Aramis had been as good as his word. He had found out for his friend d'Artagnan the convent in which Madame Constance Bonacieux was living. The news had been obtained from the invaluable seamstress Marie Michon of Tours. She had written Aramis to say that her Majesty had placed the young woman in the nunnery of the Carmelites at Béthune, a small town upon the frontiers of Artois and of Flanders.

The Gascon, of course, had been mad with joy to receive such definite news of his ladylove and to learn she was alive and unharmed. It was as good as settled among the four friends that, the moment the siege of La Rochelle was over, they should make a tour in the direction of the convent.

Now, for a long time after the return of Planchet, nothing worthy of chronicle had happened in the camp before the beleaguered city. And so the king grew more bored with life than ever, and finally determined to go incognito and spend the festival of St. Louis at the city of St. Germain. He asked the cardinal for an escort of twenty musketeers. His Eminence, who, truth to tell, often became weary of the fidgets of his Majesty Louis XIII, granted this leave of absence with great pleasure to his royal lieutenant, who promised to return not later than September 15.

When M. de Tréville was notified of this fact by his Eminence, he packed his portmanteau. Without knowing the cause of it, he remembered the great desire his four friends entertained to return to Paris. And so he fixed upon them to form part of the escort.

The Inseparables heard the news fifteen minutes after M. de Tréville himself, for they were the very first to whom he had communicated it. It was at that moment, I presume, that d'Artagnan most fully appreciated the favor the cardinal had done him in making him at last a full-fledged musketeer. For if that one thing had not occurred, d'Artagnan would have been forced to stay in camp while his comrades were away on escort duty.

It goes without saying that the imperative need the young Gascon felt for returning to Paris was concerned with the danger he thought Madame Bonacieux might run of meeting with her mortal enemy, Milady, at the convent of Béthune. Aramis, always complaisant, had therefore immediately written again to Marie Michon, the seamstress at Tours who had such fine acquaintances. And she had obtained from Anne of Austria authority for the mercer's wife to leave the nunnery and to retire either into Lorraine or Belgium. The friends had not, in fact, long to wait for an answer to Aramis' request. Eight or ten days after he had written it, Aramis had received the following note:

My dear Cousin:

Here is the authorization from my sister to withdraw our young servant from the convent of Béthune, the air of which you consider to be bad for her. My sister sends you this authorization

with much pleasure, for she is quite fond of the little girl, to whom
she intends to be of greater service hereafter. I salute you.

Marie Michon.

To this letter was affixed an order which was duly
sealed and attested, and couched in the following terms:

At the Louvre, August 10, 1628.

The superior of the convent of Béthune will place in the
hands of the person who shall present this note to her the novice
who entered the convent upon my recommendation and under my
patronage.

Anne.

The three friends of Aramis were highly amused by
his relationship to a seamstress who called the queen of
France sister. What is more, they spoke about the fact.
But then the would-be abbé, blushing to the whites of
his eyes at the gross pleasantries of Porthos, begged them
not to revert to the subject again. And he declared that
if a single further word was said to him about it, he would
never again urge his cousin to interfere in such matters.

This put a definite stop to conversation regarding
Marie Michon. Anyway, they had just what they most
wanted: the royal order to withdraw Madame Bonacieux
from the convent of the Carmelites at Béthune. At first,
to be sure, they did not see how this order was to be of any
specific use to them while they were in camp before La
Rochelle — the other end of France from their objective.
And so d'Artagnan was on the point of going to ask leave
of absence from M. de Tréville, confiding to him the true
reason for the desired permission to depart. But just
then the four friends learned that the king was to set out

for Paris with an escort of twenty musketeers, and that they formed part of the retinue.

Their joy was beyond description. The lackeys were sent on in advance with the baggage, and they themselves set forth on the morning of the sixteenth.

The cardinal accompanied his Majesty from Surgères to Mauzé. There the king and his minister took leave of each other with many ardent demonstrations of friendliness.

Although Louis XIII was desirous to travel with the utmost speed, he yet was unwilling to forego distraction. Although he was very eager to reach Paris by the twenty-third of the month, he stopped here and there to fly the magpie—a pastime of which he had long been fond. When such pauses occurred, sixteen of the escort of twenty musketeers rejoiced heartily at the relaxation thus afforded, but the other four cursed in strong vein.

At length the escort passed through Paris on the night of the twenty-third. The king thanked M. de Tréville for the manner in which his duty had been performed and allowed him to grant furloughs for four days, on condition that the favored persons should not appear in any public place under penalty of imprisonment in the Bastille.

The first four leaves of absence, as the reader may guess, were handed to the four Inseparables. And what is more, Athos obtained of M. de Tréville a term of six days, instead of four, and two added nights. For the friends set out on their adventure at five o'clock on the evening of the twenty-fourth, although as an especial kindness the captain of Musketeers had postdated the leave to read the morning of the twenty-fifth.

"Great heavens!" said d'Artagnan. "It seems to me we are making a mountain out of a molehill. I have plenty of money for horses and anything else I need for the trip. With the queen's letter to aid me I shall easily gain possession of the dear treasure I am going to seek. You fellows stay where you are and do not exhaust yourselves with useless fatigue. Planchet and I are all that so simple an exploit requires."

"We also have heaps of money left from the diamond," Athos replied quietly. "And you will do well to remember that Béthune is a city where the cardinal has given a rendezvous to a woman who, wherever she goes, brings misery in her wake. If you only had four men to deal with, d'Artagnan, I should allow you to go alone. But you have to do with that woman! And I hope to God that with our lackeys we four may be enough to cope with her."

"You frighten me terribly," said the young man. "What do you fear?"

"Everything!" replied Athos.

D'Artagnan studied the faces of his other companions and found them likewise stamped with an expression of deepest anxiety. Thereafter the friends continued on their way as fast as their horses could carry them, but without adding another word.

They entered Arras on the evening of the twenty-fifth. The young Gascon had just dismounted at the inn of the Golden Harrow to drink a glass of wine. At that instant a cavalier on a fresh horse rode out of the post yard, where he had secured his relay, and at a hard gallop took the road to Paris. As the horseman was passing through the gateway to the turnpike, the wind blew open the cloak in which he was enveloped (despite the warmth of the evening air) and half lifted his hat from his head. The traveler pulled the hat eagerly back again over his eyes.

D'Artagnan, whose gaze had been by chance fastened upon this stranger, grew very pale and let his glass fall from his hand.

"What is the matter, Monsieur?" cried the anxious Planchet. "Oh, run, gentlemen, my master is ill!"

But the young man certainly had a strange fashion of showing his illness, for as the three friends hastened toward him he tore eagerly after his horse. The friends stopped him at the door.

"Where the devil are you going?" shouted Athos.

"It is he!" cried d'Artagnan, pale with anger, and with the sweat standing on his forehead. "Let me overtake him!"

"What he are you talking about?" demanded Athos.

"He. That man!"

"What man?"

"That cursed chap, my evil genius, whom I always run across when menaced by some misfortune. The fellow who accompanied that horrible woman when I met her for the first time. The one I was seeking when I offended you, Athos. The man I saw the morning Madame Bonacieux was carried off. I saw him ride out the stable yard and recognized him when the wind blew open his cloak."

"The devil!" said Athos, ruminating.

"To saddle, gentlemen, to saddle! Pursue him and overtake him!"

"My dear friend," advised Aramis gently, "remember he is going in a direction opposite to ours. He has a fresh horse, ours are fatigued; we should thus only disable our own animals without even the off chance of catching up with his. Let the man go, d'Artagnan; let us save the woman."

"Monsieur!" shouted a hostler, running out of the post yard and looking after the unknown. "Monsieur, here is a paper that dropped from your hat! Hi, there! Hello, you, Monsieur!"

"Friend," said d'Artagnan quietly, "here is a half pistole for that paper."

"Why, thank you, Monsieur! With all the pleasure in life! Take it and welcome."

The hostler, enchanted with the good work he had done for himself, retired to the yard. The Gascon opened the paper.

"Well?" eagerly demanded his three friends in unison.

"Nothing but one word," replied d'Artagnan, disappointedly.

"Yes," said Aramis, "but that one word is the name of some village or town, you may be sure."

"Armentières," read Porthos. "I don't know any such place."

"Look!" cried Athos. "That name of a town or village is written in Milady's hand."

"Come on!" said d'Artagnan. "We shall keep that slip of paper carefully. Perhaps I didn't throw away that half pistole, after all. To horse, my friends!"

And the four companions flew at a gallop along the road to Béthune.

CHAPTER XLVIII

THE CARMELITE CONVENT AT BÉTHUNE

Great criminals seem to be the creatures of a kind of predestination which causes them to surmount every obstacle and escape every danger up to the very moment which a wearied Providence has marked for the wreck of their impious fortunes.

Thus it was with Milady. She avoided the cruisers of two nations and arrived at Boulogne without accident.

When she landed at Portsmouth, she had posed as an Englishwoman driven from La Rochelle by the persecutions of the French. When she landed at Boulogne, Milady posed as a Frenchwoman whom the English had been torturing at Portsmouth because of their hatred for France.

This great criminal had the best of all passports: her beauty, her noble appearance, and the liberality with which she distributed her pistoles broadcast. She stopped at Boulogne only long enough to post a letter of the following content:

Boulogne, evening of the 25th.

To his Eminence, Monseigneur the Cardinal Richelieu, in his camp before La Rochelle.

Monseigneur:

Let your Eminence be reassured. His Grace the Duke of Buckingham will not set out for France.

Milady.

Postscript: According to the instructions of your Eminence, I shall report at the convent of the Carmelites at Béthune, where I shall await your further orders.

The same evening Milady commenced her journey. Night overtook her; so she stopped and slept at an inn. But at five o'clock the next morning she again proceeded, and in three hours thereafter entered the town of Béthune. She inquired for the convent of the Carmelites and went thither immediately. The superior met her. Milady showed her the cardinal's order. The abbess assigned her a chamber and had breakfast served.

After the meal the abbess came to pay her a visit. There is little amusement in the life of a cloister, and the good superior was eager to make the acquaintance of her new boarder.

Milady was anxious to please the abbess. This was a comparatively easy matter for a woman who possessed such unusual graces of mind and person. Milady endeavored to be agreeable, and she was charming. She quite won over the good superior by her clever conversation and the attractions of her vivid personality. It was only after the most delightful of visits that the abbess suddenly recalled herself to the exercise of her duties as hostess.

"You have been traveling these four days, child, by your own confession," she said. "This morning you arose at five o'clock and must therefore be sadly in need of repose. Go to bed and sleep. At dinner time we shall rouse you."

Although Milady would willingly have foregone sleep, sustained as she was by the excitement which a new adventure always awakened in her heart, yet she accepted the offer of the superior. During the last fortnight she had undergone so many and such varied emotions that even if her iron physique was still capable of sustaining fatigue, her mind required repose. Rocked by the soothing hopes of vengeance upon d'Artagnan and the hated husband, the Comte de la Fère, she soon fell asleep. . . . .

She was awakened by a soft voice which proceeded from the foot of her bed. She opened her eyes and saw the abbess, accompanied by a young woman with light hair and delicate complexion, who fixed upon her a glance of sweet-tempered curiosity.

The face of the young woman was utterly strange to her, and so each examined the other with much attention, the while they were exchanging the customary phrases of politeness. The abbess introduced them to each other. When this formality was ended, as her duties summoned her to chapel, the superior left the two young women alone.

"Madame," said the novice, "I fear I have chosen an inopportune time for visiting. You were asleep; you are still fatigued."

"Well," answered Milady in honeyed accents, "what better can those who sleep wish for than a happy awakening? This you have given me—allow me then to enjoy it at my ease."

She took the novice's hand and drew her toward the armchair by the bedside. The novice sat down.

"How unfortunate I am!" she sighed. "I have been isolated here six months without the tiniest bit of entertainment. You come, and your presence here is calculated to afford me the most delightful companionship. And yet

I am expecting to leave the convent now at almost any moment."

"What? You are going soon?" asked Milady.

"I hope so, at least," answered the novice, with an expression of joy which she made no attempt to disguise.

"Have you, too, suffered persecutions?" continued Milady. "And from the cardinal, perhaps? That might have been another bond of sympathy between us."

"Oh, our good mother superior suspects that you likewise may have been a victim of that wicked priest, Madame."

"Hush!" counseled Milady. "Let us not so speak of the cardinal even here. All my misfortunes have arisen from my having said almost what you have just said before a woman whom I thought my friend, but who betrayed me."

"Ah," objected the novice, "but I am no victim of treachery—of my devotion, rather. I have been sacrificed for my loyalty to a woman I loved, for whom I should willingly have laid down my life, for whom I still would give it."

"And who has abandoned you—is that it?"

"That is what I was nearly unjust enough to believe. But now I have obtained proof to the contrary, for which I thank God! But you, Madame, you seem to be free, and if you were inclined to fly it only rests with you to do so."

"Where would you have me go, pray? I am without friends, without money, in a part of France with which I am not acquainted, and where I have never been before."

"Oh," cried the novice, "you must have friends wherever you go — you are so beautiful, and you appear to be so good!"

Milady softened her smile so as to lend it an angelic cast.

"That does not prevent my being alone and persecuted," she said, "although I have powerful friends who have at times been of value to me in the past. I have not the honor of knowing her Majesty the queen personally, but I am acquainted with a great number of her most intimate friends. I know M. de Putange, for example, have met M. Dujart in England, am acquainted with M. de Tréville."

"Do you know him?" exclaimed the novice.

"Yes, perfectly well—even intimately."

"The captain of the king's Musketeers?"

"The very same and none other."

"Why, then, you see," cried the novice happily, "we shall soon be well acquainted and almost friends. If you are on such good terms with M. de Tréville, you must have visited him?"

"Frequently!" nodded Milady. Perceiving her falsehood successful, she determined to stick to this tack.

"You must have met some of the musketeers at his house."

"Every one of them who was in any sense a familiar in his house," answered Milady. She was excessively curious to see where this turn of the conversation might lead.

"Name a few of those you know and let's see if they happen to be my friends, too."

"Well," began Milady, slightly embarrassed, "there is M. de Louvigny, M. de Courtivron, M. de Férussac."

The novice listened attentively, then, seeing that the lady paused, she asked, "Do you know a gentleman named Athos?"

Milady became as pale as the sheets in which she was lying and, although she did not lose control of herself, she could not help giving a cry. She grasped the wrist of the novice and devoured her with her eyes.

"Oh, oh!" asked that poor woman, "have I said anything to hurt your feelings?"

"No. Only the name struck me because I also know that gentleman, and it seemed strange to meet a person who knows him so well."

"Very well indeed, I am happy to say. And I know his friends, besides, MM. Porthos and Aramis."

"Really!" cried Milady, who began to feel a chill in the region of her heart. "Why, so do I."

"Well, if you know them, Madame, why not turn in that direction when you are in need of help?"

"Oh, I should scarcely claim to be intimate with any one of the three," stammered Milady. "I have simply heard one of their friends, M. d'Artagnan, speak of them very often."

"Heavens! You know M. d'Artagnan!" cried the novice, staring open-eyed at Milady. Then she could not help but remark the queer look on her companion's face and added, "By what title do you know him, Madame?"

"Why," replied Milady, embarrassed, "by the title of friend, of course—how else?"

"You are deceiving me, Madame," said the novice, "he is or he has been your lover."

"It is you whom he loves!" cried Milady.

"I?" said the novice.

"Yes—you! I know now who you are. You are Madame Bonacieux."

The young woman drew back, overcome by surprise and fear.

"Oh, do not deny it! Answer!" continued Milady.

"Yes, Madame," said the novice. "Are we rivals?"

The face of Milady was lighted with so savage a joy that under any other circumstances Madame Bonacieux would have fled from her in terror. But she was entirely overcome by her jealousy.

"Tell me the truth, Madame!" cried Madame Bonacieux with a force of which one would not have thought her capable. "Have you been or are you now beloved by him?"

"Never!" replied Milady in a voice that admitted of no doubt as to the truth of her statement.

"I believe you," said Madame Bonacieux. "But why did you cry out so, if you were not deeply interested?"

"Can you not understand that M. d'Artagnan, being my friend, has taken me into his confidence regarding you?"

"Truly?"

"And that I therefore know everything—your abduction from the cottage at St. Germain, his despair at the loss of you, his vain search for your whereabouts up to this very moment? How can I help being woefully amazed when I meet you unexpectedly face to face? You, of whom we have so often spoken together? You whom he loves as his own soul? You whom he taught me to care for before I ever saw you? Ah, dear Constance, I have found you then! I behold you at last!"

And Milady stretched out her arms to Madame Bonacieux, who from this moment saw nothing in her companion except a sincere and devoted friend. For an instant the two women held each other in a close embrace. Certainly, if Milady's strength had been equal to her hatred, the mercer's wife would never have left that embrace alive.

"You beautiful, good little creature!" cried Milady. "How delighted I am to have found you!"

The poor young woman could not possibly suspect what hideous cruelty lurked behind the rampart of that pure brow, behind those brilliant eyes in which the observer could read nothing but concern and compassion.

'Then you must know what I have suffered," said Madame Bonacieux, "since he has told you what he has endured. Still, to suffer for him is happiness."

"Yes, indeed," replied Milady mechanically. She was thinking of something else than what the mercer's wife was saying.

"Besides," continued the novice, "my imprisonment is drawing to a close. Tomorrow, or perhaps this very evening, I shall see him again. And then the sad past will all be forgotten."

"This evening?" asked Milady, aroused from her reverie by these unexpected words. "What do you mean? Do you expect news from him?"

"I expect to receive him in person."

"What! D'Artagnan here?"

"None other."

"But that's out of the question! He is with the cardinal at the siege of La Rochelle. He will not return to
Paris until after the fall of the city."

"You think so, really? Let me tell you that nothing is
impossible to my d'Artagnan, the noble and loyal gentleman."

"Oh, I can hardly believe that!"

"Just read this note, then!" cried the young woman, in
the full flush of her pride and happiness, handing Milady
a letter.

"Aha! The handwriting of Madame de Chevreuse,"
said Milady to herself. "And I always suspected there
was some secret understanding in that quarter!" She
hastily devoured the following lines:

My dear Child:

Hold yourself in readiness to depart. Our friend will see you
soon. He comes with the sole purpose of freeing you from that
imprisonment which your safety required that you should undergo.
Prepare, then, for a journey. Whatever happens, do not despair.

Our charming Gascon has just proved himself as brave and
faithful as ever. Tell him that certain people are very grateful
to him for the warning he has given.

"The letter is certainly precise and to the point,"
acknowledged Milady. "Have you any idea of what the
warning was?"

"None. But I suppose he warned the queen against
some new plots of the cardinal."

"Yes, that's it, doubtless," said Milady, returning the
note to Madame Bonacieux and letting her head sink forward on her bosom.

At that moment the hoofbeats of a galloping horse were heard.

"Can it be he?" cried the mercer's wife, rushing to the window.

Milady lay motionless in bed as if turned to stone. Unexpected events were following each other so rapidly that she was quite at a loss what to do next.

"Alas, no!" said Madame Bonacieux. "It is a man I don't know, although he seems to be turning in at the gate. Yes, there he is ringing the bell."

Milady sprang from her bed. "You are sure it is not he?" she demanded.

"Very sure indeed."

"Perhaps you did not see him clearly."

"Oh, if I were to see but the plume of his hat, only the tip end of his cloak, I should know d'Artagnan."

Milady was dressing in great haste.

"The man is entering, you say?"

"Yes, he has already come in."

"Is it for you or me he has come, I wonder?"

"Heavens! How you are trembling with excitement!"

"I admit it. I am more afraid of the cardinal than you are."

"Hush!" warned Madame Bonacieux. "Somebody is knocking."

Immediately the door opened and the superior entered.

"Did you come here from Boulogne?" she asked Milady.

"Yes," answered the latter, striving hard to retain her self-possession. "Who is asking for me?"

"A man who refuses to give his name, but who comes from his Eminence the cardinal."

"Does he demand speech with me?"

"He insists on seeing a lady recently arrived from Boulogne."

"Then let him be admitted."

"Oh, oh, can it be bad news?" cried Madame Bonacieux.

"I fear it may be."

"I shall leave you alone with the stranger, but as soon as he has gone, if you will permit me, I shall return."

"Permit you? I beseech you to!"

Milady remained alone, with her eyes fixed upon the door. An instant later the clanking of spurs was heard on the stairs, the door opened, and a man appeared.

Milady uttered a cry of joy. For this visitor was the Comte de Rochefort — the evil genius of his Eminence.

CHAPTER XLIX

TWO VARIETIES OF DEMON

"It is you!" cried Milady and Rochefort in the same breath.

"Where do you hail from?" asked Milady.

"La Rochelle—and you?"

"From England."

"How did you leave Buckingham?"

"Dead, or desperately wounded. A fanatic had just stabbed him."

"Good!" commented Rochefort with a smile. "Have you informed the cardinal of it?"

"I wrote to him from Boulogne. But what brings you here?"

"His Eminence was growing uneasy and sent me to find you."

"I landed only yesterday."

"And what have you been up to since?"

"I have not been idle."

"You never do waste any time."

"Guess whom I have encountered here."

"How can I?"

"The young woman the queen removed from prison."

"The woman d'Artagnan is in love with?"

"Yes, Madame Bonacieux, with whose whereabouts the cardinal was not acquainted."

"Of all things!" said Rochefort.

"Imagine my astonishment when I found myself face to face with her," continued Milady.

"Did she know who you are?"

"No."

"She considers you a stranger, then?"

Milady smiled. "On the contrary, I am her best friend."

"My faith!" said Rochefort. "You alone, my dear countess, can perform such miracles."

"And it's a good thing I can, Chevalier," said Milady. "Do you know what is going on here?"

"Of course not."

"Tomorrow or the day after, they are coming to get her, with an order from the queen."

"Good Lord! And who are they?"

"D'Artagnan and his friends."

"If they are not careful, we shall have to stick them into the Bastille."

"Why has that not been done already?"

"The cardinal has an inexplicable weakness for these men."

"Are you serious?"

"Never more so."

"Well, then, Rochefort, tell him this: Our conversation at the inn of the Red Dovecote was overheard by these four men. After his departure, one of the musketeers came up to my room and took by violence the safe-conduct the cardinal had given me. They warned Lord de Winter of my journey to England. They nearly foiled my mission, as they did before in the affair of the studs. Tell the

cardinal that only two of these four men are to be feared:
d'Artagnan and Athos. Aramis is in love with Madame
de Chevreuse—his secret may be of use to us if we leave
him alone. The fourth man, Porthos, is a big blustering
booby, not worthy troubling about."

"But these musketeers must be now at the siege of
La Rochelle."

"That is what I thought, too. But a letter which
Madame Bonacieux received from Madame de Chevreuse,
and which she was imprudent enough to show me, makes
me believe these four men are on the way here."

"The devil! What is to be done?"

"What did the cardinal tell you regarding me?"

"I am to take your dispatches, written or verbal, and
return posthaste. When he learns what you have done, he
will advise you as to your further actions."

"I shall have to stay here, then?"

"Here, or somewhere close by."

"You cannot take me back with you?"

"No. My orders were imperative. You might be
recognized near the camp. Your presence there would
compromise the cardinal."

"But I may not be able to remain here."

"Why not?"

"You forget my deadly enemies may arrive at any
moment."

"Are you going to let this little Bonacieux escape the
cardinal's clutches?"

"Oh, no, indeed!" said Milady with a cruel smile that
was peculiarly her own. "Remember I am her best friend."

"I may then assure the cardinal with respect to this young woman—"

"That he need not worry in the least."

"Is that all I am to say?"

"He will know what that means."

"I shall return instantly. But my chaise broke down when I was coming into Lilliers."

"Excellent!"

"What is there excellent about the accident, pray?"

"I want your chaise when it's mended."

"How am I going to travel in that case?"

"On horseback."

"You talk very comfortably about it—and the distance is one hundred and eighty leagues."

"What of it?"

"Oh, I suppose I can manage it! Is there anything else?"

"Yes. In passing through Lilliers, send me your chaise together with an order placing your servant at my disposal."

"All right."

"Have you a written order from the cardinal?"

"I have my letter of full authority."

"Show it to the abbess, Count, and tell her that some one will come and fetch me, either today or tomorrow. Say to her that I am ordered to follow the person who presents himself in your name."

"Agreed."

"And do not forget to speak harshly of me to the abbess."

"But why?"

"I am supposed to be a victim of the cardinal. I must keep the trust of little Madame Bonacieux."

"Good—I shall remember! Are you going to give me a full report of your mission to England?"

"I have already told you what is important. You have a good memory. A paper might be lost or stolen."

"Correct. Now, only let me know where to find you, so that I shall not waste valuable time in searching."

"Wait, let me reflect a moment! Ah, that will do— Armentières."

"Write that name on a piece of paper so I won't forget it," said Rochefort.

He took the scrap of paper Milady handed him, folded it, and placed it in the lining of his hat. "You may be easy, Madame," he assured her. "I shall do as children do: repeat the name as I am riding along for fear of losing the paper. Is everything now attended to?"

"So far as I know."

"Let us see. Buckingham is dead or grievously wounded. Your conversation with the cardinal overheard by four musketeers. Lord de Winter warned of your arrival in Portsmouth. D'Artagnan and Athos must be shut up in the Bastille. Aramis is the lover of Madame de Chevreuse. Porthos is an ass. Madame Bonacieux has been rediscovered. Send you my chaise at once. Put my lackey at your service. Cause the abbess to think you're a victim of the cardinal. Armentières, a town on the banks of the river Lys. Anything else?"

"I want all the gold you have. Empty your pockets."

"There you are!"

"Capital! With a thousand pistoles one can face anything."

"Adieu, Countess!"

"Commend me to the cardinal."

"Commend me to Satan."

Milady and Rochefort exchanged a smile and separated. Not long afterward Rochefort set forth at a fast pace. Five hours later he was passing through Arras.

Our readers already know how he was recognized by d'Artagnan. This chance encounter, by inspiring fear in the hearts of the four musketeers, had inspired them to fresh activity.

CHAPTER L

THE DROP OF WATER

Rochefort was scarcely gone when Madame Bonacieux entered. She found Milady with a face all smiles.

"Oh," cried the young woman, "what you dreaded has come to pass! This evening or tomorrow the cardinal will send some one to carry you away from here."

"Who told you that, my dear girl?" inquired Milady.

"I heard it from the lips of the messenger himself."

"Come and sit down close by me," said Milady.

"Here I am."

"Wait until I am sure no one can overhear us."

"Why do you have to be so cautious?"

"You will know soon enough."

Milady got up from her chair, went to the door, and opened it to cast a furtive glance down the corridor. She then came back and took a place beside the mercer's wife.

"So he played his part well, apparently!"

"Whom do you mean?"

"The man who pretended to be a messenger from the cardinal, but who is really my brother."

"Your brother!"

"Nobody must know this secret but yourself, my dear. If you reveal it to a single soul, I shall be lost, and perhaps you, too."

"Oh, gracious heavens!"

"Listen! My brother, on his way to take me away by

force, if necessary, met with the emissary of the cardinal who was searching for me. At a solitary part of the road my brother demanded of the emissary the papers he was carrying. The messenger resisted, naturally. My brother killed him."

"Oh!" exclaimed Madame Bonacieux, shuddering.

"My brother then decided to substitute cunning for violence. He presented himself with the papers as the real messenger of his Eminence, and in an hour or so a carriage will come to take me away."

"I see. It is your brother who sends the carriage."

"Certainly. But there is more to this. The letter you showed me, which you believed to be from Madame de Chevreuse—"

"Well?"

"It is a forgery."

"How can that possibly be?"

"It is only a snare to prevent your making any resistance when your supposed friends come to fetch you."

"But d'Artagnan himself is coming."

"Don't you believe it for an instant. D'Artagnan and his friends are detained at the siege of La Rochelle."

"How can you be sure of that?"

"My brother came upon some emissaries of the cardinal in the uniform of musketeers. It seems you were to be summoned to the gate of the convent in the belief you were to meet friends. You would then be forcibly carried off and taken back to Paris."

"Oh, dear God! My senses fail me when I am confronted by such a swarm of iniquities. I shall go mad!"

"Stop! Hush!"

"What is it now?"

"I hear the galloping of a horse. It must be my brother setting off again. I must wave him a last greeting. Come!"

Milady opened the casement and made a sign to the mercer's wife to join her. The young woman complied. Rochefort passed the window.

"Adieu, brother mine!" Milady cried.

The rider raised his head, saw the two young women at the open casement, and waved his hand in friendly fashion to Milady.

"Dear George!" she said, with a look on her face full of love and melancholy. She resumed her seat, as if absorbed in meditation of a purely personal nature.

"Pardon me for interrupting your reverie, dear Madame," said the mercer's wife shyly, "but how do you advise me to act? You have so much more knowledge of the world than I."

"Why, first of all," responded Milady, "it is possible that I am wrongly informed and that d'Artagnan and his friends may really be on their way to your assistance. If that is so, it is a sort of race to see who will get here ahead. If your friends are the more speedy, you are saved; if the satellites of the cardinal, you are lost."

"Ah, yes, lost beyond hope of salvation!"

"There would be a very simple means of knowing—"

"Only tell me what!"

"Conceal yourself somewhere in the neighborhood until you are sure what men they are who come to fetch you."

"But where could I wait?"

"Oh, there is nothing difficult in that. I am going to hide myself a few leagues from here until my brother comes to rejoin me. I'll take you along with me if you wish to go."

"But I shall not be permitted to leave. To all intents and purposes, I am a prisoner."

"Wait, I have an idea! As the people here think I am going because of the cardinal's commands, they won't believe you are very anxious to accompany me."

"What of that?"

"Well! The carriage will be at the door. You come to say good-by to me. Mount the step of the chaise to give me a last embrace. My brother's servant will make a sign to the postilion and we shall set off at a furious pace."

"But what of d'Artagnan if he comes?"

"Shall we not learn of it at once?"

"I don't see how."

"Nothing is easier. We shall send my brother's servant back to Béthune to place himself in disguise in front of the convent. If the cardinal's minions come, he will pay no attention to them. If d'Artagnan arrives, he will bring him to us."

"Are you sure, though, that he knows d'Artagnan?"

"Of course. He has often seen him at my house."

"Why, then, your plan is the right one. But do you intend to go far from this place?"

"Seven or eight leagues at most. That distance brings us to the frontier. At the first alarm we can leave French territory."

"Are you sure your brother's carriage will arrive here before either of the other parties comes?"

"Positive."

"Suppose the carriage comes for you when I happen to be off somewhere—at dinner or supper, for instance?"

"We'll make sure of things. Tell your good superior that you should like to take your meals with me."

"Do you think she will allow me to?"

"What possible inconvenience can it be to her?"

"And where shall I find you, say, an hour from now?"

"Here in this chamber."

"Oh, Madame, you are so kind, and I am so grateful!"

"Are you not the beloved of one of my best friends?"

And the two women parted, exchanging the most charming smiles.

Milady was glad to be left alone for an hour that she might put her thoughts into order. She felt the need of a period of silence and quiet to give a more distinct form to her ideas, which were still confused, and to decide upon some definite plan.

The most important thing was to get Madame Bonacieux away and, if it should prove necessary, to make her a hostage. Milady was beginning to have doubts as to the issue of this desperate duel of wits in which her enemies showed so much endurance.

The main thing, of course, was to keep the mercer's wife in her power. Madame Bonacieux was the very life of d'Artagnan. In case of ill fortune she would be a means of temporizing and obtaining good terms from Milady's foes. Once concealed at Armentières, it would be easy to make her believe that d'Artagnan had not come to Béthune. In a fortnight at most Rochefort would have returned, and during those two weeks Milady would have time to ponder how she could best avenge herself on the four Inseparables. She would not grow weary of the long wait, for she would be enjoying the sweetest pastime fate can afford a woman of her temperament: perfecting a beautiful scheme of vengeance.

At the end of an hour of pleasant meditation she heard a soft voice calling her. It was Madame Bonacieux. The good abbess had consented to her request—the two women were to dine together.

On reaching the courtyard they heard the sound of an approaching carriage which stopped at the gate. Milady listened.

The bell of the convent gate was rung.

"Go to your chamber," she whispered to Madame Bonacieux, "you have perhaps some jewels which you want to take along."

"I have d'Artagnan's letters," she answered.

"Well, run and get them, then. Hurry back to my apartment. We will snatch a bite to eat, for we are going to travel a part of the night and must keep up our strength."

Madame Bonacieux laid her hand upon her bosom. "My heart is pounding so, I cannot walk," she murmured.

"Courage! In a quarter of an hour you will be safe and out of danger. Remember what you now do is for your loved one's sake."

Milady ran up to her room quickly. She there gave Rochefort's lackey his instructions. He was to wait for

her at the gate. If by ill chance the musketeers should
appear, the chaise was to set off at once, circle the convent
wall, and await Milady at a little village which was situated on the other side of the adjacent wood. If, on the
contrary, the musketeers did not appear, then things were
to proceed as had already been agreed upon: the mercer's
wife was to get into the chaise as if to bid her adieu, and
Milady was to carry off Madame Bonacieux. She then
asked some questions as to the carriage. She was informed
it was a vehicle drawn by three horses and driven by a
postilion. Rochefort's lackey would precede it as courier.

Madame Bonacieux came in and, to remove any possible
suspicion on her part, Milady repeated the final part of
her instructions to the servant.

"You see," she said, when the lackey had left the room,
"everything is ready. The abbess suspects nothing and
thinks that I am being removed by order of the cardinal.
This servant has gone to give his final commands. Take
the least bite to eat, drink a thimbleful of wine, and let
us be gone."

Milady made her a sign to sit down opposite, poured
out a small glass of Spanish wine, and helped her to the
wing of a chicken.

Madame Bonacieux ate a few mouthfuls mechanically,
and barely touched her lips to the glass which was offered
her. But at the moment the glass touched her lips her hand
remained suspended—she heard a sound outside on the
road which sounded like the clank and clatter of distant
galloping. It drew rapidly nearer, and it seemed as if
almost at the same time she heard the whinnying of horses.

"Oh, dear God!" cried Madame Bonacieux. "What is that noise?"

"It is made by either our friends or our enemies," answered Milady with her terrible coolness. "Stay where you are and I shall investigate."

Milady gazed with all the keenness her eyes were capable of. It was still light enough for her to see who was approaching. At the turning of the road she saw the gleaming of laced hats and the swaying of feathers. She counted two, then five, then eight horsemen. She uttered a stifled moan. In the first horseman of the group she recognized d'Artagnan.

"Oh!" exclaimed Madame Bonacieux. "What is it?"

"It is the uniform of the cardinal's Guards. There's not an instant to be lost—fly for your life!"

They heard the horsemen thunder past the windows.

"Come on!" screamed Milady, trying to drag the young woman along by the arm.

Madame Bonacieux attempted to walk, took a step or two, tottered, and sank to her knees.

Outside, three or four shots were fired, presumably at the fleeing carriage.

"For the last time, will you come?" cried Milady.

"Oh, my God! You see my strength fails me. I cannot walk. You flee alone, Madame!"

All at once Milady paused. A livid flash darted from her cruel eyes. She ran to the table, emptied into Madame Bonacieux's glass the contents of a seal ring, which she opened with singular quickness. A grain of a reddish color fell into the wine and dissolved.

Taking up the glass with a hand which was without a
tremor, she said, "Drink! The wine will give you the
strength you need so sadly." She placed the glass at the
lips of Madame Bonacieux, who drank its contents
mechanically.

"This is not the way in which I wished to avenge
myself," muttered Milady, with an infernal smile, as she
put the emptied glass back upon the table. "But pshaw!
In this world one must do what one can." And she rushed
out of the room.

The mercer's wife witnessed her departure without
being able to follow. She was like a person who is being
pursued in a nightmare and tries in vain to move.

A few moments passed, then a loud noise was heard
at the gate. Every second poor Madame Bonacieux expected to see the returning Milady. Several times the cold
sweat of terror burst afresh from the young woman's
brow.

At length she heard the grating of the hinges of the
convent gates. The sound of boots and spurs came from
the direction of the staircase. There was a confused murmur of voices drawing ever nearer. Amid the tumult she
seemed to hear her own name called.

Suddenly she gave a great cry of joy and darted toward
the door. She had recognized the voice of her beloved.

"D'Artagnan! D'Artagnan!" she cried. "This way!"

At the same moment the door of the chamber yielded to
a shock from without, and several men rushed in headlong.
Madame Bonacieux had sunk into an armchair, incapable
of movement.

D'Artagnan threw down a smoking pistol and fell upon his knees before his dear mistress. Athos replaced his pistol in his belt. Porthos and Aramis, who held their drawn swords in their hands, returned them to their scabbards.

"Oh, d'Artagnan," cried the young woman, "it was in vain she told me you would not come! I hoped in secret. I was unwilling to fly with her."

"She? What she are you speaking of?" demanded the Gascon.

"My companion. She mistook you for the cardinal's Guards and has just made her escape. Her carriage was at the gate. She calls herself your friend, and is the woman to whom you told everything."

"Her name!" cried d'Artagnan. "My God, tell me her name!"

"Oh, my head swims—I cannot see—"

"Help, my friends!" called d'Artagnan. "Her hands are like ice. She is deathly ill. She is losing her senses."

While Porthos was shouting for assistance at the top of his powerful voice, Aramis ran toward the table to get a glass of water. But he stopped short at seeing the terrible change that had come into the face of Athos, who was staring at one of the glasses and seemed to be the victim of some grave doubt.

"Madame!" called Athos. "In the name of heaven, whose empty glass is this?"

Madame had opened her eyes under the kisses of d'Artagnan and was apparently reviving somewhat.

"She poured the glass for me and I drank," responded

the young woman in feeble tones. "I remember her name now—the Comtesse de Winter."

The four friends uttered a simultaneous cry, but the voice of Athos dominated all the others. At that instant the face of Madame Bonacieux grew livid. A fearful anguish shook her, and she sank gasping for breath into the arms of Porthos and Aramis. A convulsive shuddering shook her whole frame, the sweat rolled from her brow.

"Run! Call for help!" screamed d'Artagnan.

"Useless!" said Athos sternly. "There is no antidote for the poison that woman pours."

Collecting the last remnant of her strength, the mercer's wife took the head of the young Gascon between her hands, looked at him for an instant as if her whole soul passed into that glance, and with a choking cry caught his lips to hers. Then did her soul, so chaste and so loving, reascend to heaven from which it came.

D'Artagnan pressed nothing but a corpse in his arms. He uttered a cry and fell by the side of his beloved, as pale and cold as she.

At this juncture a man appeared in the doorway. He looked about him and saw Madame Bonacieux dead and her lover in a swoon. He appeared just at that interval of stupor which follows all great catastrophes.

"Messieurs," said the newcomer, "like myself, you are in search of a woman who must have passed this way, for I see a corpse."

The three friends remained mute.

"Gentlemen," continued the stranger, "I perceive you

do not recognize me.   I am Lord de Winter, brother-in-law
of her you seek."

The three friends uttered a cry of surprise.   At that
moment d'Artagnan opened his eyes.   He tore himself
from the arms of Porthos and Aramis, who were trying to
recall him to life, and threw himself like a madman across
the dead body of his beloved.

Athos walked to his friend, embraced him tenderly, and
said to him in his noble and persuasive voice, "Be a man,
my lad! Women weep for their dead.   Men avenge them!"

"Ah!" cried d'Artagnan, "if it be to avenge her, I am
willing to follow you now."

Athos took advantage of this moment of strength which
the hope of vengeance gave his unfortunate friend to sign
to Porthos and Aramis to go and fetch the superior.   The
two found her in the corridor, much upset by the untoward
events in her quiet house.   She summoned some of her
nuns, who, contrary to all monastic precedent, now found
themselves in the presence of five men.

"Madame," said Athos, "we abandon to your pious
care the body of this unfortunate woman.   She was an
angel on earth before she became an angel of heaven.
Treat her as one of your sisters.   We shall some day return
to pray above her grave."

And he drew away his sobbing friend.

All five, followed by their lackeys leading their horses,
took their way to the town of Béthune and stopped at the
first inn they came to.

"And now, gentlemen," said Athos, when he had ascer-
tained there were five chambers free in the hotel, "let every

one retire to his own room. D'Artagnan needs privacy to weep and to rest from his exhaustion. I shall take charge of every detail. Be easy."

"But it seems to me," objected Lord de Winter, "that if there are any steps to be taken against the countess, it is my business to take them. She is my sister-in-law."

"She is my wife!" said Athos.

At that sentence d'Artagnan unexpectedly smiled, for he understood that Athos felt absolutely certain of his vengeance or he would not have revealed the secret. Porthos and Athos looked at each other and turned pale. De Winter thought Athos mad.

"And now, d'Artagnan," continued the eldest musketeer, "if you have not lost it, hand me the paper which fell from that man's hat. Upon this scrap of paper is written the name of the village of—"

"Aha!" cried d'Artagnan. "I comprehend! That name written in Milady's own hand."

"You see, then," observed Athos, "there is a God in Heaven still!"

CHAPTER LI

THE MAN IN THE RED CLOAK

The despairing mood of Athos had yielded to a concentrated grief which served to render even more lucid the brilliant mental qualities of this strange man.

His mind was filled with but one thought: to acquit himself well of the responsibility he had assumed. He retired to his room in the inn, asked the landlord for a map of the vicinity, and subjected this to a searching examination. He discovered there were four different roads leading from Béthune to Armentières. Then he sent for the four lackeys.

He ordered Planchet, Grimaud, Bazin, and Mousqueton to set out the next morning at dawn and to proceed to Armentières, each by a different route. Planchet (whom Athos considered the most intelligent of the four) was to follow the road by which the chaise had gone. This carriage, it may be remembered, had been accompanied by Rochefort's lackey.

Athos had decided to set the servants to work spying, because their questions would inspire less distrust than any their masters might ask. Also, people of the servant class would meet with more sympathy among those to whom they would address themselves. But, best of all, Milady knew the masters and not the lackeys, whereas the latter knew Milady perfectly.

The four servants were to meet the next day at eleven

o'clock. If they had ferreted out Milady's retreat, three of them were to stand guard—the fourth was to come back to Béthune to serve as a guide for the musketeers. These arrangements once perfected, the four lackeys retired to rest.

Then Athos enveloped himself in his cloak, girded on his sword, and left the inn. At ten o'clock in the evening the streets in provincial towns are practically deserted, and yet Athos was evidently desirous of finding some one of whom he could ask a question. At last he stumbled upon a belated stroller and spoke a few words with him. The man Athos addressed started back in affright and responded only by a gesture. Athos offered the man a half pistole to accompany him on the road he had pointed out, but the pedestrian refused.

The musketeer therefore plunged down the dark street the man had indicated with his finger. He soon arrived at a crossroads and was uncertain which way to turn, so he waited some time motionless, until a night watchman made his appearance. Athos repeated to the constable the same question he had asked the former person he had met. The watchman evinced the same terror, likewise refused to accompany the musketeer, and only pointed in the direction which was to be taken.

Athos proceeded on his way and reached the suburb which was located at the opposite end of the town from that by which he and his friends had entered it. There he was forced to wait a third time, ill at ease and perplexed by his lack of knowledge.

Fortunately, despite the lateness of the hour, a beggar

appeared and asked alms of Athos. The latter offered the mendicant half a crown if he would accompany him to where he was going. At first the beggar hesitated, but at sight of the piece of silver which shone in the dusk he consented and walked on ahead of Athos.

Arrived at the corner of the street, the guide pointed to a small house which was off at one side, solitary and dismal. Athos approached the house, while the beggar, who had received his stipulated reward, ran away as fast as his legs would carry him.

Athos had to walk almost clear around the house before he could discover the door to it. The house was painted red. No lights shone through the chinks in the window blinds. Not the slightest noise indicated that the place was inhabited. It was dark and silent as a tomb.

Three times Athos knocked without visible result. At the third summons, however, steps were heard inside. The door was slowly opened and there appeared a man of high stature, pallid complexion, and black hair and beard.

The man whom Athos had come so far to seek ushered him into a sort of laboratory where he had been engaged in wiring together the dry bones of a human skeleton. The whole frame had been adjusted except the head, which lay on the table.

The equipment of the room indicated that the owner of the house occupied himself with the study of natural science. Dried lizards gleamed like emeralds set in large frames of black wood. Bunches of scented herbs, doubtless endowed with qualities unknown to ordinary men, were fastened to the ceiling and hung down in the corners of

the room.   Apparently there was no family, and no servant,
about.   The tall man alone inhabited the house.

Athos cast a cold and indifferent glance at the objects
we have described.   At the invitation of his silent host he
sat down near him.

Then he explained the reason of his visit and the
service he required of the man he had come so far to
seek.   But scarcely had he made known the object he
had in mind when the unknown, who remained standing
before the musketeer, started back with every sign of
terror and refusal.   Then Athos took from his pocket
a small paper on which were written two lines, accompanied with signature and seal.   He presented this
writing to the unknown and watched carefully to see
what would be the result.   The tall man had scarcely read
the lines, examined the signature, and recognized the seal,
when he bowed low to indicate that he no longer had any
objection to offer and that he was ready to obey.

Athos apparently had accomplished what he wished.
For he arose, went out of the house, returned by the same
route he had come, reëntered the inn, and went to his
apartment.

At dawn d'Artagnan entered his chamber and asked
what was now to be done.

"To wait," replied Athos.

The superior of the convent soon sent a servant to
inform the musketeers that the burial of the body of
Madame Bonacieux was to take place at midday.   As to
the prisoner, they had heard no news whatsoever of her.
But it seemed she must have made her escape through the

garden for her footsteps could be traced on the soil. Besides, the gate of the garden had been found unaccountably closed, and the key to it had disappeared.

At the appointed hour Lord de Winter and the four friends took their way to the convent. The bells were tolling, the chapel was open, but the grating of the choir was closed. In the center of the choir the body of the victim, clothed in her novitiate dress, was exposed. On each side of this space and behind the gratings opening into the convent, the whole community of the Carmelite nuns was assembled. They listened to the divine service and mingled their chant with that of the priests without seeing the profane visitors or being seen by them.

At the entrance to the chapel d'Artagnan felt his courage ooze away, and instead of going in he returned to hunt for Athos. But the latter had disappeared from view.

Mindful of his mission for vengeance, Athos had asked to be led to the garden. And there, following the tracks Milady's feet had made in the soil, he walked toward the gate that led to the wood. This was opened at his request, and he went out into the forest.

There all his suspicions were confirmed—the road down which the carriage had been driven encircled the woods. Athos pursued this route for some distance, his eyes fixed upon the ground. Slight stains of blood dotted the wayside here and there. These came either from the wound inflicted by a bullet upon the courier who accompanied the chaise or perhaps from one of the horses which had been similarly struck.

At the end of nearly a league, within fifty yards of

Festubert, a larger bloodstain appeared. The ground was here trampled by horses. Between the forest and this fatal spot, a short distance behind the trampled ground, were the same tracks of small feet as in the garden—the carriage had evidently stopped at this point. Here Milady had emerged from the woods and entered the chaise.

Content with his discovery, which confirmed his every suspicion, Athos retraced his steps to the inn and found Planchet awaiting him. He discovered that Planchet too had followed the road. Like Athos, he had come upon the bloodstains and had ɪoted the spot where the equipage had halted. But Planchet had plodded on farther than Athos, for at the village of Festubert, while drinking at an inn, he had learned, without even needing to ask a single question, that about half-past eight o'clock of the evening before a wounded man traveling in a post chaise had been obliged to stop, unable to proceed on his journey. The woman who accompanied him secured a relay of horses and continued on her way.

Planchet next went in search of the postilion who had driven Milady and found him. He said he had taken the lady as far as Fromelles and from there he understood she set out for Armentières. Planchet took a short cut which was indicated to him, and by seven o'clock in the morning he was at Armentières.

There was but a single inn at this place, the Post. Planchet presented himself there as a lackey out of a situation who was seeking employment. He had not been chatting with the people of the inn ten minutes before he learned that a woman had arrived there unattended about eleven o'clock the night before. She had engaged a room, had sent for the landlord, and had informed him she intended to stay some time in the neighborhood.

Planchet had no need to discover more. He hurried to the appointed meeting place, found the three other lackeys awaiting him, placed them as sentinels at three different exits of the hotel, and came to find Athos, who had scarcely been put into possession of this news when his friends returned from the convent.

"What is there to do?" demanded d'Artagnan eagerly.

"Wait!" replied Athos.

At eight o'clock that evening Athos ordered the horses to be saddled. Then he notified Lord de Winter and his friends to prepare for the expedition.

In a trice all five were ready. Each examined his arms carefully and put them in order. Athos was the last to come down. He found d'Artagnan already on horseback and growing restless.

"Be patient!" said Athos. "One of our number is still wanting."

The four horsemen looked about them in surprise, and they sought vainly in their minds to discover who this missing person might be.

At this moment Planchet brought out Athos' horse. The musketeer vaulted lightly into the saddle. "Wait for me, I shall soon be back," he cried, and set off at a gallop.

In a quarter of an hour he returned, accompanied by a tall man, masked, and wrapped in a large red cloak.

Lord de Winter and the three musketeers looked at one another blankly. Each one was ignorant as to who this man might be. And yet they were convinced things were as they should be, for this had been done by the command of Athos.

At nine o'clock, guided by Planchet, the small cavalcade started, following the route the post chaise had taken.

It was a mournful sight enough, that of these six men riding in absolute silence, each absorbed in his own gloomy thoughts, sad as despair itself, melancholy as chastisement.

CHAPTER LII

JUDGMENT

The night was black and stormy. Great clouds concealed the sky and the stars. The moon would not rise before midnight. Now and then, because of the lightning that flashed along the horizon, the road was visible as it stretched on before the riders—white and solitary. The moment the flash died out, the whole world was again wrapped in darkness.

Athos was constantly compelled to restrain d'Artagnan from outriding the rest of the small troop, for the young Gascon was possessed of but one idea—to forge ahead.

They passed silently through the village of Festubert, where the wounded lackey of Rochefort was lying, and skirted the woods of Richebourg. At Herlier, Planchet, who was leading the column, turned to the right.

On several occasions Lord de Winter, Porthos, or Aramis had tried to engage the man with the red cloak in conversation. But to every question which was addressed to him the unknown bowed without further response. The travelers thus understood that there must be some valid reason why the strange personage wished to preserve silence, and they ceased to address him.

The wind increased, flashes of lightning succeeded one another with increasing frequency, the thunder began to roar. The cavalcade fell into a swifter trot.

Shortly before they reached Fromelles the storm burst.

There remained three leagues to travel, and this distance was covered amid perfect torrents of rain.

D'Artagnan removed his hat from his head and could not be persuaded to avail himself of the protection of his cloak. It gave him a sense of pleasure to feel the water trickle down his burning forehead and over his body, that was shaken as if by ague.

The moment the troop passed Goskal and were drawing near to the Post, a man sheltered under a tree detached himself from the shadows and advanced into the middle of the road, putting his finger warningly to his lips. Athos recognized Grimaud.

"Where is Milady?" asked Athos.

Grimaud stretched his hand in the direction of the river Lys.

"Far from here?"

Grimaud held up his right hand, with the forefinger bent.

"Alone?"

Grimaud nodded his head.

"Gentlemen," said Athos, "she is alone, within half a league of us, close to the river."

They passed the village of Erquinheim and forded a rivulet. They rode on for some minutes more. Suddenly a flash of lightning illuminated the whole landscape round about. Grimaud extended his arm, and by the bluish radiance of the fiery snake they perceived an isolated cottage on the banks of the river within a hundred yards of a ferry. One window of the house was lighted.

At this instant a man jumped up from the ditch in

which he had been crouching and came toward them. It
was Mousqueton. He pointed at the bright windowpane.

"She is there," he said.

"Where's Bazin?" asked Athos.

"Guarding the door, Monsieur."

"You are good and faithful servants," said Athos.

Athos sprang from his horse, handed the bridle to
Grimaud, and walked over to the window. He signed to
the rest of the company to advance to the door.

The cottage was surrounded by a low quickset hedge
about a yard in height. Athos jumped lightly over it and
went to the casement, which was without blinds but had
half-curtains closely drawn. He climbed silently upon the
sill that his eyes might look over the top of the curtains.

By the light of a lamp he saw a woman wrapped in a
dark mantle seated upon a stool close to a dying fire. Her
elbows were resting upon a mean sort of table, and she
leaned her head on her two hands, which shone in the light
as white as ivory. Her face he could not distinguish, but
a sinister smile passed across his lips. Athos was not
deceived. It was the woman he sought.

At this moment a horse neighed. Milady raised her
head, saw the pale countenance of Athos pressed close
against the pane, and screamed. Seeing that he was recognized, the eavesdropper pushed in the window with his
knee and hand. The square panes were broken into many
pieces. Like a specter of vengeance, Athos leaped down
into the room.

Milady rushed to the door and opened it. More pale
and even more menacing than Athos, d'Artagnan stood on

the threshold. The woman started violently back, uttering a cry. The young Gascon, fearing she might have unknown means of escape, drew a pistol from his belt. But Athos raised a warning hand.

"Put up your weapon, my lad!" he ordered. "This person must be tried, and not assassinated. Come in, gentlemen."

D'Artagnan obeyed. The others entered behind him. The four lackeys guarded the door and the window.

"What do you want here?" screamed Milady.

"We want," said Athos in a solemn voice, "Charlotte Backson, who was first called Comtesse de la Fère and afterward Milady de Winter, Baroness of Sheffield."

"That is I," murmured Milady in extreme terror.

"We are here to judge you according to your crimes," continued Athos. "Justify yourself, if you can. M. d'Artagnan, you shall be first to accuse her."

D'Artagnan stepped forward. "Before God and before men," he said, "I accuse this woman of having poisoned Constance Bonacieux, who died yesterday evening."

"We bear witness to this," said Porthos and Aramis.

The Gascon continued. "Before God and before men, I accuse this woman of attempting to poison me with the wine she sent me from Villeroy. God preserved me, but a man named Brisemont died in my stead."

"We bear witness to this," said Porthos and Aramis.

"Before God and before men, I accuse this woman of urging me to murder the Baron de Wardes. As no one else can attest the truth of this claim, I attest it myself. I have finished."

And d'Artagnan passed to the other side of the room where Porthos and Aramis were standing.

"Your turn, Lord de Winter," said Athos.

The Englishman came forward. "Before God and before men," he said, "I accuse this woman of having through the medium of my servant Felton caused the assassination of the Duke of Buckingham."

"What!" cried all present with one voice.

"Yes," said the baron, "assassinated. On receiving the warning note you wrote to me, I had this woman arrested, and gave her in charge to a loyal servant, Felton. She corrupted this man. She placed the poniard in his hand. She made him kill the duke. At this very moment Felton is perhaps paying with his head for the crime of this demoniac woman."

A shudder passed through the judges at the baring of these unsuspected crimes.

"Nor is that all," resumed Lord de Winter. "My brother, who had made you his heir, died in three hours of a strange disorder which left livid patches all over his body. Sister mine, how did your husband die?"

"Oh, my God!" cried Porthos and Aramis.

"Assassin of Buckingham, assassin of Felton, assassin of my brother, I demand justice upon you. And I swear, if it be not granted me, I shall execute it myself."

And the Englishman ranged himself with d'Artagnan, leaving his place free for another accuser. Milady let her head sink between her two hands. She tried to collect her scattered wits, but her brain was whirling dizzily.

"It is now my turn," spoke Athos, trembling as does a

lion at sight of a serpent. "I married that woman when she was a young girl. I gave her my wealth and my name. And one day I discovered she was branded with a fleur-de-lis on her left shoulder."

"Oh!" cried Milady, standing up. "I defy you to find any tribunal which pronounced that infamous judgment upon me—or to find him who executed it."

"Silence!" answered a hollow voice. And the man in the red cloak stepped forward.

"What man is that?" screamed Milady. She seemed choked with terror. Her hair had become loosened and rose above her livid face as if alive.

All eyes were turned toward the stranger, for except to Athos his personality was unknown. But even Athos stared at the man in stupefaction, for he had not believed he was in any way implicated in the terrible drama that was here unfolding. The stranger drew near Milady with a slow and solemn tread so that the table alone separated them. And then the man removed his mask.

The woman examined for some seconds that pale face, framed with black hair and beard, the sole expression of which was one of stony impassiveness. Then she cried out in sudden terror, "Oh, no, no! It is an apparition from hell! It cannot be he! Help, help!" She retreated to the very wall. She screamed and turned to face the partition as if she would tear an opening through it with her bare hands.

"Who are you?" cried the witnesses of this scene.

"Ask that woman," answered the man in the red cloak.

"The executioner of Lille!" cried Milady, a prey to

insensate terror. She clung to the wall with her hands to keep from falling.

Everyone drew back from the man in the red cloak, who remained alone in the center of the room.

"That woman," he said, "was once a young girl, as beautiful as she is today. A young priest with a simple and trustful heart performed the offices of the church in that convent where this young girl was a nun. She seduced this priest. She prevailed upon him to fly with her to another part of France where they might live at ease because unknown. Money was necessary for this; neither had any. The priest stole the sacred vessels of the church and sold them. As they were preparing to escape together, they were both arrested.

"Eight days later she had seduced the son of the jailer and escaped. The young priest was condemned to ten years' imprisonment and to be branded. I was executioner of the city of Lille; it was my duty to brand the guilty man. And he, gentlemen, was my brother!

"I swore that this woman who had urged my brother to his crime should at least share his punishment in part. I suspected where the false nun was concealed. I caught and bound her, and I imprinted upon her the same disgraceful mark I had to place upon my poor brother.

"The day after my return to Lille the poor boy in his turn succeeded in making his escape. He rejoined this woman. They fled together to Berry, and there he obtained a small curacy. This woman passed as his sister.

"The lord of the estate where the chapel of the curacy was situated saw the pretended sister and fell so in love with her that he proposed to marry her. Then this woman abandoned him she had ruined for him whom she was destined to ruin, and became the Comtesse de la Fère—"

All eyes were turned toward Athos as his real name was pronounced by the narrator. The musketeer nodded to indicate the truth of what the executioner was saying.

"Then," the man in the red cloak resumed, "my brother returned to Lille. He was mad, desperate, determined to rid himself of an existence from which she had stolen honor and happiness. He surrendered himself to the authorities, and that night hanged himself from the iron bar of the loophole of his cell. That is the crime of which I accuse her. That is the cause for which she was branded."

"M. d'Artagnan," said Athos, "what penalty do you demand against this woman?"

"The punishment of death," replied d'Artagnan.

"My Lord de Winter," continued Athos, "what penalty do you demand against this woman?"

"The punishment of death," replied the Englishman.

"Messieurs," repeated Athos, turning to Porthos and Aramis, "you who are her judges, what sentence do you pronounce upon this woman?"

"The punishment of death," replied the musketeers.

Milady uttered a frightful shriek and dragged herself upon her knees toward her judges. Athos stretched out his hand in her direction.

"Charlotte Backson, Comtesse de la Fère, Milady de Winter," he said in a hollow voice, "your crimes have wearied men on earth and God in heaven. If you know a prayer, say it now. For you are condemned to death, and die you shall."

At these words Milady abandoned hope. She raised herself proudly and tried to speak, but strength failed her. She felt that a powerful and implacable hand was seizing her by the hair and dragging her along as irresistibly as destiny draws humanity. She did not, therefore, even attempt the slightest resistance, but went out of the cottage.

Lord de Winter, d'Artagnan, Athos, Porthos, and Aramis went out close behind her. The lackeys followed their masters, and the chamber was left desolate—with its broken window, its opened door, and its smoking lamp burning sadly on the table.

CHAPTER LIII

EXECUTION

The hour was close to midnight. The moon, in the early period of its waning and reddened by the last vestiges of storm, rose behind the small town of Armentières. Against the pallid light of the broken disk the village showed the dark outline of its houses and the skeleton of its high belfry.

In front of the little procession the river Lys rolled its silent waters like a stream of molten silver, while across, on the opposite side of the quiet current, a black mass of trees stood out in silhouette on the background of stormy sky, overrun with large copper-colored clouds which created a sort of false twilight.

To the left was an old abandoned mill with motionless wings outthrust, and from the ruins of this a hoot owl was voicing its shrill, periodic cry. Away from this, and to the left of the road which the dismal procession was following, there appeared a few stunted trees which looked for all the world like gnarled dwarfs crouched low to watch men who might be about at this witching hour.

From time to time a broad sheet of lightning blazed the whole breadth of the horizon, darted like a tonguing snake above the somber mass of trees, dividing the heavens and the waters into two separate parts. Not a breath of wind troubled the murky air. The soil was dank and gleaming

with the rain that had recently fallen.   The refreshed
herbage sent forth its invigorating odors.

Two lackeys were dragging Milady along.

The executioner stalked on behind them.   He in turn
was followed by the remainder of the company.   Planchet
and Bazin came last.

Milady was conducted to the bank of the river.   Her
lips were mute, but her eyes spoke with incessant eloquence,
supplicating each of those on whom she gazed.

Because she was a few yards in advance of the others,
she finally whispered to the lackeys who held her arms
pinioned, "A thousand pistoles to each of you if you will
help me to escape.   But if you give me up to your masters,
there are avengers near at hand who will see that you pay
dearly for my death."

Grimaud hesitated.   Mousqueton fell to trembling.

Athos, who had sensed rather than heard Milady's
voice, came quickly up.   Lord de Winter followed his
example.

"Change the lackeys," he ordered, "she has spoken to
them.   They are no longer to be trusted."

Planchet and Bazin were summoned.   They took the
places of their two fellows.

When the procession arrived at the bank of the river,
the executioner stepped forward and bound the hands and
feet of Milady.   At this indignity she broke her silence
and cried, "You are cowards and wretched assassins—ten
strong men united to murder one frail woman!   Have a
care, you!   If I am not saved, I shall at least be terribly
avenged."

"You are no woman," responded Athos sternly. "You are a fiend loosed from hell, and to that place we but return you."

"Virtuous souls!" sneered Milady. "He who touches a hair of my head is an assassin."

"The executioner kills but cannot murder," said the man in the red cloak calmly, rattling his enormous sword. "He is but the last judge of human wrongs."

While speaking these words he was binding her limbs. Milady gave vent to two or three cries so shrill and savage that they seemed to flee forth into the night and lose themselves in the depth of the somber woods.

"If I am guilty of the sins you accuse me of," the woman cried, "take me before a court. You are not judges."

"Why did you not accept imprisonment in an English prison when I offered it?" demanded Lord de Winter.

"Because I do not want to die!" wailed Milady, struggling with her bonds. "I am too young to die."

"The woman you poisoned at Béthune was younger than you are, and yet she is dead," said d'Artagnan.

"I will enter a cloister—I will become a nun," cried Milady.

"You were in a convent," the executioner reminded her sternly, "and you left it to destroy my brother."

Milady uttered a cry of terror and sank down upon her knees. The executioner seized her in his arms and started to carry her toward the boat.

"Oh, my God!" she shrieked. "Are you going to drown me?"

These cries were so heart-rending that d'Artagnan, who from the first had been the most eager in the pursuit of Milady, crouched down on the stump of a tree and lowered his head, stopping his ears with the palms of his hands.

"Oh, I cannot witness this awful scene!" he groaned. "I cannot bear to have this woman die thus."

Milady heard these words and caught at the shred of hope they gave her. "D'Artagnan," she called to him, "remember that I loved you!"

The young Gascon sprang up and took a step in her direction. But Athos likewise came forward, drawing his sword and placing himself in his friend's way.

"One more step, d'Artagnan," he said, "and we cross swords together. Come, executioner, do your duty."

"Willingly, Monsieur," replied the man in the red cloak. "For, as I am a good Catholic, I firmly believe that I am acting justly in performing the duty of my office on this woman."

"That is well," said Athos, and took a step toward Milady.

"I pardon you," he said, "the wrong you did me. I forgive you my lost honor, my besmirched love, my blasted existence. May you die in peace!"

Lord de Winter advanced in his turn.

"I pardon you," he said, "the poisoning of my brother and the assassination of his Grace, the Duke of Buckingham. I forgive you the death of poor Felton and your attempts upon my life. Die in peace!"

"And I," said d'Artagnan, "ask your pardon, Madame,

for having by a trick unworthy of a gentleman incited your anger. I pardon you the murder of my dearly beloved and your cruel vengeance upon me. May you die in peace!"

"Where am I to die?" asked Milady in a dull voice.

"On the other bank of the river," replied the executioner.

Then he set her in the boat. As he was going to enter it, Athos handed him a sum of silver money.

"There is the price of the execution," he said. "I do this to make it clear that we act as judges."

"Correct!" answered the man. "And now, let this woman see that I am not fulfilling my trade but my debt." And he threw the money into the river.

The boat glided away toward the opposite bank of the Lys, bearing with it the guilty woman and the executioner. The other members of the company stayed on the nigh shore of the river. They saw the boat gain the other shore; the figures in it were marked as black shadows against the red-hued horizon.

During the passage of the boat across the Lys, Milady had managed to slip the cord which bound her feet. The moment the bank was reached, she jumped lightly ashore and took to flight. But the soil was wet, and she had no more than gained the top of the bank when she slipped and fell to her knees.

Perhaps at this moment she was convinced that heaven had denied its aid to her, for she remained in the very attitude in which she had fallen, her head hanging forward, her hands clasped.

Then the group of watchers saw the executioner raise

both arms slowly above his head—a moonbeam glistened on the blade of the huge sword. The man's two arms fell with sudden force. A truncated mass sank beneath the blow.

The executioner then removed his red cloak, spread it upon the ground, laid the body in it, threw in the severed head, tied the four corners of the cloak together, raised the burden to his back, and entered the boat again.

Midstream he stopped the ferry. Suspending his grim bundle above the water, he cried in a loud voice, "Let the justice of God prevail!" And he threw the corpse into the stream.

*   *   *   *

Three days afterward the Inseparables were in Paris. They had not exceeded their furlough. They reported at once to M. de Tréville.

"Well, Messieurs," asked the worthy captain, "I hope you enjoyed your little vacation?"

"Prodigiously," replied Athos.

CHAPTER LIV

THE CARDINAL'S MESSENGER

The return from Paris to La Rochelle was profoundly dull. Our four friends rode side by side, with sad eyes and lowered heads. Athos alone would occasionally raise his brow, a flash would kindle in his eyes, a bitter smile pass across his lips; then, like his companions, he would sink back again into meditation.

As soon as the royal escort of musketeers arrived in a town, after they had conducted the king to his quarters the four friends at once retired either to their own lodgings or to some secluded cabaret where they neither drank nor gamed. They conversed only in low tones, first looking attentively around to make sure that they were not overheard.

One day when Louis XIII had halted to fly the magpie and the four musketeers had stopped at a cabaret on the highroad, a cavalier coming from La Rochelle pulled up at the door to drink a glass of wine. He cast a swift glance into the room where the friends were sitting.

"Hello!" he cried. "Is that not M. d'Artagnan whom I see yonder?"

The young Gascon raised his head and gave a shout of joy. It was the man he called his specter—it was the unknown of Meung, of the Rue des Fossoyeurs, and of Arras.

D'Artagnan drew his sword and sprang toward the

door. This time, instead of avoiding him, the stranger jumped down from his horse and advanced to meet his antagonist.

"Surrender your sword to me, Monsieur, and without resistance," commanded the dismounted cavalier. "I arrest you in the name of his Majesty the king."

"Who are you to demand that?" inquired d'Artagnan, without making a move to yield up his blade.

"I am the Chevalier de Rochefort," answered the other, "equerry of M. the Cardinal Richelieu. I have orders to conduct you to his Eminence."

"We are returning to that very person, Monsieur," observed Athos, coming forward. "Accept the word of my friend that he will go straight to La Rochelle."

"I regret that I must place him in the escort of guards who will take him into camp."

"We shall be his escort, Monsieur," added Athos, frowning. "M. d'Artagnan shall not leave us."

Rochefort cast a glance behind him. He perceived that Porthos and Aramis had stationed themselves between him and the gate of the cabaret. He understood that he was completely at the mercy of these three friends of d'Artagnan.

"Messieurs," he replied, "if M. d'Artagnan surrenders his sword to me and promises to seek at once the quarters of Monseigneur the Cardinal, I am satisfied."

"I pledge you my word, Monsieur. And here is my blade."

"That suits me exactly," said Rochefort, "for I wish to continue my journey without delay."

"If it is to rejoin Milady," remarked Athos calmly, "spare yourself the trip. You will not find her."

"Why not?" demanded Rochefort eagerly.

"Return to camp and you will discover."

. . . . Next evening, on returning to his quarters at the bridge of La Pierre, Cardinal Richelieu found d'Artagnan standing before the house he occupied. The Gascon was without his sword, but the three musketeers who were with him were armed.

As he was well attended, his Eminence looked at the quartet sternly, then made a sign with his hand for d'Artagnan to follow him. Needless to relate, the young Gascon obeyed.

"We shall wait for you, d'Artagnan," called Athos loudly enough for the cardinal to hear him.

His Eminence entered the chamber that served him as a study and signaled Rochefort to bring in the young musketeer. Rochefort obeyed and retired.

D'Artagnan made a deep obeisance and came to a standstill before the cardinal. This was his second audience with Richelieu, and he later confessed that he felt fairly sure it was to be his last.

His Eminence the cardinal remained standing leaning against the chimney breast. A table was between him and his prisoner.

"Do you know why I have had you arrested, Monsieur?" the cardinal inquired.

"No, Monseigneur, for the only cause which would naturally bring about my detention is still unknown to your Eminence. If you will have the goodness to tell me,

Monseigneur, what crimes are laid to my charge, I shall then relate what I have really done."

"You are charged with having corresponded with enemies of the realm, with having surprised State secrets, with having attempted to thwart the plans of your commander."

"And who imputes these sins to me, Monseigneur?" demanded d'Artagnan loftily. "A woman branded by justice with the fleur-de-lis; a woman who married bigamously one man in France and another in England; a woman who poisoned her third husband; a woman who tried both to poison and to assassinate me."

"Of what person are you speaking, Monsieur?" cried the cardinal heartily astonished.

"Of Milady de Winter. Your Eminence is doubtless ignorant of her atrocities, since you honor her with your confidence."

"If she be guilty of the crimes you lay at her door, Monsieur, she shall be punished," said the cardinal.

"That has already happened, Monseigneur."

"Who executed the punishment?"

"We did."

"Is she imprisoned?"

"She is dead."

"Dead! Did I hear you aright?"

"Three times she attempted to murder me, and I pardoned her. But she slew the woman whom I loved. My friends and I then took her, gave her trial, and condemned her."

D'Artagnan proceeded to narrate the whole story of

the poisoning of Madame Bonacieux in the convent of the Carmelites at Béthune, the trial in the isolated cottage, and the execution on the bank of the river Lys. A shudder passed through the frame of the cardinal, although he was not given to chills.

But suddenly the face of Richelieu, until that moment gloomy, began to clear, as if under the influence of some unspoken thought, and it recovered its look of serenity.

"So," he said, in a tone that contrasted curiously with the sternness of his words, "you four constituted yourselves judges, failing to remember that they who punish others without license are no more than murderers?"

"Monseigneur, I willingly submit to any penalty your Eminence may please to inflict upon me. I do not hold life dear. Another might reply that he had his pardon in his pocket. I content myself with saying, 'Command, Monseigneur, I am ready.'"

"By whom is that pardon signed—by the king?" demanded the cardinal in a tone of singular contempt.

"No—by your Eminence."

"By me? You are beside yourself, Monsieur."

"Monseigneur will undoubtedly recognize his own handwriting?"

And d'Artagnan handed to the cardinal the precious scrap of paper Athos had forced from Milady, and which he had given d'Artagnan to serve him as a talisman.

December 3, 1627.

It is by my order and for the good of the State that the bearer of this note has done what has been done.

RICHELIEU.

The cardinal after having read these lines, sank into a deep reverie. But he did not return the paper to d'Artagnan.

"He is speculating as to the particular way he wishes to kill me," the Gascon said to himself.

After what seemed a long while, Richelieu raised his head and fixed his eagle eye upon the frank and intelligent face of d'Artagnan. He reflected how much there was in that youth of scarce twenty-one years, and what resources his courage and his shrewdness might offer a good master. On the other hand, the crimes and the infernal genius of Milady had more than once horrified Richelieu. He had a feeling of secret joy at being forever relieved of this dangerous accomplice. He slowly tore up the paper which d'Artagnan had generously relinquished to him

"I am lost!" said d'Artagnan to himself. "Lord, Thy will be done!"

The cardinal leaned over the table and, without sitting down, wrote a few lines upon a parchment of which two-thirds was already filled in. He affixed his seal.

"That is my death sentence," thought d'Artagnan. "He is sparing me the tedium of the Bastille and the weariness of a proper trial. It is really kind of him."

"Here, Monsieur," said the cardinal to the young soldier. "I have robbed you of one full power only to provide you with another. The name is lacking in this commission. Write it in yourself."

D'Artagnan took the parchment hesitantly and glanced at it. It was a lieutenant's commission in the Musketeers.

The young fellow sank at the feet of the cardinal.

"Monseigneur," he said, "my life is yours. Dispose of it as you will. But I do not merit this favor you are bestowing upon me. I have three friends, each one of whom is more worthy—"

"You are a fine youngster, d'Artagnan," intervened the cardinal, tapping him familiarly on the shoulder. "Do with the commission what you desire. But remember, though the name is lacking, it is to you I offer it."

"I never shall forget," replied d'Artagnan.

The cardinal turned away and called in a loud voice, "Rochefort!" The chevalier entered immediately.

"Rochefort," said the cardinal, "you behold M. d'Artagnan. I receive him among the number of my friends."

The two enemies greeted one another coolly with their lips. The cardinal observed them attentively with his vigilant eye. They left the study together.

"We shall meet again, Monsieur, I hope?"

"Whenever you please," said d'Artagnan.

"I shall find an early opportunity," replied Rochefort.

"Eh?" said Richelieu, opening the door suddenly.

The two men smiled at each other inanely, shook hands, and saluted his Eminence. . . . .

"We were beginning to grow uneasy," said Athos a moment later, as d'Artagnan rejoined his waiting friends.

"Here I am, dear people," responded the Gascon, "not only free, but in high favor."

"Tell us the story."

"This evening, at your rooms, Athos. But for the moment, let us go our separate ways."

Accordingly, that evening the young musketeer re-

paired to the domicile of Athos, whom he found just fin-
ishing a bottle of Spanish wine. D'Artagnan narrated
what had taken place between the cardinal and himself.
Then he drew the commission from his pocket and said,
"Here, Athos. This belongs quite naturally to you."

Athos read the parchment. Then his face assumed one
of its sweet and expressive smiles.

"Dear friend," he said, "for Athos this is too much, for
the Comte de la Fère it is too little. Keep the commission,
my lad, it is yours. Alas, you have bought it dearly
enough!"

D'Artagnan went to the chambers of Porthos. He
found his friend clothed in a magnificent suit which was
covered with splendid embroidery. Porthos was admiring
his image before the mirror.

"And how do you think these garments fit me?" asked
Porthos.

"Wonderfully! But I am come to offer you a dress
which will become you still better."

"What is that?" asked the startled soldier.

"The uniform of a lieutenant of Musketeers."

D'Artagnan then told his friend the substance of his
conversation with the cardinal. Again he drew the commission from his pocket and said, "Here, my friend, write
your name in the vacant space and become my superior
officer."

Porthos cast a careless glance at the parchment and
then, to the great astonishment of the young man, returned
it to d'Artagnan.

"Very flattering, I'm sure," he said. "But during our

expedition to Béthune the husband of my duchess died. My dear, the coffer of the deceased is holding out its arms to me. I am to marry the widow. This is my wedding suit I am trying on. Keep the lieutenancy, dear fellow."

But a short while thereafter the young Gascon entered the apartment of Aramis. He found the would-be abbé kneeling before a prie-dieu, with his head leaning on an opened prayer book.

He described to Aramis his interview with the cardinal. He drew for the third time the parchment from his pocket and said, "Accept this commission, my friend! You have deserved it more than any other of us because of your wise counsels."

"Alas, my dear chap," replied Aramis, "our recent exploit has quite disgusted me with the military career. This time my decision is irrevocable—after the siege I am to enter the house of the Lazarists. Keep the commission, d'Artagnan. The profession of arms suits you to a T. You will live to be a brave and most adventurous captain."

D'Artagnan's eyes were wet with gratitude, although beaming with joy. The young fellow ran back to Athos, whom he found still at table engaged in contemplating the hue of a glass of Malaga before the light of his lamp.

"Well," he said, "they refused me, too."

"That is because there is none more worthy than yourself."

Athos took up a quill, wrote the name of d'Artagnan in the vacant space of the parchment, and returned it to him.

"I shall then have no more friends," said the young Gascon sadly. "Alas, nothing but bitter recollections!"

And he let his head sink upon his hands, while two large tears started to roll down his cheeks.

"You are young," answered Athos, "and your bitter memories have much time in which to change to sweet recollections."

EPILOGUE

La Rochelle, deprived of the help of the English fleet, surrendered after a siege of one year. The capitulation was signed October 28, 1628. The king made his entrance into Paris almost two months later. He was given a triumph, as if he had come from conquering a foreign foe and not Frenchmen. He entered by the Faubourg St. Jacques beneath arches of living verdure.

D'Artagnan took possession of his command. Porthos left the service, and in the course of the following year he espoused Madame Coquenard. The coveted coffers contained eight hundred thousand livres. Mousqueton was given the most splendid liveries. And thereafter he had the supreme satisfaction of doing what he had always longed for: standing on the boot of a gilded equipage.

Aramis made a trip into Lorraine. But all at once he vanished and ceased to write to his friends. At a later period they learned through Madame de Chevreuse that, yielding to his love for his real vocation, Aramis had retired to a monastery. Nobody knew, however, to which monastic house he had gone. Bazin became a lay-brother.

Athos remained with the Musketeers under command of d'Artagnan until the year 1633, when, after making a journey to Touraine, he likewise left the service under the pretext of having inherited a small estate in Roussillon. Grimaud followed Athos.

D'Artagnan fought three duels with Rochefort, wounding him three times. "I shall probably kill you on the fourth occasion," the Gascon said to him, as he held out his hand to assist the count to rise.

"It would be wiser for both of us to stop where we are," replied the wounded man. *"Corbleu!* I am a greater friend to you than you imagine. By saying a single word to the cardinal after our very first engagement, I could have had your throat slit!"

So the two embraced heartily, and bore one another no malice.

Planchet, through Rochefort's influence, was given the rank of sergeant in the Piedmontese regiment.

M. Bonacieux continued to lead an unobtrusive existence, ignorant of the fate of his wife and caring little to know what it was. One day he was imprudent enough to recall himself to the memory of the cardinal. The latter informed him he would provide so well for the mercer that he should never want for anything again. And the truth is that M. Bonacieux left his house at seven o'clock one evening to go to the Louvre. Thereafter he never appeared again in the Rue des Fossoyeurs. The opinion of those who should know about such matters was that the mercer was fed and lodged in some royal castle at the expense of his generous Eminence.